ACTS of GOD

Brian John

Gre   ~JKS
Newport, Pembrokeshire

2014

Typeset by the author in Palatino 10 pt and designed on
Apple iMac computer using Pages 4.1

Printed and bound by
The Printing House, London W1D 2EU

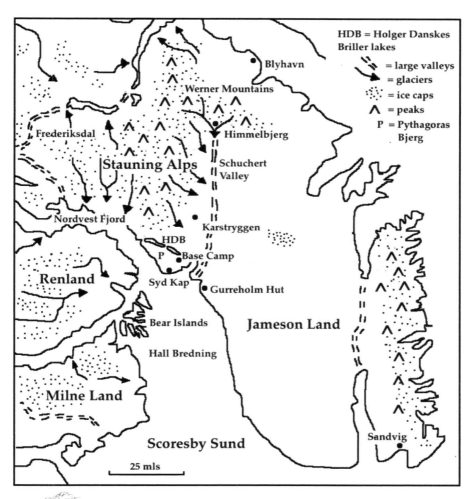

HDB = Holger Danskes
Briller lakes

↘↘ = large valleys
↘ = glaciers
⋰ = ice caps
∧ = peaks
P = Pythagoras
    Bjerg

Blyhavn

Werner Mountains

Frederiksdal

Himmelbjerg

Stauning Alps

Schuchert
Valley

Nordvest Fjord

Karstryggen

HDB

P   Base Camp

Syd Kap

Gurreholm Hut

Renland

Jameson Land

Bear Islands

Hall Bredning

Milne Land

Sandvig

Scoresby Sund

25 mls

The scene of the action. The map on the left shows the area
normally referred to as "North-East Greenland". Above is
an enlarged map of the Scoresby Land - Jameson Land area,
at approximately 72 degrees North.

CHAPTER 1
July 1962

Pavel Leskov had never killed a man before. He had been trained to do it, in many different ways, but now that the time had come his hands were shaking and there was cold sweat on his forehead. He had drunk too much vodka, and was unsteady on his feet. He was almost overcome with a wave of nausea, but then Tolstoy said to him: "Concentrate, Pavel! There won't be a better opportunity. No second thoughts. Put your whole weight on him, hold his arms and stop him from kicking. I'll look after the pillow. Now!"

It was absurdly easy. There was no struggle, and no sound. The Norwegian had been fast asleep on the bunk bed, and breathing deeply, and then there was no more breath, and he was dead. The murder weapon, a dusty old pillow filled with goose-down, was flung into the corner, and the two assassins sat back and looked at their victim, as if they half expected him to spring back to life. But he lay perfectly still. Tolstoy nodded to himself and folded his arms. "Good, good," he said, as he had done many times on the completion of some task or other since their arrival in Greenland. Several minutes passed, and it was so quiet, now that the rain had stopped, that they could hear the sound of the last water droplets pitting the soft ground beneath the roof overhang. The only other sound was that of a great northern diver, far out on the fjord. Leskov had hated that wild and lonely call ever since childhood, and he was still only partly convinced that it came from a living creature and not from a ghost. He could not take his eyes off the dead man's face. He shivered, and whispered: "Did we have to do that? He meant us no harm......."

Tolstoy put his arm around his shoulder. "We had to, my friend. God knows where he was headed for, but wherever it was, news of our presence here would have been echoing round these fjords within a couple of weeks. In a week, he could have reached the working radio in the hut on Ella Island, or he could even have walked round the coast to Blyhavn.

Tonight, he had the best part of a bottle of vodka inside him, but tomorrow he would have been sober, and inquisitive."

"You're right," Leskov shrugged. "It's done. I suppose he felt nothing. Shall we finish what we've started?"

The two men decided that the Norwegian should leave the hut dressed exactly as he had been when he entered. So with great difficulty they pulled on his soaking wet over-trousers and boots and carefully tied up his boot-laces. They fitted him into his sodden parka, with even greater difficulty. Then they carried him out into the deep evening shade and down to the shore of the lake, about three hundred yards away. That was hard work, for he was a big man. They did not try to bury him, since it was still early summer, and the permafrost, as hard as concrete, was only a foot or so beneath the ground surface. They had seen a big male polar bear on the shoreline twice during the past two days, and they had fired a few rounds over its head, to frighten it away when it had shown an unhealthy interest in the hut and its contents; it would not be far away, and they knew that it would probably be along within a few hours, attracted by the smell of death. Long before anybody else reached this God-forsaken place, there would be nothing left of the corpse but a few scattered bones and shreds of clothing. Not the first trapper in East Greenland to have come off worst in an encounter with a polar bear........

Jim Wagner looked down from his observation window, three thousand feet up on the red pyramidal peak called Himmelbjerg. The glass had only just been installed, but it was reinforced and it should, he thought, be quite capable of coping with anything that nature might throw at it. But now it was summer, the season of continuous daylight and warm sunshine. The view was magnificent, and he had still not adjusted to the clarity of the air. To the south he could see clearly, even with the naked eye, the red snow-streaked mountains of Knud Rasmussens Land, about two hundred miles away. With the biggest of his high-resolution telescopes, specially made for the project by Hasselblad, he could pick up extraordinary detail, with just a little distortion caused by the heat haze.

He looked around the room which would henceforth be his office and his private domain, as well as being the control centre for everything that went on inside the mountain and throughout the region. He grinned to himself. Yes, he thought, he would call this "Heaven" — entirely appropriate, given the celestial name which the Danes had given to the mountain.

All of his key radio and radar equipment was in place, and the work inside the mountain was almost complete. Another five or six days should do it, assuming that the weather held up. They had been lucky thus far, with three weeks of unbroken sunshine which had pushed the spring melt along more quickly than expected. They had been able to use all three passes through the mountains for the tractor trains coming over from Blyhavn on the outer coast, but it had been a bloody nuisance that too much snow had melted off the Mellem Pass, the steepest and shortest of the three. He had misjudged that one, sending the heaviest Caterpillar train that way instead of over the safer Eastern Glacier pass, just to save on distance and time. Now the damned thing was stuck forty feet down in the biggest crevasse they had ever seen in the Werner Mountains, together with all the experimental laser rangefinder equipment on the first sledge. Nevertheless, they should have sledge and tractor out within the week, thanks to the combined pulling power of three other Caterpillars, and then they would have to assess the damage.

In the meantime, there were the Oxford explorers to deal with. They would fly in to the Blyhavn airstrip on a charter flight from Iceland, and would make parachute drops of their food and other supplies into Kjove Land, their planned field-working area far to the south of the mountains. It was so remote that there was no landing strip within a hundred miles, and the only way to get there by land was by walking. So they would walk, first by following glacier routes across the Werner Mountains to Himmelbjerg, and then southwards down the Schuchert Valley into Scoresby Land. They would of course take local advice before setting off. So now, in the light of this crevasse accident on the main thoroughfare through the mountains, they would have to be sent over the Eastern Pass on some trumped up pretext, just to keep them out of the way. But they were young and tough, and mad enough to want to walk a hundred miles to their Base Camp site, across nightmarish terrain, carrying their own packs.

Wagner rather liked the eccentricity of the English, and he hoped that they would enjoy their adventure in that part of East Greenland referred to, by those who knew it and apparently without irony, as the "Arctic Riviera". They were expected within the next week, and he decided that when they arrived at Himmelbjerg he would give them, on behalf of Greenland Metals A/S, a warm welcome and a feast that would not be out of place on an Oxford college high table. It would, he thought, be a pleasure to work with them, even though that pleasure would be short-lived.

Joe Horton and Andy Petherton leaned on the starboard handrail of the *MS Gullfoss* and gazed into the mud-grey swells of the North Sea as they slid past. They were thirty-six hours out from Leith, en route for Reykjavik in Iceland. Until now, they had both been confined to their cabins, afflicted by protracted bouts of sea-sickness. They had run into a northerly gale just a couple of hours into the voyage, and had discovered why this famous old vessel was more hated than loved as it rolled and pitched in a maelstrom of old swells from the east and new breaking waves from the north. But now the wind had dropped and the clouds had dissipated, and the deck was bathed in warm sunshine.

Both men were tall and well-built, with a number of physical similarities. Horton was 28 years old, with short-cropped fair hair, intensely blue eyes and a weather-beaten face which bore traces of a violent past, including a long scar which ran from the corner of his right eye almost to his stubbly chin. He was not exactly disfigured by it, but it was quite prominent. Apart from that he was a good-looking man, and there was an intensity and directness in both his gaze and his manner of speaking that proved very attractive to the opposite sex. Petherton was a few years older, with a broad face, deep-set grey eyes and a jutting chin. When he spoke, there was no doubting either his Australian nationality or his self-confidence. He was, after all, the most highly qualified member of the party — a lecturer rather than a student. He was a man who took himself very seriously indeed, and he did not smile a lot. Horton had already noticed, on their first meeting on the quayside in Leith, that he was not entirely tuned in to the self-effacing irony and humour that ran through the conversation of his Oxford colleagues. But he would surely adapt, and for him the adjustment would be much simpler than it would be for Lars Knudsen, the Dane who had also joined the party at the quayside.

"God, I hate the sea," moaned Horton. "If the old man in the sky had meant us to spend time in places like this he would have given us either fins or inbuilt gyroscopes. He gave us neither, so that proves God doesn't exist."

"Tend to agree with you on that, mate," said Petherton with a rare grin. "Or maybe he does exist, and uses old tubs like the *Gullfoss* to give us a taste of hell, just to keep us on the straight and narrow......"

"Or maybe to punish us for our evil deeds?"

"Evil deeds? Whiter than bloody white, I am. Speak for yourself."

For a while the two of them watched a group of gannets fishing a few hundred yards from the ship, each bird wheeling high into the sky, picking its target, and then spearing down into the waves before taking off and doing it all again. Horton, who was a biologist with an enquiring mind, speculated on how, from a hundred feet up, the birds could factor in water refraction and the depth of fish beneath the surface when there were ten-foot swells and a lot of white water to cope with, not to mention the direction and strength of the wind. He wondered whether the fishing success rate might be one in five dives, or one in ten.

"Don't think too much, Joe," said Petherton, slapping him on the back. "Preserve the old grey matter for classifying all those pretty flowers you'll be collecting in Greenland."

"Huh! You're a typical bloody geologist, Andy. No understanding of the living world. Flowers are of no interest to me whatsoever -- but ask me to talk about tundra plant communities, adaptations and ecological niches and I'll bore the socks off you, any day."

"Thanks for the offer. Maybe some other time. So what brought you into this mad enterprise? Didn't you have anything better to do this summer?"

"As it happens, I couldn't possibly be doing anything better. What I discover here will go straight into my thesis — I've spent great summers on Svalbard and Ellesmere Island, and East Greenland is slap in the middle, between the two. Will the flora have more similarities with the North Atlantic islands, or with those on the west side of the ice sheet? Take it from me — a matter of vast importance to science."

"Well, it takes all sorts. So how did you hook up with Steffo and the other guys?"

"Through the Exploration Club. About eight months ago he gave a presentation on his plans for an expedition to the Scoresby Sund area, and I liked what I heard. He was looking for members with Arctic experience, and for post-grads who might bring in a bit of weight and enhance the fund-raising efforts. Expeditions composed entirely of undergraduates tend never to get off the ground. So I asked if I could join, and I was the first one to sign up."

"And you're impressed with his planning?"

"Actually, I am. Steffo's young and inexperienced, but he's a smart bugger, and his preparation has been pretty meticulous. He's put so much into the planning, at the same time as preparing for Finals, that it's probably cost him a First. He doesn't seem to mind. You can never plan for every eventuality, but he's taken advice from all over the place, and he seems to me to be a fast learner. We'll see how he gets on in the field."

"I'm surprised the university didn't ask you to be leader, Joe."

"That's not how things work in Oxford, Andy. Those who dream up expeditions to wild places tend to be the ones who lead them — which is fair enough, since they're the ones who have the vision and the motivation. And they are the poor sods who have to put in God knows how many hours of hard grind to get their projects off the ground — including scientific approvals, transport planning, fund-raising, organizing rations and equipment, and God knows what else. I have no aspirations to be in charge. In the third year of a doctorate it's as much as I can manage to get out of the lab, let alone organize a two-month expedition to Greenland."

"Has Steffo thought of everything?"

"Well, I went on a Bristol University expedition to Svalbard a couple of years back, and that was a bloody shambles by comparison, I can tell you.

It was a miracle we all got out of there alive."

"Maybe we'll need a miracle here too……."

"Doubt that. This expedition has a nice mix of youth and experience — with a Dane on board as a gesture to international goodwill. But how did you get involved, Andy? From what I can gather, the whole trip was in danger of being called off, but then along you came, and Griff Mortimer as well, and everything suddenly fell into place."

"Nah — it wasn't that simple, Joe. The boys were having financial difficulties, that's for sure. But that was mainly because the funders wanted the science programme to be beefed up a bit. They wanted more geology and more zoology — and so did the Danish government, apparently. The call went out, and after two seasons in West Greenland on mineral prospecting, I was in the right place at the right time. Without even meeting me they asked me to join, and after a bit of thought I said yes."

"Serendipity, they call it. But didn't you have a summer all mapped out for family holidays and so forth? I heard that you're married, and that there are two little daughters………"

A shadow came over Petherton's face. "They'll cope on their own, and I'll probably be having a hell of a lot more fun than they are." The big Australian spat over the rail into the sea, and chose not to elaborate.

"Running away from something, Andy? They say that everybody who goes to Greenland, either on the Sledge Patrol, or as a miner, or as an expedition member, is running away from something."

"Not me, mate. Running away isn't my style. Let's call it moving on, shall we? So what are you running away from?"

"Quite a number of things, as it happens. I'll tell you some time, when you have a few days to spare."

It was time for supper, and since they had eaten no food at all since leaving Leith, both men felt hungry. Having confirmed that the wind from the north was still dropping and that the swells were reducing in size, they went below to join their colleagues.

Paulus Arke sat at the water's edge at Syd Kap, gazing out across the sound of Hall Bredning towards the Bear Islands, maybe ten miles away. Surrounded as he was by extraordinary beauty, he should have been happy, he thought — but his heart was as heavy as if he had lost a loved one. The deserted village where he had spent virtually the whole of his life was now as silent as midwinter. The residents had been "advised" to leave, and to move to the village of Sandvig near the mouth of Scoresby Sund — and since they had no option in the matter, they had gone......

The *Nanuk* was at anchor, a couple of hundred yards offshore. The sun was low, but he could still sense its golden warmth on his face. The last of the clouds from yesterday's summer storm were hanging on over the high snowfields on the Renland plateau, as if reluctant to release their grip. But he knew that they would be gone within the next hour or so, together with the last of the fresh snow. Down here at sea level he and his friend Christian Kunak had sat out the storm in this place of memories, in the house which his great-great-grandfather had built. They were content that the northerly gale had pushed all the sea ice and iceberg fragments across the bay, leaving them with the clear water that they needed in order to get back to Sandvig, 120 miles away. He thought that there must have been big waves on the Bear Islands, for just a few hours. Now the water was mirror-calm again, and even the monstrous icebergs stranded in the shallows in the middle of the sound seemed to be asleep.

The bronze colour of the sea reminded him of one of the sections in the stained glass window behind the altar of the church in the village. But that was a church, built for the little community by the Danes, using timber and iron and glass and concrete brought in by sea some forty years ago. Inside it, with his family and friends around him, and with the sounds of his favourite hymn echoing around the rafters, he felt close to God. Well, maybe a little bit closer to God than he was already. Somehow, he thought, it was not right to be contained within those walls, with the wide sky blocked by a corrugated iron roof, shut off from the sounds of the dogs and the gulls and the wind by the whining of that wretched harmonium and the endless ramblings of the priest. Here, at Syd Kap, everything was real. Here he was as close to God as it was possible to be, without being in Heaven.

Further along the shore, Christian was walking along on the gravelly beach, near the rusting winch that had always been used for hauling up narwhals, seals and walruses. He had his hands behind his back, with his head bowed, and he was lost in thought. Paulus watched him for a while, and then closed his eyes.

Remembered sounds came to him, as if in a dream. He thought that he heard the wailing of Eva Kulik's new baby, who cried a lot, and the snarling and yapping dogs behind Mikkel's house, and the laughter of the four small boys who had a secret place high up on the hillside, and the gulls fighting over the remains of a narwhal which had been cut up on the smooth sloping rocks across the bay. A mother was shouting in the distance. Somebody else was using a hammer to do some repairs, and an old woman was sharpening a flensing knife. He knew that it was a flensing knife, because the sound was unique. And he knew that it was an old woman, because the rhythm of the sound came from decades of experience. Einar, the oldest man in the community, was singing that old hunting song of his, beating out the rhythm on two sticks. Joseph's youngest boy was throwing stones at a piece of wood floating ten yards offshore. Pieces of brash ice brushed against one another in the wavelets, sounding for all the world like miniature bells. His father had told him many years ago that this was the sound of "laughing ice", but he always thought that the sound, when heard from a long way off, was more like small children singing…………..

Paulus was pulled out of his reverie as the acrid smell of woodsmoke and rendered harp seal blubber hit his nostrils, carried along the shore by a breath of wind. Their job was done for now, and they had skinned and butchered the fifteen seals shot on the Bear Islands within the past three days. They could have taken more, but had run out of time with the approach of the storm. So they had rendered all the fresh blubber into oil in Mikkel's big iron cauldron. The skins and the meat, and the crispy residues of the blubber taken from the hot cauldron, were already on board the boat. They would return for the twenty barrels of oil whether the Americans liked it or not, whenever they could escape from Sandvig. The *Mikkelsen*, owned by his uncle, would suit their purpose, for she had ample room in her hold.

Christian whistled and waved to him from the beach. It was time to go. Time to leave this sacred place once again to the foxes, the skuas and the gulls, who would fight over the seal remains until there was nothing left. He got up slowly and stiffly, feeling very tired after several days of backbreaking work. He sensed that there were tears on his cheeks.

The younger Russian was surprised by the speed at which the cloud evaporated from the shore of the lake, allowing a shaft of sunlight to break through into the dim interior of the trappers' hut where he was sitting. That was a freakish occurrence, for there was only one very small window. It did nothing to lighten his spirits, and if anything it made matters worse -- illuminating, in his mind, the minute details of yesterday's appalling crime which he and Maxim Tolstoy had committed on that poor Norwegian trapper who had been in the wrong place at the wrong time.

The sunbeams also revealed something on the floor of the hut. Leskov picked it up and looked at it. It was a faded and creased photograph which showed an elegant blonde woman dressed in a heavily embroidered folk costume, and in front of her a little girl with a shock of curly blonde hair and laughter in her face. The girl was very pretty, and seemed to be about five years old. The woman had her hand on the child's shoulder. Behind the two people there was a tree -- maybe an apple tree -- in full blossom, and a wooden hut made of horizontally placed rough-cut logs and roofed with turf. Leskov looked at the photo for a long time, and noticed that the hand in which he held it was shaking. Now he remembered. In the middle of their drinking session with the Norwegian, the poor fellow had taken out the photo from his pocket and showed it to them proudly. Communication had been difficult, but he had pointed at the woman and said "Hilde!" and at the little girl whom he named Fricka. Leskov could not be sure of it, but probably they were wife and daughter, photographed in happy times on some little farm in the Norwegian countryside. Wife and daughter. Now widow and orphan. He could not take his eyes off the happy, trusting and carefree face of the child, and thought of his own little sister who was the same age……….

14

The wretched Norwegian had burst in on them without even knocking, while they were poring over their maps and photographs and planning their route across the mountains. Was one supposed to knock politely at the door of a trappers' hut hundreds of miles from anywhere, in the middle of a deluge, when one arrived without warning? On balance, he supposed not. He might have walked straight in himself, if he had been out in that storm, exhausted and soaked to the skin, and if he had seen smoke coming out through the chimney pipe. And he might have expected a warm welcome from the inhabitants, especially if he had had no contact with other human beings for weeks or even months.

In the event, he and Maxim had been so surprised by the dramatic entry of this bedraggled apparition that they had quite literally been rendered speechless. And although they had recovered their equilibrium sufficiently to give the Norwegian a cup of vodka and something to eat, it had quickly become apparent that they had not the slightest chance of maintaining the pretence that they were Norwegian trappers, since they patently knew very little about traps and baits and the preparation of pelts, and only spoke a few words of Norwegian. They had evaded questions and procrastinated for as long as possible, helped by the facts that the fellow was so tired that he could hardly stand, and that he had a liking for vodka. So they had laughed with him, got him drunk, packed him off into the bunk bed next to the stove, and done away with him in cold blood while he was sleeping like a baby.

It was now eight days since the sealer *Nabokov* had managed to battle through the sea ice to reach the head of Alpefjord, having at last found a narrow strip of open water close to the cliffed shoreline. Under a blanket of cloud, the vessel's captain had managed to stay well clear of the American and Danish ships and planes coming and going between Blyhavn and the outside world, and the Russians were sure that they had come through undetected. After being dropped off, the two men had had a nightmare journey along the shores of two ice-dammed lakes called Dammen and FGuresø. At last, with the aid of a portable inflatable craft and a little outboard engine, they had reached the entrance to the glacier-cut valley which would take them to Frederiksdal and Nordvest Fjord -- and give them access through the Stauning Alps to their destination.

By the time they had reached the broad entrance to Frederiksdal they had run out of food, and they were exhausted after crossing the snouts of innumerable small glaciers and fighting their way across meltwater streams that seemed always to be in spate. At last they had sunk their little boat and its engine, as planned, and had found the trappers' hut. It was just about habitable, and was used only occasionally by the Sledge Patrol and by trappers during the winter hunting season. Nobody had bothered to repair it for years, and although the black tarred felt on the roof was still capable of keeping out the weather, the felt that had once covered the planking walls had been ripped to shreds by polar bears intent upon forcing an entry. They had decided to rest up for a few days and to supplement the tinned rations found in the hut with some fresh meat and eggs. They had been lucky with their hunting, having bagged between them three geese, a muskox and two Arctic hares. They had planned to feed up well, and to take with them as much cooked meat as they could carry, since they were not sure how successful their hunting would be from this point on. Then the storm had come, the Norwegian had appeared from nowhere, and they had been forced to kill him.

During the preparations for their mission Leskov had been told something about the mysterious code of honour that bound these solitary trappers into an arctic brotherhood. There were few enough of them in East Greenland -- maybe twenty Danes and half a dozen Norwegians -- to remain largely unnoticed by officialdom. Like the barnacle geese and golden plovers they moved about according to the dictates of nature, but not all of them stayed for the summer, since their serious hunting was almost always done when the sea ice was thick and when they could travel with their sleds and dog teams. They seemed to prefer the company of their dogs to that of human beings. Theirs was a life on the edge, for they put up with extraordinary deprivation and coped with deadly danger every day of their working lives. They hunted for Arctic foxes and polar bears, and like the Inuits they lived off seals and muskoxen. To a certain extent, there was competition between them, but there were unspoken rules about hunting territories, and nobody knowingly hunted on another man's patch. No trapper would ever steal from a cache of furs and skins left in a hut by someone else. There were even secret codes which these nomads used when they visited their regular huts, which were spaced at intervals of about thirty miles throughout the great wilderness of the East Greenland fjords. A trapper would know from a symbol chalked onto a doorpost or a rock that so-and-so had been in a particular hut two weeks ago, and was headed for Daneborg, or wherever, and would be back again in five weeks. If you came across a trap, you knew whose it was because every man had his own unique design. Food stocks in the huts were always replenished if possible, and a fire was always laid in the stove by the man about to depart, ready to be instantly lit by the next man to arrive, whether or not he was in trouble. Friendship, mutual trust and respect were the watchwords of those who belonged to this community of strange and self-sufficient men -- and it would have been unthinkable for any trapper to refuse to help another in need. It would have been even more unthinkable for any one of these men to harm another — and it was this thought that now haunted Pavel Leskov, who knew that he had betrayed a trust as sacred as that which bound Judas Iscariot and Jesus Christ. That wretched creature had not actually killed his Master, but now, in the cause of this thing called duty, he, Pavel Leskov, had the blood of an amiable and innocent man all over his hands. And not just his hands. He felt that it impregnated every pore of his body, and stained his soul. And to make matters worse, he could not get out of his mind the image of an elegant Norwegian woman and a little girl with blonde curly hair and a cheeky smile.

As for Tolstoy, he was seriously worried about his colleague's black mood. He was thankful that the vodka bottle was empty. He hoped that once they got moving again, after another good night's sleep, they could forget about trappers' huts and corpses and polar bears, and concentrate on the job in hand. They had some hard walking and climbing still to do, travelling so light that there was no room for error or delay. But that was what they had been trained for, and they still had more than two months ahead of them, in which to accomplish their mission and to reach the pick-up point on the shore at Gurreholm, not far from Syd Kap, on the tenth day of September.

CHAPTER 2
July 1962

At last *MS Gullfoss* had stopped rolling, and although it was still pitching and hammering its bows into big swells most of the passengers had recovered their balance and their appetite. The eight members of the Oxford University expedition congregated at the far end of the restaurant and managed to consume everything that the kitchen staff put on their plates. They enjoyed a stream of good-natured banter. Joe Horton remarked that this was the first time they had all been together in one place, upon which Rowland Linney, the party's marine biologist, laughed and said: "Well, Lars and me have been gathered together here in the saloon ever since we left Leith, waiting for the rest of you to turn up. Excellent food, good company, and some mountainous seas to look at through the window. And some jolly Icelandic girls, heading home for the holidays. Very entertaining, it's been. I reckon this sea-sickness thing's all in the mind, and that those who suffer are just looking for sympathy........."

"Bullshit!" said Gwyn Hughes, the Welsh glaciologist from Cambridge, with mock outrage. "You two are just freaks. Normal people throw up in Force Ten storms, especially when they're only a couple of hours out from port. Speaking for myself, I'm a sensitive soul, and I don't like my equilibrium to be disturbed. Give me a nice solid glacier to stand on and I'm happy. The sea moves too much."

Stephen Hanna, the Scottish leader of the expedition, gave a great guffaw. "No room for sensitive wee souls on this trip, boys, that's for sure. And we're all going to have our equilibrium disturbed, if the history of expeditions to East Greenland is anything to go by. But I'd like to have a short briefing with everybody in the saloon in half an hour, to run through some of the practicalities. Are we happy with that?"

The were all pleased with the idea, and thirty minutes later they gathered around three of the fixed tables in the saloon, intent on learning more about each other and about the plans for the coming weeks. Prior to departure, communications between the various expedition members had not been easy, partly because the leader had been heavily involved in Geography Finals and partly because the final make-up of the group had only been determined a fortnight before. The four Oxford men (Hanna, Linney, Horton and Whiteside) knew each other reasonably well, having held many planning meetings in college bars and in Hanna's room in Jesus College. Indeed, three of them had worked very closely — while the leader was sitting his exams — with Horton's girl-friend Susanna Smith on packing food supplies and equipment ready for transport to Leith Docks, and on ensuring that everybody had the tickets they needed to get to Leith in time for the departure of *Gullfoss*.

Lars Knudsen, the Dane, was on the expedition because he had met Horton at an international botany conference the year before and because they had got on well together; and in spite of his youthful appearance he seemed to know as much about living and working in East Greenland as any European alive, after two years with the legendary Sledge Patrol and two other summer seasons as a mineral prospector.

The selection process for the team had been haphazard and therefore rather risky, with personal contacts and recommendations taking the place of formal interviews. That was the way with university expeditions — and on the whole it worked out well, since social misfits and megalomaniacs tended not to be very interested in prolonged periods of physical discomfort and extreme exertions in unexplored wildernesses in the company of strong-willed and adventurous companions. That having been said, when eight men were thrown together in this fashion for eight weeks or more, there was always the possibility of personality clashes, and they were all well aware that very small niggles could — if not dealt with quickly — escalate into major issues that could affect the morale of the whole group. Those who snored, farted, habitually burned the soup or evaded washing up duty were asking for trouble, in spite of the fact that tolerance was, and is, one of the great virtues of an expedition member. As leader, Hanna would have to look out for incompatibilities and for signs of resentment or discontent, and he would have to make up work parties in the field in such a way that the potential for small niggles and big arguments was minimized.........

"Right, boys, let's start," said Hanna. "Glasses all well filled? Enjoy your wee dram while you can — it'll be iced water once we arrive in Greenland." He was physically the biggest man in the party, built like a bull and with a rugby blue to his name. He had fair hair and blue eyes, and even after a few days away from his razor, there was the making of a considerable beard on his chin. His roots were on the island of South Harris in the Outer Hebrides, and he was a fluent Gaelic speaker. He had an ebullient and confident manner, but Gwyn Hughes, who enjoyed people watching, thought that he was essentially quite a shy man. But all the indications were that he was well-liked by the others, and well respected too, since he was an expert skier and mountaineer, with several sessions as an outdoor pursuits instructor under his belt.

"First things first. It's great to have you all on board, and good to have you all together in one place after all the ups and downs during eighteen months of planning. As you all know, this thing almost didn't happen — a month ago we were still short of our four thousand quid target, and thought we'd have to call the whole thing off, but then after a welter of phone calls and undiplomatic activity things suddenly fell into place. The addition of Andy and Griff gave us the extra academic clout we needed — so a big "thank you" to you two guys for agreeing to come on board at such short notice."

"Is a toast in order, my dear old fruit?" asked Peregrin Whiteside. "Whether it is or not, let's raise our glasses to Andy and Griff, for giving up the exotic delights of an English summer just to help us all have a bloody miserable time in Greenland....."

The others laughed, banged the tables, and drank to the health of the two late additions, who looked just a little embarrassed. Joe Horton could not resist reserving a little of his laughter for Whiteside, who was far and away the most eccentric member of the team. He was a big man with unruly fair hair, good-humoured blue eyes and a ruddy complexion arising from either too much alcohol or too much fresh air. He was clearly from a wealthy family, and would not have been out of place in a novel featuring Wooster and Jeeves; but there was not a trace of arrogance about him, and he admitted in private conversations that his privileged background — including an Eton education — had given him more misery than pleasure.

He wore an extravagant silk cravat tucked into the neck of a black and white Norwegian woollen sweater, and it was apparent to all and sundry that he was not in the least concerned about what others thought of him or his dress code. He claimed that he did not really need an Oxford degree at all, since his future was already mapped out for him on his vast family estate, and said that he would be well pleased if he could reach the end of his course without being sent down on the grounds of incompetence or inappropriate behaviour. He apologized profusely for the fact that father was a foreign office minister in the Tory government, and said that the Old Man was not best pleased about his obvious sympathy for the ideas of Karl Marx. He was clearly no scientist, and it was his objective on this trip to conduct a population census of migratory birds. He thought he could just about manage that, once he learned which bird was which. So he would not contribute a great deal to the sum total of human knowledge. But, thought Horton, he might well prove to be a rather valuable member of the team, since he had an impressive record as a climber and had spent time with the British Antarctic Survey. When it came to roping techniques, crevasse rescues, and river crossings, he might just turn out to be the man who would keep his companions out of harm's way; and whenever he looked at him Horton was instantly impressed that this jovial buffoon was not quite as scatty and naive as he made out.

"And another toast, while we're about it," said Hanna. "To Rowland, Joe and Perry here, for all the hard grind they put in while I was stuck in those blasted Examination Schools..........."

Again tables were banged and ale was quaffed, and Rowland Linney shouted above the racket: "And don't forget that good woman of Joe's — Susanna Smith, the sex goddess of the Woodstock Road. She's been amazing over the last few weeks, with letters flying off all over the world and with God knows how many phone calls being subsidized by her long-suffering father. Now that we're here and she's still in Oxford, I have to say I quite miss her!"

"Careful, Linney," grinned Horton. "She's mine. Or at least I hope she is, and hope she still is when we all get home. Never fear — I've already thanked her in private. Now, can we please get back on track?"

Hanna pressed on. "First, the expedition prospectus. You all had copies before we left, with details of personal CVs, work programme, rations, equipment and so forth. More by luck than judgment, it looks as if the prospectus still stands. We'll arrive in Reykjavik on the day after tomorrow, and we'll stay in the youth hostel for two days while we get everything ready for the flights to Greenland. It'll be all hands on deck. First we have to get all five tons of our equipment, which came out on the last *Gullfoss* sailing, through customs in the dockside bonded warehouse and over to the hangar at the airport. There we have to separate out the delicate stuff that has to be carried or sent over to Himmelbjerg by plane from all the rest, which needs to be sorted according to our detailed list into ten parachute loads, each weighing about 200 kilos. No deviation — if a load is too heavy the parachute won't work properly, and we might well find the load on the ground, smashed to smithereens. We'll need help from the Icelandair staff on padding and roping up the bundles, and we also need help with getting the parachutes. Lars will be invaluable in liaising with the Icelanders, since most of them understand Danish better than English. We've got an indication that the US Air Force in Keflavik will lend us the ten parachutes — but that still has to be confirmed, and the parachutes will have to be picked up from the US air base. As soon as we're ready, we'll fly out in two chartered DC3 flights to Blyhavn. The second flight will carry the ten parachute loads, and once we land at the airstrip we will have a couple of hours at most to get everything ready for the drop. We just have to pray for good weather — if the cloud base is too low for flying across the Werner Mountains, we're stuffed, since we only have the DC3 for one day. Some of us will go with the aircraft and tell them exactly where the drop is to be made, as close as we can manage to the location we've chosen for Base Camp..........."

"What happens if there are strong winds?" asked Petherton.

"Well, my dear fellow, I watched some drops in the Antarctic," said Whiteside. "The best that can happen in strong crosswinds is that the loads are scattered over a vast area. Bloody nuisance. The worst that can happen is that the loads get dragged along on the ground after landing, in which case, we'll have to cope with some nasty damage."

"That's my understanding too," said Hanna. "We just have to trust in the good judgment of the pilot and crew of the aircraft. OK — once the loads are down, and we are all back at Blyhavn, and the aircraft has gone, we'll sort ourselves out and sleep in one of the mining huts as arranged by Lars. We'll leave the theodolites and other delicate equipment at the airstrip for the Greenland Metals light aircraft or the helicopter to take over to Himmelbjerg. Then we'll start walking, and use one of the Caterpillar tractor routes over the mountains — they are all pretty safe, and are used for hauling out the milled molybdenum ore from the mine on sledge trains. But we'll have very heavy packs — maybe up to 50 lbs each. If nothing else, the walk will get us fit, and we hope we can do it in two days. Any questions?"

"What about safety?" asked Griff Mortimer. "I noticed in the prospectus that we have no radio and no firearms. Doesn't that make us rather vulnerable?"

"Perhaps I can come in here?" asked Knudsen, the man with the greatest local knowledge. "Back-pack radios are useless in East Greenland. I've tried them, using standard military models. They're heavy, unreliable, and they hardly ever give you a transmission range of more than twenty miles. As for firearms, they're more trouble than they are worth, given that I have never yet encountered a polar bear in a summer field season. And how many guns would we carry? One? Two? Ten? Once we're at work, we'll be scattered all over the tundra, and a gun at Base Camp is no good to me if I encounter a polar bear thirty miles away somewhere up in the mountains."

"That was our judgment too," said Horton. "We did a somewhat unscientific risk assessment, and decided that we'd be better off travelling light and staying well clear of nasty predators."

Hanna nodded. "Quite so. So we settled on a good supply of emergency rocket flares and smoke canisters in case anything goes wrong, and we'll have to depend on the guys at Himmelbjerg spotting one of them if they are used. Now then — I'm almost done. Just a few more details. If all goes according to plan, we'll stick to the programme we laid out. Once we're through the mountains and near the snout of Sirius Glacier, we'll walk up to the Himmelbjerg mine, pick up our equipment, and then plod down the western side of the Schuchert Glacier and Schuchert Valley to the Base Camp site. God knows how long that walk will take us — four days if we are lucky and if the weather holds. Phase One of the programme will run from July 8th to the 18th, on which date we'll all meet up at Base, review our findings, and start on Phase Two immediately. If the canoes are undamaged after the parachute drop, and if sea conditions are all right, four of us will then work on the Bear Islands for ten days, while the other six work from Base Camp. In Phase Three, in the first couple of weeks of August, we'll split into three groups, with four of us paddling up Nordvest Fjord to Frederiksdal while two go over to Jameson Land. On the principle that somebody should always be at Base Camp, Rowland and Joe will work from there while the rest of us are away having adventures. After that, we have two more phases of work, but we'll leave those for now; and it's probably wise to assume that they will need to be modified anyhow because of bad weather or other unforeseen events. Whatever happens, there'll be a pickup at Syd Kap around 5th September, and we are booked to get away from Sandvig on the *Kista Dan* two days later. Queries?"

"Thanks, Steffo," said Lars Knudsen, sitting back in his chair. "That all sounds perfectly feasible. All we need now is good weather and good health."

"Top up your glasses, boys," said Hanna. "There are a few more wee things I want to mention........"

There was a scramble for the bar, but Joe Horton stayed put since he still had half of a double whisky in his glass. He watched the others and speculated idly on the dynamics within the group, trying to work out where instinctive friendships might be forged and where points of friction and even flashpoints might occur when the team started to encounter discomforts and difficulties in the field.

"A penny for your thoughts," said Gwyn Hughes quietly, as he returned to the table with his filled glass. "You have a mysterious grin on your face. More enigmatic than the Mona Lisa, you are."

Horton laughed. "That's no grin. Apparently I always look like that when I'm thinking. I was just pondering on what an ill-assorted group we are. But we have some really good chaps on board — and I think I'd trust my life to most of them."

"Most, but not all?"

"Well, there's you for a start. I'm an Oxford man, and you're from

Cambridge. If I was to fall in the water and look as if I was about to drown, would you really haul me out?"

"I'd like to think that I would overcome my prejudices and do the right thing, Joe. Besides, I covet that bloody great knife you carry in your belt, and wouldn't like to see that go to the bottom!"

"You are too observant for your own good, Gwyn. I thought it was invisible. It will come in handy one of these days — just you wait and see. So I can count on you. That's good to know. As for our friend Rowland Linney, I'm not sure how somebody that frail and wet behind the ears ever got onto this expedition. I hope he can pull his weight and carry his loads without buckling at the knees."

"Guys with that sort of wiry build often have fantastic stamina. He's as scatty as hell, but he's got a first class degree, and had half a dozen research papers published while he was still an undergraduate. There's not a lot he doesn't know about ring seals and harp seals."

"Well, that's very reassuring," chortled Horton. "If I ever have to eat one of them I'll ask him how to cook it. Seriously though, I hope he doesn't need too much looking after. If he was to be left on his own anywhere in East Greenland, I think I might be concerned for his safety. With his stringy whiskers, wild hair and staring eyes, he looks more like a mad nuclear scientist than a timid zoologist………"

"Don't judge people too quickly, Joe. Hidden depths and all that. You and I will get a few surprises before we're through with this expedition, that's for sure………"

The others were now back at the tables with drinks in hand, and so Hanna continued with his briefing. "A few things of a general nature, if I may. First of all, you must excuse my Scots manner of speaking — I'd be happier speaking Gaelic, but today I have to go with the flow. If there's anything you don't understand, ask Joe. He and I have spent so much time together that he actually understands most of the things I say."

"Correction. **Some** of the things you say," said Horton with a grin.

"Very well — I'll speak slowly. Practicalities. First, the Greenland Metals mine. The guys there have been incredibly helpful so far, and Lars has been able to contact some of those he's known for years, in order to line up assorted bits of assistance. But we mustn't assume that they'll always be around to do things for us — so we must try to be as independent as possible. They've a commercial operation to run, and just a couple of months to get their minerals out to the coast and shipped away before the ice closes in again in September. Their light aircraft and helicopter will be in use all the time on their own projects, and there may also be some aircraft and research vessels at work in our field areas, doing mineral exploration and mapping work. Some of that will be work done by various Danish government agencies. We'd best keep out of their way, and we shouldn't expect any logistical help from them at all. As for the Danes, they've been very helpful to us in giving us consents for our field programme and so forth. We probably won't see anything of the Sledge Patrol guys — they'll be holed up in Daneborg, way up north, waiting for their beloved deep freeze to return so that they can get out onto the sea ice with their dog teams. We might see something of the Danish Administrator who looks after our area — he's based in Sandvig. Then we come to the Greenlanders. Some of them might appear out of the blue, but we hear that the little settlement at Syd Kap has been abandoned — we aren't sure why. They've got some houses there, and there's a good modern house which was built by the government, and which we have permission to use. There's also a big hut at Gurreholm, on the Jameson Land side of the Schuchert estuary. We have permission to use that too, if we want to. By all accounts it's in a pretty good state of repair."

"There are a few other prospectors' and trappers' huts as well," said Knudsen. "They're very small, and some of them have been almost destroyed by polar bears, but they're useful as emergency shelters, and some might even contain food supplies which may or may not be edible."

"Back to the Inuits. If we do meet any of them communication will be difficult — but some of them will be able to speak Danish, and if Lars is around we should be able to get on with them all right. Correct?"

"Quite correct, Steffo," nodded Knudsen. "I don't know any of the people from Sandvig, but some of my old friends on the Sledge Patrol are very fond of them. They are by all accounts gentle, peaceful people — quiet and shy, and difficult to get to know, but trying very hard to come to terms with the modern world of ships, planes, science, mining operations and so forth. And we mustn't forget alcohol and infectious diseases too —

both responsible for social upheavals. We'll do well to remember that the inner part of Scoresby Sund, where much of our work will be concentrated, has a profound spiritual significance for the Greenlanders. Hall Bredning, just off Syd Kap, is a traditional fishing ground. It's also at the entrance to Nordvest Fjord, whose black waters are almost a mile deep. It's a place which holds the spirits of their ancestors, and which must not be defiled. Please, friends, remember that if you will."

"So how do we avoid contaminating or desecrating their sacred territory?" asked Griff Mortimer with a heavy frown on his brow.

"I can only guess," smiled Knudsen, "since they're not very forthcoming with others who seek to understand their beliefs. But as I understand it, the thing which they hate most of all in their sacred places is violence and any signs of conflict left in the landscape."

"But how can that make sense?' persisted Mortimer. "They kill polar bears, seals, walruses and narwhals all the time, whenever they get the chance. That seems pretty violent, to my way of thinking."

"That's where you're wrong, Griff. Their killing of animals is almost a ritual, and as I understand it, they see their hunting activities as a part of their contract with the natural world. They have huge respect for the spirits of the animals, and seem to think that those which die during their hunting trips give themselves to the hunters in exchange for the protection of the environment and the continuation of the old ways. No — the violence they hate most of all goes with the military apparatus which they seem to associate most of all with the Americans. When I was in Jameson Land some years ago, an American C-130 Hercules aircraft flew straight over Sandvig village, just a few hundred feet up, scaring the living daylights out of everybody, not to mention hundreds of dogs. The pilot didn't need to do that — he was probably just trying to impress people, or showing off, on his way up to Blyhavn. The Greenlanders asked me what the aircraft was for, and I tried to explain that it was in Greenland to protect them. "Protect us? From whom?" they asked. "Well, from the enemy," I said. "But we have no enemies," they said. They were angry and mystified, and in the end I fear I gave up on the conversation, and had to walk away with tears in my eyes. I was sad not because of their naivety and innocence, but because of our own insensitivity and stupidity.........."

There was silence for a while, before Hanna resumed his briefing. "Thanks for that, Lasse," he said. "An appropriate reminder that in East Greenland we'll be working in a very alien environment — alien in many different ways. On the military front, we shouldn't be too surprised if we see signs of activity. Nowhere escapes the influence of the Cold War — not even Greenland. There are a number of military bases on the west coast, close to the United States and Canada, and a few on the ice sheet as well. Some of the NATO or American bases are top secret, and you only have to read the newspapers to know that the Russians are prowling about too, especially along the North Atlantic fringes of the Arctic sea ice, using vessels which they traditionally refer to as sealers or trawlers or oceanographic research vessels. They're generally not armed, but they are sure as hell crammed full with sophisticated gadgetry and manned by military personnel. The Foreign Office asked us to stay well clear of any military exercises or any other military activity — that seemed to be a bit of a strange request, but now I've done my duty and passed it on."

"I think I want my money back," grinned Linney. "We've been conned into believing that we were going on a jolly walking holiday in a pristine wilderness, and now you tell us we'll be stuck in the middle of a bloody shooting range..........."

"Too late," said Horton. "Your hundred quid's already spent. I think the chap from the Foreign Office was just following the party line — he probably says the same thing to every expedition that sets off from Britain, no matter what part of the world they are heading for. We probably won't see a single ship or plane for the whole of the time we're in the field."

"Some final points about safety," said Hanna. "Some of you guys know this far better than I do, but our field area is a place that deserves the utmost respect. The most dangerous thing we'll encounter is the Schuchert River, the biggest and most violent river in Greenland. It's fed by the meltwater from at least eleven glaciers, and it will be at its highest precisely during our weeks in the field. It's uncrossable in its lower reaches, but crossing might be possible high up in the valley, above the Roslin Glacier, during cool weather and in the middle of the night when melting rates are low. Otherwise, for God's sake don't attempt to get across it, even with ropes. There are plenty of other streams which are dangerous too, and please make sure that ropes are used properly on every single crossing. When we're walking from Blyhavn to Himmelbjerg we'll have several difficult river crossings to do, and Perry will give us some intensive training in the methods to be used. All right, Perry?"

"It's in the schedules, old fruit. Happy to help if I can."

"Then we have glacier climbing and sea canoeing as other potential hazards. Please, everybody, use ropes, ice axes and crampons on glaciers at all times. We've got the right gear and we must use it properly. Again, we can get some practice in when we're walking over the Werner Mountains. As far as the sea is concerned, we have a lot of canoeing to do, and quite a few trips as well on the small inflatable craft which will be dropped at Base Camp in one of the parachute loads. Just one thing to remember. Don't go into the water. Not ever. Especially if you are wearing cold weather clothing, waterproofs and boots. We have lifejackets with us, but they're actually completely useless. If you are in a canoe which goes over in the sea, in deep water, you can expect to live for maybe ten minutes at most — but after two minutes you'll probably be incapable of helping yourself."

"God, Steffo, you are a bundle of laughs this evening, aren't you?" said Gwyn Hughes. "But quite right you are. This is all about risk management — and I agree that one must develop a healthy respect for the environment we'll be working in. If something we're planning to do looks, in the cold light of day, to be too risky, then we must all learn to back off. Greenland is no place for macho behaviour. Those who are prudent are the ones who survive to tell the tale."

"Well said, friends," nodded Knudsen. "I've no wish to attend any funerals or memorial services either during this trip or afterwards. Respect for the wilderness is rule number one. Prudence at all times is rule number two. And the third rule is this: look after your comrades. If we obey those rules, we'll enjoy the most wonderful few weeks of our lives, and return home a little older and a lot wiser."

"So, my dear fellows," said Whiteside in a voice thick with emotion, "we've heard many wise words this evening, and we must keep them in mind at all times. I think another toast is in order. Raise your glasses if you will, and drink to the success of the 1962 Scoresby Sund expedition, and to a safe return for all men of goodwill."

They stood, and repeated the toast, and touched glasses, and then drained them. And then they talked far into the night.

Jim Wagner was well pleased, since news had come through that the Caterpillar in the crevasse in the Mellem Pass was not too badly damaged, and that hardly any of the electronic equipment on the sledge had been lost. If the weather held, they should have everything away from the Pass and delivered to Himmelbjerg within a few days. But they would wait until the Oxford explorers had come and gone, since they would probably be sharp-eyed buggers who would see everything and ask too many questions for comfort. Those fellows would probably start their trek over the mountains tomorrow, he thought, since their parachute drops had clearly gone according to plan. He had seen the Icelandair DC3 on its way south, and on its way north again an hour later, and Larry Bishop, the Himmelbjerg radio operator, had made radio contact with the pilot and confirmed that parachute dropping conditions had been perfect. They had been lucky, for the weather forecast was ominous for the next few days........

Wagner decided to go for a walk on the glacier while the going was good. He followed the steeply sloping passage down from his observation room, went down the steps past the ore crushing plant and noisy diesel generators, crossed the vast cavern which had once been used for the mining of mineral ores, and eventually emerged from the dim electrically-lit interior of the mountain into the bright sunshine. He breathed deeply, filling his lungs with the cool crisp air of the pristine wilderness in which he was now stranded for two or three months. He was not as fit as he used to be, and had mixed feelings about descending to the mine entrance, since it meant he would have to struggle all the way back up again later on — a climb of over 800 feet. He still felt resentful that the assholes in the Pentagon had not given him a big enough budget to pay for a lift on the inside of the mountain, on the grounds that such luxury would give rise to "unwarranted suspicions" about what was going on there.

For a while he chatted with some of the American and Danish engineers who were putting the finishing touches to the iron door at the mine entrance. Then he wandered along on the clean ice surface for twenty minutes or so, before sitting down on a ridge of moraine to enjoy the warmth of the afternoon sun. He took a sip of Jack Daniels from his hip flask, and thought that all was well with the world........

"Boss! " came a shout from one of the huts on the moraine near the mine entrance, a couple of hundred yards away. "Can I have a word?"

Wagner recognized the voice as that of Larry Bishop, who must have been told by one of the other men of his whereabouts. He waved his arm in the air, in acknowledgement. "Sure, Larry," he shouted. "Come on over."

Bishop hurried across the ice and settled down onto the stony moraine next to his boss. "Message just in from Keflavik," he said quietly. "I've just finished unscrambling it."

"I'm giving myself half a day off, Larry, and I'm feeling very mellow. Can't it wait?"

"Afraid not, Boss. High priority, top security rating."

"Aw, shit! Go on then, tell me the worst."

"You know that Russian sealer 60 miles north of Jan Mayen which was spotted a fortnight back by the U2 from Keflavik?"

"Yep. Sculling about in waters where there ain't any seals, as usual. So?"

"They spotted it moving westwards, towards the Greenland coast, as soon as the winter pack ice began to break up. Then the cloud increased and they lost sight of it. Anyway, yesterday the cloud over most of the North Atlantic cleared, and the sealer has disappeared......."

"Things don't just disappear, Larry."

"The problem is that they haven't seen it for ten days or more. It hasn't gone back to Murmansk, that's for sure. There's still a thick blanket of cloud all the way along the Greenland coast from Sandvig to Daneborg, over the pack ice belt, and the powers that be reckon the sealer has found a lead and has come in towards the coast, somewhere to the north of here."

"Bugger! Are they on to us?"

"HQ doesn't think so, but it can't be ruled out. We listen to all their messages, and they listen to all of ours. As far as we know, they haven't cracked our June or July codes. Problem is, we haven't cracked theirs

31

either, so we have no advantage. "

"OK," said Wagner slowly, with a deep frown on his brow. "So they are snooping. Not my problem, Larry........"

"Afraid it is, Boss. Keflavik says that if the sealer is in the pack ice belt, or even in the fjords, it's off their patch and onto yours. As you may recall, when you took this job it was on condition that all decisions here would be yours, without interference from Keflavik, Sondrestrom or Camp Century."

"Quite right you are, Larry. The buck stope here. But I don't have the resources to investigate — they fucking well know that."

"Of course. But they promised to keep the U2 flights going, in the hope of catching a glimpse if there should be a sudden break in the cloud. They'll let us know at once if they see anything. In the meantime, the General says he'll try to come over to Blyhavn within the next three weeks for a progress report, weather permitting."

"Progress report?" snarled Wagner. "Don't the bastards trust me?"

"Nobody trusts anybody in this business, Boss, as we all know. Anyway, it's no bad thing for them to be up to speed — it means you're a bit less exposed if anything goes wrong."

Wagner grinned suddenly. "Wise words, Larry. Here, have a sip of Jack Daniels. There's great comfort to be had in the Holy Spirit........"

Seventy-two hours into the walk across the Werner Mountains, Petherton was the first one to collapse from sheer exhaustion. That was not surprising, given that he was the oldest in the group. They were all on their last legs, staggering erratically one after another through knee-deep slushy snow, encumbered with thirty-kilo packs, and suffering from heavy physical demands the like of which none of them had ever encountered before. They were roped together in two groups of four. They had had no sleep at all since leaving the airstrip at Blyhavn. The storm that had been chasing them down the glacier from the col had finally overtaken them, and as the wind accelerated to gale force the snow came with it, reducing visibility to less than ten yards. Seven of the men in the line had been trying to use the deep water-filled footprints made by their colleague who led the first group, but now even the effort of lifting one foot at a time, one agonizing stride after another, was too much for them. Hughes and Mortimer, on either side of the Australian, tried to drag him to his feet, but he gasped: "Just give me a minute or two to catch my breath, boys, and I'll be all right..........."

Several of the others subsided into the snow, grateful for a moment's rest, and Joe Horton, who was the last man in the second line, wondered what the young leader would do. They were only three days into the trip, and all of his decisions thus far had been spot-on. This time, as Horton watched him closely, Hanna got it right too. With a minimum of discussion, he decided that they had to put the tents up and get some food into their stomachs before trying to catch up on lost sleep. The leader, who was in truth less fit than some of the others, having spent the last few months preparing for his final exams, somehow found the strength to disconnect the ropes binding the men together and to help them out of their cumbersome pack harnesses. "Right, boys," he said. "We've got no option but to camp where we are, and let's hope there isn't a yawning crevasse right under us. We could head for the edge of the glacier where there might be some shelter near a ridge of moraine, but getting there might be more risky than staying put."

Peregrin Whiteside nodded. "Agree with that, old man. Let's do it."

Within a few minutes they had three tents up, with snow piled onto the snow-flaps and ice axes holding a few essential guy ropes in place. They used their pack-loads as wind breaks on the up-glacier side of the tents, and then crawled inside, two or three to a tent, in the hope that their combined weights would suffice to prevent the flimsy cotton structures from taking off as the wind thundered around them. They had no time, or inclination, to unpack sleeping bags and mattresses. In each tent they got a Primus stove going, melted some slush and cooked up a pot of whichever dried soup came to hand in the food rations. Then they huddled together for warmth and sipped at their steaming mugs, fighting to stay awake as they consumed the contents. Linney had fallen asleep in a sitting position even before the soup was ready, and had to be woken up and forced to drink it.

Suddenly Whiteside shouted: "Now then, my dear fellows! Time for a treat!" He dived into the depths of his rucksack and emerged with a lump of currant cake, wrapped up in greaseproof paper. It was rather battered, but in good enough condition to be cut laboriously into eight slices with the aid of a trusty Swiss Army knife. He handed some over to the inhabitants of his own tent and then delivered slices to the others as well.

"Quite excellent," said Gwyn Hughes, with a burp. "Perry, you are a bloody genius, and generous to boot. No wonder you were staggering, with all that extra weight on board. Where the hell did you get a cake from, in Greenland?"

"Bribery and corruption, old fruit. There was this nice lady in the galley of the *Gullfoss*, on the way over, and we got chatting, as one does......" They all roared with laughter. Then, soaking wet from perspiration and wet snow, they tried to sleep.

Four or five of the lucky ones did manage to nod off, but after three hours of extreme discomfort the groundsheets were running with water and the weight of fresh snow was such that the space inside each tent was halved. Suddenly there was a noticeable change to the pitch of the strumming on the guy ropes, and the deep-throated roaring of the gale gave way to something more akin to an ominous growl. The more experienced men in the party appreciated that this lowering of the windspeed gave them an opportunity to move downslope away from this middle part of the glacier, where snow accumulation and melting were more or less balanced, and where underfoot conditions were always horrendous. This lull might not last for long, and there might not be another break for four or five days. Hanna, who had not managed to sleep, decided to strike camp. After a few minutes of shouting and cajoling, everybody else was awake and out of the tents, and although the snow was still falling they managed to get everything, including three sodden tents, stuffed back into their packs and were ready to go. Roped up again, and with visibility still no better than ten yards, they set off down a gentle gradient, knowing that the change from knee-deep slush to firm glacier ice could not be that far ahead. They had all decided against wearing crampons, because they were worthless in such wet conditions, and they had all dispensed with their gloves, because they were saturated and did nothing to keep their hands warm.

It was then that Hanna went down the crevasse. He had been in the lead, roped up properly in a group of four and prodding ahead with his ice axe, but suddenly the snow bridge that had been taking his considerable weight gave way, and he was gone, causing the first of his colleagues on the lead rope to pitch forward into the slushy mess of the glacier surface as the rope snapped tight. But they had done everything by the book, and once the first men in the line had taken the weight and secured the rope, Whiteside instinctively took charge of the situation, with the implicit approval of everybody else. He approached cautiously and stared down through a neat circular hole into the void. He could not see Hanna, but the Scot yelled up from the depths to say that he was all right, and that he was jammed between blue ice walls.

"Are you injured?" shouted Whiteside. "Legs and arms moving all right?"

"Yes, I think so. But my right leg's numb and seems to be jammed in an awkward position........"

"Is it painful? Can you move your right foot about?"

After a long delay, Hanna shouted back: "No pain, and the foot seems OK."

"That's a relief. Have you still got your ice axe?"

"Yes — the loop's still around my wrist. But it's not going to help me to get out of here. I'm totally stuck — I think my pack is stopping me from falling further."

On hearing that, Whiteside released the rope a little, and discovered that his colleague's assumption was quite correct. "That's bloody bad news, old man," he shouted into the echoing depths. "It's much easier to pull up a dangling man than one who's jammed. I'd better come down and give you a hand."

The rescuer, who had claimed before they left Blyhavn to have been into more crevasses than hot baths in his twenty-four years, could not work out the alignment of this particular fissure, and was afraid that if they did not define its edges somebody else, with or without a rope, might go through the snow bridge. So he began to excavate with his ice axe, causing vast quantities of slush to rain down on Hanna, who was not amused. But eventually the edges of the five-foot wide crevasse were revealed, and they were able to concentrate on a rescue. Now they could see Hanna quite clearly, about twenty feet down. They fixed a second rope to a couple of embedded ice axes while Whiteside fitted crampons to his boots. Then they let him down until he was close enough to their fallen colleague to assess the situation and to work out a strategy for getting him and his pack safely up to the surface.

Luckily there was enough light for Whiteside to see what was going on, and after a few minutes of trying to release Hanna, or at least move him into a less contorted position, he shouted up to the surface: "Pull Steffo's rope as tight as you can, and fix it so that he doesn't fall any further! Then send me another rope for his pack.........." Down came the extra rope, and the rescuer braced himself across the crevasse while he helped Hanna to wriggle clear of the shoulder straps of his bulky pack. It was exhausting work, and he had to stop frequently to catch his breath. Then the rope was affixed to the pack, and it was hauled up to the surface by the others. Hanna was now able to move, and to assess the extent of the damage to his own body. There was a lot of blood about, but Whiteside discovered that it had all come from superficial grazes and cuts to his head and hands, caused by contact with sharp and brittle projections of blue ice on the sides of the crevasse. Repairs would have to wait until they were back on the glacier surface. Then four colleagues -- Horton, Knudsen, Petherton and Hughes -- took the strain, and inch by inch the big man, uttering a string of Scottish Presbyterian oaths, was lifted through a cascade of meltwater and lumps of slush to the surface.

Just as Hanna got to the lip of the crevasse and was grabbed by the others, Petherton lost his footing and fell onto the glacier surface with a cry of pain.   Lars Knudsen, who had been filming the rescue on the expedition's movie camera, abandoned that task and jumped to his side. "Andy, what's the matter?" he asked, as he lifted him into a sitting position.

"My bloody back again! What a drongo........." moaned Petherton. "An old Aussie Rules injury, I think. Hasn't given me any grief for fifteen years or more -- I'd pretty well forgotten about it."

"Damn!" said Linney. "A man with a busted back. Last thing we needed in our current predicament."

Horton gave his colleague a withering look. "Not Andy's fault. Things happen. This could have clobbered any one of us -- we probably all carry old injuries of one sort or another. Take it easy for a few minutes, Andy, and we'll see how you feel then."

"Hey! You buggers! How about me?" came a voice from within the crevasse; and in response they managed to pull Whiteside out too, very wet and tired from his exertions, but otherwise none the worse for wear.

"Bloody good, Perry!" said Hughes, slapping him on the back as he stood and shook slush and water from his unruly blonde hair and then tidied up his silk cravat. "I'm very impressed. This is an expedition of all the talents — thank God we've got somebody who knows how to get into a deep hole and back out of it again.."

After ten minutes Hanna had regained his composure and confirmed that his legs and arms were in good working order. He punched Whiteside on the arm, and said: "Thanks, Perry. Appreciate that — and I know how hard it was for you down there, braced as you were across the abyss. I had plenty of time to look around, and I couldn't see the bottom. It must be at least a couple of hundred feet deep. If ever you need rescuing, just let me know. I owe you one.............."

"And the whole thing recorded for posterity!" gushed Knudsen. "While you fellows were working flat out, I had the film camera rolling. It'll be great for my Hollywood block-buster. Action sequences are important, especially since almost everything else I'll be filming will be mundane work, and pretty boring by comparison."

Ten minutes later Hanna had been cleaned up and repaired by Mortimer, the expedition's medic, using assorted bandages and plasters from the small medical kit they carried with them. But he was wet and cold, and wanted to get moving. It was still snowing, and the wind was picking up again. They had to go on. Petherton was back on his feet, stretching and grimacing and insisting that he was all right. He confirmed that he could still walk, in spite of complaining of dizziness; but when he tried to lift his pack onto his back so that the trek could continue, he was clearly in great distress. So the other seven members of the party split his load between them, leaving him with an empty pack. As for the rest of them, their packs were now grotesque, with assorted extraneous items tied on with light rope. Each man's pack could only be lifted into position with the help of others; some of them were certainly in excess of sixty pounds.

At last, with Hughes taking the lead, and with Petherton at number three in the second roped line where he could be carefully watched, they set off again. They crossed the crevasse at a point where it was less than four feet wide, and where there was a thick and solid snow bridge. Two or three times the injured Australian almost stumbled and fell while suffering from more dizzy spells, but after about an hour they noticed that the slush which they cursed with every step was thinning -- and suddenly they walked out of it onto crisp blue glacier ice. Simultaneously the wind dropped and the snowfall stopped, and as they watched in amazement the enveloping cloud started to break up into wraiths which danced upwards and disappeared into thin air, to be replaced by shafts of sunshine. Within a few minutes the cloud that had enveloped them was all gone from their immediate vicinity, and as they watched it rolled back up the glacier towards the col which they had crossed seven hours earlier.

Now, as they stood in bright warm sunshine, the view which opened before them was something none of them would never forget. They helped each other out of their pack harnesses and then used the packs as chairs as they adjusted to the light and drank in the life-affirming essence of East Greenland.

"Good God!" murmured Hanna. "Even better than the Cuillins from Loch Eishort..........."

On either side of them, breaks in the evaporating cloud gave them glimpses of improbably sharp rock pinnacles high on the valley sides, draped in fresh snow but now streaming with water as the melt set in. To the south, they could see all the way down the Schuchert Valley and its vast river, five miles wide and fifty miles long, and supplied with a never-ending torrent of sediment-heavy meltwater by the glaciers of the Stauning Alps and the Werner Mountains. It was a braided river made up of a myriad of shifting channels which were so swiftly blocked with boulders and rolling stones that a map of it today might be quite different from that of yesterday or tomorrow. Lars Knudsen, who knew it well, said that its fearsome reputation was based partly on the sheer volume and speed of the water flow and partly on the abundance of boulders rolling on its bed, which were quite large enough to break a leg. If that was not enough of a deterrent, the water was so heavily laden with sediment that it was impossible to judge the depth of individual stream segments from the banks; there were hidden pools and temporary cataracts everywhere. Some of the expedition members would have to try to cross the river in its higher reaches at some stage, but that was something to worry about later on...........

Beyond the mouth of the river the weary explorers could see the wide expanse of Hall Bredning, in the inner part of Scoresby Sund, its water glittering in the sunshine, littered with patches of sea ice and with thousands of icebergs of all shapes and sizes. And beyond that, they could see the strange little archipelago called the Bear Islands and the plateau ice-caps and mountain peaks of Renland, Milne Land and Knud Rasmussen's Land. For those who had not been to East Greenland before, the clarity of the light was awesome. They knew from their mental maps of the terrain that the most distant peaks were almost 250 miles from the Sirius Glacier on which they were standing. Away to their right there was an even more spectacular landscape, dominated by the glaciers, snowfields and summits of the Stauning Alps, some of which were the highest and most difficult alpine peaks in Greenland. About twenty were already climbed and recorded, but there were still dozens of virgin peaks there, unmapped and even unobserved. They would leave those to be conquered by the frivolous members of the climbing fraternity, said Hughes with disdain in his voice.

"Huh!" said Whiteside, with a broad grin on his ruddy features. "My dear fellow, frivolous those mountaineers may be, but if I'd not learned more than a little from them about crevasse rescues, our esteemed leader might still be stuck down in that big icy crack. Some climbers are afflicted by a death wish, but they jolly well have their uses, I can assure you from experience."

An hour later, at the junction between the Sirius Glacier and the Schuchert Glacier, the eight weary explorers turned right and set off towards the red mountain called Himmelbjerg, the site of the Greenland

Metals molybdenum mine, where they were due to collect the delicate surveying and glaciology equipment which the mining company had flown in from the coast. Its Cessna aircraft, fitted with ski landing gear, flitted back and forth several times a day, and other trips were made by a helicopter; and Lars Knudsen, who seemed to know everything and everybody, had made the arrangements. Hanna was reassured by the thought that Petherton could soon be properly examined by the mine doctor; and although the invalid protested that he would quickly walk off his injury, the leader was prepared to take no chances.

At nine o'clock on a fine summer morning the seven fit men, accompanied by another who was obviously in some distress, saw the pyramidal peak of Himmelbjerg ahead of them, flanked by the valleys of the Schuchert and Arcturus Glaciers. In reality they were looking at the end of a long mountain spur, but its sheer bulk and spectacular red colouring made it stand out from all of the other summits and ridges in this part of the Werner Mountains. It seemed to shimmer in the sunlight, and Hanna said: "Hmmm. It does look a bit ethereal. I can see now why the early explorers called it "the mountain of heaven." On the other hand, it's not exactly beautiful……………"

"Agree with that, Steffo," said Linney, tugging on his stringy beard. "To me, it looks a bit intimidating, and even threatening."

"Well, all mountains look threatening to you, Rowland," grinned Mortimer. "You're obviously one of those lowland people, most comfortable down at sea-level, or preferably beneath it, looking at seals. Seriously though, a miner at Blyhavn told me that the proportions of the mountain and the colour are down to the presence of a huge "ore body" in the rocks. There are exceptionally high concentrations of molybdenum and other ores here — that's why this mountain's such a valuable asset for Greenland Metals A/S."

They plodded on up the glacier, with Himmelbjerg becoming an increasingly dominant part of the landscape ahead of them. Now they could see more and more detail on its steep rock surfaces, including fractures, small landslide scars, and even individual veins of intensely red and orange rock which they assumed to be the most valuable concentrations of minerals running back into the heart of the mountain, where the mining operations were taking place. They could see several small openings where the miners had burst through from the interior, presumably for ventilation purposes, and close to the summit of the mountain, well over a thousand feet above the surface of the glacier, there seemed to be a larger opening where they could see sunlight glinting on a sheet of glass. The walkers could not resist speculating about it, but Mortimer was again able to act as the purveyor of sound information. "They've got a radio room up there," he said. "The chap from Blyhavn told me that in the past they've had terrible problems with radio communications because of the high surrounding peaks and because of interference from the mineral ores inside the mountain. So they've had to put new aerials right on top of the mountain and build a new radio shack as high up as possible, to minimize magnetic interference."

"So that's involved very heavy investment," said Hughes. "It looks as if Greenland Metals is here for the long haul........"

An hour later the men saw the mining settlement ahead of them, perched high on a bank of moraine and scree at the foot of the mountain and on the Arcturus Glacier flank. They knew that the men at the Blyhavn airstrip ironically referred to this place as "the ski resort" because this was where most of the investment was nowadays. But one could hardly have imagined anything less likely to be used for recreation. No shops, no roads, no entertainments -- just a collection of red prefabricated huts on wooden platforms, scattered here and there on slight terraces that had been carved out for them, and connected by precarious footpaths.

Suddenly the explorers got the shock of their lives when they heard a small dog barking. They could hardly believe their ears, and while they tried to work out where the sound had come from a Jack Russell terrier came bounding towards them across the ice, with its tail wagging furiously. That was surreal enough, but then a dapper middle-aged gentlemen carrying a cane walking stick appeared from behind a ridge of moraine, looking for all the world as if he was out for his Sunday constitutional in a leafy park in Copenhagen. He wore a trilby hat on his head, and was dressed in cavalry twills and a tweed jacket. "Good morning, gentlemen!" he shouted in perfect English. "I've been expecting you. I'm Alfred Jensen, the mine doctor. This little creature is Hamlet, who protects me from polar

41

bears. You're late, I think...... no doubt because of the storm?"

They all shook hands and exchanged names, nodding in the manner of Danish gentlemen, and the doctor was informed of Petherton's unfortunate accident. "Oh dear," he said. "Bad business, so early in your great adventure. But we'll get you into the sick bay, Mr Petherton, and we'll see what we can do to get you back to fitness."

Thirty minutes later Petherton was in the sick bay, dosed with painkillers, and was fast asleep. The others, who were now so exhausted that they could hardly stand, let alone make polite conversation with the mine personnel, were given a hut with bunk beds and clean blankets and sheets, and were told by Dr Jensen to catch up on lost sleep. They dropped their packs, put out their tents and sodden personal gear to dry, and collapsed onto their beds. Then they slept for fourteen hours.

Paulus Arke and Christian Kunak were not amused. Since leaving Syd Kap in *Nanuk* they had made good progress across the mouth of the Schuchert River, where the sheer volume of water coming out into the fjord tended to push icebergs and ice floes offshore. But then the wind had swung to the west, and they had been forced by a dense mass of moving ice floes to pass closer and closer to the coast of Jameson Land, where there were too many shallows for their liking. *Nanuk* was not as good in thick sea ice as some of the older wooden Sandvig vessels like the *Mikkelsen* and *Ymer*. Its hull shape was all wrong, and in any case the glass fibre outer shell was too flimsy to cope with serious bow collisions with brash ice and floes, and incapable of resisting strong sideways pressure should the boat ever get trapped in a field of heavy moving slabs up to fifteen feet thick. Paulus liked it anyway. He had bought it with the aid of a government grant, and it was perfect for summer hunting and fishing trips. He had used it a lot, for net fishing in the shallows near the Bear Islands, and for hunting narwhals and seals. It was twice as fast as the Mikkelsen, with a shallow draught and a reliable modern diesel engine, and because it was only six yards long it was very maneuverable.

But now there was no escape from the ice, which was moving so much that even if they had tried to enter a lead, the floes on either side of it would surely have closed and crushed the boat. There were just three places on this coast where they might avoid disaster — each one a small lagoon near a river mouth with a sand bar a little distance offshore. Each lagoon was deep enough to take a boat the size of the *Nanuk*, and each sand bar was substantial enough to resist the pressure of ice floes driven onshore by the wind. The first of these havens was ten miles away, not far from a place called Draba Sibrica. Paulus had no option but to open his throttle and race along parallel to the beach, twenty yards offshore, in the hope of reaching safety before the ice crushed them against the edge of the land.

On five occasions the boat went aground, and they had shut down the engine for fear that the propeller would be smashed; but each time they managed to push the flimsy vessel clear of the grounds, and each time they thanked God that the sea floor here was made of sand rather than boulders or jagged bedrock. After half an hour they reached their haven, and managed to force the boat over the protective sandbar and into the quiet lagoon, much to the consternation of fifty or more moulting pinkfoot geese which habitually used it as a refuge from Arctic foxes at this time of year, when they were unable to fly.

An hour later the tortured mass of sea ice, incorporating fragments of brash ice and bergy bits from broken icebergs, ground its way onto the shoreline. The noise would have amazed anybody unused to floating ice in its myriad forms — but for Paulus and Christian it was perfectly familiar, and simply a nuisance. The deeper fragments grounded first, and some of them were tipped over as the shallower floes exerted the incalculable pressure which Paulus and Christian knew only too well, having seen other boats crushed and having watched boulders the size of houses rolled along by similar advancing ice fronts as if they had been footballs. But now they were safe, and there was nothing for it but to tie up the boat against the edge of the lagoon and sit tight until the wind changed and the ice decided to move out into the centre of Scoresby Sund again. They were more bored than frightened, having learned since childhood that as far as nature is concerned, you take whatever comes at you, with equanimity.

They were stranded for three days, during which time they lived off cooked pinkfoot goose and emergency supplies from the boat's galley. But while they sat on the shore and waited, they experienced a miracle. By some quirk of currents and tides, just a few hours after their arrival a large open water pool opened up just beyond the protective sand bar, even though the sea ice remained anchored to the land both to north and south. The water was no more than twenty feet deep, but it was the only place for maybe twenty miles where large sea mammals could come to the surface to breathe, and suddenly a group of twenty-six narwhals appeared (they knew there were twenty-six, since they had plenty of time to count them) and remained in residence, snorting and jostling for position and frequently thrusting their strange single twisted tusks far above the water surface. Some of the tusks were at least ten feet long. They had never seen so many narwhals in one place before, and they had never seen animals with tusks so magnificent. This was a true entrapment or "sassat" which happened maybe once a century in the waters of Scoresby Sund. It was the stuff of legend. If the two men had carried out a slaughter — as they could well have done with their rifles — they would have made their fortunes, for each narwhal tusk was at the time equivalent in value to five perfect polar bear skins. But they knew that they did not have the means to take the tusks from the carcasses of any animals they might have killed, and they certainly had no need for the meat and blubber from so many magnificent creatures. Without speaking of it, both men knew that while the financial gain of a narwhal slaughter would have been great, the cost in terms of wasted resources would have been quite unacceptable. So they took the visitation as an omen, and sat on the shore and watched the creatures for hours on end without speaking, lost in wonderment.

Professor Frazer Smith sighed contentedly as he settled into his deck chair in the shady garden of his home on the Woodstock Road in Oxford. After a week of rain a heat-wave had arrived, and it was now too hot to think or to do any of the manual jobs that were needed around the house. He stretched out his legs and closed his eyes. He was exhausted, as he always was on the completion of the annual round of examination marking and meetings of the Board of Examiners. Now it was all over — and the examination results, including five firsts, would be published in Schools tomorrow morning.

He sipped at his cup of tea and snoozed for a while. Then he thought he might as well check to see if there was anything important in the pages of the latest *Oxford Times*. He picked it up from the garden table and browsed idly through its pages. His attention was grabbed by a large photograph of a group of cheerful young men dressed in climbing gear, standing in front of a passenger ship called the *Gullfoss*. Some of them were bearded, and others were smooth-chinned. The caption said: *"The eight members of the Oxford University Scoresby Sund Expedition 1962, about to embark on the MS Gullfoss from Leith in Scotland, on the first leg of their journey to East Greenland."* Beneath the photo there was a prominent headline with the words: *"OU Greenland Explorers Set Out on The Adventure of a Lifetime."* The Professor recognized some of the faces in the photo, so he read on. The article ran as follows:

For the first time since the War, an OU expedition has just set foot in the icy wastes of Greenland, with eight men intent upon discovering new territory and completing an ambitious programme of scientific work in the area around Kjove Land and Scoresby Sund, about a hundred miles inland from the east coast.

It is reported that the party has now landed at Blyhavn airstrip from the Icelandic capital Reykjavik and has embarked upon its first major challenge — a walk of more than 120 km across the ice-covered Werner Mountains and thence along the immense Schuchert Valley into the area where Base Camp will be established. Using a chartered DC3 aircraft, the expedition members have completed a parachute drop of supplies into their key fieldworking area, which is very remote from the nearest airstrip. Now, carrying all of the supplies needed for a week of trekking across hostile terrain, the explorers are on their own, braving several glacier crossings and torrential meltwater streams and without any radio contact with the outside world.

The members of the expedition are as follows:
Stephen Hanna (22), Jesus College, leader and geomorphologist.
Gwyn Hughes (27), Cambridge Scott Polar Research Institute,

glaciologist.
Rowland Linney (23), Magdalen College, marine biologist.
Griff Mortimer (30), Sheffield University, zoologist and medic.
Andrew Petherton (35), Brisbane, Australia, and Imperial College London, geologist.
Joseph Horton (28), Merton College, botanist.
Lars Knudsen (23), Copenhagen University, ecologist and photographer.
Peregrin Whiteside (24), St John's College, ornithologist.

The leader, who is the youngest member of the expedition, has just completed Geography Schools and hopes to commence work towards his doctorate degree during the next academic year. In addition to the wide-ranging scientific skills of the expedition members, most of them have mountaineering and cold-climate survival skills, and seven of them have previous polar experience in either Antarctica or the Arctic. Three members have previously worked in Greenland, and the Danish member of the party, Lars Knudsen, has spent two winter seasons with the famous Sirius Sledge Patrol.

The expedition has been awarded the status of an official Oxford University Expedition, and its budget of around £4,000 has been met through personal contributions from members and through grant aid from the university, individual colleges, the Mount Everest Foundation, the Royal Geographical Society, and the Rockefeller Foundation. In addition, much of the party's food and equipment has been generously donated by sponsors.

Speaking just before leaving Oxford on the two-week journey into the field area, leader Stephen Hanna said: "We have planned this trip as carefully as possible, and have received wonderful support from our sponsors and from the University. We can never promise that nothing will go wrong, because we are going into a very hostile environment, but we have top class people in our party, the most sophisticated lightweight food supplies ever used on an expedition of this type, and the best available camping, canoeing and mountaineering gear. Yes, this will be an adventure, but our number one priority is scientific work, and we anticipate that after our return several months of work will be required to analyse samples and write up our results. We can promise that we will make a wide range of fascinating new discoveries, and we look forward to reporting these in detail on our return to Oxford."

It is anticipated that the expedition will return to Oxford in mid-September, after ten weeks in the field.

Professor Smith grinned to himself, and put down the paper. He turned to his daughter, who was reading the Sunday newspaper in the shade of an ancient pear tree. "Susanna," he said, "can I ask you something?"

"In a minute, Father, when I've finished this article."

He smiled to himself and watched her for a while. She was getting prettier by the day, he thought, and as she blossomed into womanhood she was looking more and more like her mother, with grey-blue eyes, unruly blonde hair, and a smile that reduced every young man who met her to a quivering wreck. Since Marian had died two years ago, father and daughter had grown very close, and he wondered how long it would be before the inevitable gulf would open up between them as she asserted her independence of spirit. She was already showing plenty of that, and he was not sure that he knew how he would deal with the inevitable emotional crises that would come as she played off one red-blooded suitor against another and eventually came to a view as to which one offered the best value.......

"This article in the *Oxford Times*," he said, when at last she looked up. "One of yours?"

"Of course it is. Who else has the inside story on the Scoresby Sund expedition? I am after all their press officer, if that doesn't sound too grand."

"Well, I must congratulate you. Nicely written — concise, informative, and mercifully free of purple prose. You have the making of a good journalist, once you get fed up of working in Blackwells."

"I've no intention of getting fed up with the bookshop, Father. I like it there, and the pay as a junior reporter on *The Times* would be nothing short of an insult." She laughed. "And I have to be honest. There was a lot of rather purple prose in the piece, but the Editor cut it out. He's the one who has the making of a good journalist."

"Fair enough. That's a nice photo of the lads before departure. But one thing confuses me. I thought there were six of them last time I looked — and now there seem to be eight."

"Oh, you're seriously out of date. Don't you remember Joe being here one evening, some months ago, feeling pretty miserable and saying that the expedition might not happen? They needed about £4,000 and they were a thousand pounds short, which meant that they didn't have enough to pay for the DC3 charter and the parachute drops. Then Prof Adrian Davies stepped in and contacted the Rockefeller Foundation in America, and they agreed to put up the last thousand on condition that the science programme was strengthened. They wanted a geologist involved, and more zoology as well. They also wanted more Greenland experience in the party. After talking to Steffo, Prof Davies put out some enquires and found two extra chaps, Andy Petherton and Griff Mortimer, who agreed to join the party at rather short notice. So along came the Rockefeller grant, and the rest is history."

"So why was Adrian Davies involved in all of this?"

"Because every accredited OU expedition has to have a senior academic as "home member" as a guarantee that things are being properly run — and as a contact in the UK in case things go wrong out in the field."

"Of course. That all sounds sensible — and Davies is a very experienced man. You've heard from Joe that they've landed safely at Blyhavn and started on this crazy walk?"

"Yes — he got a letter out to me somehow or other, so I was able to build his news into the article."

"You're fond of him?"

Susanna blushed. "Of course I am. Hadn't you noticed? Or have you been too busy with exams and so forth to notice how much time we've been spending together?"

"I stand rebuked. Sorry, darling. I am not a very good father, I'm afraid. I should be more attentive — but for what it's worth, I like him too. It's good to see a grammar school boy doing well. A bit rough around the edges, but considerate, intelligent, and very determined, if I'm not mistaken. He'd be a good strong counterbalance to your wild impulsiveness. Do you think you might marry him?"

"Father!" she scolded. "It's far too early for such thoughts. I'm too young and innocent to settle down, and I have you to look after, since you're not very clever at looking after yourself. Anyway, he's over there and I'm over here for the next ten weeks. That's a long time, and there's no knowing what'll happen to disturb the course of true love."

CHAPTER 3
July 1962

Griff Mortimer was the first to wake, and when he started moving around inside the hut with the delicacy of a trapped walrus there was no way that the others could remain asleep. It turned out to be mid-morning, although this had little significance. The continuous daylight and a slight lowering of temperatures during the small hours had already led the members of the party, on the trek across the mountains, into a pattern of working and walking by "night" and trying to sleep by day. Alfred Jensen knocked on the door and looked into the hut. "Good morning, gentlemen!" he said. "I trust you've slept well? Good, good. I've been asked to inform you that in one hour's time, when you've completed your ablutions, Jim Wagner, who's the man in charge here, invites you to lunch in hut number three. That's the mess hut. You can't miss it — there's a sign over the door that says "Nibelungen Arms." Ha! Somebody put it up in jest a few years ago, and it's still there. Rather a good joke, I think. I hope to join you there when I've completed my treatment of Mr Petherton -- assuming that he wakes up before too long."

By the time the bell rang, summoning the expedition members to the canteen hut, they had been able to absorb something of the atmosphere of the place. They discovered that there were about sixty people on the site, and were intrigued that most of the miners seemed to be American. That was maybe not surprising, given that Greenland Metals A/S was a Danish subsidiary of an American mining corporation. They exchanged greetings and chatted with some of the inhabitants, who were all perfectly friendly and welcoming -- and very impressed that the expedition members had walked over the mountains from Blyhavn, carrying their own supplies. By contrast, all of the miners had been flown in by the Bell 47J helicopter which apparently made five or six trips back and forth every day, weather permitting. The place was as filthy as mining settlements everywhere, with bits of timber, cables, oily rope and rags, tin cans and Coke bottles scattered about across the moraine surface. There were scores of forty-five-gallon drums of diesel fuel stacked well away from the huts, and there was a smell of diesel in the air. In the distance, somewhere inside the mountain, a big electricity generator was working hard. There was no vegetation of any sort to mask the impact of the works of man. The mine entrance had a heavy iron door which was closed. A narrow gauge railway track ran from the main tunnel and out along the crests of maybe a dozen ridges of quarrying spoil, which were constantly being extended by more excavated debris carried out on strings of small tipper wagons. On the edge of the glacier, three yellow Caterpillar D8 tractors were parked, with half a dozen covered sledges behind each one. Some of these sledges were being unloaded. Other Caterpillars with damaged tracks and dented cabs were parked three hundred yards away, out on the flat surface of the glacier, bearing testimony to the dangers of motorized transport in the glacier environment. There were some damaged sledges too, with tarpaulins over their loads. There were big crates everywhere, piled up on platforms cut into the unstable moraine. Some of these looked as if they carried mining machinery and others held scientific equipment, explosives and food.

When the men turned up at Hut Three mine manager Jim Wagner was already there, together with several others including Dr Jensen and the helicopter pilot Art Ruckle. Three tables were laid out for the guests with bone china plates, metal cutlery and proper wine and snaps glasses, and at the far end of the room was another table heavily laden with all of the things that one might expect of a traditional Danish "smørrebrød"-- cold meats, salads, prawns, pickled herrings, cheeses, five or six different breads, a large smoked Arctic char, pots of pate and caviar, sliced eggs and even slices of roast muskox meat delicately prepared. There were several exotic desserts incorporating fresh cream, a fruit bowl piled high with fresh grapes, apples, pears, oranges and bananas, and another table of beverages including five or six top-quality wines, a crate of Carlsberg lager, fruit juices and the inevitable Danish akvavit. Gwyn Hughes, who fancied himself as a man of the world, and who had encountered Danish cuisine before, was mightily impressed by both the range and quality of the items on the menu and the manner of their presentation -- which would, he thought, have done credit to the Grand Hotel in Copenhagen. He particularly liked the look of the wines. Wagner was clearly not a man to be satisfied with normal canteen fare, and the cook who flitted in and out of the hut sporting a white chef's hat and a red and white striped apron looked ludicrously out of place in this scruffy hut perched on a Greenland moraine........

Hanna surveyed the scene from the doorway, and received out of nowhere a flash of inspiration that this was a Last Supper, prepared for some purpose other than hospitality and conviviality. His eyes met those of his host, which narrowed for an instant, and then the moment was gone.

"Come on in, guys!" shouted Wagner, louder than was strictly necessary. "Slept well, I hope?" Hanna confirmed that indeed they had, and there followed a round of jovial introductions during which it transpired that three of the guests in the hut were senior mine managers and that one was Harald Keppel, the District Officer from Sandvig, who had flown in specially to meet the Expedition members. The Dane was a very tall man, fair haired and blue eyed, and at about 30 years old much younger than one might expect for a senior government official. Andy Petherton was missing from the assembly, but when his colleagues enquired after his health Dr Jensen said: "Don't you worry, gentlemen. I've examined him carefully and there's no serious back injury. However, I want him to remain in bed for at least another day while I conduct blood and urine tests just in case of some internal damage. I think he'll recover completely, and should be able to rejoin the expedition very soon." Then Wagner said: "Sit! Sit! You deserve a bloody good meal after that epic glacier walk of yours. Tuck in and drink up -- you've another asshole of a trek ahead of you! And please call me Jim. No formalities around here."

So they loaded up their plates, and sat, and were about to tuck in when their host tapped on a glass with his knife until he had silence. Hughes somehow managed to suppress a guffaw when he noticed that Hanna already had his mouth open, with a tomato on the end of a fork about six inches away from it. There was a long pause, and as the new arrivals watched in amazement Wagner put his hands together under his chin, in the manner of a three-year-old saying prayers at the side of his bed. The American closed his eyes and said: "For friends and fellowship, and for what we are about to receive, may Jehovah make us truly grateful. Amen." They all repeated the Amen, and then they got stuck into everything that the Good Lord had provided. In no time at all the hut was reverberating with the sounds of cutlery on china, clinking glasses, laughter and animated conversation.

Hanna noticed at a very early stage in the proceedings that their host was over-generous when it came to the dispensing of alcoholic drinks, given that his guests planned to set off on the long trek down the Schuchert valley as soon as the meal was finished. He also noticed that Linney and Mortimer were showing more enthusiasm for the white wine than was appropriate. So he said: "Thanks, Jim, for your amazing hospitality. I hope this doesn't sound churlish, but can we go easy on the alcohol, boys, since we have to find our way off the glacier and down into the valley within the next few hours, with rather heavy packs on our backs?" Harald Keppel laughed, and the two explorers took the hint. Wagner laughed too, but it was a forced laugh, and Hanna noticed that his eyes were deadly serious. The young Scot found that interesting.

Gwyn Hughes got up to replenish his plate, and pondered on the peculiarities of the man who was their host. Jim Wagner was not the sort of mine manager he might have expected. He was a short man, well built and maybe fifty years old, with a ruddy freckled complexion, red hair with streaks of grey in it, and green eyes. There was nothing exceptional about his clothes — he wore jeans and a denim shirt, and he had well-used working boots on his feet. He wore a very large gold ring on the index finger of his right hand. On balance, he would not have looked out of place on the streets of Limerick. But he was American through and through, with a southern drawl that was difficult to place, and a manner of speaking that was precise and somewhat intimidating, even though every sentence seemed to be punctuated with profanities. There was a wild energy running through his veins. When he spoke, his words were accompanied by animated and exaggerated gestures, and his eyes flitted about restlessly, giving Hughes the impression that he missed nothing, and that he might not be the most amiable or relaxed of bosses for the workers in the mine. Overall, thought the Welshman, it might not be a good idea to get on the wrong side of this particular American, no matter how convivial and civilized he might appear. As for the ostentatious grace recited at the commencement of the meal, it was intriguing, to say the least, that this apparently sincere Christian gentleman incorporated a string of profanities into almost every sentence. And the use of the word "Jehovah" in the grace in place of the word "Lord" — was that a matter of no importance, or did it say something about Wagner's system of belief?

As the conversation rolled on, the visitors learned less than they might have expected about their hosts. Wagner's colleagues who worked at the mine called themselves "engineers" but were strangely reluctant to describe exactly what they did day by day. Horton asked if he and his fellow travellers could have a look inside the mine but Wagner politely refused that request, saying that the Greenland Metals insurance cover specifically excluded non-employees from any of the work areas inside the mountain. But he was happy enough to describe what was going on in the tunnels and mineral extraction chambers, and passed around a dozen photos which showed how the mineral ore was dug out by special excavating machines, then crushed in a central "facility" close to the diesel generator plant before being loaded and transported on the miniature railway system within a seven mile network of tunnels.

But while the explorers were surprised by the unwillingness of their hosts to talk about mineral mining and ore crushing, they were flattered by the amount of interest shown in their own expedition. They were asked about their personal details and about the minutiae of their own personal research projects over the coming weeks, and were intrigued to learn that both Keppel and Wagner had copies of the Draft Expedition Research Schedule which had been finalized just before the group set off from the UK a couple of weeks earlier.

"Wow!" said Hanna. "I'm impressed. There were only four copies of that schedule. One's in a box dropped by parachute onto our Base Camp site. One was sent to the Danish Government; one rests with our home member, Prof Davies in Oxford; and the last one was sent to the Royal Geographical Society in London."

Harald Keppel grinned. "Perfectly normal procedure, I can assure you, Mr Hanna. The Government routinely passes on to us all of the key information on expeditions working in the field; that's entirely prudent, in case anything goes wrong and in case somebody or other has to be rescued. In some cases, if we know a research programme, we can actually help with transport and so forth -- and I think the mining company carried your theodolite and delicate equipment over the mountains for you?"

"Indeed they did," said Hanna. "And we're very grateful for their generosity."

"Our pleasure," said Wagner. "Greenland Metals is always informed too, especially in this area, since we have field parties out and about the whole time, and we don't want any confusion over logistics and camp sites. And hell, we sometimes undertake seismic exploration work involving explosive charges, and we don't want you guys getting in the way. That wouldn't be very good for your health. Anyway, my old friend Adrian has asked me to look after you especially well.........."

"You mean you know Prof Davies in Oxford?"

"Of course. An old drinking buddy of mine. You shouldn't be surprised -- he's a field geologist, and I'm a mining engineer. People like us meet at conferences and exhibitions all the time. I even dined once as his guest on the high table at that Balliol College place of his. Seriously weird, it was. The most surreal experience of my life.........."

They all laughed, and the conversation flowed easily. Joe Horton developed a relaxed and pleasant rapport with Harald Keppel, who was sitting opposite him at the table, and mentioned to him that, according to the Icelandair staff in Reykjavik, theirs was the only expedition needing a flight into Blyhavn this year. Apparently there were no other scientific groups and no climbing parties either. Why was this, asked Horton, when last year there were no less than eight expeditions to Scoresby Land and Jameson Land? Keppel explained that no other consents were given because no other expedition this year was of sufficient quality -- besides

54

which the logistics at the Blyhavn air strip were flat out in support of official Danish Government and Greenland Metals geological exploration in the Stauning Alps and Jameson Land. This programme involved the use of helicopters, Norseman seaplanes and other light aircraft doing aerial photography for the first ever 1:100,000 map of the area. Also, he said, there was construction work on the runway and port at Blyhavn, in anticipation of more mining developments and export of ore since, according to Jim Wagner, the molybdenum market price was currently going up like a rocket. They simply could not handle too many additional "frivolous" flights carrying university expeditions and mountaineering teams, given their limited facilities.

After a couple of hours the explorers had eaten so much that they could hardly move -- but Hanna knew that they must get going, since the weather was still fine. They wanted to walk in the cool of the night, when temperatures were down a few degrees and when meltwater streams were lower than they were in the heat of the day. So they thanked their hosts profusely for their extraordinary hospitality, and prepared to take their leave.

Before they left, Keppel and Wagner asked them all to sign "blood chits" indemnifying the Danish Government, the regional authorities and Greenland Metals A/S in case anything should go wrong or in case anybody should have an accident. They all agreed to that, on the basis that all the members of the party had long since accepted the risks involved in working in this hostile wilderness, and that they had in any case expected to look after themselves come hell or high water. They explained that they had ten Schermuly emergency rocket flares visible from over 50 miles and also six smoke distress signals. But they had no radio; communications difficulties were too great in the fjords, and all of the radios which they had investigated before departure were far too heavy to carry. They agreed with Wagner that if there should be an emergency, rockets would be sent up at 8 pm, when the sun was low and far round in the north-west, giving twilight conditions which should ensure that the rockets would be seen. The mine boss promised that he would have somebody on watch at eight o'clock every evening, since there was a direct line of sight from Himmelbjerg all the way down the Schuchert valley to the base camp area.

He also promised that the geologists and other fieldworkers on various ships and planes in the fjords over the coming weeks would be warned to keep an eye out for them, and for emergency signals in particular.

An hour later, replete and refreshed, and assured that their colleague Petherton was in good hands and well on the mend, the five members of the Base Camp party heaved their massive packs onto their backs and waved their farewells to civilization. They had accepted Wagner's offer to use the chopper to fly Petherton in to the field area just as soon as Dr Jensen passed him as fit.

As they walked down the glacier Rowland Linney said: "Now that was very strange. You know what we were told in Blyhavn about the western and middle passes over the mountains being impenetrable because of heavy snow?"

"Yes, we know. That's why we did the Eastern Glacier route, twice as long and in the event a bloody nightmare. So what of it?"

"Well, before we left I got talking to one of the Caterpillar drivers. He's twice my age, but he saluted and called me sir!"

"Congratulations, Rowland. You are the sort of fellow who obviously inspires respect..........."

"I'm aware of that. But this was very strange. He told me that he'd just come over the western pass, and that it's been virtually clear of snow for the last ten days."

"How many glasses of that white wine did you drink, Rowland?"

"Just four, as it happens. But I'm not so sozzled as to imagine things. That's what he said. Cross my heart and hope to die."

Jim Wagner was snoozing in his office close to the summit of Himmelbjerg, enjoying the warmth of the summer sun as it streamed through his observation window. He had eaten and drunk too much in the company of those guys from Oxford, in defiance of his recent resolution that he would live more healthily. He had put on two stones since arriving in Greenland, and he determined that any day now he would start an intense physical exercise regime. Maybe he would do some jogging on the glacier. This desk job was interesting enough, but his real home, in his heyday, had been the helicopter gunship, swooping low over a green tropical canopy...........

The telephone rang. He answered it, without taking his feet off the desk. "Yes?"

"Hi, Jim. Art here. Are you alone?"

"Why would I not be? I was trying to have a bit of a siesta. The Doc says it's good for me."

"Sorry to disturb you. Thanks for the feast. Bloody good. Pity we can't eat like that every day..........."

Wagner laughed. "Fat chance of that! You haven't seen my budget — NATO is the tightest outfit since arses were invented. Anyway, it's back to iron rations till September. Just as well — we have work to do. Tell me what you thought of our honoured guests."

"They'll do. All pretty wet behind the ears, I'd say. All with their bright red anoraks and orange waterproof trousers, looking like characters straight out of a Disney cartoon film! One of them said that was so that they could be seen from a great distance in case of emergency....."

"Yep — I liked that too. Get used to it, Art. In the world that they come from, safety is everything. In the world that we come from, camouflage is everything. Anyway, the technicolour outfits suit us very well indeed.........."

"Can't disagree with that," said the chopper pilot. "The guys themselves? Well, Linney, the skinny one with that mousy beard, looks as if he couldn't find his way around a laboratory, let alone the wilds of East Greenland. An amiable kid -- spent God knows how long talking to Jensen about the symphonies of some guy called Nielsen. I kid you not. I thought that was bloody funny........."

"And the leader, Steffo Hanna?"

"Also wet behind the ears. He seems bright enough, but I doubt we'll have any problems with him. Told me he would rather speak Gaelic than English. He's a strong bastard, by the look of it — been down a crevasse already, and looks a bit battered, but he plays rugby and says he has ambitions to play for Scotland. I think he's got a soft centre — engaged to be married, and comes from a close family on some God-forsaken island way out in the Atlantic. Seems quite religious — maybe you and he can have a theological discussion some time, Jim........"

"Keep my fucking beliefs out of this, Art."

"Sorry, Jim. Only joking. And that tall one called Horton, with a scar on his face? He's lived a bit, I reckon. Did you see the big knife in his belt? Probably knows how to use it. Sharp eyes too -- I reckon he doesn't miss much. Plays the harmonica, so he says!"

There was a loud guffaw from Wagner. "You don't say?" he spluttered. "Next thing you'll be telling me is that one of the others has got a bloody violin in his rucksack............"

"So I shouldn't worry about him, if I was you. Then Hughes, the glaciologist. The one with the black curly hair and the big beard. Can't see much of the bastard's face, what with all that hair about. But he's been around too. Doesn't miss a thing. Questions, questions, all the time. One to watch........ Oh shit! I've just noticed the time — I'm supposed to meet the next flight in from Keflavik in ninety minutes. Anything you need from the airstrip?"

"Tell that new guy in the stores that I could do with another crate of Heineken, if that won't put you over the weight limit."

"Will do. Catch up later. Over and out."

Having put the phone down, Wagner felt inclined to continue with his siesta. He sighed, closed his eyes, and folded his arms across his chest. Then the phone rang again.

He was irritated. "What the fuck is it this time?"

"Boss, this is Larry. There's news of that Russian sealer."

"Ah........ OK. What's the deal?"

"Coastguard first spotted her on their radar, and then the U-2 from Sondrestrøm found her and tracked her when the cloud thinned a bit. She went into Alpefjord, and might have been stuck there for a few days."

"Alpefjord? That leads nowhere -- hellishly remote. Why there, for God's sake?"

"To put in some equipment? Your guess is as good as mine, Boss. Anyway, she's now come back out again, and is having a hard time in thick pack ice just off Ella Island."

"Did the captain put anybody ashore?"

"Not as far as we know, Boss. It's possible, but HQ thinks they are just trying to pick up our communications in and out. They have come into the fjords before, for just that purpose. Last summer they did it twice."

"Then, it didn't matter. Now, sure as hell, it does. Their communications?"

"Highly sophisticated. There were a lot of coded messages while they were in Alpefjord, but HQ hasn't cracked them yet. They've kept radio silence for the last twelve hours. She's listening and recording."

"Shit! Is she still moving?"

"Yes, at maybe a couple of knots. She's surely very powerful, with an ice-strengthened hull profile. The Coastguard think she's the *Nabokov* — they've played cat and mouse with her before. Bloody good ice captain. She's heading for Sofia Sound, round the north side of Geographical Society Island. "

"As I suspected. Too close for comfort. If she gets any closer, she'll see and hear all the action at Blyhavn."

"She might have done that already, Boss."

Wagner scrutinized a map on the office wall for a couple of minutes, during which time Larry Bishop knew better than to say anything. Then he asked: "How deep is the Sound?"

"Deep enough. Three thousand feet, give or take a few."

"Any trappers wandering in the area, or at Ella Island or Myggbukta?"

"I took the liberty of making enquiries. No Danes, as far as we know. Three of them are at Blyhavn, and that's where the new Sledge Patrol guys are as well, getting trained up for next winter. There's just one Norwegian named Olav Tusvik who leaves his dogs up at Daneborg every summer with the met station guys, and goes off wandering."

"Have you checked him out?"

"Not in detail. He has a wife and daughter in Norway, not far from Bergen. He's probably as naive and romantic as the other trappers. Seems like he's a bit more of a nutter than the others. They say he talks about his "communion with nature", and nobody ever knows where he is........."

"OK -- we'll just have to take a chance on him being out with the fairies. What's the ice like outside Myggbukta?"

"Very light at the moment, by all accounts," came the reply. "The gale has broken up the pack, and there are big leads everywhere. If the captain wants to take the ship out of the fjords, she'll be away and into international waters within a few hours."

"Hmm.... and back again, whenever she feels like. Decision time. Larry, I feel threatened, and I don't like to be threatened. Pentagon?"

"Permission confirmed. They guess the Soviets won't say a word."

"Denmark?"

"Not informed. Shall I call Copenhagen for clearance?"

"No. Sometimes, with small children and allies, it's better that innocence is protected............"

There was a long pause, and then the voice on the telephone said: "Not sure I agree with that, Boss."

Wagner slammed the desk with his fist, and shouted: "Fuck you, Larry! Your job is to obey orders, and not to fart out your bloody half-baked opinions from your asshole. Get that?"

"Yes, Boss. Sorry I spoke out of turn."

"OK -- OK. Just don't get me pissed off again. You wouldn't like to see me when I'm angry. Now then. What about Keflavik?"

"Three planes on standby."

"OK. Get the best possible fix from the U2, and tell them to do it. Ring me again to report, when it's done."

Wagner put down the phone. His feet were still on the desk, but his hands were shaking. He needed to calm down, and he breathed deeply. For a few minutes he was lost in thought. Had he made the right call here? A decision made in anger? No -- it had been rational and dispassionate, as ever. It had been the only possible call in the circumstances.

Then he rolled a joint, lit it, and took a few drags.

Fifteen minutes later, he had recovered his composure, and felt distinctly mellow. This was starting to get interesting, he thought, and the summer climate and pace of life in East Greenland were, all things considered, more congenial than they were in Vietnam. There weren't even any insects, up here in the mountains. Better food too. Never did like rice. No flesh pots here, but then one couldn't have everything. This business with the sealer had given him an adrenalin rush, not exactly like those of the old days, since he was not actually staring death in the face, but it had felt good. Anyway, he was certain that he was the right man, in the right place, at the right time. He could cope with — and indeed control — every situation that might arise over the coming months.

Then he knelt beside his desk, clasped his hands together like a cherub, and prayed.

Paulus and Christian were at last moving easily through clear water towards Sandvig, the place that they must now start referring to as "home". Suddenly, twenty miles from shore out in the middle of Scoresby Sund, they spotted a group of five or six harbour seals hauled out on an ice floe that was about three hundred yards long. Immediately Paulus throttled back the engine although they were still about half a mile away from the animals. They did not even discuss whether they should try to kill at least one of them. The seals were fair game, unlike the narwhals which had snorted and frolicked in that pool of open water on the Jameson Land coast. Paulus raised his eyebrows, and Christian smiled and nodded. Greenlanders will almost always hunt an animal that is moving, but more to the point, they can never resist the temptation of hunting one that is asleep. Two men, two rifles, and no problems with taking the kills home; so the target was agreed as one seal each, if they shot simultaneously.

Paulus stopped the engine on the approach to the floe, and the two men made the boat fast with an embedded anchor. They were still about two hundred yards from the seals, but could not see them because there were several rough pressure ridges on the floe surface. They jumped out onto the ice, carrying just their rifles and their square white camouflage "screens" stretched on light wooden frames, which they used to make themselves invisible when crawling across the ice. Each screen had a single hole in the middle of it, big enough to peep through while moving forward, and also to take the business end of a rifle. They settled down behind a pressure ridge and waited for thirty minutes, just in case the seals had been alerted by the sounds made by the boat during its approach and contact with the floe. They had learned, from bitter experience, that patience is a greater virtue in a hunter than a good eye and an ability to move as silently as a ghost. Then Paulus peeped over the top of the pressure ridge, and saw that the seals were still there, apparently fast asleep. But the creatures were just a yard or so from the edge of the floe, which meant that they could be in the water within a second or two if they should be spooked. Paulus and Christian would get just one shot each, and they needed to get closer. With infinite slowness, pushing their while camouflage screens in front of them, they slid along across the ice surface, using their elbows and knees for propulsion. They stopped frequently, wherever they could find a dip in the ice surface or a small pressure ridge to hide behind. After forty minutes of painstaking and infinitely patient approach work, they stopped about fifty yards from the animals. One of them raised its head, looked around, and relaxed again. Christian nodded to his friend, and whispered: "You take the one on the left and I take the big bull with the dark spots. On the count of three...." They took aim, but as soon as Christian said "One" they heard a deep-throated roar from the south, causing all five of the seals instantly to panic and drop into the sea. Out of nowhere three jet fighters thundered directly overhead, only a couple of hundred feet above the sea, causing the two men instinctively to drop their rifles and cower down, assaulted, frightened and angry.

When the hellish roar of the airborne killing machines had been dragged away towards the north, both of the hunters beat their fists into the white sea ice in frustration. They had seen fighter jets before, but never this close, and like the other Greenlanders of Sandvig they hated them, for they were symbols of arrogance and power — and of an obsession with violence that they could not comprehend. "Americans?" asked Paulus.

"Of course," replied Christian. "And now this place is their playground..........."

Nothing more was said. Despondently, the two men picked up their white camouflage screens and their rifles, and walked back across the ice floe towards the *Nanuk*. Paulus looked at his friend, and saw that there were tears in his eyes — and they were not just the tears of a hunter who has lost his quarry. As for himself, there was a deep fury raging in the pit of his stomach.

CHAPTER 4
July 1962

The first few hours were almost too easy, as the explorers walked down towards the snout of the Schuchert Glacier on firm, clean ice free of crevasses and all but free of meltwater streams too. On the glacier there was a cool breeze, and no mosquitoes. That helped to clear heads and settle stomachs after the excesses of Jim Wagner's farewell party. But then they were forced to cross the labyrinth of ridges, hills, depressions and lakes around the rim and snout of the glacier -- and that was dangerous, for no matter how stable the surface moraine looked, they knew that there was melting ice not far beneath their feet, and that slope collapses could happen at any time. They got off the glacier and onto the solid ground of the green valley side without major incident, but then they got the shock of their lives when three fast jets came up from the south-east in tight formation and roared overhead, flying so low that they could see the pilots. Hughes recognized them as USAF Phantoms like those he had seen in the skies around Cambridge, except that these were fully armed. The aircraft thundered northwards up the Schuchert Valley, following the route of the glacier in a smooth banking operation, and then they disappeared into the heart of the Stauning Alps. Peace was restored.

"What the hell are they doing up here in Greenland?" asked Linney. "They went straight past Himmelbjerg, well beneath the mountain tops. Must have frightened the life out of the miners, if any of them were out and about on the glacier."

"War games," said Mortimer. "A week ago, when we borrowed our parachutes from the Keflavik air base, courtesy of those nice Americans, there were fast jets and bombers all over the place. One of the airmen told me that they're on alert all the time, and that they often do low-altitude training flights over East Greenland when the weather's good. Bloody cheek, disturbing the musk-oxen like that........"

Whiteside laughed. "Well, old fruit, what about my delicate nerves?

I came to Greenland for a bit of peace and quiet, and look what happens."

Half an hour later they heard the jets again, far away to the north and apparently at high altitude, but they did not see them.

After that, the seven comrades pressed on with a journey that became increasingly difficult with every hour that passed. They had to come to terms with the three inescapable problems: the heat, the mosquitoes, and the meltwater streams. Walking when the sun was high overhead was almost unbearable, given the bulky packs that they were carrying and given that they could not strip down to bare torsos and legs for fear of being eaten alive by the clouds of mosquitoes that accompanied them. They had made one elementary mistake at Blyhavn before setting off on their walk, by placing all of their insect repellant cream into the parachute loads, in an effort to save on weight. Stupid, very stupid. Now they were made to suffer, and within twenty-four hours of leaving Himmelbjerg they had all been stung so many times that they sported angry inflamed rashes on faces, necks and bare arms. Horton's face was so swollen around the eyes that he could hardly see where he was going. They tried to stick to the principle of walking during the small hours and sleeping during the heat of the day, but when the sun was high it was too hot to sleep inside the tents, and even though they had mosquito nets to protect them the insects seemed to find ways of getting through, and the torment continued day and night, inside and outside. The only respite they had was during the crossing of the Roslin Glacier which flowed down from the mountains to the west and out onto the floor of the Schuchert Valley. On the ice surface, there was a blessed cooling breeze -- and no mosquitoes. But as soon as they reached the grassy valley side again, on the south side of the glacier, the mosquitoes returned and the torture resumed.

Larry Bishop pushed his head around the door of the observation room. "Boss, there's a U-2 reconnaissance report from Keflavik, about the sealer."

Jim Wagner looked up from his telescope, through which he had been following the slow and erratic progress of the explorers who were now about eighteen miles away.

"About time too. What took them so long?"

"The Russians are doing a lot of jamming at the moment. They use some quite sophisticated techniques, and have two other vessels referred to as sealers a hundred miles off Jan Mayen. They're loaded with surveillance and communications gear, and I'd sure like to have a look at some of it............"

Wagner held up his hand, irritated with the digression. "So they are worried about the disappearance of the ship?"

"Assume so, Boss," came the reply. "They probably don't know that she's gone down. All they know is that she's not responding to messages."

"So what's the report say?"

"Timed at five hours ago. The message has taken this long to get through and be decoded. There's a wide oil slick halfway along Sofia Sound, but not much debris. The jets went in very low and very fast. One missile was all that it took, and she sank like a stone. Big missile, small ship. We assume that they didn't get a message out before she was hit."

"Of course they got a message out. They must have picked up the planes before the rocket was fired. Maybe just an emergency signal — no time for details."

"All will be revealed, Boss. I'll keep listening."

Wagner nodded. "OK. So that dirty business is out of the way. The slick will gradually disperse, once the wind gets up. The Soviets won't say anything, since the sealer was in the fjords without any consent from the Danes. Anyway, that was no bloody sealer. They know it and we know it. Still, I feel sorry for those poor bastards who are now at the bottom of Sofia Sound........."

"How many, Boss? A crew of eight or ten on a ship of that size?"

"And the rest. The innards of that pretty lady were packed full with electronics. Thirty men, at least. May they sleep in peace. Now then, it's probably time for supper."

On the third day Mortimer went down with heat exhaustion. After resting for an hour he managed to stagger on with the help of his companions, and since he was the expedition medic he decided that he should be soaked to the skin with icy water next time that they came across a meltwater stream. So when they reached the river at the mouth of Kortedal they doused him from head to toe -- and that seemed to work, for his temperature dropped, and after resting for another couple of hours he was able to continue with the river crossing. But within six hours Linney also collapsed, and this time things were much more serious, for he had a high temperature and was physically sick several times. They decided that he was suffering from both heat exhaustion and the toxic effects of thousands of mosquito bites. They were seriously worried about him; he was skinny enough at the best of times, and they had always been concerned about his stamina, but now he would be losing even more weight.

They had to stop and pitch camp immediately, in what was effectively a rocky desert. They tried to make the patient as comfortable as possible, but it was difficult to cool him down, for there was no water within striking distance and at 4 pm it was the hottest time of the day. Hughes went off with a polythene water container to find a pond or a small stream, and Linney protested that he would be all right; but over the next four hours his condition deteriorated to the point where he was delirious, and Hanna had to consider the possibility of an evacuation. The leader consulted with Joe Horton, who was already emerging as his right-hand man. They had very little food left, and they knew that if two men were to walk back to Himmelbjerg for help, in a hurry, they would have put themselves in danger and might even have placed at risk the future of the whole expedition. They would certainly have been highly vulnerable during river and glacier crossings. Should they put up an emergency rocket and call in a rescue helicopter from the mine? It was touch and go, but in response to Linney's pleading, and with Horton's agreement, Hanna deferred a decision for a few more hours. He also knew that the helicopter from the mine could appear at any moment, carrying a fully recovered Andy Petherton to join his colleagues. If Linney's condition did not improve, Art Ruckle might agree to fly him out, without any need for emergency rockets and major adjustments to the field programme.

At midnight Hanna and Horton, who were sharing accommodation in the smaller tent, agreed that it was still too hot to sleep under canvas.

However, they realized that all five of their colleagues were fast asleep in the other tents, and that for them sleep was the best medicine. So they crept slowly into the open air, wrapped their heads in wet towels in a fruitless attempt to deter a few of the million mosquitoes swarming around them, and sat on a big flat rock about forty yards away from the camp site. They were in no mood to enjoy the view or appreciate the subtle shifting colours of the night-time mist that swirled around the mountain-tops, illuminated by the low sun. "Well, my friend," said Hanna. "This is not a lot of fun, is it?"

"We didn't come here for fun, Steffo. We came here, as you may recall, to have an adventure and to launch our brilliant academic careers.........."

"Professors Horton and Hanna! I like it! I wonder where we'll end up? America? Not for me, anyway — Edinburgh or Aberdeen, maybe. Good Geography Departments in both places. Morag doesn't want to leave Scotland, and when we get married I'll have to respect that."

"Bullshit! She's young, and so are you. Everything will change, just you wait and see. You've flown a long way from Scotland already, although your roots are obviously still on the island of Harris. She'll do the same, and she'll discover that the world south of Gretna Green and Berwick-on-Tweed isn't entirely populated by savages."

The big Scot grinned. "You may be right. I'll do my best to drag her away. And Susanna? She's a bright spark, and I bet she wants to see the world."

"Not so fast! We aren't even engaged yet. And I have still to find out whether she's good in............."

"In bed?"

"Well, yes."

"She's a very sexy lass, and bright, too. She's pretty good everywhere else, from what I can see, so I think you're quite safe on the bedding front. Move quickly when you get home, Joe, before she gets snapped up by some smooth bastard from Balliol or Christ Church."

"Well, I'm doing my best to keep her onside. I managed to get a letter off to her in Blyhavn, when we were passing through."

"You did? How the hell did you manage that? I didn't see a posting box at the airstrip."

Horton grinned. "No problem. When I was in the Marines, I was renowned for my ingenuity."

Hanna got up and threw a stone at an Arctic fox which was showing too much interest in the open food box a few yards away from the tents. It scampered away, sat down, looked at them, and yawned. They both laughed at its impudence, but then became serious again. "So what's the assessment thus far, Professor Hanna?" asked Horton. "Should we be satisfied, or disgruntled?"

"I think the former, Joe. On balance, I'm pretty gruntled. It's bloody tough, and I don't think I've ever been so tired in all my life, even when we were pushed right to the limit in those training sessions before the Varsity Match. I puked at the end of every session. But then we went straight into recovery, with carefully controlled diets and so forth. The agony was always short-lived."

"Your puking was not in vain, my good man. You got a blue out of it, and a narrow victory at Twickenham."

"Not complaining. But here it's pretty unremitting…….."

"Agreed. Very character-forming, I'm sure. But anything Scott of the Antarctic can do, we can do better."

"Bad comparison, old man. Remember that he died because of bad judgement and insane patriotism. I intend to stay alive. Mind you, I could do with a nice Scottish blizzard right now."

Horton threw another stone at the fox, and almost hit it. Then he said: "Seriously Steffo, how are we doing? D'you think you've made the right calls?"

"You're not doubting my leadership qualities, are you, Joe?"

"Far from it, mate. Everything spot on, in my judgment. But a word in your ear. With this level of exhaustion, it's all too easy to get things wrong — to take stupid risks, or to lose concentration………. Happens in the Marines all the time."

"I'm sure you're right. For what it's worth, Gwyn had a word with me when we were at the mine. Very complimentary, he was, not just about our careful planning in Oxford, but about my prudence as leader. I appreciated that, coming from a Cambridge man."

Horton grinned. "Well, that's reassuring, coming from a guy who's been on five or six other Arctic expeditions. But prudence? Don't see much of it myself. Bloody casualties everywhere. You down a crevasse and covered with bruises and scratches, Andy with a damaged back that may yet leave him permanently disabled, and Griff and Raymond down with heat exhaustion and toxic shock. Who's next?"

"You're a miserable bastard, aren't you? Cheer up, man! Remember that we are still pretty unfit — all of us. Just you wait — these small setbacks, and the physical challenge of these first ten days, will sort out the men from the boys!"

"Spoken like a true leader! Don't worry -- I'm just winding you up........"

Hanna got to his feet and slapped his colleague on the back. "We needed sound people, and for the most part I think we've got them. But good field researchers are not necessarily the best leaders. Neither Rowland, or Griff, or Lars could organize a Mother's Union tea party, unless I am very much mistaken. The others could lead in an emergency — you could, Joe, and so could Gwyn Hughes. As long as you two are on my side, we'll be all right."

"Count me as a blood brother, Steffo. That sounds like a perfect mix of innocence, experience, incompetence and enthusiasm, purely by chance. What about Perry Whiteside?"

"Top man, without a doubt. He pretends to be a bumbling idiot, but he's bloody smart. When I'm next gazing into the jaws of death, I want him at my side."

"And Andy Petherton? Opinionated, highly intelligent, and with us, I suspect, because he's escaping from a broken marriage and a pretty chaotic personal life. He's a hard man to read. The Aussie accent doesn't help.........."

"Give him time, Ed. I quite like him — interesting fellow. We haven't seen him at his best, that's for sure, and to get a back injury before we even reached Base Camp was hard for him to take. A severe dent to his pride. But there's still a long way to go on this little escapade of ours."

"So that's the world sorted out for now. By the way, d'you realize how ludicrous you look with that wet towel wrapped round your head?

Fancy a cup of tea and one of those inedible biscuits?"

By 4 am Linney had recovered enough to start walking again. Since they were now within twenty-five miles of the Base Camp site, where the parachute loads were waiting for them, Hanna decided to make a depot of every bit of equipment they could spare, leaving Linney with a load light enough to manage in his current groggy state. They found a gravelly terrace close to their camp site and then draped a bright orange tent over the pile of odds and ends, using heavy stones to keep it in position should the wind pick up. They called it Desert Depot. They were confident that it could be seen from a couple of miles away at ground level, and very easily from the air. On that basis, and planning to come back and pick up their gear at a later stage, they pressed on.

River crossings were sometimes impossible and always challenging. The walkers were now familiar with the fact that there were great differences in water levels between daytime, when ice melting was at its peak, and night-time, when parts of the glaciers were in deep shadow. They had some idea where the biggest streams were, and tried to plan their walking schedules so they they crossed them in the small hours -- but that was not always possible. They also concluded that it was impossible to cross any of the meltwater streams if the water was flowing in a single channel or rocky gorge, and that they had to find locations where the rivers were braided or split up into many channels where they ran out onto the floor of the Schuchert Valley. Their routine, once tested, remained the same throughout the walk. Somebody without a pack and connected by a rope would venture out into the torrent at a place that looked auspicious, using an ice axe as a third leg. Often he would be forced to retreat, and sometimes he would be swept away and hauled to the bank on the rope. On successive days Gwyn Hughes was swept away and had to be rescued -- soaked, cold and angry. After that Hanna took the lead, since he was a much bigger man who had a better chance of keeping his footing. If he did get across the first channel, it was easier for those who followed to send across rucksacks by rope and to cross themselves in relative safety, using the ropes to help maintain balance. While they were quite literally learning the ropes, they crossed in bare feet, with the idea of keeping their boots dry; but that proved to be a lousy idea, since there was so much debris rolling along on the beds of these rivers, invisible because of the milky turbulence of the water, that they were lucky to escape serious leg and foot injuries. In some of the streams that had multiple channels, they used the full 200 feet of their rope with two or three belays, with those on gravel islands trying to secure the safety of whoever was in the water. The routine was repeated over and again, countless times over the five days, and the time spent on making downstream detours and in actual river crossings was probably equivalent to the time spent on walking across open country. The only consolation was that if they had been a week earlier, with the spring melt at its peak, some crossings would have been impossible.

On the evening of day four, with the last of the big glacial meltwater streams behind them, and with Linney continuing to regain his strength, the little band of brothers pressed on. Three of them had bleeding blisters, but they had walked through the pain, and were past caring. Sometimes they spoke, and sometimes not -- but Joe Horton noticed that a tight bond was developing between the seven of them, built on mutual respect and dependence, and maybe upon the fact that each one of them had at some stage been hauled back from certain death in an ice-cold meltwater stream on the end of a rescue rope. They were now virtually out of food, having planned for just three days of walking. They had to cross what they referred to as "The Gobi Desert" -- still in stifling heat and still plagued by mosquitoes. There were extensive gravel flats and even sand dunes which made walking with heavy packs exceedingly difficult -- and the total lack of surface water was a curse. Now they were not just hungry and exhausted, but suffering from severe dehydration as well.

As they moved southwards there was a subtle shift from a landscape dominated by mountains and glaciers into one where there was more greenery and more animal life, even if clearwater streams were in short supply. They saw Arctic foxes and Arctic hares quite frequently, and noticed that some of the animals had summer coats which were more brown and grey than white. They made many sightings of geese and other birds, and assumed that most of them must be nesting in the more boggy areas of Jameson Land, to the east of the Schuchert River. They also saw four small herds of musk-oxen, strange primitive beasts with shaggy coats and heavy horns; but the animals were very shy, and kept their distance.

Even in the most barren areas there were traces of past animal life — reindeer antlers, skeletons and skulls of fallen musk-oxen, picked clean by the ravens and other carrion eaters, and wispy lumps of super-fine musk-ox wool which Mortimer insisted on collecting, since one day he wanted a musk-ox sweater to be knitted for him by the girl of his dreams............

They climbed up onto a high limestone plateau called Karstryggen -- the last major obstacle of their walk -- and found themselves walking on a wide expanse of clean limestone, bleached and baking in the heat of the sun. It was a weird landscape, with red boulders the size of houses scattered about on the gleaming white limestone surface, just where they had been dumped by ice thousands of years ago. At one stage Horton complained that the soles of his boots were melting, and he was not joking. They needed to drop down into a narrow limestone gorge as they plodded southwards, and suddenly Gwyn Hughes, who was in the lead, shouted: "Hey boys, look over here!" and promptly disappeared from sight.

He had found a limestone cavern, the entrance of which was so small that it would not have been noticed by anybody either a yard or two to the right or left of his route through a jumble of limestone blocks. They all squeezed inside, to discover that the cave was a spectacularly large one, maybe thirty yards across, with feeder tunnels running away from it into the distant darkness. Shade at last! They dumped their rucksacks and allowed their eyes to adjust. There were bones everywhere, and also several reindeer antlers and three musk-ox skulls with massive horns still attached. The cave had clearly been used for centuries and maybe even millennia by wild animals, including wolves, since some of the bones had teeth marks on them. There were no stalactites and stalagmites, but in one corner of the cave there was a clay floor with something even more precious -- a pool of fresh clear water fed by a trickle from a crevice in the rock. Like nomads encountering an oasis in the middle of the Sahara, they scooped the water up and splashed it all over their bodies, laughing like small children. They doubted that it was safe to drink from the pool because of all the animal remains scattered about, but the running water deeper into the cave tasted wonderful. They drank deeply, filled their water bottles and then luxuriated in the cool mosquito-free darkness for maybe half an hour, stretched out on smooth limestone slabs.

Invigorated, they marched on, to receive an ever greater boost to their spirits from the view which they encountered when they found themselves on top of a substantial limestone cliff. Suddenly they were looking down from an altitude of about 2,000 feet across Kjove Land towards their destination near the edge of a wide green expanse of tundra. Down to their left they could see the rolling uplands of Jameson Land, on the other side of the uncrossable maelstrom of the Schuchert River. Here the braided river was almost five miles wide; and its never-ending deep-throated roar hit them with great force although they were about six miles away from it. That sound was all-pervasive, and they knew that it would be there, in the background, for the whole of their stay in this part of East Greenland. It was frightening, since it was a constant reminder of the hostility and danger of the environment that they had chosen to spend time in; but there was also something strangely reassuring about it.

To the south, across the iceberg-studded inlet of Nordøstbugt, they could see the full sweep of Hall Bredning, with pinnacled tabular bergs moving with infinite slowness out of Nordvest Fjord even though the water was glassy calm. Every now and then a sharp retort or a low grumble of thunder reached their ears, having travelled more than twenty miles from icebergs as they collapsed or rolled, adjusting to the inexorable processes of melting beneath and above the waterline. And on the other side of the water they could see the high plateau of Milne Land, capped with ice caps and spewing outlet glaciers down towards sea level, around sixty miles away. Then towards the west the nearest of the peaks of the Stauning Alps were shimmering in the heat haze, with ranks of jagged pinnacles of black rock, one ridge crest behind another, fading towards a distant horizon. And right ahead they could see the massive bulk of Pythagoras Bjerg, beautifully triangular and as high as Mount Snowdon, dominating the rolling glaciated plateau on which some of the expedition members planned to conduct their field research.

At last, the parachutes! Hanna thought he could see them through the binoculars from a distance of maybe five miles -- minute flecks of red, yellow and orange in the dusty green vastness of the Greenland tundra. The men had been looking for them for several hours as they plodded across an undulating wasteland which they had already named "The

Prairies", comprising gravel patches, boggy fen, meltwater streams and lakes. The journey, which should have taken them three days at the most, had now taken them five, and they had been walking for an average of fifteen hours per day, without shade or shelter of any kind, and without the cooling balm of night. They had not seen a single cloud since those storm clouds had evaporated over the Sirius Glacier. They were completely exhausted; they had no food left in their packs; and they had long since given up worrying whether their feet were wet or dry. They had had hardly any sleep since leaving Himmelbjerg, and in response to Hanna's excited outburst Hughes mumbled: "Huh! Probably a mirage or a delusion, Steffo. Medically proved, it is, that when chaps are totally clapped out, they see things. For example, I can see a glass of ice-cold lager on that rock over there." They giggled like idiots, and pressed on.

The whole journey to Base Camp had been undertaken under a merciless sun, which never once set beneath the horizon. But now, with the parachutes acting as their homing beacons and as their incentives to keep going, the men finally staggered up to the patch of gravelly ground where they lay, all within a radius of about fifty yards. They were duly impressed with the skill of the Icelandair pilot and his crew who had kicked them nonchalantly out of their hired DC3 aircraft about ten days before, during the course of six runs across the site. First, they threw down their rucksacks and dived into the boxes that contained the insect repellant. That brought them instant relief from the plague that had afflicted them ever since they had stepped off the Schuchert Glacier. Then they found a food box and put Linney in charge of cooking breakfast -- or was it supper? Their watches told them that it was 3 am, but their body clocks were so confused that they really did not care. And while Linney got two Primus stoves going out in the open, Mortimer and Hughes started to unpack the parachute bundles while Hanna decided exactly where their Base Camp should be located, on a wide gravelly patch a few feet above and about two hundred yards away from a cluster of small freshwater ponds which they referred to as "Parachute Ponds." Then they put up their tents, ate a huge supper, and slept for fifteen hours.

Pana Naukun was feeling his age. In his time, he had been the best hunter at Syd Kap, but now his eyesight was going, and his joints were stiff, and his fingers were not as nimble as they were. Carving was difficult for him, and he was grateful that he could use modern tools including metal chisels, hammers and knives -- in contrast to the old days, when he had been forced to use whatever sharp and heavy things he could get his hands on. He looked out of the window of his wooden hut on the edge of the Sandvig settlement, and saw that there was a thin mist over the sea, hiding the more distant icebergs which were grounded in the shallows. There was too little sea ice for comfort, and he knew that there was a very wide coastal belt of ice-free water this year, with open water outside Kap Brewster and Kap Tobin. He could feel the moisture in the air, and he knew that soon the weather would break, and the rain would come.

He returned to his work, and two hours later he was finished. He held in his hand a very small carving, about three inches tall, which was so grotesque that it would have terrified a small child. It was made from part of a walrus tusk, and it had a head that was as large as its body, with sharpened teeth and staring eyes and no ears. The lower part was more like a skeleton than a body made of flesh and blood, with protruding ribs, an exaggerated pelvis, and claws instead of feet. Pana had reluctantly drilled a small hole through the top of the skull, as if inviting somebody to thread a cord or a leather thong through it. He was uneasy about that, but that is what he had been guided to do, and he had long since learned not to question the things that came to him when he was outside of his own body. He placed the little creature on the table in front of him, and closed his eyes. He knew immediately that it was very powerful, and very evil.........

He was a Christian, of course, like all of the other Inuits who lived in Sandvig, but before he had been moved with his family from Syd Kap to the village with its church and its resident priest they had had only occasional encounters with the new religion, and while he had great respect for it and for its emphasis on peace and love, he saw no reason to discontinue the old ways. Even when he had been a small child, his parents had recognized that he had an instinct for spiritual things, so one of the names he had been given -- and the one he chose to keep -- meant "a god who cares for souls" and also "which way?" He had another name too, known only to a few in the village. That was Tuullik -- the Inuit name for the great northern diver, the bird whose spirit he carried inside himself. Even as an old man, he was still not sure which way was the right way, but he was more certain about which way was the wrong way, and there was something going on in the countryside round about that was evil. He felt it more and more strongly every time that he spoke to his spirits, and three days since he had known that he had to make a **tupilak**. He had not made one for at least fifteen years. He had tried to resist, but it was inevitable. So he had made it. And now it had to be delivered. But first, there were certain ceremonies to be completed.......

Three hours later, at breakfast time, Pana knocked on the front door of Harald Keppel and his family, down in the centre of the village. A small daughter opened the door, rubbing her eyes. "Good morning, Anyu, pretty one," said the old man in his own language. "Is your father up and about? If, so, please might I talk with him?"

The little girl nodded and invited him into the front room that Keppel used as an office, and shortly afterwards the tall Dane came in, still holding a breakfast sandwich in his hand. "Good day to you, Pana," he grinned. "You're up bright and early this morning! What can I do for you?" Then he saw the expression on Pana's face, and realized that the old fellow was in no mood for cheery greetings or frivolity of any sort. He had not shaved, and he looked exhausted. "You've been up all night?"

The old man nodded. Keppel knew what that meant, for the two of them were good friends, and while he had been taught prior to his Greenland posting to be intolerant of shamanism and all things related to the old beliefs among the older generation, he respected Pana as one of the gentlest and wisest men he had ever met. So he said: "I won't ask questions, and will assume that there's something you wish to do for the good of your people. Correct?" The old man nodded again.

"Let's sit down, Pana. I can finish my breakfast later on."

So they sat facing one another. Pana was a man of few words, and he came straight to the point. "Harald, you are going to Blyhavn in the near future?"

"Yes, next week, with the government helicopter. There's a meeting in the Sledge Patrol Hut which I must attend."

"Will the American be there?"

"Which American? There are quite a few of them working at the airstrip and at Himmelbjerg."

"The one from the red mountain."

"Yes, that'll be Himmelbjerg. The man in charge there is Jim Wagner. Of course, he will be present."

"He will be the one. Will you please give him this, from me? You needn't say where it came from." Pana reached into the deep front pocket of his parka and pulled out a small brown paper parcel, only about six inches across, tied up with string. There was no writing on it. He handed it to the Dane, who had a good idea what it contained, but thought it unwise to seek confirmation.

Pana's business was done, and he needed some sleep. He nodded. Then he stood up and said: "Thank you, Harald. You're a good man, and you understand us."

As he went through the door he turned back to Keppel and said: "You promise?"

"Yes, Pana," said the Dane quietly. "I promise."

When they woke, early on the evening of 13th July, Hanna remembered that it was his birthday, and insisted on his birthday rights -- no cooking and no washing up. The others reluctantly agreed to that, but insisted that he should act as quartermaster instead, checking all of the parachute loads for damage, getting the big tent which they called "The Palace" erected, and starting to secure food supplies, scientific instruments, fuel and other essential items in different locations beneath bivouac sheets where they would be safe from the rain which would eventually come. Additionally, they would not all be lost if -- heaven forbid -- they should ever suffer from a fire at the camp. As they untied the bundles and checked the loads, they found remarkably little damage -- the jerrycans of paraffin were all safe, as were the food boxes, the small inflatable craft, the 2 HP outboard motor, and the two canoes. There was a broken paddle and some damage to the struts of the Klepper, but Whiteside said that could easily be repaired.

As they worked around the camp site, in preparation for eight weeks in residence, they were greatly surprised by the sound of a light aircraft. Then they saw the Cessna 172 from Blyhavn, flying very low as it approached. On its first pass they saw Dr Alfred Jensen in the passenger seat, smiling and waving. The Base Camp party responded by waving and giving exaggerated thumbs up signs. Then the aircraft made one more pass, during which they saw Dr Jensen toss out a small box on a miniature parachute made out of a table cloth. The plane swung northwards and headed back towards Himmelbjerg. On recovering the tin box, Mortimer found that it contained a wonderful freshly baked birthday cake with icing, and a bottle of brandy. There was a message inside the box which said "Petherton better. Will send him with chopper tomorrow or next day. Happy Birthday, Steffo!" -- but on the outside of the box there was a single word written hastily in black marker pen, probably by Dr Jensen just before it was sent on its way. The word was "BEWARE!"

Later on, as the seven men tucked into Hanna's birthday supper, there was an animated discussion. What on earth did Jensen's message mean? Was it joke of some sort? Was there a polar bear about, or some other sort of danger? They all enjoyed the cake, but they had to agree that they were mystified by the warning, and by the fact that the people at Himmelbjerg -- presumably including Jim Wagner -- knew the birthdays of the expedition members. This meant they must not only have been in possession of the expedition's work schedule, but also of passport details and the full expedition prospectus, which contained the CVs and personal information about all eight members of the party.

After two days of settling in the Base Camp party was beginning to feel at home. The place was in good order, and they had set up routines and rotas that seemed to work, for cooking, washing up, water carrying and waste disposal. They had completed a few reconnaissance walks, and the five individual research programmes were under way. They all got on well enough. Stephen Hanna seemed to grow in stature day by day, both physically and in the estimation of his colleagues, who had already lost any reservations they might have had about his leadership qualities. Joe Horton was a quiet and somewhat mysterious figure, with an air of authority about him which elicited respect and even reverence from the others. There was something dark in his character which the others could not quite work out. But he was the one to whom Hanna turned when he needed reassurance or advice. Gwyn Hughes was ferociously intelligent and studious to a fault, but he was well liked because of his maturity and calmness, and because he empathized strongly with others, as well as being very observant and perceptive. Without making it too obvious, he kept a weather eye open for Rowland Linney, who was certainly destined, in later life, to be the archetypal scatty professor. Linney had several published papers to his name in learned zoological journals before he reached the age of 20, but he was entirely disorganized in his personal life, and they all worried about him in the wilderness because he seemed to have no sense of direction. "Spatial awareness?" he had said once. "No time for such luxuries........" Mortimer, the zoologist from Sheffield University, was the oldest of the group, and to some degree the odd man out. He was withdrawn and occasionally moody, and did not find it easy to talk about himself and his family and personal relationships -- but he seemed happy enough, and he was in seventh heaven when he told the others about a herd of fifteen muskoxen which seemed to have taken up residence on the plateau around Pythagoras Bjerg, and recounted his intention to track their grazing movements in minute detail.

On the 15th July Horton and Whiteside left Base Camp and made a forced march all the way back to Desert Depot, a full 25 miles away, since they had work to do in the valleys running southwards out of the Stauning Alps. Just as they reached the depot, late in the evening, the chopper appeared from the north. Art Ruckle, the pilot, spotted them and landed, and out climbed Andy Petherton, recovered and refreshed, and eager to get on with his own fieldwork programme. He had with him his rucksack and personal gear, including the geological equipment he needed for taking and recording rock samples. With a grin, he also unloaded a box of bread, fruit and assorted luxury items. "Courtesy of the Himmelbjerg sick bay," he said. "Invalids get special rations, and the cook insisted I should take these with me to assist in my full recuperation. If you guys are kind to me, I might share them with you........."

"My dear fellow, I'm very partial to dark chocolate. In exchange for a lump a day, I will tuck you in at night and tell you bedtime stories, and provide whatever other services you require.........."

Horton laughed. "Be careful what you promise, Perry! These bloody Aussies have strange tastes and weird habits, especially after weeks in the outback."

The four men had a brief conference, and it was agreed that Petherton would join the two biologists in working from a new camp site a few miles away, on the west side of the Schuchertdal river plain. They would work from that camp for four days, and then return to Base. That having been agreed, Ruckle took off in a whirlwind of dust and returned to his depot adjacent to the red mountain.

One evening, after supper, the residents of Base Camp were together in "The Palace". This was the only tent big enough to stand up in, and they had already established a pattern of using it for meals when the weather was bad, and for cooking and the storage of daily rations. One corner was set aside for scientific equipment and for the field samples which were already starting to accumulate. The conversation turned to Himmelbjerg, and Hughes said: "Strange place, that red mountain. Did you notice when we were there that there were no stockpiles of milled molybdenum ore or any other extracted minerals? One would expect them to be outside rather than cluttering up valuable space inside the mountain. At Blyhavn, when the lead mine was working, they had a crushing plant inside the mountain, in a specially widened chamber, and there was some gear for processing out the lead concentrate, which then went out as nicely packed pellets ready for shipping."

"What's your point, Gwyn?" asked Mortimer. "There, they were after lead, which is hellish heavy. Here they're after molybdenum......."

"......... which is maybe lighter. I don't have a clue -- I'm no geologist. But did you see anything that looked as if it was on the way out? I didn't. On the other hand there seemed to be a lot of stuff coming in, on those

Caterpillar sledge trains."

"Agreed," said Linney, "now that you come to mention it. But they are certainly digging a lot -- look at all those piles of debris being carried out on the little railway lines and trucks. Gold? Diamonds? Uranium?"

"Not the latter," said Hanna. "Nasty stuff. If they were digging for that, there would be drums of yellowcake somewhere. And there would be signs of much higher safety standards, and radioactivity symbols and so forth. Didn't see any of that."

Then Knudsen chipped in to the discussion. "But why that massive iron door across the entrance to the main tunnel? I thought that was weird -- there's nothing like it in the mines at Blyhavn. Are they trying to keep something out, or something in? It's not as if there are all sorts of undesirable people just wandering past on the glacier, who might just pop in and do a bit of petty thieving!"

"My thoughts entirely," replied Hughes. "And another thing. My old man is a stock broker in New York, specializing in metals -- and he told me just before we left, when we were talking about our field programme and so forth on the phone, that the price of molybdenum was tumbling, with no bottom in sight. He said that a number of global mining enterprises -- really big players in the market -- had gone bust because they had over-invested in dodgy molybdenum enterprises in remote places."

"Strange. Didn't that fellow Wagner tell us over our exotic lunch that the world price of molybdenum was rocketing upwards, and that there were now big profits to be made from their sort of operation?"

"He did. Heard it myself, from the horse's mouth."

"Maybe mining operations have a long lead time," said Mortimer. "I reckon that the Greenland Metals company is speculating that the price for concentrate cannot go any lower, and that the boom is just around the corner........."

Hanna had a deep furrow on his brow. "You may be right, Griff. But there's another issue that bugs me. You know those pictures of the mining operations that Jim Wagner showed us? Well, I'm pretty sure I've seen more than one of them before, when we were doing some background work for the expedition. I think they were photos from another mine, a gold mine in West Greenland......."

81

"But why on earth would he want to pass those off as photos from Himmelbjerg? Doesn't make sense."

"It makes perfect sense," retorted Hughes. "If he's hiding something, he has to hide it, using whatever diversionary and evasion tactics he can devise. He probably took us for a bunch of gullible students."

"Which is what some of us are, my dear fellow," grinned Linney. "It's only when one puts all these bits and pieces together that they stack up into something intriguing, if not downright dodgy. There's yet another thing that caught my eye at the red mountain -- did you notice the letters "NAPRE" stencilled onto the sides of many of the boxes?"

"Can't say I did," said Mortimer. "But what of it anyway? Probably the code letters of the transport company bringing all the supplies in from Iceland? Northern Associated Product Removals Europe — or some such thing."

"That sounds reasonable. But thinking of logistics, we have that bloody Mellem Pass issue. When we walked in over the mountains, why were we sent all the way round over the Eastern Glacier Pass on the pretext that there was impassably thick snow on the Mellem, only to get told later by one of the Caterpillar drivers that it was quite clear over there? Something was going on, I reckon, that Wagner didn't want us to know about."

"You have a nasty suspicious mind, Gwyn."

"So my mother told me, when I was two years old. And another thing......"

"Good God, old man, you are on a bit of a roll here....."

"Indeed I am. When our DC3 came in to Blyhavn from Keflavik, you guys might have been looking the other way, but from my side of the plane I could see a hell of a lot of earth moving and construction machinery next to the runway, behind a big ridge of spoil. It wasn't visible after we'd landed. I had a word with the pilot about this after leaving the aircraft, and was told the length of the runway was being doubled to two thousand yards. That's well over a mile. I asked him why. "You can guess if you like," said the pilot. "But I'm not at liberty to say.............""

As if on cue, the animated discussion over cups of coffee in The

Palace was interrupted by the deep drone of a heavy aircraft. They tumbled outside, but could see nothing. The sound came from far away to the north-west, somewhere over the Stauning Alps. Gradually the drone faded away. "So what the hell was that?" asked Hanna.

"I have an uncle who lives in Wiltshire," said Hughes. "Been to visit him many times. So I know that sound as well as any of the locals. I'll bet my bottom dollar that was a USAF Hercules, just out from Blyhavn and off over the ice sheet to Summit Camp..........."

"What goes on there?" asked Linney.

"Well, there's a lot of weather and a lot of ice. It's near the summit of the ice sheet, and is five hundred miles from anywhere. It's more difficult to get to than the South Pole. I know from some of the recent conferences in the US that the place is crawling with meteorologists and glaciologists, putting up with incredibly tough conditions but doing excellent work."

"Who says it's excellent work?"

"Well, the Americans do. But here's an interesting thought. I'm a glaciologist, and I'm pretty well informed on everything that's going on in the literature, but come to think of it, I've never seen a single published paper from Summit Camp, nor heard a single conference presentation........."

The meeting in the Sledge Patrol Hut at Blyhavn was an interminable one, with a long agenda dealing with dog sledges, breeding programmes, annual budgets, postal deliveries, new recruitments and a myriad of other petty issues as well. Keppel was there because he had to be, as the senior Danish Government official from Sandvig; and Wagner was there, by invitation, because he wanted to be fully informed about who was in the district, what their movements might be over the coming months, and what they would be doing. He prided himself on his meticulous planning, and though he hated meetings, he saw it as his duty to be involved in everything that happened at Blyhavn. Keppel rather resented that, since he had no official status in East Greenland affairs -- but like a good diplomat he held his tongue.

The meeting droned on, and when it was over, and the participants were enjoying a cup of coffee together, Keppel took Wagner to one side. "Jim," he said. "I've been asked by a certain gentleman in Sandvig to give this to you personally. I promised to oblige, so here you are."

He handed over Pana's little parcel, and Wagner gave a radiant smile. "A present, Harald?"

"I have no idea," lied Keppel. "I'm just the courier here."

Wagner tore the little parcel open, to reveal the grotesque **tupilak** carved out of walrus tusk. "Say, that's great!" he enthused. "I like it! Naive design and crudely made, but what d'you expect out here? Fancy myself as a bit of a connoisseur of native art. I got a good luck charm like this one back in Vietnam, from a whore in a brothel in Saigon. Hot as the fires of hell, she was. She said she loved me, and that I needed protecting. Anyway, best thing that ever happened to me. I hung it round my neck, and after that, Harald, with hell to pay going on all around me, I came through without a single injury. I kid you not -- not a fucking scratch. I lost that little carving somewhere, so I'll wear this one round my neck, to protect me from all those evil spirits prowling on the tundra!" He chortled at his own joke. "What d'ya think?"

"Your choice, Jim," said Keppel evenly. "Now then, can I pour you some more coffee?"

Afterwards, the lanky Dane strolled along the dusty track leading to the old mining settlement, enjoying a quiet smoke, content in his own company. In the distance he heard the weird and haunting cry of the great northern diver, as he knew he would.

CHAPTER 5
July 1962

Horton and Whiteside were starting their work just below the snowline on a steep spur above one of the smaller glaciers of the southern Stauning Alps, just a few miles to the west of their camp site. They were in good spirits, for they were above the mosquito zone. The going was good, and since the weather was still in perfect Arctic Riviera mode the views around the full circle of the compass were fabulous. Horton had his eye on some cliffs further along on the mountainside which he thought might reveal to him some of the secrets of limestone plant communities, and Whiteside was trying to work out whether the small brown bird he could hear in the distance was, or was not, a meadow pipit. Suddenly, without warning, they heard a sharp thudding sound on a long snow slope above them, followed by a low rumble. They realized immediately that the whole of the snowbank had given way, and that an avalanche at least two hundred yards across was hurtling down towards them. They turned and fled, and managed to scramble onto a small rocky tor which stood just a few feet above the rest of the ground surface. They were just in time, and they watched in horror as the powder snow, behaving just as a flood of water might have done, flowed around their little sanctuary on both sides and then ran away down the slope. Then it was over. It had lasted for no more than a couple of minutes, and it left the previously clean upland ridge littered with snowy debris and with stones and boulders which had been dragged along in the descending torrent.

The two colleagues were thoroughly shaken by the experience, and they stayed where they were for a few minutes in the hope that there would be no more collapses from the snowfield above them. The broken snow face was about three hundred yards away, and when Whiteside examined it through his binoculars he said that it still looked very precarious. They decided to retrace their steps as rapidly as possible, and for five minutes they ran, staggered, crawled and climbed across the chaotic jumble of snowy debris that the avalanche had left behind on the gently inclined crest of the spur. At last they reached the relative safety of the rocky scree and moraine outside the avalanche zone, and collapsed onto the ground, gasping for breath. "God, that was a bit too close for comfort," said Horton when he had regained the power of speech. "Never seen an avalanche in that sort of situation before......."

"Me neither," said Whiteside. "Out of the blue, well into the summer, and not even in an avalanche gully. I've learnt a lot about avalanches over the years, but this just goes to show that one's always got more to learn. You all right, my dear fellow?"

"Yes, fine. Just a few bruises from that mad scramble. Let's take some photos. Gwyn knows all about snow and ice, and when we meet up again at Base he'll be very interested in this little episode............."

So they photographed the avalanche scar and snowslide material, and made detailed notes about the nature of the event, after which they were in no mood to continue their day's work on lime-loving plants and meadow pipits. They had after all come within an inch of losing their lives, and they felt that they deserved the rest of the afternoon off.

Rowland Linney sat on a large rock near the shore of Nordøst Bugt, about four miles from Base Camp. The sun was high, and if it had not been for the mosquitoes he would have taken his shirt off. There was a gentle breeze from the east, and that meant stable weather at least for the next day or two. A couple of hundred yards away a large flock of barnacle geese was grazing on the grassy flats near the shoreline, and across the bay he could see half a dozen musk-oxen, widely separated as they often were when there was nothing in particular to threaten them. All was well with the world. He enjoyed being on his own for a while, since there was virtually no privacy at Base Camp. He lay back on his rock and closed his eyes, and listened to the Ice Symphony.

They were all fascinated by it, for it went on day after day, round the clock. There was hardly a moment when the ice was silent, thought Linney, and while some of the sounds came from the small brash ice fragments disturbed by waves on the shoreline just a few yards away, others were carrying across the waters of Hall Bredning on the breeze, telling of gigantic catastrophic events over sixty miles away. In the distance there was always the low hollow thundering of the Schuchert River as it dropped towards the sea, underpinning and supporting all the other sounds that reached his ears. It reminded him of the long drone in the Prelude to *Das Rheingold*, but without those silly Rhine maidens. The real iceberg sounds were distributed up and down through the octaves -- sometimes in the bass part of the register, like distant quarrying explosions faintly heard, sometimes as a sharp tenor crack echoing off the fjord walls, and sometimes as a long sustained baritone rumble rolling across the ice-studded waters. One learned to live with these sounds, in an infinite number of variations, but sometimes one could be genuinely surprised and even frightened by a great thunderclap coming out of nowhere, maybe sustained for a minute or more, before it faded with equal suddenness into nothing. He thought that he could hear the March to the Scaffold from the Berlioz *Symphonie Fantastique* far away across the water. In his mind's eye he saw distant armies marching to the accompaniment of muffled drumbeats, or black thunderclouds riven by lightning as ferocious storms spent their fury between the high containing walls of distant fjords. And then he heard the little sounds, coming from ice on the receding waterline as the tide dropped: the constant hollow dripping of meltwater, the quiet drumming of wavelets beneath ice overhangs, and the melodic chattering and tinkling of small ice fragments drifting about in the expanses of brash ice which moved in and out according to the whims of winds, waves and tidal currents...........

Linney snapped himself out of his reverie. He had work to do, and the tide had now dropped far enough for him to walk out across the mud-flats in search of the shellfish and crustaceans which were near the bottom of the food-chain and which maintained the Hall Bredning population of seals. So he strode out with his folding shovel and light rucksack full of collecting bottles, navigating between stranded small icebergs and brash ice fragments and scanning the ground surface for interesting creatures. He had forgotten that in a shallow bay like Nordøst Bugt the big grounded icebergs become increasingly unstable as the water that supports them is drained away; so he should not really have been surprised by what happened next.

He happened to be looking up at the time, and saw it happen, no more than 400 yards from where he stood. An old and rotten iceberg about the size of an office block disintegrated with an explosive force that almost took his breath away, causing massive avalanches of pulverized ice to cascade down into the water and even throwing up fragments of solid ice which splashed down more than twenty yards away. Larger ice slabs smashed into the shallow water as the remnants of the berg reared up like a wounded sea monster, slowly at first and then with staggering speed for something so huge. Waterfalls carrying thousands of tonnes of white water cascaded off its glistening flanks as Linney watched with eyes wide and mouth agape, hypnotized by the spectacle. That was his undoing, for he realized too late that a huge foaming wave was now racing across the mud-flats towards him. He dropped his shovel and his bottles and ran for his life. The water was shallow where the wave was generated, and since water depth decreased as it raced towards the shore, it built up until it was more than ten feet high. Frantically Linney tried to keep ahead of it, but he slipped on the mud and had to grovel and crawl towards the distant green shoreline, looking over his shoulder towards the rolling wave and gasping for breath as terror replaced wonderment in his eyes.

Then the wave picked him up and rolled him about as he fought for air and desperately tried to work out where the water surface was. Afterwards, he would have no recollection of the length of time that passed while he was submerged -- all he recalled was a maelstrom of black muddy water and fragments of ice, some of them far larger than him, as he was tumbled over and over, quite incapable of doing anything to protect himself. Then with a final roar the wave poured over the beach on the western shore of the bay and across the green tundra as its energy was dissipated. Linney felt himself face down on a carpet of rough greenery, being pushed inland by a flood about three feet deep. Then there was a moment of calm before the water started to pour back down towards the mud flats, threatening to drag him with it. But somehow he managed to fill his lungs with air, and then found enough strength in his bruised and bleeding hands to grab hold of the tangled prostrate branches of dwarf willow and dwarf birch which he found all around him. Then the water was gone, leaving him high and dry. Several other waves followed, but they were all much smaller, and did not reach the shoreline.

By some miracle he was still alive. He coughed water from his lungs and took in great gulps of fresh air. He lifted his head and then gingerly sat up as he assessed the situation. He discovered that his arms and legs functioned as they should. He was covered in blood, from the lacerations and scratches on his hands, arms and head. His trousers were shredded, but he still had his boots on, and his torso had been protected by his heavy corduroy shirt. At last he stood up, to survey the scene of desolation all around him -- and saw thousands of fragments of ice, some of them bigger than cars, scattered over the green tundra for three or four hundred yards inland. The streaming waters had taken away his scientific equipment, and he knew that he would never see it again, but by another miracle he could see his warmer clothing and his pack frame dry and undisturbed, on the rocky knoll where he had not so long ago done his daydreaming.

Then the full significance of what had happened to him hit home, and his legs gave way as he shivered violently. Shock, he thought, this is what shock does to you. Just be patient, and it will pass...........

For some minutes he knelt as he recovered his composure, then he staggered to his feet again and headed for his possessions about a hundred yards away. He knew that he had to get out of his wet garments, or at least out of the bits that were left dangling from his body, and into the warm clothes that he had left on the stone. He also knew that he had to keep moving if he was to avoid hypothermia. So he dressed his wounds as best he could, and bound up the worst of them with strips of fabric from his shredded trousers, and set off for Base Camp. As he walked, he thought it prudent to thank whichever deity had been responsible for his survival.

––––––––––––––––––––––––––

Horton, Whiteside and Petherton were back at Base Camp, after a successful and not uneventful first phase of research work. The eight members of the expedition were now together for the first time since their nightmare journey across the Werner Mountains, and there was much discussion about the close shaves experienced by three of them. Hanna was angry about these incidents which could have resulted in loss of life, but he was reluctant to criticize because, as far as he could see, all three of his colleagues had not been culpable in any way. Nonetheless, he urged caution at all times, and pleaded for a heightened awareness of potential risks from any quarter. "If you ever put yourselves in harm's way," he said sombrely, "accidents can happen. So for God's sake think ahead, read the landscape and the weather, and expect the worst -- and then celebrate when nothing happens." He was greeted with silence. At last, Joe Horton said: "Amen to that, Steffo. Well said. Cup of tea, anybody, to celebrate the fact that we are all still alive?"

Next day Horton, Whiteside and Knudsen were striding along at a good pace on the edge of the Schuchert River gravel flats, a few miles from Base, when Horton began to laugh.

"Thought of a funny story, old fruit?" said Whiteside. "Share it with us, if you will."

"No joke at all, Perry. I was just thinking what an ill-assorted bunch of clowns we are on this expedition. English, Welsh, Scottish, Australian, Danish -- like a bloody United Nations, we are. Sometimes, when Steffo speaks with that thick Scottish accent of his, he could just as well be speaking Gaelic for all I know............"

"Oh, I don't have any problem with it," grinned Knudsen. "Maybe that's because both he and I are descended from the Vikings. Kindred spirits, as I think you say in English."

"And Andy back there, like Ned Kelly on the outside and Adolf Hitler on the inside."

"Don't be so quick to judge. He's just a typical Aussie -- he enjoys making a noise, and stirring things up. It's a sport for him, and probably has been ever since he gave up playing Aussie Rules."

"Well, I still think it's a miracle that we all understand each other, and get on pretty well."

"That's not so surprising, is it?" asked Whiteside. "Steffo pulled us together because he thought we'd make a good team. So far so good......."

"So what brought you on board, Perry?" asked Knudsen.

"I met Steffo at the Exploration Club. We got chatting about the Antarctic -- it's his intention to go there one day. So I gave him some of the lowdown -- I did my stint as a FIDS gash hand before getting a place at St John's."

"Gash hand, Perry?   Now who's talking a strange foreign language?"

Whiteside laughed. "Apologies, my dear fellow. A gash hand on an Antarctic base is the lowest of the low, and yet the most important person around. He looks after everything that the incompetent scientists are incapable of understanding -- dog handling, sledges, repairs, cooking, putting up tents, getting people out of crevasses........ You name it, I've done it."

"That sounds like the sort of job I should have done, given my background," said Horton. "Very humble beginnings, I had. But I get a distinct impression that you were born with a bloody silver spoon in your mouth, Perry. So how come you were a gash hand in Antarctica, instead of going for a commission at Sandhurst?"

"Steady on, old fruit! That sounds a bit resentful, if I may say so."

"Sorry, Perry," replied Horton. "Didn't mean it to come out quite like that. But maybe, if I'm honest, I am a bit resentful of people like you. The way you talk, like somebody out of a Woodhouse novel. The way you look, with that silk cravat round your neck, come hell or high water. Can't help it. For me, life has always been like wading through shit, uphill. Two steps forward, one step back, over and over again."

"So what makes you think it hasn't been a bloody uphill battle for me too?"

"Well, money might not buy happiness, but it certainly helps........"

Whiteside stopped and looked Horton in the eye. "Let me put you in the picture, my dear fellow. Can't do much about my way of speaking — that's the way I am. My childhood was totally weird -- a sick mother, who's still alive, and still sick, three older sisters who argue incessantly, and a father who's always spent more time in London and the House of Lords than on the family estate. He has a mistress who has a vast apartment in Mayfair. Everybody in the world knows that. I'll inherit the estate, if I get out of here alive, when Father dies. For the record, it's the Netherhall Estate in Lincolnshire, five thousand acres, twenty-two tenant farmers, and so many accumulated debts that when Father dies most of the land and buildings will have to be sold off or given to the National Trust. It's expected of me that I'll find a wife with a magnificent pedigree and broad hips, and produce a male heir. Mother already has a monstrous female in mind, and there will be hell to pay when I give her the push. Not looking forward to it at all, my dear fellows. In fact, it will all be a bloody nightmare. Had enough of nightmares. Eton was a nightmare too -- hated every minute of it. And, Joe, you are jealous because I was born with a silver spoon in my mouth?"

Whiteside was shaking with emotion, and Knudsen saw that he was close to tears. Instinctively he put a hand on his colleague's shoulder, and at last he took a deep breath and managed to smile. "Sorry if I get emotional sometimes, chaps. But I'll tell you that my time in the Antarctic was the happiest ever, when I was doing really useful things. And it was even better because I was twenty thousand miles -- give or take a few -- from home. Can't tell you how important that was. Father has always thought me to be as thick as two planks. I don't think I'm stupid, but I just hate academic work -- but give me a mountain to climb, or a river to cross, and I reckon I'm close to Heaven. D'you understand that?"

"I do, Perry," said Horton quietly. "Maybe we are two of a kind. And I'm sorry for speaking out of turn like that. I always was too quick in jumping to conclusions, and in passing judgment on others. I've rather a lot to learn............"

"Think nothing of it, old fruit. I think that on this jolly jaunt of ours, all of us have rather a lot still to learn."

And with that, the three men turned and strode southwards again, in silence.

Stephen Hanna was well into his research programme, working on raised beaches and other evidence of the changing positions of land and sea over the millennia since the end of the last big glacial episode. He had made some exciting discoveries during his early reconnaissance trips, and now he was working on a series of old deltas which looked in the landscape like gigantic steps running from sea level up to an altitude of more than 300 feet in the lower part of the Gurreholm river valley. With Lars Knudsen as his assistant, he was working six or seven miles from Base Camp. They had a two-man tent and supplies for four days with them while they completed their surveying work with a theodolite and other equipment. Their last task for the day was to walk the couple of miles from their camp site down to the shore, so that they could establish sea level. This would be the fixed point they would use for working out all of the terrace altitudes on the "delta staircase."

It was about 7 pm, and they were enjoying a mellow evening as the sun rolled round to the west over the mountains and ice caps of Renland. They had timed their visit to coincide with high tide, and now they were walking along the shore looking for a suitable spot for measurements. They were both mindful of what had happened to Linney a few days since, and still wondered whether he should really have predicted the collapse of one or more large stranded bergs out there on the mud flats on a falling tide............

At any rate, they determined to be ultra-cautious in making their own assessments of the risks which faced them in this estuarine environment, and promised themselves that nothing dramatic would ever happen to them. Then they heard a sharp crack, followed by a low rumbling sound that lasted for fully two minutes. Something big had happened far out in Hall Bredning, maybe out of sight behind Syd Kap Island. They were on full alert, and Hanna moaned: "Oh no! Not us too? That would be too weird for words......." The stood still for fully two minutes more, listening intently.

But nothing happened, and it became quiet again. The two colleagues continued their walk along the shore. They took out a pair of binoculars and scanned the water surface in the bay, looking for long swells that might signal danger. A few minutes passed. Then they heard a low murmur a long way off, which gradually became louder. They exchanged glances, and as they did so they noticed that the water was draining away from the beach until it was maybe six feet beneath high water mark. "Bloody hell! Run!" shouted Hanna, and the two of them sprinted away from the shoreline as fast as their legs would carry them, given that they were wearing heavy walking boots and rucksacks full of surveying equipment. "As high as possible," gasped Hanna. "Onto that ridge of moraine!" They turned to catch their breath and looked back, and then they saw the swells coming -- maybe four or five of them, one after another, rolling up through a vast field of brash ice fragments towards the beach and building as they came.

Frantically the two men scrambled onto the moraine ridge which had been their objective, and reached it just as the swells turned into breakers and tumbled onto the shore where they had been walking. Within seconds there was water and brash ice everywhere as the breakers roared across the surface of the tundra, ripping up greenery and littering the landscape with bits and pieces of ice which had been formed maybe millennia earlier up on the vast expanse of the Greenland Ice Sheet.

The two men feared that the worst was about to happen as the swirling soup of water, ice, mud and plant debris lapped around their hummock of moraine, making an island of it; but it came no higher, and at last they exhaled with relief as the water began to subside. Incredibly, they lost no equipment, and did not even get their feet wet. For several minutes they sat still, without exchanging a single word, as they regained their composure.

Since Hanna was a geomorphologist, he recorded the effects of the tidal wave that had almost overwhelmed them in as much detail as possible. Knudsen took many photographs while his colleague made copious notes on the extent and duration of the short-lived flood, the size of the waves (as far as they could assess them), the dimensions and weight of the ice fragments carried inland, and the damage done to the plant cover and the ground surface. Then, still chastened and even a little shocked by their near-death experience, they walked back to their camp site at about 10 pm and cooked up a large pot of beef curry.

Afterwards Hanna did not feel like sleeping. While Knudsen settled into his sleeping bag and fell into a deep sleep, he wandered off from the tent and sat on a rock, where he listened to the chords of the ice symphony in the distance as it drifted eerily across the landscape, punctuated by bird calls. Somewhere, very far away, there was a single great northern diver..........

"In my humble opinion, Dr Jensen is psychic," said Mortimer, with a grin on his face. "Unusual for a doctor maybe, but when we got here he warned us to beware, and I think he'd picked up on some mysterious vibes that told him we would have some close shaves. So that's my theory, and I'm sticking to it."

"Stuff and nonsense," said Joe Horton. "Doctors are very rational fellows, not given to mumbo-jumbo. And from the little we've seen of Dr Jensen he seems to have his feet pretty firmly planted on the ground. What d'you think, Andy? You got to know him better than the rest us us, up at Himmelbjerg."

"Well, he seemed quite normal to me, and he's a good doctor. I doubt that he spends time talking to the spirits of the ancestors as the Inuits do. But you never know -- we'd best be open to all possibilities..........."

They were all relaxing in "The Palace", drinking copious amounts of coffee and exchanging notes on work targets achieved, adventures in the field, and the merits of the boxed food rations which Hanna had assured them were the best in the world in terms of calorific value, nutrition per pound of weight, variety and taste.

After a fortnight in the field, those who had decided to go for the bearded look were looking stubbly and uncivilized, and only Knudsen was keeping to a routine of shaving every second or third day. Clothes were already starting to show signs of wear and tear, and although the weather had been good there were wet clothes hanging up on the clothes-lines which were draped between and inside all of the tents. They all looked forward to the next phase of the expedition in which visits to the huts at Syd Kap and Gurreholm might allow them to swap some of their expedition dried food supplies for tinned things like carrots, potatoes, beetroots and even peaches -- as well as having the luxury of bunk beds to sleep in and accommodation in which they could actually stand up straight. "I had a nightmare last night," moaned Gwyn Hughes. "I dreamed that I was in a bivvy on some glacier or other, suffering in the cause of science, while you lot were in a little hut on a rock, just out of reach. You were all lounging about on feather beds and sitting at tables and eating the same things as you do at home. Then Eskimo Nell turned up and provided her services for the night, and after that you had fresh crusty bread with Oxford marmalade for breakfast! And all I could do was watch. I could even smell the crusty bread. Absolute hell, it was."

"That's all a bit deep, old man," grinned Whiteside, "When we get home, I'll put you in touch with my shrink."

The quality of the conversation rapidly deteriorated. Soon there were gales of laughter echoing around the Kjove Land tundra as the eight colleagues enjoyed each others' company and pushed out of their minds their past discomforts and assorted adventures.

Then Whiteside reported that within half an hour of his arrival at Base he had planted a garden containing lettuces, radishes and carrots, using three packets of seeds brought all the way from home in the depths of his rucksack. This brought hoots of derision from those who had not observed his gardening activities. They claimed that there was not the slightest chance of the seeds germinating, let along providing them with salad for supper later on in the summer. Whiteside reacted with suitable outrage. "Oh ye of little faith!" he spluttered. "I will jolly well eat all the salad myself, if that's the way you want it. I've done everything by the book — beautiful sandy tilth, copious dressings of musk-ox manure, and just the right amount of water. Anyway, this is in the nature of a scientific experiment which far outweighs in importance all the other rubbish going on here, supposedly in the name of science. If it succeeds, this will be the most northerly lettuce patch in the world, and will find its rightful place in the Guinness Book of Records. The Nobel Prize for Science will be mine, and then you'll all look pretty stupid........"

"Speaking as a botanist," laughed Horton, "I think you should be hauled before the Royal Society Ethics Committee for irresponsible meddling in a delicate ecosystem. What if these lettuces thrive, and grow to giant proportions, and escape? They might take over the tundra within a few years, and in response there might be an explosion in the Arctic hare population, and the evolution of a new breed of super-bunnies. What then? Law of Unforeseen Consequences, and all that."

But it was inevitable that the conversation should eventually drift back to those occasions on which no less than five of the expedition members had stared death in the face -- and frivolity disappeared as they tried to analyse the risks which they had already taken and the means by which they might avoid other accidents during the rest of their time in Greenland. They clearly could not simply abandon their fieldwork and spend the rest of their time sitting at Base Camp. But Lars Knudsen, as an old hand in this harsh environment, reminded his colleagues that he had never seen anybody die, either in his seasons with the Sledge Patrol or during his trips with the Lauge Koch geology field parties. "This is a STRONG country," he said, speaking very slowly and deliberately as he always did. "It might have a gentle smile on its face, and it is of course so beautiful that some men cannot bear to drag themselves away -- but when it is angry it can snuff you out faster than I can snuff a candle. So be aware and alert at all times, my friends, and seek to plan ahead and predict what nature is about to do. So far, if I may speak as an old man, I'm very impressed with your planning and your decision-making. For that, Steffo, I congratulate you. You're a young man, but you have a wise head on your shoulders. Let's therefore be prepared for almost anything, let's use discretion and know when to abort rather than persist, and above all else, let's look after one another." He was not smiling any more. In fact he was shaking with emotion. And for a long time after he had finished his little speech, there was silence in the mess tent.

"Hey, boys," said Rowland Linney. "What's that? I'm sure I can hear something. It's very far away, I think. A deep thumping sound.""

Hanna, Hughes and Mortimer stopped in their tracks and listened for a minute, but decided that they could hear nothing, other than the sound of the waves and the wind. They were on Island Number Eleven, the largest of the Bear Islands, looking for moraines, seals, and traces of musk-ox occupation. Phase Two of the expedition was safely under way, and the four men had travelled across the open water of Hall Bredning in the two heavily-laden canvas canoes in just three hours, blessed by a gentle following breeze and mercifully ice-free water. They had set up camp on the northernmost of the islands, so that they could get back to Syd Kap quickly and easily, should they need to use a window of opportunity in a spell of bad weather. In the event the weather had remained good, and they had spent three wonderful days in this magical archipelago of complicated coves and straits, sheltered harbours, rocky ridge crests and hillocks smoothed by the inexorable sliding and grinding of millions of tonnes of ice over many thousands of years. They had used the canoes to paddle about between one island and another, and their field notebooks were bulging with observations and measurements. The islands had been named "Bear Islands" because some explorer had presumably seen polar bears here long ago; and Linney was convinced that there might even be one somewhere on the islands even now, for it was clearly a favourite hauling-out place for the ringed seals that made up the preferred polar bear food supply. The others hoped that that was just a fantasy, and were relieved that they had thus far seen no sign of any prowling and starving monster.

Just now they were waiting for the wind to drop and for the waves to subside, for an easterly gale was screaming down from the ice sheet under a high sun and a cloudless sky, as it often did during the months of July and August. They were not worried. They had plenty of work to do, and they knew that the wind and the waves would die down as afternoon passed into evening, allowing them to get back onto the water and to navigate a safe route on the lee side of the islands back to their camp site. The four of them got on well together, and even the normally reticent Mortimer was livelier and more relaxed than they had ever seen him. Hanna had decided that because his colleague was quite a shy fellow, he felt intimidated and even dominated when all eight of them were talking either frivolously or seriously, and that he was a great deal more comfortable when in a group of three or four men whom he liked and trusted.

Suddenly Hughes stopped examining the stones on a spectacular ridge of moraine and held up his hand. "I can hear it too," he said quietly. "There **is** something!" So they all stopped and listened, and bit by bit, through the sounds of the storm, they picked up the fragmentary but persistent beat of a small boat engine as it came closer. After a few minutes Hanna said: "That's a sound that belongs in my soul and brings a tear to my eye. I was brought up with it on the Isle of Harris. A hot-bulb single cylinder engine, if I'm not mistaken. Runs on paraffin or anything else. It never breaks down. A nightmare to start, but never goes wrong. Perfection, in a wilderness like this one. Seriously, I would trust my life to it."

They all stared out to sea, assuming that the little boat must be coming up from the south -- presumably from Sandvig. At last they saw it, a bright red speck far out, tossed by waves that must have been ten feet high, dodging in and out of the great bergs that sailed before the gale like a thousand galleons under full sail. Sometimes they saw it, and sometimes not; but it drew closer and closer, and at last they could see that it was a small cutter maybe twenty feet long, with a single mast towards the bow and a substantial wheelhouse towards the stern. It passed quite close to the island on which they were standing, and although the four men shouted and waved there was no sign that anybody on the little vessel had spotted them. It passed through a narrow sound between two of the lower islands, taking advantage of momentary shelter from the waves, and then moved north again, out into the waters of Øfjord. The men knew that it must be headed for Syd Kap, the old Inuit settlement from which they themselves had pushed off in their canoes just a few days earlier. The cutter was a couple of miles to the north when it passed a huge tabular berg no larger or inherently more dangerous than any of the others it had passed on its stormy voyage. But suddenly there was an immense clap of thunder out of nowhere, and a slice of the berg several hundred yards long simply sheared off its flank. As they watched in horror, the detached section tumbled over sideways into the stormy water as the remnant of the berg heaved itself upwards like a giant white whale coming up from the depths. A single huge wave, far bigger than anything they had ever seen before, surged away from the scene of the catastrophe. The little red boat could only have been a hundred yards away, and it did not have a chance. As they watched, it was lifted, rolled and then swamped by a giant foaming roller. One second it was there, and next second it was gone. All that was left was a swirling maelstrom of brash ice and berg fragments as the tidal wave dissipated and the storm waves reasserted themselves. There was a strange smell in the air, which they put down to the boat's exhaust fumes and maybe to an explosion of the red-hot engine as the boat went down.

The four men stood in a state of shock, horrified and terrified -- and mortified that there was nothing -- absolutely nothing -- that they could do. Their emergency rockets were at their camp site, about three miles away, and there was no way that they could get back to Syd Kap with the canoes, to raise the alarm, until the wind had dropped and the sea had subsided. For another couple of hours they paced back and forth on their desert island, in no mood to speak, let alone work. Linney thought that he had never before experienced such gloom, and Mortimer was so moved by the disaster that he sat for an age with his head in his hands, moaning "Oh no! Oh no!" over and over again. Later, when the sun had set and the wind had eased a little, they were back at their camp. They waited until precisely 8 pm and then set off a flare and a smoke canister, in the hope that somebody at Himmelbjerg might see the pyrotechnics. They ate their supper and waited until midnight for a response, but there was none, and at last they had to conclude that nobody had seen their signals. They cursed the inefficiency of the miners who should have been keeping watch, and they cursed the fact that they had no radio.

The wind continued unabated for two more days, and the four men were effectively stranded on the islands. There were a few spells of lighter winds, but the waves kept on rolling, and they did not dare to risk a crossing with the canvas canoes until they could see every razor-sharp piece of brash ice amid the waves and take evasive action. Much as they were appalled by the tragedy which they had witnessed, they decided at last that they could not just sit around, and so by consensus they got on with their work.

On the 28th of July Linney was on the northern shore of one of the smaller islands collecting marine samples when he made a gruesome discovery -- the body of an Inuit, washed ashore by the waves. He alerted the others, and they thought that they owed some sort of a duty to the missing seamen to search for any of the others who might also be washed ashore.   So they set out, in spite of the ongoing stormy weather, to examine some of the other shores of the Bear Islands as well. They found three more bodies of Inuit men in widely separate locations, all dumped by the waves which were driving directly onshore onto small rocky islets from the scene of the accident. All were dressed in traditional Inuit garb, and all appeared to be quite uninjured. They had simply been swept away from the boat as it went down, and must have died by drowning or from hypothermia.   Linney took careful photos of the bodies and particularly of the faces, in the hope that this might in due course aid identification.

But what to do now?   There was really no choice in the matter -- they must give all four of the Greenlanders good Christian burials, since that was certainly what their families would have wanted.   They would have liked to carry the corpses to one central location where they could be buried together, but they had no way of moving dead men from one island to another since all they had were two small and very unstable canoes as their means of transport.   So the bodies had to be buried more or less where they had been found.   The four colleagues spent the best part of a day trying to scrape elongated holes in the thin and stony soil, but that was easier said than done, since they had no strong shovels with them and since they always hit permafrost at a depth of 2 feet or less. They covered each body as best they could, and then piled on loose stones to make an elongated mound -- knowing full well that polar bears would find the human remains as soon as the fjord froze over in the autumn — if not earlier. At each burial Hanna, who was a good Scottish Presbyterian, said a simple prayer, and they recited the Lord's Prayer, and then tried to sing the only hymn for which they remembered the words:

Guide me, O thou great Jehovah,
pilgrim through this barren land.
I am weak, but thou art mighty;
hold me with thy powerful hand.
Bread of heaven, bread of heaven,

feed me till I want no more;
feed me till I want no more.

Open now the crystal fountain,
whence the healing stream doth flow;
let the fire and cloudy pillar
lead me all my journey through.
Strong deliverer, strong deliverer,
be thou still my strength and shield;
be thou still my strength and shield.

When I tread the verge of Jordan,
bid my anxious fears subside;
death of death and hell's destruction,
land me safe on Canaan's side.
Songs of praises, songs of praises,
I will ever give to thee;
I will ever give to thee.

Hanna knew it best, having belted it out in the back of rugby team buses on more occasions than he cared to remember, usually lubricated by alcohol and never with any attention paid to the words. The famous tune called *Cwm Rhondda* had been all that mattered. But now they did listen to the text of Williams Pantycelyn, and on each of the four occasions on which they tried to deliver the hymn, they failed to get to the end, as they were struck by its strangely appropriate words and as they choked with emotion.

When the last of the burials was done, they stood close together in silence for several minutes, arms around each other, in one last act of respect and reverence for four peaceful and innocent men who had been entirely comfortable in this environment and whose lives had nonetheless been snatched away by some monstrous freak of nature. They were completely exhausted, both physically and emotionally. Then they realized that the wind had stopped, and that the waves were diminishing at a speed which was hard to credit. They knew that within a few hours there would be a glassy calm on the sea. Without even discussing it, they knew that they had to abandon their research programme and take the opportunity now presented. So they jumped into their canoes, paddled as hard as possible back to their camp site, and started to dismantle the tents. There was no thought of either eating or sleeping. Those activities could wait until they were back at Syd Kap.

It took them four hours to canoe back to the old Inuit settlement, negotiating around great expanses of brash ice on the way and working hard to give all big bergs a wide berth. Some of the biggest, with keels extending for perhaps 800 feet down into the dark depths of the fjord, were still moving very fast, pushed by a strong current flowing out towards the distant entrance of Scoresby Sund. They reached Syd Kap at 8 am, dragged up the canoes onto the gravel beach, and walked into the one building that was in good repair -- the office used by the Danish Administrator on his visits. They had already named this "Hotel Paradiso". Hughes and Hanna prepared a quick meal from the first of their food boxes that came to hand. Then they slept for 5 hours, and got back onto the water, still driven by the urge to tell somebody -- anybody -- about the tragedy that they had witnessed and become a part of. Still very tired and having to cope with floating broken ice that had been driven onto the Syd Kap coast during the gale, they did their best to hug the shoreline back to Nordøstbugt and the mouth of Konglomeratelv.

Having made the canoes safe well above high water mark, they heaved their essential gear onto their backs and trudged back across the featureless Prairies to Base Camp.

CHAPTER 6
August 1962

The camp site was a shambles, with untidy sleeping bags lying about in the sleeping tents and with unwashed dishes on the ground where they had been left following the last meal in the open air. Hanna was beginning to think that some disaster had befallen his colleagues, and said so, but Linney said: "Not so fast, Steffo. You're obsessed with disasters. Nothing's happened. There hasn't even been a visit from a polar bear. The tent entrances are nicely zipped up and the mess tent's in good order. Just get used to the fact that some of your colleagues sleep later and worry less about tidiness than you do!" The young leader had to accept the truth of his colleague's observations. Nonetheless, as they reinstalled themselves at Base, and put up their tents in their old positions, the new arrivals were more than a little apprehensive -- and they were greatly relieved when they saw two figures in the distance, walking at a leisurely pace across the tundra from the direction of Nordøstbugt.

Those who returned to Base were Whiteside and Knudsen, who had been using the small inflatable boat with its outboard motor to investigate the characteristics of some of the smaller icebergs stranded in the bay. Everything had gone smoothly, said the Dane. Then he continued: "And we've got some excellent film footage in the can. There are remarkable colours on some of those bergs when you get up close. But don't you worry about me putting myself in danger -- the camera has an excellent zoom, and I always try to use it, which means I can stay well away from fragile bergs with overhangs."

When pressed on strange events, Whiteside said: "There were none, as far as we could tell, old fruit. We did hear one exceptionally load roar from far out in Hall Bredning some three or four days ago, but there's nothing exceptional to report. Windy, and pretty rough out in the bay. But on lee shores no big waves, and not even any big swells when we were out in the inflatable. East Greenland at its most benign."

"And not before time, if I may say so," smiled Hanna. "Maybe the earth spirits have now done their mischief, and will leave us in peace......"

Shortly afterwards Horton returned from the plateau, where he had been making good progress on his botanical project. He said that Petherton was taking advantage of the good weather to complete some geological mapping near Pythagoras Bjerg, and that he would be back soon. By the time supper was ready, they had all returned, and when they had eaten and washed up they assembled outside the mess tent as the Bear Islands party related in full the appalling events surrounding the sinking of the little red cutter from Sandvig and the deaths of the four Inuit hunters. Lars Knudsen was particularly affected by the news, and sat silent and white-faced until the story was completed. Then he got up and walked away without saying a word, and for more than an hour the others watched him as he strode back and forth around the Parachute Ponds with his head bowed and his hands clasped behind his back. They all knew that their Danish colleague had a very special bond with the Greenlanders, and Linney thought of trying to comfort him in some way, but as he got up Hanna put his hand on his shoulder and said: "Leave him, Rowland. He needs time on his own. Let's get another couple of rockets off instead."

At 8 pm, they set off the first Schermuly rocket flare and watched it climb up to a thousand feet or more before it burst into a swirling ball of red light and smoke which they were sure would be visible from at least fifty miles in all directions. They followed it as it descended slowly on its parachute. Precisely ten minutes later they sent up another, certain that there should be some response from Himmelbjerg. As they had done on the Bear Islands, they waited until midnight in the hope that a light aircraft or helicopter might appear, but the only sounds to reach their ears as the sun slipped down behind the peaks and snowfields of Renland were the distant roar of the Schuchert River and the sounds of the pinkfoot geese and the loons on the eastern lake of the Holger Danskes Briller. Once again, they swore about mine workers being untrustworthy and incompetent, and as they climbed into their sleeping bags they all felt angry and despondent.

Next morning, over breakfast, the expedition leader had to make

105

decisions. Five days had now passed since the sinking of the Inuit boat, and Hanna was forced to conclude that there was nothing to be gained by sending two men to Himmelbjerg, which would take another three days at least. They all agreed that somebody at Sandvig must have been aware that the red cutter and its crew were missing, and that a search party would soon be sent out. So they jointly decided, reluctantly, to press on with their work programme in modified form -- with the proviso that somebody should be at Base Camp at all times, in case a search party should turn up. They would make constant checks with Syd Kap, in case another boat should put in an appearance. The expedition members agreed with all of this, and Petherton and Horton said they were happy to work from Base for the next ten days or so, while carrying on with their work around the plateau and the Holger Danskes Briller lakes.

The expedition work schedule had made provision for two men to cross the bay to Gurreholm on the Jameson Land side of the Schuchert Valley, using the inflatable craft -- and Hanna reckoned that Linney and Mortimer could get a lot done in what was a relatively safe environment. The Jameson Land coast was, after all, low and sandy, with no major hazards on it -- and it would be easy for them to explore from the Gurreholm hut, which was one of the largest and most comfortable research huts in East Greenland. All being well, the two of them would travel to Gurreholm whenever sea ice conditions were suitable.

Once this had all been worked out to everybody's satisfaction, Linney grinned and said: "Griff and I seem to get all the luck on this expedition, don't we? We get to live in that mansion on the other side of the river, and we even get to use the little boat with an engine. Kayaks and tents are relics from the past."

"Huh!" said Mortimer, with a grin. "Enjoy your comfort while you can, Raymond. As for me, there's work to be done over there. I'll be out and about all day and every day, whatever the weather, returning to the hut each evening and expecting to find a nice steaming supper waiting for me on the table."

Whiteside and Knudsen, in the Klepper canoe, eased their fragile and heavily-laden craft onto the small sandy beach at the head of Nordbukten (North Bay), on the northern shore of Nordvest Fjord. A couple of minutes later the Granta also slipped onto the beach, with Hanna and Hughes resting on their paddles. "At last, at last," said Hughes. "Having overcome all obstacles, we set foot upon the promised land."

"Now that we are on dry land again, can I admit to a sense of relief?" asked Hanna, easing himself out of a canoe cockpit which was never intended for a man of his size. "Seriously spooky, that was, with just the thickness of a bit of canvas between us and the fjord bottom almost a mile below."

"Take it from me, old fruit," grinned Whiteside, "that water depth is immaterial. Not worth thinking about. If you had gone in, you would have died just as quickly even if the water had been just ten feet deep."

"Very reassuring, I'm sure," said Knudsen. "But if one is going down one might as well take with one the memory of a rather splendid landscape............"

The four friends were very tired, having paddled for three days with minimal rest all the way from Nordøstbugt -- a direct distance of over sixty miles along one of the most hostile shorelines in the world, distinguished in part by glowering walls of rock that plunged straight down from an altitude of over four thousand feet directly into the depths of the fjord. There had been many of those walls, for they were paddling along the outside of a fjord bend against which all of the fearsome erosive power of the Nordvest Fjord Glacier had been concentrated during one glaciation after another over millions of years. They were reminded again and again that this was the biggest and deepest fjord in the world. They had given these undercut and over-steepened walls, sometimes over five miles long, names such as "Hells Bells", "Black Death" and "Skydive", on the assumption that maybe one day some idiot would be mad enough to want to climb them, but they had been scared to death of them, knowing that if they had encountered any difficulties while passing beneath them, it would have been quite impossible to get out of the water and onto dry land. They might even have been struck by one of the boulders which they saw falling straight down into the sea from overhangs high overhead. They had passed a few small bays and inlets where glacial meltwater streams ran out into the sea, and they had camped and rested in two of those, one near Storm Point and the other to the west of the surging glacier which the Danes called Løberen (The Sprinter). Knudsen explained its name, and Hughes said it was known to be one of the fastest-flowing glaciers in the world. Their camp sites had been magnificent, on grassy banks just above high water mark, and they had been reluctant to leave either of them because they had been blessed with perfect weather and because of the indescribable beauty of the middle section of this mighty fjord. But on each occasion they had eaten, slept, and moved on. Near the floating snout of Løberen they had been forced to paddle through a vast expanse of brash ice and icebergs, which was almost suicidal in canoes with rubberized canvas skins -- but they had breathed deeply and gone for it, and the gods had smiled on them. What with all the detours, and the attempts to bypass enormous tabular bergs and to work through fields of brash ice, they reckoned that the actual distance they had paddled was well over a hundred miles.

Having eased themselves out from the tightly-packed cockpits of the two-man canoes, they jogged along the beach for a minute or two as they attempted to get some circulation back into their legs. The fragile vessels were great work-horses, and they had managed to squeeze five hundred pounds of food and gear into each one, over and above the weight of the two paddlers; but they were certainly not made for comfort, and they loved and hated them in equal measure.

All four of them were now delighted to be in the business of real exploring. They had no maps of this area, and no aerial photographs; and they had no idea, when they set out from Base Camp, what to expect. So now they took stock of their surroundings. They were in the western corner of a broad bay almost a mile wide, flanked by steep valley sides and with a flat gravel floor built up over the centuries by a complicated braided pattern of rushing meltwater streams. It was in truth a sterile place, but it looked safe enough, and so they established camp on a stretch of springy turf adjacent to a stream of clear clean water.

The intention was to explore the long valley system of Frederiksdal, which ran north-westwards for fifteen miles to a huge free-standing mountain called Trianglen, and then for another twenty miles north-eastwards to the shore of the ice-dammed lake called Furesø. Some of the early explorers, said Knudsen, had visited this valley after sailing up the fjord from Syd Kap, and certainly some geology field parties had been here with their helicopters; but the only other people who ever came here under their own steam were occasional trappers who came to the Furesø hut in the depths of winter, with their dog teams. So the explorers looked forward eagerly to discovering the valley's secrets and mapping the extent of the scores of small glaciers that tumbled down from the flanking plateau ice-caps towards the valley floor. Most of these glaciers ended high on the valley sides; but they had heard that some of them had snouts right down on the Frederiksdal valley floor, maybe making the valley impassable, and maybe not. They were prepared for anything......... or so they thought.

Next day, having left the canoes and a depot of food and other items at Nordbukten, they set off. The first part of the valley was a slog, but then it became very beautiful, with soft turf underfoot, interspersed with dry tundra similar to that of Kjove Land which would, before long, provide a rich harvest of bilberries. The scenery became more and more spectacular, and as they came into an area of scattered moraines and small lakes the bird life became very rich, with sizable flocks of barnacle geese and pinkfoot geese and abundant small waders and other ground-nesting species which Whiteside tried to give names to. There seemed to be several pairs of ravens in the valley, and they thought they saw a white-tailed eagle circling high overhead. Ptarmigans were abundant too, and they were surprised to find gulls, terns and even skuas more than ten miles inland, probably scavenging for eggs and chicks around the nesting areas used by the geese in particular. As they approached the great bend in the valley which was overlooked by Trianglen they realized that the mountain peak was actually at a complex junction of five valleys, one of which ran back to the inner reaches of Nordvest Fjord. The one that they were determined to follow ran north-eastwards, and now that they had reached the highest point on their exploratory trek, having walked and climbed fifteen miles in the day, they pitched camp close to the col in the shadow of the triangular peak.

It was Hanna's turn to cook supper, and while he slaved over a hot Primus stove the others relaxed in the warm evening air, swearing -- as ever -- about the swarms of mosquitoes that surrounded them, but not seriously bothered any more, since they had good supplies of insect repellant and since they had in any case developed a degree of immunity against the bites. Whiteside was sitting on the ground and leaning against a large rock as he idly scanned the distant hillside with his binoculars, and he suddenly sat up straight and subjected something or other to intense scrutiny. "Well, bless my soul!" he exclaimed. "I would never have believed it! Reindeer! Over there beyond that long lake -- about a dozen of them!" The others looked, and they all confirmed that Whiteside was not suffering from hallucinations. There they were, grazing peacefully as they moved quietly across a verdant terrace a few hundred feet above the valley floor. "First record for East Greenland since about 1870, if I'm not mistaken. There are lots of reindeer antlers lying about everywhere, but everybody says they are centuries old. Maybe they aren't -- not here, anyway. All the texts say that reindeer have been extinct right down the east coast, although there are a few in the north and on the west coast, where they can come in over the sea ice from Canada. Absolutely top class, chaps! This makes the whole expedition worthwhile, no matter how crap the rest of our so-called scientific results may be.............."

"No supper for you tonight, Perry" said Hanna, waving a plastic spoon. "Nobody insults my scientific results like that and gets away with it. If you are hungry, go off and get yourself a reindeer steak."

"Not allowed, my dear fellow. Strictly protected, they are. So I fear that I will have to put up with your disgusting hot mush that purports to be beef stroganoff, just like the other suffering souls in this party. Seriously though, this shows that Frederiksdal is indeed an isolated wildlife paradise, cut off by high plateaux, mountains and ice caps, incredibly difficult to get into, and close enough to the ice sheet to have an extraordinary microclimate. I wouldn't mind betting that summer temperatures are higher here, and snowfall is lower, than almost anywhere else along the East Greenland coast. Come to think of it, before we left England, I looked at one of the Danish aerial photos of this area, taken in June 1960. Most of the landscape was snow-covered, but

Frederiksdal was snow-free. This is the real Arctic Riviera."

"So, my dear Professor Whiteside," grinned Hughes, "what will you do about Frederiksdal? Tell the world about it, turn it into a wildlife refuge, and have the tourists flooding in, or keep it as our secret paradise?"

And so the conversation bubbled on over supper, until it was late in the evening and the light began to fade.

Art Ruckle and Larry Bishop poured cups of coffee for themselves and settled down in the Himmelbjerg mess room. They were the only ones there. Outside two Caterpillar tractors were moving off over the glacier towards the Mellem Pass, each one hauling four sledges of crushed ore, just for the benefit of anybody who might be watching.

Both men preferred to be out here, in one or other of the huts on the moraine where the light was bright and the air was fresh. Ruckle, in particular, disliked the inside of the mountain, where it was stuffy and dusty and claustrophobic and where there was a constant hum of machines — the main generator, the drilling machines, the crushing plant, and God only knows what else. It was not such a problem for Larry, he thought; radio men spent their whole lives holed up in dark corners, hunched up in front of buzzing and crackling radio sets with flashing lights, delicately balanced dials, switches and buttons, shut off from the world by their headsets, and endlessly talking to people they did not know and could not see. On the other hand, he mused, maybe Larry thought the life of a helicopter pilot was equally strange, where one had no option but to sit in a glass bubble beneath a set of noisy and madly rotating blades, lifting off and setting down on schedules dictated by other people, living with danger every moment. Did radio operators live longer than helicopter pilots? Maybe, maybe not........

"You're very thoughtful today, Art," said Bishop. "A dollar for your thoughts."

"Not worth a dollar, buddy. Just daydreaming. But I like it out here in this hut. Bright sunshine coming through the window, great view, peace and quiet. I'll make the most of it. Got to be back at Blyhavn by three this afternoon."

"Boss going with you?"

"Yep. Some meeting or other with somebody coming in from Keflavik."

"Top brass from NATO. I picked up the message in the shack."

Ruckle shrugged. "Progress review, I suppose. Last time I spoke to Jim, he seemed pleased enough. The Oxford guys haven't suspected anything so far. But there were a few choice words flying around; apparently he was was not best pleased with what happened down near the Bear Islands."

"I know. I handled the radio traffic. Not best pleased? That's the bloody understatement of the year. He was apoplectic. God knows how many expletives I had to remove from his messages, to avoid offence to those nice people in the Pentagon."

"So what was the problem?" asked Ruckle.

"Not sure of the details, but he was mad with Captain O'Brien on the **Ellsworth** for doing Experiment One-Five while the Oxford guys were on the islands making maps and so forth. He calmed down a bit when O'Brien insisted that they had got away with it, and that it was only a few Greenlanders who got killed."

Ruckle frowned. "He spends a bit too much time being mad with people these days, Larry. That worries me. In Vietnam has was as cold as ice. I don't like to see him melting."

"He seemed pretty cold when he went off with you over the mountains to Frederiksdal a few days ago. He had a job to do, and he was going to do it."

"And he did it too, without a moment's hesitation," said Ruckle. "God knows what the consequences will be. Somebody else's problem, I guess."

"You don't get to where Jim is without knowing when to take the glory and when to shove the blame off onto some other poor jerk............"

"Larry, you should have seen the bastard when we came back! Like a kid who'd just had his first ride on a roller-coaster. He smoked a couple of joints in the chopper, on the way home......."

"That's not good, Art. He says a joint a day keeps the doctor away. I told him the other day to go easy, and he almost bit my head off. Is he ill, d'you think?

"I know him better than anybody, but he's as tight as a clam. Of course he's bloody ill. Not physically maybe — but inside his head. That's why they took him home from Vietnam and gave him this desk job. Out there, he was starting to get erratic. Alfred Jensen looks after him, but he's the old sort of doctor, and won't say a word to anybody else about what's wrong, or what his treatment is."

Bishop gave a wry smile. "So he depends on Jensen to keep him alive, and hates his guts at the same time."

"With reason. I don't trust Jensen either. Asks too many questions. Come to think of it, the Boss doesn't trust any of the Danes. Maybe that's why they are rumoured to be moving out of here in a couple of weeks, to look after Blyhavn instead. Not that Blyhavn needs looking after. Plenty of guys there already."

"I can confirm all that, Art. I handled the messages, in and out."

Early in the morning, for the first time in his life, Hanna was woken by the sound of howling wolves. He knew that they were wolves, since he had heard recordings of them on the radio -- and the eerie howling, with answering calls, from far away down the valley towards Furesø, could really have come from no other animal. Soon Whiteside, who was sharing the tent with him, was awake too. "Unbelievable!" he exclaimed, as he scrambled out of his sleeping bag and into the cool morning air. "First, reindeer, and now wolves. They're supposed to be extinct too, although there are occasional rumours of sightings up north, around Dove Bugt and Germania Land.........." Then the wild and awesome sound of those ultimate creatures of the Arctic tundra came rolling up the valley again, and Whiteside was lost for words. After a few minutes the howling stopped, and while they ate breakfast and packed up in readiness for another day's walking, they heard nothing other than a few geese and angry terns within half a mile of their camp site. Now there was no holding Whiteside, for he was determined to see the wolves at close quarters and maybe get some photographs of them before the day was done -- and he wanted pictures of the reindeer too, if they had not strayed too far from the place where they had been spotted on the previous evening.

As the explorers made slow progress down the valley the going became increasingly tough. They were forced to scramble along the rocky shore of an ice-dammed lake for about two miles, and then they had to negotiate an area of ice-cored moraine, meltwater streams and very unstable slopes as they skirted the snout of a small glacier which was so heavily crevassed that they could not possibly have crossed it without crampons and ropes. They saw several small herds of musk-oxen in the middle section of the valley, and while they were eating their lunch close to the snout of another small glacier they spotted the reindeer at last. The animals had moved high up off the valley side and onto the edge of the plateau near the snow line, much too far away to be approached, but Whiteside obtained some consolation from the fact that he was able to count them accurately. There were fourteen, including four calves, and he was pleased by that indication that the herd was breeding and was intent upon survival.

They pressed on, and noticed that a white-tailed eagle was wheeling maybe five thousand feet up, above the valley floor. Whiteside looked at it through his binoculars. "That big fellow isn't going anywhere," he murmured. "It's got its beady eyes fixed on something on the ground. Maybe a big carcass — polar bear or musk-ox, or maybe a reindeer? Maybe it's the same carcass that has attracted the wolves. This is very exciting, my dear fellows! Nature red in tooth and claw, and all that guff........."

Before long they heard the wolves again, now very much closer. They scanned the valley ahead of them with their binoculars, and then they spotted the creatures not far from a very small hut near the Toscano Glacier. Not even Knudsen had known that there was a hut in this particular location, but they were not too surprised, since there were many huts in unrecorded locations, some of them new and habitable and others built by trappers more than fifty years ago and now substantially destroyed by weather and polar bears. Thirty minutes later they approached the hut, which proved to be about fifteen feet long by ten feet wide, with two small windows facing south and a door on the eastern side. The windows had external shutters, which were fixed in the open position. The roof was steeply pitched, and made of rough planking partly covered with creosote paper that had been shredded by the wind. The walls were protected up to a height of about four feet by banks of turf and stone, which served as a primitive form of insulation. A metal flue pipe passed through one of the walls and then extended above roof level, held in position by crude brackets. All in all, the hut looked perfectly serviceable.

The men now saw that there were six wolves in the pack, apparently preoccupied with something about 400 yards further down the valley, below the hut. They dumped their rucksacks on the ground at the side of the little building, and went to investigate. The animals were reluctant to give way as they approached, but at last they did leave, only to sit on a low knoll a hundred yards away, howling. The men all knew enough about wolves to be sure that they would not attack. They all thought they were magnificent, and they particularly admired a big white male in prime condition. He was clearly the leader of the pack.

Whiteside, who had seen wolves at close quarters in Canada, was now convinced that that they would find the gutted and half-consumed carcass of a large mammal, as he had speculated earlier. But then he and his colleagues recoiled in horror with the realization that the animals had been feeding on two human carcasses.

Both had been dismembered by the wolves. One torso was about a hundred yards from the other. There was not much left of them, and scraps of clothes, bones and bits of flesh were scattered over a wide area across the gravelly tundra. Some of the bones had almost been stripped clean by the wolves. Hanna walked towards the nearest torso and almost stepped on a leg with a boot still attached to it, half hidden in a patch of dwarf birch. The remains seemed remarkably fresh, and the stench of rotting flesh and innards was almost unbearable, causing both Whiteside and Hughes to retch uncontrollably.

The men were shocked into silence, but at last Hanna turned to Knudsen and said: "My God, Lasse, I can hardly believe what we're looking at. Ten minutes ago, this valley was Paradise. Now it's like something straight out of Hieronymus Bosch. Bloody unbelievable. Before coming out here I'd never been anywhere near a dead body, and now in the space of a couple of weeks we've buried four drowned Inuit hunters with our own hands, and it looks as if we'll have to try to bury whatever remains of these two poor buggers."

Knudsen nodded. "Agreed, Steffo. A nightmare to end all nightmares. Let's go back to the hut and try to work out what to do next. It looks as if Gwyn and Perry need to get away from this carnage anyway, at least for a few minutes."

The four of them walked back to the hut in silence, and sat on the gravel near the open door. They hardly dared to look inside, for fear of what they might find. At last they managed to focus enough to discuss their gruesome discovery. While they talked, the wolves stayed where they were, and started to howl again, this time sending shivers down their spines.........

The consensus was that the dead men had been attacked by the pack of wolves, maybe not more than three or four days ago. The human remains that they could see on the ground were fresh and putrid because the days were still very warm and because night-time temperatures had still not started to dip below zero, even in the deep shade. Hughes suggested that the men -- whoever they were -- might have been attacked by the wolf pack and that they had then tried to get back to their hut before being dragged down and killed, one after the other. Hanna and Knudsen nodded their agreement with that hypothesis, but Whiteside shook his head. "Sorry chaps," he said, "but I find that hard to believe. I was in northern Canada a couple of years ago in an area populated by wolves, and got to learn quite a bit about them. It's highly unlikely that they would go after human beings unless they were completely starving -- especially if there were two human beings together. They aren't really hungry at this time of year -- they've been feasting on eggs, goslings and so forth for the past few weeks. In the winter it might be a different matter. Wolves seem to know that human beings often have guns. A pack of only five or six animals would not go after two targets at the same time. They would go after one, maybe, if they were desperate, but if they pulled a man down they would instinctively all help to kill him rather than allow some members of the pack to go after somebody else. I don't buy the idea........."

"Well, how else do you explain what has gone on here?"

"God only knows. Perhaps we'd better do some detective work, since I don't suppose there is such a thing as a Greenland CID."

So they systematically scoured the area across which the body parts were littered, and made a number of interesting discoveries. They found another three boots, badly damaged by the wolves in their attempts to get at the flesh that had been contained inside them. Whiteside found a blood-spattered waterproof watch that was still working, and took possession of it since his own had been destroyed during one of the Schuchert Valley river crossings. Without examining it carefully, he strapped it to his wrist. They found two hunting rifles on the ground, each one not far from a torso. Both of the guns were Henry semi-automatic .22 Armalite AR-7 survival rifles, which Whiteside said were favoured by the hunting and trapping community and by the US Air Force because they were compact, accurate and robust. When he examined them he found no obvious distinguishing marks. But both weapons were fully loaded, and since there were no cartridge cases or abandoned clips in the vicinity Whiteside assumed that no shots had been fired by the two men before they had been killed.

"More and more bizarre," said Hughes. "If these guys were attacked by wolves, and if they were carrying their rifles, why the hell didn't they fire at the animals and try to defend themselves?"

"Agreed, Gwyn," responded Hanna. "They couldn't have been surprised by a wolf attack, since there's no tree cover here for the pack, and no darkness either. They **must** have seen the animals before they got killed."

"Unless the animals attacked when this whole area was lost in thick mist or low cloud?" mused Whiteside. "But that doesn't figure either. The weather over the past fortnight has been bright and clear the whole time, with just a few wisps of early morning mist.........."

They went back to the hut and confirmed that it had recently been lived in. The stove was cold, but there were ashes inside it, so it had been used for either warmth or cooking. There were clothes scattered about on the two bunk beds and on a couple of rickety chairs, but none on the floor. Some garments were hanging on a hook behind the door. So the place had not been ransacked by anybody in a hurry, or by someone intent upon theft. There was a pile of animal skins in a corner, and some bits of a recently butchered muskox in an open wooden box outside the door. The place was untidy, but was no worse than it might have been if any of them had been in residence. There were the remains of an unfinished meal on the table — some remnants of meat and beans on two plates, and two cups half filled with cold black coffee. They found a good supply of tinned foods in the cupboard. Most of the tins had Danish labels on them, and some were dated to 1955. They looked as if they might have come into Greenland via Blyhavn as part of a routine resupply operation five or six years before, and the two dead men must have used quite a few of them if the pile of empty tins outside the door was anything to go by. That meant that they might not have carried much food of their own. On a shelf near the stove there was a small cardboard box containing half a dozen clips of bullets for the rifles.

Although the door of the hut was open, the wolves had not touched either the muskox meat or the food on the table. "Not surprising," said Whiteside. "I've been told that wolves don't like huts. They stay clear of them if they can -- they're much happier out in the open. But if this door had been open for quite a long time, Arctic foxes would certainly have been inside, helping themselves. So -- we're talking about just a few days, during which time the wolves have tucked in at their leisure and kept other predators like ravens and foxes at bay."

Then Hughes made another discovery -- scuffed footprints on the sandy gravel outside the hut, suggesting that the two inhabitants were maybe running **away** from the hut, down the slope of the valley, when they died. "Could one have been chasing the other, maybe?" asked Hanna. "Trappers are pretty mad fellows, living a tough life, close to the edge, in incredibly remote places, just for the sake of selling a few polar bear and Arctic fox skins..... perhaps one of them went off his rocker, or perhaps they had a quarrel, with one going after and shooting the other?"

"Not a possibility, old chap," said Whiteside. "As we've seen, the clips in the guns are full. No shots were fired by these weapons during this particular episode."

"As I understand it, the trappers in this area usually work alone, not in pairs. Maybe one of these fellows was trying to muscle in on the other one's patch?"

"Don't buy that either. In the hut there are two plates on the table, and two unfinished meals. They were living in the hut together, and something disturbed them while they were in the middle of their lunch or supper."

"So were they Danish trappers, or surveyors, or what?" asked Knudsen.

"I'm inclined towards the latter, old chap," said Whiteside. "As you'll probably confirm, trappers hate walking, especially in the summer, and especially when they don't have their dogs with them. And they hate straying more than a mile away from the coast, because their natural territory is the flat sea ice and the adjacent shoreline, in the depths of winter. Here we're a good fifty miles from the sea, and I wouldn't mind betting that men with dogs and sledges have never been here since the hut was built. I think it's probably an old emergency shelter, for summer use only, built by one of the very earliest geological mapping parties..........."

"So were they Greenlanders, on a hunting trip, after musk-oxen or reindeer, or maybe even collecting goose eggs?"

Whiteside pondered for a moment, and then said: "`Possible, but unlikely. It's a forty or fifty mile walk into this valley, from whatever direction you choose. If they had come in from Nordbukten, as we did, there would have been traces of their arrival on the beach — maybe even a couple of kayaks pulled up from the water line. There was nothing. And I don't think Greenlanders would have been so stupid as to allow themselves to be attacked by wolves. Anyway, all the items in this hut look like the sort of things that any of us might have worn or used — there are no real Inuit items of clothing, so far as I can see."

"I agree," said Hanna. "And there's no way they could carry big lumps of meat — or even quantities of eggs — away from here and back to Syd Kap or Sandvig. They could have left a cache of meat as dog food, I suppose, ready for collection next winter, but where would they have stored it, and how would they have protected it from roving polar bears, wolves and foxes? Meat collected in the winter freezes instantly and is usable many months later, but meat collected in the summer has a tendency to go putrid..........."

"An Arctic mystery -- and a gruesome one at that," moaned Hughes. "We'll probably never get to the bottom of it. So what do we do now? Steffo, you are the man in charge here. Decision please?"

"My own instinct," said Hanna, "is to photograph the evidence, such as it is, and then to bury as much of the bodies as we can find, hoping that the wolves don't dig up the bits and pieces. Once we've done that, I suppose we'd better carry on with our work programme......."

"Agreed," said Knudsen. "We can't bring dead men back to life, and we have to try to do the civilized thing. There's no point in rushing off back to Base Camp and trying to attract attention by sending up some flares from there. Nobody will be expecting these two fellows and nobody will be missing them. I suppose that Keppel or somebody like that might have a register of the trappers currently at work in the fjords, but mostly they work with dogs in the winter, when they make occasional contacts and look out for one another. Chaps who are at work in the summer without their sledges and their dogs are obviously at risk -- and probably some of them die from bear attacks and accidents. The risk goes with the job.............."

"Should we put up an emergency signal from here?" asked Hughes.

"Total waste of time," said Whiteside. "We've only got one emergency rocket flare and one distress smoke signal canister with us. If we set them off here there's not a hope in Hell that anybody will see them -- we've got a big chunk of the Stauning Alps between us and Blyhavn and Himmelbjerg, including the highest peaks in Greenland. Anyway, we agreed to use the signals only as guidance, if we hear or see a helicopter or a plane that's looking for us."

"Fair enough. But those bloody howling wolves are getting on my nerves. Let's use the guns to scare them off. Then we can give these fellows the last rites."

They took possession of the guns, fired a few shots in the air to scare off the wolves, and set about the grim exercise of gathering up the human remains with their bare hands. They all felt that it was almost as gruesome as trying to clear up on a battlefield where people had been blown to bits by high explosives. They worked for about three hours, ranging across an area of about eight hundred square yards. Hanna found the task especially difficult, in spite of being a big man who prided himself on his toughness; he was overcome with nausea and vomited several times. They found a shovel in the hut and took turns in using it to dig two shallow graves near the gable end, down to the top of the permafrost layer, and then tried to put the right bits into the right graves. It would have been easier to put all the bits into a common grave, but that did not even occur to them, so intent were they on doing the "right" thing. They tried to cover the body parts with all of the scraps of clothing which had been blowing about in the wind across the scene of the carnage. It was not easy for the four men to keep their spirits up, and they made slow progress with their gruesome task, eventually becoming resigned to the fact that their anoraks and trousers were streaked with human blood, hair and bits of flesh. Whiteside tried to lift the gloom by saying to Hughes: "I think you should change career, my dear chap. No money in teaching glaciology, and most of your students would much rather be somewhere else than listening to you for hours on end. You're very good with a shovel. Undertakers and gravediggers are in great demand in Greenland, so I hear........." The Welshman gave him a frosty look, and he never did finish the sentence.

At last, when they could find no more bits and pieces of bodies and shreds of clothing, they washed their hands in a small stream not far from the hut. Hanna asked: "Haven't we got any more clues as to the names or the origins of the deceased? God, I sound like an undertaker talking. One should mark graves if one can, with crosses or plaques or something else appropriate."

"Let's finish this first," replied Whiteside. "I've had my fill of body parts and scraps of flesh. When the graves are sealed up, we'll have another look inside the hut, to see if there are any clues as to who these guys might have been." The other three nodded, and they had already started to push the gravel and stones back into the shallow graves when Hughes said: "Hang on a minute, chaps. Let me take a closer look at those two skulls. I know nothing whatsoever about forensics, but let's see if there is any room for simple deduction.............."

He lifted the two skulls from the graves and tried to clear away some of the blood and gore from the matted hair still attached to the two scalps. He found that very difficult, and was almost overcome by another wave of nausea, but then, after close scrutiny, he said: "Progress. One of these guys had blonde hair and the other had brown hair more or less the same colour as yours, Perry. That means they were not Greenlanders — their hair is always pitch black."

For several more several minutes he continued with his examination. Then he groaned. He looked up and said very quietly: "Oh my God. I was afraid of this -- each of these skulls has a single bullet hole in it. Large calibre, serious damage. Bone fragments everywhere. Shots fired from above and behind, if I'm not very much mistaken. Each of these poor sods was running away from the hut when he was killed, and was shot from the air. That wouldn't have been possible from a plane, and so we are presumably talking about a manhunt from a helicopter which was flying down the valley, more or less in the direction of our own approach on the ground. What's more, the slaughter involved somebody who was using a machine gun."

CHAPTER 7
August 1962

Rowland Linney and Joe Horton were striding along the top edge of the big alluvial fan between the western and eastern Holger Danskes Briller lakes. They were travelling light. They were just a few miles from Base Camp, and they had promised their colleague Andy Petherton that they would be back by mid-afternoon, releasing him from watch duty to get on with some of his own fieldwork. Griff Mortimer was five miles away to the north, tracking a musk-ox herd in Gurreholmsdal. Mortimer and Linney should have crossed to Gurreholm by now, but onshore winds had packed so much sea ice and icebergs into Nordost Bugt and the Schuchert Estuary that using the flimsy inflatable boat would have been suicidal. So they were stuck at Base Camp, where they were happy enough to work closely with their colleagues.

The two men liked this valley, which cut a great gash through the landscape all the way from Kjove Land to Nordvest Fjord. It had no glacier in it now, but it had clearly been excavated by a huge stream of ice maybe a million years ago. It had steep sides about two thousand feet high, and its most prominent features were two rock buttresses, one on either side of the trough, which soared up to three thousand feet. Normally their summits were swathed in cloud, but today they were lit by bright sunshine.

There was a small gorge with a clearwater stream in it close to the point where the gravelly river fan met the mountainside scree slope. Clearwater was a valuable asset; unlike the cloudy or milky water that came from melting glaciers, it was drinkable. So this was a perfect spot for lunch, and Linney and Horton settled down to eat their normal lunchtime ration of biscuits, cheese, and sardines followed by dried fruits and chocolate, all washed down with a swig or two of water from the stream. They chatted for a while about their work, and then Linney said: "Joe, can I ask you something personal?"

"Go ahead, Rowland. I have no secrets."

"Well, that's just it. I've noticed that you don't often talk about yourself and your family. International man of mystery, and all that. Some people like to be mysterious, and maybe you're one of them. You do have a family?"

A shadow passed across Horton's face. He thought for a moment, and replied: "I do. Of a sort. My father was not a nice man. I hardly remember him — he left my mother when I was five, at the beginning of the war. I think he was an alcoholic. I remember my mother weeping a lot, late at night when she thought I was asleep and he was still out with his cronies. She was scared to death of him, and I think he beat her. Sometimes she had bruises all over her face and arms........."

"Oh God, I'm sorry to hear all that, Joe. Apologies for asking — it must be very hard for you to talk about these things."

"No, no. I should probably talk about them more often, and exorcise my demons. I trust you, Rowland, so I don't mind telling you."

"I appreciate that, and won't betray your trust. Did your father beat you as well?"

"Strangely, he didn't. I think he was quite fond of me, but he was too old for marbles, let alone football. Anyway, in retrospect I think he was most violent late at night, when I was tucked up in bed out of harm's way."

"But you must have had some happy times?"

"Oh yes. When my father disappeared — God only knows where he went — my mother was transformed. Maybe he was called up for Army service, and was blown up on some battlefield or other. Suddenly the two of us started having fun, in spite of the war. She started to sing, and tell me stories, and we played together. We lived in Nottingham, and she had a job in an an armaments factory. Shift work, long hours, blackouts, air raids. A lot of the time I was looked after by the neighbours, but there was a great feeling of camaraderie and community. Somehow or other, I think I was protected from really seeing what the war did to people. I saw bomb damage, of course, but never any damage to people, apart from a few grown-ups with bandages round their heads, or hobbling about on crutches. We kids spent hundreds of hours in the air raid shelters, playing games. Does that sound absurd?"

"Not at all. I envy you........."

"You envy me?" spluttered Horton. "There's not a lot in my childhood to envy, I can assure you."

"Well," replied Linney, "my childhood by comparison was utterly secure, and dull, and well regulated. I was too young to remember much about the war, except for scuttling under the stairs now and then with my two sisters when the sirens were going off, and I remember the gas masks and the ration books and the tin helmets — but it sounds to me as if you really experienced life in the raw and learned rather a lot about humanity."

"It didn't feel like a privilege to me at the time, Rowland, and it still doesn't to this day. Was your father in the army?"

"No — in the Navy, doing secret work with mines. Because of that, he never saw active combat, and I can remember him living at home for a lot of the time, except near the end of the war when he was posted down to the south of England. Thinking of military things, weren't you once in the Royal Marines?"

"Yes, I was. National service in the Navy and then I joined the Marines. I learned a hell of a lot — sabotage, signals, survival skills, special operations and so forth. At first I thought it was wonderful — highly disciplined, exciting, and with great camaraderie among my mates........."

"I sense a "but" coming along, Joe."

"Correct. I was in 45 Commando. Then came the Suez War, and we were sent into Port Said. November 1956. We used helicopters to go in, and there was such a bloody shambles that we were landed in a football stadium that was under the control of the Egyptian Army. Like something out of a comedy show. It's a miracle that any of us got out of there alive. There was hand-to-hand combat, and we lost five men. God knows how many they lost — I probably killed a dozen myself. One doesn't count. My face was sliced open by a bayonet, and I suppose I was lucky not to lose an eye. Blood and gore, and men screaming. Another chopper came and lifted us out, under heavy fire, and then........." Horton's voice cracked, and he did not finish the sentence. Instinctively,

Linney put his hand on his colleague's shoulder.

"Don't say anything more, Joe. You've said enough, and I've heard enough." There was a long silence, during which Horton got up and stood with his hands in his pockets, gazing at nothing in particular, far away.

Then he turned to his colleague and said: "I might as well finish what I started, and to hell with the Official Secrets Act. When the Cease Fire came and we were pulled back, I and two other guys caused a near-riot in our debrief sessions by criticizing the wholesale bloody incompetence of the Port Said commando operation. We were all in a state of shock, I think — and in retrospect we were lucky not to be court-martialled. Then I heard that our commanding officer, Paddy Wilberforce, had put in a detailed citation recommending me for a DSO medal — almost unheard of for a junior rank. I must have been slightly off my rocker at the time, but I said that if it went through, I would refuse it publicly as a protest against the bumbling idiots in high command who had caused the deaths of my best mates. To cut a long story short, that led to me being quietly invited to leave the Marines with a clean record in the spring of 1957. Looking back, best thing that ever happened to me. The Navy helped me to get a place at Bristol University and gave me a grant to read botany, and I followed that with a research fellowship at Merton. So I'm one of those strange people referred to as "mature students." Everything else you know."

"Good God, what a story, Joe. You look like a man who has done some living in his time, but I could never have guessed the half of it."

"No repetition to anybody else please, Rowland?"

"I promise."

Then Linney leaped to his feet, grinned, and said: "Our esteemed leaders would be mightily displeased if they saw us nattering here for hours on end when we should be working. Shall we proceed?" Horton nodded, and they packed the remnants of their lunch into their light rucksacks, filled their water bottles, and went on their way.

Half an hour later the two colleagues were walking beneath the rock face of the northern buttress, overlooking the western of the two lakes, when they heard something that sounded like an overhead thunderclap. They looked up and saw that the rock face was disintegrating above and just ahead of them. At first, it looked to Horton like a slow-motion sequence in a disaster movie, but then he saw things in real time, and he yelled: "Rowland! For God's sake, back the way we came!" They turned, dropped their rucksacks, and sprinted back along the rough gravel surface of the fan, but they did not have a chance. The whole mountainside was on the move, and within seconds they were overwhelmed by a wave of noise and dust which rolled ahead of millions of tons of displaced rock. They dived behind a bank of scree in the hope that it might give them some cover, and then they were hit by rolling, bouncing and flying rocks. They cowered together on the ground, closed their eyes instinctively and tried to cover their heads. They could feel the ground itself vibrating beneath them. The air was so thick with debris that they could hardly breathe, and when Horton dared to open his eyes for a second or two he saw that almost all of the daylight had been blotted out, and that rocks the size of cars were spinning through the air over his head. Then, as suddenly as it had started, it was all over. There was an eerie silence, broken only by the sound of a few stray boulders bouncing downslope and by the echo of the landslide thunder bouncing back from the cliffs on the other side of the valley. By some miracle they were not buried, and the main mass of debris appeared to have been diverted away from them by a long mountainside gully.

Horton realized that apart from a gash on his head, he was uninjured. But when he looked at his companion Linney, he knew that there was a major problem. It looked as if he had been hit by at least one flying or rolling boulder, and although he had assumed the embryo position as he tried to protect himself, he was now perfectly still. Horton thought at first that he was dead, but then he saw that he was still breathing regularly. He knew that it might be dangerous to move him, but had no option but to push the poor fellow aside in order to extricate himself from the rubble that almost covered them both. He rolled and shoved the bigger stones away and cursed the fact that he did not have the energy to throw them clear. Was he really as weak as a baby, or were the stones really heavier than any stones he had ever encountered before? He shook his head and paused for a moment, vaguely aware that both his mental agility and his physical strength had been damaged. He told himself that he must not panic. He breathed deeply, in spite of the fact that the air was still so filled with dust that he could see no further than ten yards. Then he continued to dig with his bare fingers. Eventually he managed to ease himself out of his stony trap, and began to move the stones that still partly buried Linney. Then he moved him gingerly so that he could try to assess his injuries. With a sinking heart he saw that his right leg was broken and twisted grotesquely and that there was some sort of injury to his chest, maybe incurred when a boulder rolled over him. He remained unconscious, and still blessedly free of pain.

For some minutes Horton coughed uncontrollably because of the dust still swirling around him. There was blood all over his hands, coming mostly from his lacerated fingers, and some of his finger nails were broken. He shook his head again and tried to focus. He had no option other than to make Linney as comfortable as possible and to get back to Base Camp so that he could summon help. The rucksacks that the two men had been carrying were lost without trace, and there was nothing that he could use as a splint. He was afraid that if his colleague regained consciousness while he was away, he might try to move and worsen the damage to his leg. He took off his own shirt and tore it into strips, and after clearing away more stones managed to get his companion into a lying position, and to rearrange the broken leg so that the foot was more or less pointing in the right direction. As he did this, he was almost overcome by a wave of nausea, and was forcefully reminded that he was not cut out to be a doctor. He knew that he had to use the left leg as a splint, and so he bound the two legs together as tightly as possible. Then, having confirmed that the patient was still breathing easily, he took off his own anorak and trousers and placed the garments over him, knowing that if he regained consciousness he would be in deep shock. Then he built a little cairn on a boulder directly in front of Linney, so that he would know that help was on the way -- and indeed to guide a rescue party back to the place where the accident had happened — or at least to the place where the casualty lay.

Horton climbed up onto the chaotic surface of the landslide and tried to fix in his own mind the location of the cairn. At last, the dust was settling, and visibility was improving by the minute. The landscape had been altered out of all recognition, and all he could see, for maybe half a mile in front of him, was a rippled or ridged surface of waves and hollows made up of boulders and rock debris that had come down from the mountainside. He saw that he was standing not far from the eastern edge of this chaos. He looked up and saw the gigantic scar on the mountainside left when the slope had collapsed. When he was reasonably sure that he could find his way back again, he turned towards Base Camp, which was about eight miles away, and set off to fetch help.

About three hours later Andy Petherton was striding down the eastern slope of the plateau. As Base Camp came into view he saw a ragged figure wearing just a pair of boots, a torn sweater and a pair of underpants staggering up to the tents. He was obviously exhausted, for he stumbled and fell to the ground, and took a couple of minutes to get up again. Then the figure went into The Palace and came out with something in his hands, and an emergency rocket streamed up into the sky, releasing its red ball of incandescence to warn the world that something terrible had happened. Not much chance of it being seen from Himmelbjerg, thought Petherton, since it's the wrong time of day and the sun is still far too bright...........

"Where the bloody hell have you been, Andy?" shouted Horton when Petherton arrived. "I thought you were supposed to be here on watch?"

"Hey, back off, mate," replied Petherton, sounding resentful. "Sure it's my turn, but it was bloody boring here all on my own, and I had work to do. So I've been doing some more mapping, but never more than twenty minutes from the tents. If a helicopter had come down the valley, or if a boat had come in to Syd Kap, I'd have seen them and been back here quicker than Jack Robinson."

"OK -- sorry, Andy. That's fair enough. But we have one hell of a problem. You heard the landslide?"

"Couldn't miss it. I actually felt the ground shake. But I thought it was on the coast somewhere. I knew that none of us was over that way today, so I just carried on with my mapping.........."

"We were caught in it. Underneath that peak between the two

129

lakes. It's a miracle we're still alive. Rowland has a horribly broken leg and I think he might have internal injuries as well. He was unconscious when I left him. We have to get back to him, whether or not anybody comes down from Himmelbjerg to help us............."

Five minutes later the two men were on their way back towards the scene of the accident, after leaving a note on the table in the mess tent in case Mortimer should turn up at Base. Horton had put some fresh clothes on. They were carrying the folding stretcher that had been included in the medical kit, various painkillers and sedatives, and also a Primus and some fuel and food. A smoke grenade was another crucial item, in case they needed to give guidance to a rescue helicopter. They did not dare to carry too much, for fear that their loads would slow them down. Progress was slow enough as it was, because Horton was so weak that he could hardly place one foot in front of the other. But he had to walk with Petherton, since the Australian could not possibly have located their injured colleague on his own.

Just as they reached the big ridge of moraine at the eastern end of the lakes, they heard a distant drumming in the air, and knew that the Himmelbjerg helicopter was on its way. At last it was close enough for them to see it, flying low across the head of Nordøstbugt. They set off the smoke grenade, and the swirl of orange smoke soon caught the attention of the pilot, who wheeled to the west and came straight towards them. They recognized the machine as the Bell 47 from the mine, and identified a flattish patch on the top surface of the moraine. After checking it from all sides the pilot motioned to them to stand well clear, and put the chopper down. The man who jumped out was Dr Alfred Jensen, and after a hasty conversation with the two expedition members, he said: "Sorry gentlemen, but we've got extra fuel tanks and medical gear on board and we can only take three men including the pilot. Andy, I suggest you wait here until Joe comes back. Joe, climb in and take us to where the injured man is lying. Assuming he's still alive, we'll strap him to a stretcher and take him to Himmelbjerg or maybe Blyhavn. I'm afraid, Joe, that you'll have to walk back to Base for the second time today." Horton shrugged and climbed on board, grateful that somebody else was now making decisions. With a cursory wave to Andy Petherton, they took off again.

From the air, Horton and Dr Jensen could see the full extent of the landslide, and they were horrified. They located the area within which Linney was lying, and Art Ruckle, the pilot, brought the machine in close enough to see him stretched out in a little hollow with a chaotic jumble of huge rocks on all sides. Ruckle brought the machine across the area time and again, searching for somewhere flat enough to land; and at last he decided to take a chance on the summit of a ridge of boulders which appeared, to Horton's eyes, to be too small to pitch a one-man tent on, let alone land a helicopter. But this was the sort of challenge that mad helicopter pilots relish, and Horton saw that his knuckles were white as he went down tentatively, tested the stability of the ground surface, and finally switched off the engine. All three of them breathed a sigh of relief. They were a couple of hundred yards from the injured man, and they had to fight their way across wickedly unstable piles of loose rock to reach him, sending precariously balanced boulders crashing downslope over and again. Luckily, none of them was carried away in these miniature avalanches, and at last they reached the little cairn that Horton had built as a rescue beacon. Linney was still alive, but still unconscious, and there was a trickle of blood from his mouth. Horton could see straight away that Dr Jensen was very concerned for his life. The doctor gave him two injections, and then, working as fast as they dared, they strapped him onto the stretcher, and somehow carried him to the helicopter. Once he was safely tied in, Ruckle started up the engine. Before he took his place next to the pilot, Dr Jensen stood with Horton on the boulders a few yards from the machine, as the rotors built up speed over his head.

"Never fear, Joe," he shouted with not much reassurance in his voice. "We'll do what we can. If we can't help him here, we'll get him to Reykjavik where they have facilities that are second to none."

"Thank you, doc," said Horton, yelling to make his voice heard above the sound of the air-slicing blades and the rising pitch of the motor. "We really appreciate your kindness. Please thank Jim Wagner on our behalf."

"I'll be happy to do that, Joe."

"Should we abort the expedition, d'you think?"

"How can you do that?" shouted the doctor, aware that Ruckle wanted to take off. "You presumably have men scattered about all over the fjords.......... You'd better continue, but I told you to be careful."

"I know that. But we do seem to be rather accident-prone."

"This was no accident, Joe," said Jensen more quietly, so that Horton could only just hear him above the din. "This makes me very angry, because it was attempted murder."

Then the doctor climbed into his seat and strapped himself in. When Horton had scrambled clear of the takeoff zone, the machine lifted off and wheeled away along the shore of the lake.

Horton was rooted to the spot. Had he really heard that from Dr Jensen, or had his words been distorted somehow by the overwhelming racket being made by the helicopter? Deep in thought, he gathered up those things worth keeping from the scene of the accident, stuffed them into his rucksack, and set off to where Petherton was waiting for him on the moraine about four miles away.

From a viewpoint near the Gurreholm River, Mortimer had followed the drama more or less from beginning to end, with the aid of his binoculars. He had heard the distant rumble of the landslide, and then seen the cloud of dust that had risen from it, swirling up to an altitude of several thousand feet. Later on he had seen the flare that Horton had sent up from Base, and with the realization that something was seriously wrong he had dropped everything and started to run -- insofar as running is possible while wearing heavy-duty boots -- back towards Base Camp. He had been crossing the silt-laden torrent near the mouth of the Gurreholm River when he had first heard and seen the helicopter, and he had watched with growing dismay as it had diverted towards the plume of the orange smoke flare and had continued to the place where the landslide had occurred. Then, as he had stumbled across the bleak tundra landscape of the Prairies, he had seen the chopper once again, heading directly for Himmelbjerg.

When he arrived back at Base, he found Horton sitting disconsolately on the ground outside the mess tent, so exhausted that he could hardly keep his eyes open. Petherton was inside, preparing something to eat. Between them, in rather jumbled fashion, they told the whole story of the landslide, the accident and the rescue. Horton did his best not to allow his deep sense of foreboding to spread to the other two, and he was determined not to share with any of them the parting words of Dr Alfred Jensen, at least until he had thought about them calmly, in the cold light of day. Neither did he want to share the fact that he felt a very special bond with the quiet and somewhat eccentric biologist from Edinburgh, with whom he had shared so much immediately before the landslide had roared down on top of them. But they picked up on his gloom anyway, and Mortimer in particular felt a desperate, deep fear that he might never see his friend Raymond Linney again.

There was nothing more to be done for the time being -- other than to try and catch up on lost sleep. That night Horton was sharing a tent with Griff Mortimer. In the middle of the night he woke with a start, and as he tried to work out what had woken him, he realized that in the sleeping bag next to him Mortimer was sobbing quietly. He said nothing, and tried to get back to sleep, but thought: "Oh my God, what's going on here? Some of the currents in this stream of events are running seriously deep............."

In the morning, it was Petherton's turn to make the breakfast, and by 10 am he had managed to get the others up and out of their tents and tucking in to a sticky hot substance with raisins in it, which he referred to as "Australian porridge." The conversation turned to the Frederiksdal party, and before he could bite his tongue Horton heard himself saying: "Lucky bastards! Off they go, swanning up the fjord in those canoes, leaving us to cope with one bloody disaster after another back here at base. Right now, instead of being here to sort out this mess, three of them are probably sitting in the sun with their mugs of morning tea, while the other cooks bacon and eggs in one of those cosy trappers' huts......."

"Take it easy, Joe," said Mortimer. "That's not entirely fair, even if spoken in jest. This is no time for resentment -- and who knows? They might even have problems of their own to cope with."

The Frederiksdal party completed the burials of the two murdered men, or what was left of them, and gave them a simple burial ceremony. For Hanna and Hughes, this was becoming a habit. As before, they recited the Lord's Prayer and sang "Guide me oh thou great Jehovah" -- but this time everything felt strangely forced, for they knew absolutely nothing about the deceased apart from the fact that they were not Greenlanders. As if in response to the hymn, their little ceremony was followed by a chorus of howling wolves in the distance.

They examined the hut carefully, and at first found no solid clues as to the identity of the victims. There was a cotton bag containing a rolled-up lightweight tent, big enough for two men. In another cotton bag there were the domestic essentials — two plastic mugs, lightweight cutlery, two plates, a primus stove and a couple of aluminium pots for cooking. Outside the door there was a small plastic jerrycan containing about a gallon of paraffin. There were some ropes, crampons, and ice axes, but no pack frames or rucksacks containing personal effects. They wondered whether somebody else — maybe the murderer — might have visited the hut and removed them because they had contained something important. They wondered what else might also have been removed.......

Then they found a Norwegian flag, neatly folded inside a small polythene bag, placed near the mountaineering equipment. "The mystery deepens," said Hanna. "Maybe they weren't trappers or hunters, but Norwegian freelance climbers, planning a few first ascents in the Stauning Alps? I gather that these guys always have their national flags with them, to wave about on each summit while their companions take lots of photos.........."

Knudsen nodded. "That's true. And the Norwegians still feel a bit sore about the way that Greenland was given to my country when they thought they had a better claim -- that was before the last War. Maybe they want to get their own back by conquering and naming unclimbed peaks?"

"No way," said Whiteside. "Sorry, my dear chaps, but there isn't enough proper gear in the corner to climb one peak, let alone twenty. Nothing at all for rock or ice climbing -- no pitons, hammers, carabiners, shackles, slings and so forth. This stuff was meant for walking on glaciers, not for getting up high. Anyway, nobody but a total idiot would try to tackle some of these peaks over seven thousand feet without proper backup. Two chaps on their own equals suicide. The Danes would never give permission -- they always expect climbing parties to consist of at least six people. In any case, Keppel told us at Himmelbjerg that there aren't any climbing groups in the Alps this year."

"So they weren't Inuit hunters or Norwegian mountaineers. Trappers, as we first thought? There've always been a few Norwegian trappers in these parts."

Whiteside shook his head. "Don't like that idea either, the more I think about it. Those animal skins in the corner. I've had a look at them, and they weren't collected by proper trappers. There are four Arctic fox skins -- worthless, because the animals were shot with their summer coats, and even more worthless because they are full of knife holes and still have fat and flesh left on them. Those skins weren't collected by professionals. I could have done better myself..............."

"So, if these poor buggers weren't after animals or first ascents, what the hell were they after? Valuable minerals? Were they geologists or surveyors?"

Nobody had an answer to that, so they decided to do some more investigations. Back in the hut, they found a soiled and frayed envelope about twelve inches square, on top of a cupboard and hidden beneath a stack of food tins. Apparently it been missed by whoever had searched the hut. Inside it they found about a dozen vertical air photos just like the ones used by their own expedition. They were readily available, sold openly by Danish Geodetic Institute and used for map-making. They looked through the photographs and recognized much of the territory covered. Then there was another surprise. Between two of the photos they found another one which was much smaller, with stains and cracks on its glossy surface. It was a photo of a fair-haired and very beautiful woman in a folk costume, with a small girl standing in front of her. There was nothing written on the back of it, but Knudsen said: "Somebody's rather gorgeous wife and daughter, I presume. And look at the background, boys -- if that isn't Norway I would eat my hat, if I had one."

"You have to be right, Lasse," replied Hughes. "Ties in with that flag. So we're back to the Norwegian connection?"

They resumed their examination of the air photos. On the back of them they noticed some stamped imprints -- and the language was not Norwegian, Danish or English. "Hmm..... Some very strange letters," said Hanna. "Looks like Russian to me. So, a couple of Norwegians using aerial photos obtained in the Soviet Union? Stranger and stranger."

"At least this confirms that they weren't trappers," said Hughes. "No genuine trappers would carry air photos around with them. They're tough bastards, those guys, even if some of them might have wives and daughters. They know how to survive in this sort of terrain. They have their own special landscapes imprinted in their minds. Air photos are just for wimps like us -- and glossy prints like these wouldn't survive for ten minutes out in the field in the winter."

"We've already disposed of the trapper idea," said Whiteside. "But look carefully at this photo. D'you see what I see?" He carried the photo from the dark interior of the hut to the door, where there was bright sunshine. "Here's the Schuchert Valley, and here's the big moraine in front of the Roslin Glacier. Here's Himmelbjerg, with a blue cross inscribed solidly on it with a ball-point pen. And how about this? If you look carefully you can see four faint lines scored into the surface of the photo, all crossing at the location of Himmelbjerg. Could they be compass or radio signal bearings? On the back of the photo, written with the same pen, is something that looks like PG1."

"PG1 --- now where have I seen that before?" asked Hughes, wrinkling his brow. "I know! I'm sure that was stencilled onto some of the boxes we saw lying around at Himmelbjerg!"

"Impressive, Gwyn. You're an observant bugger. I just noticed the ones that had NAPRE on them."

"So we conclude that they were field geologists or surveyors, at least one of whom might have been a Norwegian, maybe flown out from Himmelbjerg with the Greenland Metals helicopter," said Whiteside, with some satisfaction. "Looking for gold, maybe? That would explain the murders. People always get murdered when they find gold -- in films, anyway."

"Daft idea," said Hughes. "Are you suggesting that somebody

came out here with the helicopter, dropped them off, and then came back again after a few days to murder them?"

"Well, why not?" mused Knudsen. "They might have been in possession of very inconvenient information, meaning that they had to be got rid of. And PG1 might mean "position number one" where gold has been found?"

"Seems reasonable -- we were told that Himmelbjerg is a molybdenum mine -- but maybe that's just for propaganda purposes. What if they've found the world's largest gold resource deep inside the mountain? That would explain all the investment, the air traffic back and forth, the secrecy surrounding the place, and even that big iron door to the tunnel. D'you think the East Greenland Gold Rush is about to start?"

"Yes! I like it!" said Whiteside. "And I've just had another inspiration. D'you remember when we had that big party at Himmelbjerg, hosted by Jim Wagner? Hut Three, the canteen, is referred to by the miners as the Nibelungen Arms. I know you lot are ignorant sods, but those of us who are into cultural things are fully aware that in some boring old opera the Nibelungs were dwarves or goblins or something, slaving away deep down in the earth and mining gold, for the making of a gold ring which contained all the power of the universe. The guy who gave that name to the canteen must have known something that we don't know......... "

"And the man who composed the opera," added Knudsen with a wry smile, "was one Richard Wagner."

"Sheer fantasy, boys," said Hanna wearily. "Adding two and two and making five. We've been over all this stuff about minerals before, a couple of weeks ago. Anyway, if these poor dead buggers were geologists, where are their maps and their geological samples? All stolen by whoever landed in that helicopter? Where are their geological hammers and other surveying instruments and hand lenses? None of this makes sense......... "

Still not convinced that they were on the right track, the four colleagues needed to delve deeper. They looked at the mountaineering equipment in case there were any brand names or other identifying features on them, and given yet another surprise. They found that in

137

several places, on the metalwork, there were bright shiny patches. "Very interesting," murmured Hughes, when he had examined them minutely. "These things did have brand names or code numbers stamped on them originally, but they have been laboriously filed away. So — the dead men went to great lengths to preserve their anonymity. There's no way they could have been trappers or mountaineers — this begins to smack of military involvement. Let's take a look at those clothes again."

When they examined the clothes scattered around in the hut, they found an assortment of shirts, sweaters, trousers, socks and underclothes, two windproof parkas and waterproof jackets and over-trousers belonging to the deceased. There were two knitted balaclavas intended for use in seriously cold weather. None of the garments had any distinguishing marks on them — there were no embroidered logos, name tabs or brand labels on waistbands or collars. But on close examination the men found the places where these labels had been affixed before being cut away. When they examined the sleeping bags on the two bunk beds, they discovered that they too had had their labels removed. "Well, I'll be buggered!" said Whiteside. "This is taking anonymity to somewhat obsessive lengths, in my humble opinion. These chaps must have been spies, or maybe members of some special forces unit. Surely they can't have been Norwegians, since they are supposed to be friendly with both the Yanks and the Danes. We have to conclude, my dear fellows, that the dead men were citizens of the Soviet Union."

The others nodded. But they still had no idea as to why they might have been shot. They needed yet more evidence, so they searched on the up-valley side of the hut well clear of the area across which the human remains had been scattered. About fifty yards away, on a low gravelly mound, they found two parallel impressions made by something heavy. "A helicopter has landed here," said Whiteside. "Not a very big one. Big enough for two or three people, maybe."

"The Bell 47J that we saw parked up at Himmelbjerg, when we paid our visit?"

"Quite possible. But that's a very popular model. There may be several of them — or other similar choppers of a similar size — at work in the fjords. It might even have come down from the north, or in from the

138

coast. Might even have been based on a naval or research ship."

"So a helicopter turns up here, causing the two guys in the hut to abandon their supper and to run off down the valley," said Hanna. "Somebody in the helicopter kills the pair of them with machine gun fire. Then the helicopter lands, since the assassin wants to make sure they are both dead?"

Whiteside nodded, and Hughes said: "So far so good."

"Maybe it came here when we were paddling up the fjord?" asked Knudsen. "Do you remember that we heard what we thought was a chopper, very far away, but simply assumed it was one of the geology field parties somewhere off to the north? It may just have been coming here, with a purpose........."

On a hunch, Whiteside wandered off and examined a patch of ground about thirty yards further up-valley from where they stood, and found there a scatter of new bullet cases. "This confirms everything, boys," he said. "This is what you get when you give a ten or twenty second blast from a machine gun. Death a couple of hundred yards away, and debris here. The helicopter must have been hovering above this spot when the executioner went about his work." Then he picked up one of the cases and zipped it into an inside pocket of his anorak.

"I suspect, boys, that we are not going to get very much further with this," said Hanna. "Let's call it a day — I'm bloody exhausted. Geologists, trappers, climbers, Inuit hunters and field surveyors don't remove all the name tabs off their clothing, and file the batch codes and makers' imprints off their weapons and mountaineering gear. These fellows were intent upon complete secrecy and anonymity. So they must have been Russian agents on some sort of mission, maybe trying to maintain a pretence of being trappers, just in case they bumped into somebody or other out here in the wilderness. But somebody knew that they were here, and came looking for them. I think that Himmelbjerg was their planned destination, and that they were murdered just as they were about to set off across the Stauning Alps, planning to travel light, and to use the glaciers as their highways."

CHAPTER 8
August 1962

At Base Camp, Joe Horton was feeling a great deal better, after two nights of decent sleep. He regretted the feelings of resentment that he had harboured against absent colleagues. Anger and frustration had got the better of him, and he apologized to the others as they shared lunch in the mess tent. "No worries, mate," said Petherton. "We all get frazzled now and then, and that mother and father of a landslide the other day took a lot out of you. Shock and exhaustion combined. Bloody miracle you coped as well as you did. Matter closed."

They had to be in the tent because the weather had broken at last. High cloud had started to drift in from the east on the day before, followed by twelve hours of high winds from the same direction. Then the wind had stopped, to be replaced by a deluge. Joe Horton had grinned and said: "Typical East Greenland weather, my friends, as I understand it. We're lucky to have had more or less unbroken sunshine until now. The Danes apparently call it "ice sheet weather" when the pressure's high and the wind howls down towards the coast from the interior. But if the westerly wind carries on for long enough, it pushes the sea ice away from the coast, and the ice-free coastal strip becomes very wide, and then at last that lets the weather in from the Atlantic. In Britain we get the wind and the rain together. In East Greenland they get the wind first, and then the rain, maybe for many days without a break." Petherton had nodded, and commented that the Frederiksdal party must be having a miserable time, coping with this deluge with just two small tents as protection. But they all knew that there was at least one small hut in the valley, and hoped that they might have been able to use it as a sort of exploration headquarters.

There was nothing much that the three men could do until the rain eased off, and they all agreed that they needed a rest. So they got on with writing their diaries, writing letters to their families, and collating field notes and the samples that had been collected. They washed some of their clothes and trimmed their beards. Horton had many botanical samples of his own which needed to be catalogued and labelled, and when he watched the others at work he was impressed by how much had been achieved in spite of the near-disasters and disruptions that had punctuated their time in this peculiar wilderness which seemed to combine the attributes of both heaven and hell. He was intrigued by the changing moods of his two colleagues -- how they interacted, what they talked about, and how they behaved. All seemed normal enough on the surface, although there was less laughter and repartee than there had been at the beginning of the expedition. This was understandable, given their concerns about the fate of their colleague Rowland Linney. He was the archetypal bumbling academic, naive in the ways of the world, unsuccessful with women (if his blushing confessions were to be believed), obsessed with his work, and incapable of assessing risks and benefits as he moved about in this dangerous environment. Horton felt a sort of paternal responsibility for him -- and realized that following the landslide he was weighed down by a powerful sense of guilt for leading him into a hazardous location and failing to protect him properly. Illogical and even absurd, he knew, but human beings were strange creatures........

He was not sure whether the warnings and accusations from Dr Jensen had any direct relevance as far as his companions were concerned. Surely none of them -- all perfectly sound fellows as far as he could see -- was involved in some sort of treachery or betrayal? And how on earth could a landslide be interpreted as attempted murder? The whole idea was preposterous. If you want to murder somebody, you do it with a knife or a gun, or maybe shove somebody over a cliff when nobody else is looking. Maybe Dr Jensen was himself deranged or paranoid? Maybe only nut cases applied for medical jobs in places like this, and got them? Or did the doctor know something about Blyhavn and Himmelbjerg that he was not prepared to divulge? It was all very confusing.

So how reliable were his colleagues? Knudsen was quiet and self-contained, and not easy to get to know; he thought a great deal, and said little. Of the other three in the Frederiksdal party, he could not imagine any of them being involved in treachery of any sort. Hanna was so open and easy to read, and so obviously desperate to look after his colleagues, that he cannot possibly have been involved in any subversive activity. Whiteside was a jovial buffoon with hidden depths and a father involved in government politics. Could he be a spy, working for MI5, or even for the Russians? Possible -- but what was there to spy on, and to what end? And the Welshman Gwyn Hughes. A quiet man who missed hardly anything, and who seemed to be remarkably well informed on many things that had nothing to do with glaciology. Could be be a source of danger to the others? Unlikely, but there were many things going on in East Greenland this summer that were not what they appeared to be. The other two -- Petherton and Mortimer -- were easier to read. Petherton was almost a caricature of The Man from Down Under: an open book, direct, outspoken, self-confident, and quite intolerant of the opinions of others. But he had a soft side, and yesterday, when they had all been talking about quite intimate things, there had been a tear in his eye and a choke in his voice when he talked about the breakdown of his marriage and the loss of access to his two daughters following protracted divorce proceedings. And Mortimer? A strange fellow -- not particularly close to any of the others, but pleasant enough, and in Horton's judgment very sensitive to the atmosphere within the camp and concerned for the welfare of his friends. He had a distant sadness in his eyes, and Horton could not work out where it had come from. Most of the time he was the sort of person who made no decisions and went with the flow, but yesterday there had clearly been an argument with Petherton while they had carried some food boxes to a depot five miles away, and afterwards the atmosphere had been so tense between them, for a while, that there had been icicles on the steam from the tomato soup. Joe Horton had been in enough tents in remote locations with stressed comrades, over the years, to know that very small things can sometimes turn into gigantic disputes. Nothing surprised him any more. So he watched, and listened, and pondered.........

The incessant rain was making the camp site near Trianglen very uncomfortable. Hanna had suggested to his companions that they should get well away from the scene of the two deaths which had caused them so much grief, and that they should forget about pressing all the way through to the glacier-dammed lake of Furesø. That would have been exciting, but not particularly productive in terms of research results. Instead, the young leader had proposed that they should get back to the great triangular peak at the bend in the valley and work in the smaller valleys radiating out from there. Within easy striking distance there were four glaciers that could be studied, and enough wildlife to keep the two biologists happy as well. So it had been agreed.

They had closed the window shutters and secured the door of the hut, having thrown out all the muskox meat and other perishable food in the knowledge that it would soon be demolished by the wolves and other carrion eaters which inhabited the valley. They had left everything in the hut more or less as they had found it. Then they had set off up the valley again, carrying all their own gear, the two Armalite rifles which they had found on the ground, and some evidence relating to the identity of the two dead men, including the photo of the Norwegian woman and her daughter. Now they were stuck here, on a grassy bank on the col in the shadow of the mountain as the rain sluiced down so heavily that the flysheets sagged onto the inner two-man tents, causing pools of water to collect on the groundsheets and to soak sleeping bags and clothing. There was no point in trying to work in such weather; visibility was down to zero and their scientific instruments would give them no meaningful results anyway. They had no option but to sit it out, using their Primus stoves as often as they dared in order to keep warm if not dry.

Their discomfort was increased by the presence of the wolf pack. When they had left that accursed hut behind to retrace their steps back towards Trianglen, they thought at first that the wolves had slunk away towards Furesø. They had heard them howling in the distance, and even Whiteside had said: "Good riddance to those buggers. I thought it was rather exotic to have wolves around the place, but having seen their eating habits at close quarters I've gone right off them. Give me a nice cuddly Arctic hare any day............." They had been plodding along in single file when Hughes had looked up and exclaimed: "Oh my God, here they are again." And there they were, about two hundred yards away, all six of them trotting along at exactly the same speed. When the men stopped, the wolves stopped. When they resumed their walk, so did the wolves, keeping their distance. For the men, being shadowed in this way was a surreal and even ghostly experience. At first they were not frightened, and indeed they knew that it was extremely unlikely that six wolves would attack a party of four men with guns, but they were more than a little apprehensive. The white dog wolf that led the pack was an impressive creature, far bigger than any of the huskies which Hughes and Whiteside had worked with in the past. As they walked, they started to fantasize about him, and Hanna said: "D'you think, chaps, that the old white devil harbours a deep resentment against us for burying what was left of their feast, the other day?" The others laughed, but suspected that there might have been more than a grain of truth in what the big Scot had said.

That night, and for the next three nights, as the rain continued without a break, the wolves kept their distance. They just sat at their stations, apparently disinterested in hunting, or eating, or doing anything else. Most of the time they were as silent as phantoms, but every night, around midnight, they howled. They also howled whenever Knudsen thought it might be an idea to keep up spirits by playing a tune or two on his harmonica. It was as if they knew that the sound, bouncing off the vertical cliffs in this great amphitheatre in the mountains, would sink into the souls of the men in the tents, who were still trying to banish from their minds the sights and sounds and smells encountered near the Toscano Glacier hut.

Art Ruckle was feeling depressed. The rain was still sluicing down, and it had been his misfortune to arrive at Himmelbjerg with some spare parts for the generator just as the cloud base dropped, trapping him in this God-forsaken hole until it was safe to fly again. The met people had got their forecast wrong again — probably because they were not used to rain in East Greenland. So he sat in the mess hut for hours on end, reading cheap paperbacks, chain-smoking and drinking far too much black coffee. He didn't drink alcohol and he didn't do joints either — but he was so fed up that he was seriously considering whether he should change his habits and get a bit of pleasure into his life. Today he sat in the mess hut again, on his own. He couldn't even do any work on the chopper, because it was parked out in the open, with water streaming off it, and roped down in case the wind sprang up unexpectedly. Everybody else seemed to have jobs to do inside the nice dry mountain...........

"Hi, Art," said Larry Bishop as he came in, shaking the water off an umbrella. "All alone, I see. I hoped you would be. Can I have a word?"

"Sure, Larry. Good to have somebody to talk to."

The radio operator poured himself some coffee and sat down. "I'm worried about the Boss."

"Well, you've told me that before. As for me, I'm worried about myself. That's enough to be going on with."

"Get serious, Art. You sit here quietly and read westerns and soft porn while I have to handle everything that goes in and out of this place."

"I thought that was all classified?"

"Yep — it is. It's not so much the messages. They are all routine enough. But I'm worried about what's going on in the background."

"What's going on in the background? With this bloody rain over the last three days nothing is going on anywhere. For all I know, the world out there on the other side of the mountains has ceased to exist."

"You know that the Boss has moved out of his hut on the moraine and gone to live in that observation room up on the top of the mountain?"

"Yes, I knew. The guys down here seem happy enough about that. He's off their backs now, and they're all much more relaxed, as far as I can see."

"He's got a bed up there, close to that big window of his, and he takes all his meals up there. The cook has to take them all up to him. Grumbles like hell, he does......."

"Who? The cook? Or the Boss?"

"Both of them, as it happens. But this ain't funny, Art. Suddenly he's got isolated, and I don't like it when a man gets isolated."

"A lot of commanding officers get isolated, Larry. Goes with the job, I reckon."

"But d'you know why he moved up there, Art? I'll tell you. He was in Hut Ten, sharing it with four other guys, although he had his own room. Suddenly he decided that since it wasn't the highest one on the moraine, it showed a lack of respect from the quartermaster. So he tore him off a strip and said he would move to a place more appropriate to his status, where he could keep an eye on things, twenty-four hours a day. Now he spends virtually all his time staring out of those bloody telescopes of his, trying to pick up things that are happening more than fifty miles away. He probably watches those Oxford guys even when they go behind a boulder to have a shit."

"Okay. I see your point. He's an old friend. I might just have a word........"

"Sooner rather than later, Art, if you will. I ain't no shrink, but I reckon we might be looking at a lethal mixture of paranoia and delusions of grandeur. He's a bit too fond of that bloody label that was put on him as a joke, if you ask me. The more time he spends alone, the more I think he's likely to precipitate some disaster or other."

"He doesn't control everything, Larry. He just carries out orders. But I agree that he has to be fit to complete what's been started. If his mind goes walkabout, we're all in the shit together."

"And while we wallow in it," said Bishop with a hollow laugh, "he'll be taken to Heaven, where he will rest in the bosom of Jehovah."

"How did you know that, Larry? He thinks nobody knows about his religious beliefs."

"Well, I do, anyway. The other day I had a long message that came in after midnight. It needed an immediate response, so I thought I'd take it up to him rather than ringing it through. When I went in he was on his knees at the side of the bed, saying his prayers."

"Well, that's nice. After some of the things he's done in his life, he needs to be saved. And a devout commanding officer is always a good thing."

"Up to a point, Art. I apologized for breaking into his devotions, and thought I would get blasted to smithereens, but he smiled like a bloody angel and invited me to sit on the edge of the bed with him. Then we had a surreal conversation about religious beliefs."

Ruckle chuckled. "You should be flattered. Not many people get to share Jim Wagner's innermost thoughts........."

"And thank God for that. I was brought up as a Baptist, and have sat through a good many sermons in my time. I tend to think well of Christians, Art, although I am, shall we say, somewhat backslidden. I'm used to hearing Baptist ministers talking about things like love, compassion, forgiveness, respect, sacrifice, and so forth. You know the sorts of things." Bishop looked around nervously, and lowered his voice. "But I'll tell you, Art, I was in a daze when I came out of there, because it seemed to me that his theology stopped before he even got out of the Old Testament. I got this bloody rant that went on for almost an hour, about the evil empires of communism, and about the wrath of God, and the fires of Hell, and retribution, and avenging angels, and the end of the world............"

At last the rain had stopped, and with a steady offshore wind blowing the coast around Nordostbugt and the Schuchert estuary was clear of ice. Mortimer and Horton took the inflatable and started to explore the coast of Jameson Land, luxuriating, in their leisure time, in the comforts of the spacious Gurreholm hut. They were working on musk-ox movements, ornithology and botany in the semi-arid tundra, which was now looking positively verdant after the rain. Each man was working on his own, to pre-arranged schedules in case anything should go wrong. But accidents were unlikely here, since there were no steep cliffs, no glaciers, no big meltwater streams, and no rolling icebergs. In truth, they felt safer here than they might have done in the centre of London or Oxford during the Christmas shopping season.

While scanning the landscape with his binoculars, Mortimer spotted the largest herd of musk-oxen he had ever seen -- at least twenty animals including five calves, led by a magnificent bull. He followed dead ground as he approached them, walking as quietly as possible, and keeping downwind. When he next spotted them, he was very close, and they were grazing peacefully in a narrow rocky gorge. He was obsessed with the idea of getting the best musk-ox photos in the world, and he even thought he might sell them to the *National Geographic* magazine and make his fortune. It was also his intention to firmly demonstrate his scientific credentials to his colleagues, who seemed to doubt his knowledge of animal behaviour. He stood up and approached the beasts, certain that they would get into the standard defensive formation with the cows and immature males in a tight group, the calves behind, and the dominant bull in the centre, facing the threat. He was about thirty yards away from them, and approached quite confidently in the knowledge that muskoxen were actually quite timid although they looked fearsome. They would snort and paw the ground with their hooves, and then they would turn and run away. However, Mortimer had failed to observe that the herd was in an enclosed rocky gorge, and that there was nowhere for the animals to escape to. He did get some excellent photos -- but then, when he was about ten yards away, he saw through his camera lens that the big bull was coming straight at him. He turned and fled, but stumbled and fell to the ground, to be rolled over and trampled by the bull and the rest of the animals as they rushed past him in panic. The dust settled. He was left battered and bruised, and bleeding profusely. He knew he was lucky to be alive. There was an agonizing pain in his left ankle, and he was convinced that it was broken. He was two miles from the Gurreholm hut. But he had his whistle -- and later on, when he failed to turn up for supper, Horton heard his signals, found him where he had fallen, and carried him back to the hut with difficulty, given that he was a tall and heavily built man.

Mortimer was himself the expedition medic, and so he had to instruct his colleague on how to deal with his injuries. Horton dressed the cuts and bruises as best he could, leaving Mortimer swathed in bandages. Although his ankle was now very swollen, the diagnosis was that it was probably twisted rather than broken. Horton considered taking him back to Base with the inflatable craft -- but then realized it was best for him to remain at the Gurreholm Hut, which was much more comfortable than a soggy tent. So the two men stayed put, with Mortimer confined to quarters while the botanist continued with his work, ranging far and wide across western Jameson Land and the eastern edge of the Schuchert Valley. Over the next three days the invalid came to admire his colleagues enormously, for he was considerate and compassionate, and looked after him very well while pressing on efficiently with his own research. Within two days he was able to hobble about with the aid of a stick, and he thought that in another two days he could throw the stick aside and start to pull his weight once more.

The two Gurreholm residents had eaten their supper and completed the washing up. They were sitting at the table near the window, sipping at their mugs of coffee and gazing out across the vast expanse of Hall Bredning, which was lit by an evening light as opalescent as mother-of -pearl. There were no waves or ripples on the surface of the sea, and not a whisper of wind. Even the barnacle geese on the marshy areas near the hut were quiet, and neither man was inclined to break the silence. For thirty minutes or so neither said a word. Then Horton said, quite out of the blue: "Griff, what brings you to be on this trip with this bunch of idiots?"

Mortimer laughed. "Same things as you, I suppose, Joe. A love for the Arctic, and a fascination with its living inhabitants. In my case, polar bears and musk oxen......."

"Yes yes, that's all understood. But what are you running from? I have this theory that we're all running from something."

"Running from boredom, maybe. Nothing much else to run from, apart from Yorkshire weather."

"A woman? A family from hell? A dark secret?"

Mortimer shook his head. "Nothing so interesting. I'm from Rotherham, and leave behind me a mother who dusts the house endlessly, and cooks and does the washing, and a father who's head of a primary school........."

"Still living at home then?"

"Well, sort of. I'm hardly ever there. I've got a permanent post in the Sheffield Zoology department, and I've got a room in one of the halls of residence. Small but adequately appointed, according to the university handbook."

"No ex-girlfriend who's just dumped you?"

Mortimer flushed slightly. "Now that would have been exciting. No such luck. My encounters with the opposite sex have been -- shall we say -- casual. So what about you, Joe? Why are you here rather than at home with your family?"

Horton laughed. "The simple answer is that I don't have a family. But there's far more to it than that. You and I have sat here for half an hour without exchanging a single word, drinking in the beauty of an East Greenland evening. And we've done that quite naturally, without feeling any need to speak. Perhaps we're kindred souls......."

Mortimer smiled. "I'm not sure of that, Joe. I take your point that you cannot find this sort of peace anywhere else in this frenetic modern world of ours. What I mean is this — don't you miss your girl friend Susanna?"

"Of course I do — and I think of sex as often as the next man. But now and then one needs space. That's why I disappear off to the Arctic whenever an opportunity arises."

"And Susanna doesn't mind?"

"Not as far as I know. We have a great time together, but we aren't even engaged. So far so good...... She knows I suffer from Arctic fever, and accepts it as others might accept some strange medical condition. How many more years of travel do I have left in me? Ten, at the most. Maybe Susanna hopes that when I return home from each trip to the far north I'll be transformed from a mean-spirited and miserable old bastard into the kindest and gentlest of husbands. And there's one thing I've discovered already from my time in the Navy -- long absences work wonders for one's sex life....."

Mortimer looked slightly embarrassed, and changed the subject promptly. "And your parents, Joe?"

Horton grinned. "My mother's still alive and well. I've been in so many scrapes since I left home that whenever I go to see her she seems genuinely surprised that I'm still alive."

"But how will Susanna and your mother react when they hear about the appalling things that have happened to this expedition? Too terrible for words — how d'you tell them about those poor Greenlanders who were drowned and washed up on the Bear Islands, or about the other Acts of God that have brought all of us within an inch of losing our lives, or about poor Rowland almost being killed? That troubles me. Surely you can't portray those as Joe's jolly adventures?"

The smile disappeared from Horton's face, and he closed his eyes. When he opened them again, a minute later, Mortimer saw that they were filled with tears.

"I'm sorry, Joe," said the invalid. "I didn't mean to upset you like that........."

"Don't apologize, Griff. This is more to do with me than it is to do with you. Perhaps, when one loves too much, and lives too much, one loses sight of the real world.........."

With that, Horton got up from the table and went outside, and walked back and forth on the beach for a very long time, as the light faded.

Next morning there was still not a breath of wind, but a bank of low grey cloud had materialized from nowhere, and visibility out across Hall Bredning had reduced to almost zero. The two inhabitants of the Gurreholm Hut could not even see the ubiquitous icebergs which thundered and rumbled and cracked in the distance. Then they heard another sound, from a single-cylinder boat engine a long way off, approaching from the south and apparently hugging the shoreline. Was this the long-awaited search party, sent out to discover the fate of the vessel and its crew who had been lost off the Bear Islands? Horton and Mortimer went down to the shore, and watched as a small cutter with a cabin came gliding out of the mist. It looked as if it was intent on going straight past, but then the man at the wheel spotted the two figures on the beach and slowed the vessel to a stop. He nudged the vessel forward in to the shallow water until the bow was on the beach. The boat, painted bright green, was called the *Ymer*.

Mortimer sat on a bank at the top of the beach while Horton went down a grabbed a line which was thrown ashore. The invalid had a dull ache in the pit of his stomach, knowing what was probably coming. Two young Inuit men jumped down onto the beach, with the faintest of smiles, and started to talk rapidly in their own language. Horton could not understand them, and shrugged. An older man came out from the wheelhouse and stood on the prow, leaving the engine thumping quietly in standby mode, and looking down at the men on the beach. He spoke Danish, and it transpired that Horton remembered a few words of Norwegian from his time in Svalbard; and somehow, with the aid of many gestures and signs, the two men managed to communicate. The older man, whose name was Joseph, hopped down onto the sandy beach, and he and Horton continued their conversation while standing at the water's edge. The Greenlander said they were searching for their colleagues who were expected back at Sandvig five days ago. They had left on 8th August, and had had a difficult journey because of exceptionally large quantities of brash ice. He explained, furtively, that they had been waiting for grey overcast weather, so that they could not be spotted from the air or indeed from any other boat. Horton nodded, and deduced that they were also smart enough to know that radar signals could get very confused with so many icebergs about. Joseph was clearly very nervous, and said that they were not supposed to be in Hall Bredning as it was banned territory. "Who says so?" asked Horton. "The Americans," came the reply.

Then Horton, using a mixture of Norwegian and English words, had to tell the searchers the bad news -- that the boat and the four men on board were lost on 25th July, and that they were now buried on the Bear Islands.

The three hunters stood stock still for a moment as their worst fears were confirmed, and then all three of them broke down in tears. The two inhabitants of the hut did what they could to console them, but it was not easy, given the language difficulties that afflicted all of them. They led the poor fellows up to the hut and gave them some hot tea and something to eat at the table in the living room. At last they recovered enough to explain, with the aid of a pencil and some pages from a field notebook, why that small cutter had been at the Bear Islands when the iceberg had collapsed almost on top of it. The lost boat was called the *Mikkelsen*. Apparently the men on board had been trying -- in defiance of a ruling from the authorities -- to pick up twenty barrels of seal oil left at Syd Kap when the resident families had been forced to leave. They were reluctant to say anything more, and neither Horton nor Mortimer wished to press them.

It transpired that on board the *Ymer* they had some post for expedition members, which they had planned to leave at Syd Kap in the Danish Administrator's hut. While Mortimer remained indoors and tried to converse with the Greenlanders, Horton went back to the boat with the youngest man, who handed over a bundle of envelopes tied up with string. On top of it was a folded piece of paper containing an anonymous hand-written note. He extracted it and read it quickly. It said: "*Read and destroy. Signals via Sandvig Radio. Linney in coma, sent to Reykjavik. Dr Jensen dead - fell into crevasse near mine. Grave dangers. Take great care.*" Horton frowned and placed the note in his pocket. When he got back to the living room the Greenlanders were explaining, with great difficulty and more drawings, that there had been much helicopter traffic between Sandvig and the airstrip at Blyhavn, too far away for the expedition members to have heard or seen anything of it. Even more interesting, there were two big American vessels in Scoresby Sund, one an icebreaking research vessel and the other a submarine -- doing some sort of research. Horton was incredulous -- a submarine? That meant the involvement of the US Navy......

Suddenly the Greenlanders rose to their feet and indicated that they would now go back to Sandvig as the bearers of terrible news for the families of the four lost men. They would return in about a week to Syd Kap, with the grieving wives, in the hope that somebody could show them where the graves were located. It was clear to both Horton and Mortimer that no power on earth would keep them from doing their duty. At this point Mortimer, who had played virtually no part in the preceding conversation, was so moved that his eyes filled with tears. With Horton's help, he told the Greenlanders that he was one of those who had buried the dead men, and he promised them that he would go with them if his twisted ankle had healed sufficiently for him to get about. "I'll count it as a privilege and a duty," he said gravely to Horton, "to show the Greenlanders each of the four sacred places, and to stand with them in respect for four innocent lives lost." As he spoke, he was shaking with emotion, and had to struggle to get the words out.

Then, with the three Inuit men back on board, the *Ymer*'s ancient engine was revved up, and she went back along the way she had come, to deliver bad tidings to four of the Sandvig families. In the evening, when Horton was alone in the kitchen preparing supper, he held a lighted match under the note from the Sandvig radio operator and sent it up in flames. When they had eaten, the two residents looked at the bundle of mail. There was nothing for Mortimer, but there was one letter for Horton, from his mother. While he read it quietly on his bunk bed, his colleague sat alone at the table with a cold cup of coffee in front of him, holding his head in his hands.

When it stopped raining in Frederiksdal the world became beautiful again. The men stepped outside their sodden tents and saw that there were patches of low cloud all around them, evaporating as they watched, under the benign influence of the sun. Within an hour the sun had broken through to bathe the valley floor in blessed warmth, as the last of the cloud lingered high on the valley sides. Their first priority was to get their stinking anoraks and trousers washed, for they had not yet had the chance to scrub away the last traces of blood and body parts. They dragged their bedding and clothes out of the tents to dry in the fresh air, and while doing this they suddenly realized that the wolves had gone. It was almost as if they had really been phantoms all along, now vanquished by the rays of the sun. They never saw them again, although later that day they did hear them howling, so far away that the sound was barely audible above the sound of the cascading streams which had sprung into life all around them during the protracted deluge.

For the next three days, in much better weather, the four men managed to do good work on the small glaciers that spilled down into the valley from the high plateaux, using for the first time the ice-drilling equipment which had been a nightmare to pack and carry. They managed to obtain fifteen ice temperature readings which Hughes pronounced to be of earth-shattering importance. He refused to elaborate, to the great relief of the others. Then the party trekked back to Nordbukten, preparing to wait until conditions were just right for the return journey along the shore of the fjord. They arrived at the place where they had left their depot and saw that a stiff wind was blowing directly onshore, with breaking waves making the launching of fully laden canoes from a shelving sandy beach impossible. So they pitched their tents and prepared some supper. By 10 pm they observed that the weather was back to normal. The wind dropped to a gentle breeze, and then to a whisper, and then it was gone. The waves faded away as they watched, and by midnight the fjord was glassy calm. There was a lot of brash ice in the bay, pushed in by the onshore wind, but they thought that they could negotiate a way through it. They looked at each other, and Hanna said: "Right, boys, shall we go for it?"

An hour later they were on the water. There was more ice about than they had estimated, so progress was slow, but they made about ten miles before the wind started to pick up again under the influence of the morning sun, and so they put ashore in the bay near the island of Magetuen. They pitched camp on a grassy knoll near the beach, close to the ruins of an ancient Inuit settlement. It was close to perfect, with a clearwater stream just a few yards away; and their contentment was increased further when Whiteside spotted an Arctic hare and shot it with one of the Armalite rifles. That was supper (or was it breakfast?) sorted, and when they had eaten it they had to accept that the sea was once again too rough for canoe travel. They slept for a few hours, lazed in the sun, and watched the seals and the seabirds that appeared to be quite numerous in this part of the fjord. By 11 pm the water was calm enough for them to resume their journey, and they headed through the narrowest part of the fjord, where it was less than four miles wide and over 5,000 feet deep. They had to be careful, since there were many tabular bergs from the vast Daugaard-Jensens Glacier streaming through the narrow gap, some of them colliding and seeming to jostle for position. The biggest of these bergs had a vertical ice face almost half a mile long and three hundred feet high. They heard various distant crashes, creaks and rumbles as usual -- but nothing was close enough to cause concern.

Two hours later they were through the most dangerous part of the fjord and were happy to see that they had regained a stretch of the coast

155

where the trough sides were steep but no longer vertical or overhanging. They were are paddling smoothly and confidently about 100 yards offshore when they sensed a slight vibration in the water, and before they could react there was a thunderous explosion. As they watched, a huge tabular berg about half a mile away started to keel over. They knew that there would be enormous swells coming from this one, and Whiteside shouted: "Straight to the shore, for God's sake!" Frantically they paddled towards the base of the cliffs. They sensed the waves coming behind them, and although they were experienced enough to stop their canoes from being rolled, they were picked up and propelled towards the shore at frightening speed on swells that were bigger than anything they had ever seen before. If the water had not been so deep, the waves would certainly have broken, and they would have had no chance. As it was, the swells simply picked them up and dropped them down violently onto a small rocky beach at the foot of the cliffs. The canoes were instantly smashed to pieces, and in the maelstrom of streaming water, bits of wood and canvas, expedition equipment and possessions, all four men scrambled for handholds on the smooth rock and tried to prevent themselves from being dragged back down into the black depths. Knudsen screamed as he lost his hand-hold and started to slide back towards the edge of the shelf, but Hanna managed to grab the hood of his friend's anorak with one hand, and then another swell came and pushed the pair of them upwards again. Several other swells hit them, but they were smaller now, and somehow they managed to fight their way towards a cluster of huge boulders at the foot of the fjord wall. There they cowered as more water poured over them. Then it was all over, in less than a minute. When they dared to look up, they saw that there was no trace of their canoes on the smooth rocky ledge that had in effect saved their lives. Everything was lost -- food, camping and cooking equipment, cameras, clothing, scientific gear, samples -- everything. Knudsen was furious because his harmonica was lost too. Some flotsam and jetsam was floating about in the water fifty yards offshore, but nobody was inclined to try to recover it. They knew that full immersion in the waters of Nordvest Fjord would kill a human being in two minutes or less. They were all soaked to the skin and deeply traumatized, and it occurred to

Whiteside — who knew too much for comfort about Arctic survival — that they would probably all die anyway.

"Are we all intact, boys?" asked Hughes. The other three confirmed that they were unharmed apart from cuts and bruises.

"So what now?"

"Have we all still got boots on our feet?" They checked, and found that by some miracle, they had.

"Right, my dear fellows," said Whiteside, assuming control of the situation. "Excuse me if I boss you about, but the Good Lord sent me here for precisely this eventuality. I'm a bit rusty on some of the theory, but let's see what we can put into practice."

"Fire away, Perry," said Hanna. "I'm bloody cold, and I want to go home."

"Right. Off with all clothes, and then try to wring every last drop of water out of them. If we don't do that, we'll all die from hypothermia."

They obeyed instructions, and then put out their garments onto the sloping rock surface in the hope that the sun might help to dry them. They were lucky that the sun was now sliding up over the distant peaks of the Stauning Alps, bathing their prison with bright light if not much warmth. For twenty minutes, they hopped about on the rocks, stark naked, and did a physical exercise routine under the command of a hard taskmaster. That got their circulation going, and at last, when they started to get cold again, Whiteside allowed them to put their sodden clothes back on. They yelled and cursed as the ice-cold fabric came into contact with warm flesh, but at least the clothes were now simply wet, having previously been streaming with water.

They had to move if they were to survive. The sun was getting higher with every minute, and the weather looked settled -- and the four men knew that they had to walk or crawl all the way back to civilization. Base Camp or the Frederiksdal hut? The latter was certainly closer, but because of its grisly and morbid associations not one of them wanted to return there. So Base Camp it had to be. Their clothes would have to dry out as they climbed and walked. There was no vegetation on the rocky ledge. They had no food, and no means of making a fire. They had no ropes. Nobody would be worried about them yet because they were only one day late, according to the expedition schedule, and in the Arctic nobody worries about a day or two. The fjord sides were over 3,000 feet high -- and between their precarious rocky ledge and their destination there were some sheer and even overhanging precipices interspersed with steeply sloping rock faces littered with scree. Their biggest obstacle was Løberen, the rapidly moving and heavily crevassed glacier with a snout that was afloat in the fjord; they would have to cross it without ropes, ice axes or crampons. But that was for the future; just now they had no option but to climb up to the plateau and to keep on moving eastwards, whatever physical obstacles they might discover. They were at least thirty miles from base. There were two consolations: one was that they were not physically trapped, and the other was that they were well fed and as fit as they had ever been. They could see above them a steep and narrow gully running diagonally up the cliff face and leading eventually, so they thought, to a sort of bench on the way to the plateau. They faced the immediate prospect of serious -- and even life-threatening -- rock-climbing from the first minute of their journey from hell.

"Right then, chaps," said Whiteside. "We're as ready as we ever will be. Follow me, and try not to look down. Shall we begin?"

CHAPTER 9
August 1962

Following his strange conversation with the Greenlanders, and the reading of that hand-written note, Joe Horton was a deeply worried man. He had picked up that the poor fellows were very frightened indeed, and that there was something going on which neither they, nor the explorers, fully understood. The Himmelbjerg "mining" operation had already aroused their suspicions. They had seen and heard American military aircraft, and now there was apparently an exclusion zone in the Greenlanders' own hunting grounds in Hall Bredning, enforced by the Americans and patrolled by US naval vessels. Dr Jensen had warned them of something, and he was now dead. Coincidence? His intuition told him that it was not. And accidents -- one after another, from which all but poor Rowland Linney had, by some miracle, come through unscathed. Now Linney had been rushed to hospital in Iceland. That did not sound good. And now another warning, from an unknown friend in Sandvig.........

He chose not to share his new information or his fears with Griff Mortimer, on the basis that he had enough to worry about as it was. Anyway, he seemed to be on the verge of a breakdown, following the encounter with the Greenlanders. But news of that encounter had to be carried to Base Camp, and there was mail to be delivered. The two men talked over breakfast, and Mortimer urged his colleague to take the inflatable back across the bay, to deliver the letters and to discuss developments with whoever was in residence. They both assumed that the four members of the Frederiksdal party would by now have returned. "I'm fine on my own here, Joe," he said. "There's plenty of food, and if I rest up for a couple more days I'll probably be able to walk again. I can hobble about quite well already, and the swelling's going down. As it is, an invalid in a small inflatable is a bloody bad idea, and I'll be holding you back during your walk back to Base Camp from the shore. Bugger off, and come back and fetch me when you're ready."

The shoreline between the Gurreholm Hut and Kjove land was still clear of ice, and so Horton packed up quickly, and made the journey in the inflatable boat without incident. When he arrived at Base Camp he found only Andy Petherton in residence. The Australian reported that he had walked up onto the plateau frequently, looking out over the expanses of Hall Bredning and Scoresby Sund. He thought he had seen a small cutter once or twice, but very far away and nowhere near Syd Kap. He was mystified, he said, by this apparent lack of concern for the missing seamen. Horton then explained that the search party had already been to Gurreholm, and had gone away again. At that, Petherton pressed him so hard to pass on all the details of what the Greenlanders had said that he decided, on the spur of the moment, to be economical with the truth. "It wasn't easy to understand anything, Andy. They speak no English, and neither Griff nor I speak Danish or Inuit. We tried to communicate through gestures and grimaces, and when they realized that their friends were dead, they had tears rolling down their cheeks, for God's sake! Poor buggers. They were in a hell of a state. We gave them some tea and something to eat, and they babbled on while they were getting back onto their boat. All we could gather was that they'll return with the families as soon as they can manage. But first they have to get back to Sandvig, and the ice out in the fjord is seriously thick just now. It's all been blown offshore by this easterly wind coming across Jameson Land."

Horton said nothing more, and Petherton knew better than to press him. They looked at the bundle of mail, and saw that all of the letters were for the men who had set off with their canoes two weeks ago. Horton stuffed them back into his rucksack for safe keeping, and the conversation turned to the four absentees. They were beginning to get worried. But they knew that they simply had to sit tight and wait. After all, in Greenland everything took longer than anticipated, and if they were a week late arriving back from Nordvest Fjord, nobody would be too surprised. Horton thought about returning immediately to pick up Mortimer, but then the wind changed and the ice came back in, and for better or for worse the invalid was effectively trapped in his cosy convalescent home on the Gurreholm shore.

Two days passed. The two men at Base Camp did not get on particularly well, since they thought they had little in common. In truth they had too much in common; they were both intelligent, highly opinionated, intolerant of others, and reluctant to talk about themselves. Each was a natural leader, forced for the purposes of this expedition into a subsidiary role, and each suspected that the other had dark secrets to hide. But they made the best of the situation and got on with their own work programmes. Horton found a place where he could cross the Gurreholm River without assistance, and once he had got a fixed rope in place he was able to make his way on four occasions to the long peninsula of Landtungen to collect plants from the limestone community. Petherton worked on the plateau each day, mapping the complicated rock outcrops which might, on analysis, contain some valuable mineral concentrations.

They met up each evening for supper, and enjoyed the luxury of a sleeping tent each -- so the reality was that they did not have to spend a great deal of time together. Horton tried to be open and enthusiastic about his own research findings and hypotheses, and hoped to get some response, but there was little reciprocation from Petherton, who would not even show his colleague his field maps and samples, on the grounds that he wanted to tidy them up and get them right before going public with his results. "Secretive bastard," Horton thought. "Either he doesn't have a clue what he's doing up there on the plateau, or he lies in the sun all day, or he's found diamonds and is afraid we'll slit his throat if we find out about them." But life was too short, he thought, for endless speculation about the abilities and the motivations of his colleague. In any case he had found three plants that were first records for Greenland, and he considered that to be a matter of far greater interest and importance.

On their second evening together, Horton got bored of talking about nothing in particular, and decided to find out a little more about his colleague. As they sat on a couple of convenient rocks near their tents, enjoying a late mug of coffee, he asked: "Andy, I've been wondering what brought a Brisbane boy like you over to the UK? I know there's a lot of traffic in the other direction, with good deals for those who want to emigrate Down Under, but I've never come across another Aussie

161

academic either in Bristol or Oxford........"

Petherton laughed. "Come off it, Joe. We aren't that much of a rarity. I've come across quite a few since arriving in Pommyland. Some from Monash, Melbourne, Sydney, Macquarie and so forth. People move about during their academic careers. But in my case, you can blame a woman."

"Ah, I did wonder, from some of the things you've said."

"I was young and naive, and she was gorgeous. Her name was Jessie. Still is gorgeous, come to think of it......." He paused, and frowned, and looked away. After a while he cleared his throat and continued: "Anyway, she was a Queensland research student studying eucalyptus tree mutations, after the war. She was from Hobart. You would have got on with her like a house on fire. You botanists talk this strange language full of incomprehensible words."

"Not just botanists, Andy. You geologists are the worst of the lot. So you met and got married out there?"

"Nah — we got engaged. Then she wanted to come to England. She wasn't too keen on Brisbane — too hot and sticky, she said. But I suspect she wanted to see Stonehenge, and old castles and churches and so forth — and she had relatives in Norwich."

"So you followed her to the UK?"

"Yes — the most bloody idiotic thing I ever did. But I had no family in Oz, so no reason to stay there."

"So your parents have died?"

"Afraid so. Both killed in a bush fire, when I was ten."

"Oh hell. Sorry to hear that, mate........"

"That was before the war. During the war I was in an orphanage. Prefer to forget that. I was called up in 1945 and never saw active service. Then I got into Queensland University, in Brisbane, and met Jessie in '49. I was a bit of a larrikin at first, but then I was head over heels, or arse over tit, as we say in Oz — so I got my degree and then applied for a research grant at Imperial College, for a doctorate on limestone sedimentary processes......"

"Clear as mud, Andy."

"As it happens, a good deal clearer. No mud. Limestone comes from pristine crystal-clear tropical waters, coral reefs and all that."

"And you caught up with Jessie again, and got married, and started a family?"

"Something like that. Two girls, Sally, who's seven, and Kathleen, who's five."

"Hey," said Horton, "that must be interesting, having two daughters. You're a lucky man........."

"Lucky man?" shouted Petherton, jumping to his feet. "It's been a bloody disaster, from the beginning. Jessie turned out to be a bitch — couldn't cope with me going off on fieldwork trips and so forth. Greenland a couple of times as well, for prospecting with AMR....."

"AMR?"

"Arctic Mineral Resources. Much bigger than Greenland Metals. Bloody good pay. I thought we needed the money......"

"So.......... things started to fall apart?"

Petherton was pacing back and forth, with his face as black as thunder. He still had a half-full mug of coffee in his hands. He took a sip. "She wanted me at home all the time," he said, with a break in his voice. "Bloody unreasonable. A guy needs a bit of time with his mates."

Horton shrugged. "Can't comment on that, Andy. I've never been able to hang onto a girl friend, let alone a wife and a family."

"As it happens, neither have I. Two years of hell, that's what I've been through. The trouble with women, Joe, is that they don't understand men........."

"It takes two to tango, Andy."

"Three, as it happens. Or four, or five."

"What? Were you bloody mad?"

"Probably. Well, a man has his needs. Anyway, the bitch has got her divorce, and she's off back to Tassie with the girls. Maybe she's gone already. I don't care a fuck......."

"I think you do, Andy. Maybe not about your wife, but about the girls."

At this, Petherton roared like a wild animal and flung his plastic coffee mug as far as he could into the distance. Its contents cascaded out onto the gravel before it fell to earth. "What the hell do you know, Joe?"

he shouted. "Fuck all, you lucky bastard!"

And with that he strode off across the bleak gravelly tundra towards the bay. When he came back three hours later, Horton was in his tent, fast asleep.

Susanna Smith was working in the garden at the back of the house on a sunny, breezy afternoon when she thought that she heard the door-bell ring. She assumed that her father would answer the door, but he had obviously failed to hear the sound, for the bell was rung again, more persistently. She went through the house and opened the door, to be confronted by a middle-aged man in a dark suit, accompanied by a younger woman wearing a grey skirt and a smart jacket. They both wore badges in their lapels, and neither of them was smiling.

"Miss Susanna Smith?" said the man.

"Yes, that's me. What can I do for you?"

"May we come inside? We'd appreciate a word in private."

Susanna was no fool, and she had been brought up to be naturally cautious when in the presence of strangers. So her eyes narrowed, and she said: "And may I ask what your names are, and whom you represent?"

The two of them looked slightly discomfited by this show of resistance, but the woman responded: "My name is Mary Ellison, and this is Jonathan Harries. We work for the Government."

"How very pleasant. So do many thousands of others. May I ask which branch of the Government?"

"The Home Office."

"And how do I know that?"

"We have our badges here," said Harries, pointing at his lapel. "We're only allowed to wear these while on official business. As you can see, they have our photographs on them. You can see that we are the people whom we claim to be."

Susanna was supposed to be intimidated by this, but she was beginning to enjoy herself. She was every inch her father's daughter.

"Will you please hand your badges over so that I can examine them properly? One hears so much these days about doorstep tricksters and con artists!"

"I fear that we are not allowed to part company with our badges at any stage.........."

"Well, in that case, I bid you good day," said the young lady politely, making to close the door.

The man spluttered: "But Miss Smith, this is an urgent matter of state, and we must talk to you now rather than later. We need to ask you certain questions."

"Then please give me your badges. I'll show them to my father, and if he approves, I'll invite you inside for a chat. Otherwise, I'm afraid you'll have to go away and make a proper appointment to see me."

The two officials exchanged glances, and Harries shrugged. This young lady was obviously going to be troublesome. But they had to do what they had been sent to do, so they took off their badges and handed them over. Susanna took them, smiled sweetly, and left them on the doorstep while she went upstairs to the study, where she was certain she would find her father fast asleep. It was, after all, a Sunday afternoon, and he always had a siesta on Sunday afternoons. She came downstairs after five minutes, followed by a middle-aged and balding man who was rubbing his eyes.

"My father says you can come inside to the living room," she said brightly. She showed them in and sat them down, and left them with her father while she went to make a cup of tea for the guests. Professor Smith took care not to introduce himself. He was still holding the badges. He took a pen and a notebook from the sideboard and after scrutinizing the photographic identity cards closely, wrote down all the details. This took some time. The two officials became increasingly agitated. "Excuse me sir," said the woman, "but you are not supposed to do that."

"Oh indeed? Is there a law against it? I write everything down for future reference, since my memory isn't what it was." When he had finished writing, he handed the ID cards back. "Now then, Agent 24986, which agency do you work for? MI5, I presume?"

"I'm not supposed to tell you."

"Come now. You are among friends. My lips are sealed."

"I fear that you will have to guess."

The Professor shrugged. "Suit yourself. I'll check things out tomorrow. I had just hoped you would save me a little work."

Then Susanna came in again, poured out some tea and offered each of the guests a slice of currant cake. There was an awkward silence, and then her father said: "You have some questions for my daughter, I think?"

"In private, if you please, sir," said Harries. "This is a matter for her ears only."

"Oh, I think not, Mr Harries. I never leave my daughter alone with strangers. Very protective, I am. You just carry on and ask away, and I'll sit here and listen."

The two agents looked extremely disgruntled, but they knew that their usual tactics of intimidation and mystery were not going to get very far with this particular and rather formidable father - daughter combination. Harries said at last: "Very well. Miss Ellison here will ask some questions, and I'll just keep a record of the proceedings, if I may."

"Please carry on. I am sure my daughter will be entirely honest with you, whatever this might all be about. I too will make some notes of the proceedings, if I may."

Miss Ellison looked like a frightened chicken, but she composed herself, cleared her throat, and then started on the interrogation. "You are Miss Susanna Smith of 423 Woodstock Road, Oxford?"

"I've already confirmed that for you."

"And you act for the Oxford University Scoresby Sund Expedition 1962?"

"I don't act for them at all. I've helped them out as unpaid secretary, and I rather grandly refer to myself as their press officer. I've sent out a few things to the local papers, although for the most part their editors are entirely disinterested."

"Very well. And you sometimes make phone calls on their behalf?"

"Of course. Mostly to do with grant applications, or pestering local stores for free food supplies, or making travel arrangements. I never make any calls from the bookshop where I work, and only ring people up when I'm here at home."

"Very well. And did you make phone calls from here on 13th and 14th of July on which you sought certain information?"

"I might well have done. I try to make phone calls during my lunch break, if I can. What do you mean by "certain information"?"

"I mean classified information, Miss Smith. Relating to certain organizations and individuals."

Susanna flushed, and could not make out where this was leading, but her father stepped into the fray. Quite calmly, he said: "Miss Ellison, are you suggesting that it is a misdemeanour, or even a crime, to ask for classified information?"

"Well, not exactly......."

"Let me help you. The answer is that it is not. Otherwise a small child could be prosecuted for looking at a prototype military aircraft and asking: "Daddy, what aeroplane is that?" The whole idea is preposterous. It may be a crime for the holders of classified information to divulge it to others, if they have sworn under the Official Secrets Act, but that is quite another matter. Would you not agree?"

Miss Ellison gave her frightened chicken look again, and then looked to her colleague for help, which was not forthcoming. So she cleared her throat and continued. "You are technically correct, Mr Smith. Now, may I continue? Miss Smith, did you contact the Danish Embassy in London on 12th July to ask about military activity at the Blyhavn airstrip in Greenland?"

"Gosh, that's about a month ago. I can't remember the date, but yes, I did ring the embassy. My boyfriend Joe, who was one of the expedition organizers, asked me about that, and I tried to find an answer for him. Do you have a problem with that?"

"Miss Smith, I am asking the questions. Did you then make certain telephone enquiries about an organization with the initials NAPRE?"

"Yes. As far as I recall, nobody in this country had heard of it."

"Why was that of interest to you?"

"Because Joe had seen those letters stencilled onto the sides of crates and boxes at the airstrip, and was intrigued. Nothing more than that."

"So when you got nowhere you rang a lady called Eleanor Smith in

America -- in Chicago?"

"Yes, she's my cousin. You know a remarkable amount about my phone calls, don't you?"

"We have our methods, Miss Smith. You were very persistent with this search for information, weren't you?"

"I like to follow things through. My father says I have an enquiring mind. Anyway, there was absolutely no problem in America. Ellie found out all about NAPRE straight away — it's all on the public record, once you know where to look. While she was about it, she checked out the background of a fellow called Colonel Jim Wagner, who is described as Executive Director. That's all easily available too in the records of the US Marines — so she rang me back and gave me all the information I wanted."

"And did you transfer this information back to Greenland?"

"Of course. When we are apart, Joe and I exchange letters whenever we can."

"Hmm — that was not a very good idea, Miss Smith..........."

"Sorry — I'm mystified," said Susanna with a flush on her cheeks and a quiver in her voice. "I wrote a personal letter. Should I have submitted it to your office for prior approval?"

"No, no — thankfully we live in a free country, and we do not allow censorship. But just one other question, Miss Smith, if I may, about your political views........."

At this point, Professor Smith stood up. There was fury in his eyes. "Miss Ellison and Mr Harries, this interview is at an end. I now invite you to leave. I'll not have my daughter intimidated and threatened by people about whom she knows nothing and whose credentials are questionable to say the least."

The two agents had no option but to get to their feet, upon which the Professor ushered them towards the front door. Before he opened it for them, he said: "You have obviously not been very well briefed, and I have been remiss in not introducing myself properly. My name is Frazer Smith, and I'm the Wilberforce Professor of Jurisprudence in the University of Oxford. I'm also a special advisor to the Parliamentary Cross-bench Committee on Human Rights. I know your names, and I have all your details. If this house is bugged, you have twenty-four hours to get your devices out of here, and I want confirmation in writing. If I, or my daughter, ever hear from you or your colleagues again, and if anything should happen to my daughter as a result of this interview, you may take it as a promise from me that I will have your guts for garters."

Miss Ellison and Mr Harries did not know how to respond to that, and went through the door with scowls on their faces, without saying another word. They climbed into a black limousine that had been waiting for them, and it accelerated away towards the city centre. When they had gone, and the front door was closed, father and daughter stood in the hallway and embraced. "Daddy," whispered Susanna, "I'm frightened. What on earth was all that about?

"I've no idea, darling," said the Professor, "and I suspect it might be almost impossible to find out. But something's going on in Greenland, and I'm seriously worried about what might be happening to those young men.........."

On the thirteenth day of August, Horton managed to make the crossing to the Gurreholm Hut, where he found Mortimer hobbling on a pair of makeshift crutches fashioned from two spare planks found in the store room. He was much recovered, and in good spirits. Horton thought that the solitude had done him good. Without incident, they returned to Base Camp. Later on, when the three men were sitting together in the mess tent after supper, the conversation turned to Mortimer's encounter with the musk-oxen. The invalid admitted that he had been careless in a potentially dangerous situation, but when he described the details of his close shave Petherton could not hold his tongue. "Griff, are you completely mad?" he asked. "I'm no zoologist, but I do know that muskox herds are normally six to eight strong, because bulls can only control so many cows and calves. A herd with twenty animals is exceptional, and would have to be controlled by a very powerful and aggressive bull. You should have known that. Surely that bad-tempered old bugger gave you the usual warning signals before charging?"

"Well yes, I suppose he did," said Mortimer defensively. "I was just a bit too keen to get some classic photos........"

"And your camera?"

"Smashed to bits under the thundering hooves, I'm afraid."

"Hmm. A lot of pain and not much profit then. But thank God you are OK. No sign of the boat carrying the grieving relatives, I suppose?"

"Gurreholm has a pretty good view right across to the Bear Islands. While I was there on my own, I saw nothing and heard nothing, except for icebergs falling to bits. They could turn up at Syd Kap at any moment, on the way to the islands."

Petherton frowned. "But why Syd Kap? Why don't they go straight to the islands and get it all over and done with?"

"Because they don't know where the graves are," said Mortimer quietly. "I promised that I'd go with them, dodgy ankle permitting, and show them the precise locations. A sort of native guide, if you like......."

"Bloody hell, Griff!" exclaimed Petherton. "Haven't we got enough problems as it is, without you swanning off on an extended funeral party? The next thing we know, we'll have the Pope over here, swinging incense about and conducting an open-air mass!"

Horton, who was listening intently, noticed that Mortimer became flushed and agitated, finding it hard to hold his tongue, so he intervened. "Andy, that's not fair! This is their country, and they have their beliefs that we must respect. As a matter of fact they're not Catholics, but Lutherans, like most of the practicing Christians in Denmark. If the wives want to come and say farewell in their own traditional way, who are we to judge? Human decency demands that we help them if we can."

"Agreed, Joe," said Mortimer in measured tones. "Love is the same the world over, and so are family ties. If I died out here, and was buried somewhere accessible, I dare to hope that my wife would wish to come from England to see my grave, and to say goodbye. Is that so hard to understand? Wouldn't your wife do the same, Andy?"

"As it happens, mate, I doubt that very much," replied Petherton with a black scowl on his face. "Anyway, she isn't my wife any longer.. ...."

Horton held up his hands and said: "Now then, boys. This is

getting a bit personal. The Inuits will do what they want to do, and there isn't much we can do about it. By the way, Andy, I forgot to tell you one more piece of news that we got from the Greenlanders. I'm not one hundred percent sure of this, but I think they tried to tell us that Rowland has been taken to a proper hospital because his injuries were too severe to be treated at Blyhavn. I definitely heard the word "Reykjavik" in the middle of a lot of other words I didn't understand. And I also think they tried to tell us that Dr Alfred Jensen has died after falling into a crevasse on the glacier near the mine."

Mortimer frowned. "This is news to me, Joe. I was there when we talked with the Greenlanders, and I don't recall any of that."

Horton held up his hand and said: "I know, Griff. Mea culpa. That young Greenlander told me this when I went down to the boat with him to fetch the mail. I was uncertain of the truth of it because of our language problems, but having mulled it over I think that was the gist of what he said. For better or for worse, I chose not to tell you, since you were in a hell of a state as it was, coping with all that raw emotion from three men who had lost their friends............"

"Fair enough, Joe. That was considerate of you."

There was a long silence, for all three of them had liked the mine doctor. Horton broke the silence. "Terrible, terrible," he murmured. "A real gentleman who loved his job. You knew him better than the rest of us, Andy. He put you right after your accident on the glacier............"

"He did, he did," said Petherton quietly, with an expression on his face that Horton could not read. Then without another word, he got up and stormed out of the tent. That surprised his colleagues, for Petherton was not given to public shows of emotion. They watched him go, and Horton said: "Let him be, Griff. He's more upset than I might have expected. There are things in his life that are giving him a hard time. So, what else are we surprised about? As for me, I've spent ages mulling over the news about that American submarine."

"I'm not as surprised as you," replied Mortimer with a shrug. "There have been nuclear submarines in the fjords before. They come in for exercises, and seem to like testing their equipment in iceberg-infested waters, especially where there are big icebergs with keels going down to

171

fifty fathoms or more. Here it's not much of a challenge at all, since they can pop up to the surface at any time -- remember that just a few years ago the *Nautilus* went all the way under the Arctic ice and popped up at the North Pole."

"Well, that's good to know," muttered Horton, with some bitterness in his voice. "If we get stranded because the winter ice sets in early this year, perhaps the bastard Yanks will be kind enough to pop up here and rescue us."

Harald Keppel looked at the old man across the table in his office. When Pana came to see him, there was usually trouble brewing either in Sandvig or in one or other of the small satellite settlements a few miles away. He left most domestic matters to the old man, who normally dealt with them quietly and efficiently, with the help of the other village elders, by invoking ancient traditions and codes of behaviour which he, as a foreigner, would never fully understand. So this would be something different. Deep down, he knew already what it was. But he asked anyway. "What can I do for you, Pana?"

As usual with the old fellow, he wasted no time in getting to the point. "Harald, the families of those who died when the *Mikkelsen* went down must be allowed to visit the graves on the Bear Islands. And we must also fetch those barrels of seal oil from Syd Kap."

Keppel had known what was coming, but his heart sank anyway. He leaned forward and looked the old man directly in the eye. "Pana, you know that there's a ban on all shipping movements in the fjords for this summer season. The government in Copenhagen has approved it, and even your own regional council has said yes. So they'll have to wait."

"They will not wait, Harald. With or without your permission, they will go. More than two weeks have passed since their relatives died. The bears will take the bodies. It's important that before that happens, certain ceremonials are completed........."

"I appreciate that, Pana. But can't the families wait until the fjord is frozen? In November it'll be possible to travel on the ice, and then there'll be no conflict with the instructions that I have on my desk. As it is, I'm likely to get into serious trouble for allowing Joseph and the two boys to slip out in the *Ymer* a few days ago, when they went off to find out what had happened."

"You can't watch every boat in the bay for every hour of the day, Harald. The Greenland Department can't blame you simply because some of your parishioners went off to do their duty, as they saw it."

"Maybe you're right, Pana. But they could have got into serious trouble. They might have been arrested by the captain of that American ship........and they might even have been harmed. I'm more concerned about them than I am about my own career. "

"I thought, Harald, that we were free men in this country? This is our country, and not yours, and you are here by invitation, because you promised to protect us and to give us this thing that you call "democracy." Under what law would an American ship's captain be able to arrest three men from this village who are going about their lawful business, in the face of a family tragedy?"

Keppel sighed. This was getting complicated. He was trying to defend something for which he had no sympathy at all, and now he was caught in a pincer movement, with pressure on the one side from Copenhagen and Himmelbjerg, and on the other from this old and very intelligent fellow called Pana Naukun. It was not a very good idea to cross swords with Pana. In any case, he was inordinately fond of him. He sighed again. "Very well, Pana. Let's see if we can sort this out. Will you agree with me that the men in the *Mikkelsen* did not really need to go off for those barrels of seal oil at Syd Kap precisely when they did?"

"The oil is theirs, Harald. They must fetch it and sell it. They need the money. You Danes keep on telling us that we must enter the modern world and buy things and sell things instead of just hunting and drinking alcohol........."

"Yes yes, Pana. I know all of that. What I mean is this. The oil isn't going to disappear or go bad. Not even the bears can get at it in those barrels. They could have fetched the barrels later on, in September, after the departure of the Americans and before the winter freeze sets in."

"I see your point, Harald........"

"Of course, the fact that the boat was too close to that iceberg when it fell to bits could not have been foreseen by anybody. But that's another matter -- what's done is done. An Act of God, as the lawyers call it in England. Now we have four dead men in their graves, each one on a different small island. And four families who want to visit them. I'll tell you what I'll do. But first, will you use your influence to stop any attempt to fetch the barrels of seal oil before the Americans have gone?"

Pana looked at his friend for a long time, and then nodded. "Very well. I think I can do that for you. What do I get in exchange?"

"I'll turn a blind eye if the *Ymer* goes out again with four wives on board, on a humanitarian mission. I'll probably lose my job if anybody in Copenhagen ever finds out, but sometimes a diplomat has to make diplomatic decisions. Between you and me, Pana, I'm in love with this place and its people, which probably makes me a very bad Administrator."

He smiled bleakly. Pana said nothing, and his face registered no emotion. He stood up, leaned over the table, shook Keppel's hand, and left the room.

Ten minutes later the operator from the Sandvig radio station pushed his head around the door of the office. "Harald, message from the Greenland Ministry, probably in response to yours of a couple of days ago. Excuse me for barging in like this -- it seems urgent."

He handed the typed message over, and hovered near the door while Keppel read it. Then he asked: "Do you want me to wait while you draft a reply?"

"No thank you, Erland. I understand what they are reporting, and so do you. No reply necessary."

When the radio operator had left, Keppel read the message again, and placed it onto his desk with a groan. Things are coming to a head, he thought. This is what the message said:

HIGHEST SECURITY ENCRYPT AND DESTROY
Greenland Ministry Copenhagen
cc MoD London, FO London, PG1, NAPRE HQ
To Keppel Sandvig 15 August 1962

Confirm receipt message. Transmitted London. After FO / MoD assessment personal involvement UK Prime Minister requested and agreed. Message from Prime Minister as follows: "14.08.62. Regret news unfortunate accident Linney and loss Inuit vessel. Appreciate concerns re safety of OUSSE members. Your request abort NAPRE programme on safety grounds considered in depth. But strong Pentagon pressure re alliance solidarity / national security. Agree therefore PG1 request to continue and complete NAPRE programme as planned, even if collateral damage."

No media contacts permitted. All news management via Copenhagen and London.

ENDS

REPEAT HIGHEST SECURITY NO PAPER COPIES

Keppel got up from his desk and strode around the room, deep in thought, for the best part of an hour. Collateral damage -- was that the latest euphemism used by the Greenland Ministry? He knew that he had in his possession the modern equivalent of a medieval death warrant, personally signed off — in the national interest — by the British Prime Minister. The paper copy should not have been made by the radio operator. He, as the named recipient, should of course now destroy it. He went back to his desk, picked it up, and folded it carefully. Then he put it into his pocket and went outside.

They were on one of the highest sections of the fjord side, with a two-thousand foot vertical cliff below them, when Whiteside, who was in the lead, lost his footing. They should have gone higher up, onto the plateau edge where the slope was gentler, but they were so exhausted that they could not face climbing even a few hundred feet more, and so they had started taking risks by traversing slopes that were really far too steep for men without ropes and climbing gear.

Whiteside was crossing a smooth sloping slab of rock, but it was covered with loose rubble, and his feet went from under him. Loose scree and moraine is dangerous at the best of times, and even more dangerous when it is just a couple of inches thick and rests on a smooth rock surface. He screamed, and Hughes, who was following him a little lower down, saw that he was sliding inexorably down towards the edge of the precipice, with no means of stopping himself. Without thinking, he flung himself on top of his colleague as he slid past, and by some miracle of physics the combined weight of the two men provided sufficient friction to arrest the slide. For an age they lay there, gasping and terrified, afraid that any move might start them sliding again -- but Hanna and Knudsen, with terror in their eyes, managed to kick away enough loose debris to obtain reasonable footholds on the rock surface, and inch by inch they managed to pull them back to safety. They struggled to reach a broad ledge about thirty yards further along the slope, and there all four of them collapsed.

"Bloody hell!" moaned Whiteside after several minutes of uncontrollable shivering. "That was a bit too close for comfort. Thanks, Gwyn. Good to see that glaciologists have their uses........."

"Think nothing of it, old man. Sliding coefficient of friction. Buy me a Guinness when we get back to Base Camp."

The four of them laughed hysterically, but their legs were now so weak that they had no option but to wait for half an hour before pressing on.

They were two days into their journey, and they had eaten only a few bilberries since they had been shipwrecked. They had already lost track of time, and they were settling into a pattern of walking or climbing until they were exhausted, finding somewhere to shelter, huddling together while they tried to sleep for a few hours, and then doing it all again. They had prayed for something substantial to eat on the occasions when they had been forced to drop down to the valleys near sea level -- maybe an old food depot left by trappers or geologists -- but they had found nothing. However, the weather was holding, and although the temperatures on the plateaux and upper valley sides were now dipping well below zero during the small hours, they were walking for most of the time in bright sunlight with a fresh westerly breeze whenever the sun was high. Good drying weather, said Lawson, celebrating the fact that their

176

clothes were no longer dripping with fjord water. On a number of occasions they had been up over 5,000 feet and had been forced to slog through the snowpatches that clung to the plateau edges; and once or twice they had even managed to admire the view, which from that altitude had been truly amazing. Once they had caught a glimpse of a ship far below and about ten miles further down the fjord, and assumed it might be one of the geology support ships which Jim Wagner and Harald Keppel had referred to long ago, when they had enjoyed a sumptuous feast at Himmelbjerg........... Perhaps it was not so strange, but they now talked — and dreamed — more about food than they did about sex.

They had had three narrow escapes in addition to the one in which Whiteside had almost gone over the edge. The first one had been on their initial climb up from the narrow rock bench down at fjord level, when Hanna had sent a great boulder crashing down into the fjord and had almost gone with it. The second had occurred as they made a four-hour crossing of the surging glacier called Løberen, when Knudsen, who was lighter than the others, had almost been washed away in a surface meltwater stream. And the most recent had been when a snowbank on the plateau above Stormpynt had given way beneath all four of them, dumping them into a melt stream which luckily did not have enough force to sweep them away inside its echoing tunnel. By the time of this latter incident they were no longer bothered whether they were wet or dry, for they could see before them the deep trough containing the twin lakes of Holger Danskes Briller -- and beyond that, they would find Base Camp. Now they could perhaps relax a little, for they had climbed about 30,000 feet in all, up and down over and again, and from here on the route was downhill. But Whiteside was a hard taskmaster, and although they were weak from hunger and from extreme physical effort, he continually urged them to keep focussed and to watch every step, especially when scrambling down steep gullies and scree slopes which could be set in motion by the slightest mistake.

On the morning of 16th August the four members of the Frederiksdal party scrambled down their final bank of scree and felt beneath their feet the soft green turf of the little bay at the western end of the lakes. They reckoned from the position of the sun that it might be about 10 o'clock in the morning, and Whiteside confirmed this since he was the only one who had a waterproof and functioning watch. They slumped onto the grass, and were so exhausted that Hanna thought they might not be able to cope with the final fifteen miles of their journey. Within a minute or two, both Knudsen and Hughes were fast asleep. Whiteside, however, had incredible reserves of energy, and having observed that there were seals close inshore, he deduced that there were fish in the vicinity, and that some Arctic char might be heading up the clearwater stream towards the lake in order to spawn. He found a deep pool in the river, between two stretches where there were turbulent whitewater cascades. He nodded to himself when he saw that there was an overhang in the bank, just beneath the water level. He lay down on the turf, with his arm in the water. Then, after a few minutes, he gave a great shout, and as if by magic there was a gleaming fish, about eighteen inches long, flapping about on the grass.

"Breakfast, Steffo!" he chortled. "First decent food for four days. You've still got your knife -- be a good chap and clean it for us while I get a fire going."

"Fire, Perry? What are we going to burn, and how will you light it?"

"When you've cleaned the fish, gather up those bits of wood lying around the old Inuit camp site over there. Then get me some tinder -- seeds, dead twigs, leaves, bits of dried grass, all so dry that you can crumble them into dust between your fingers. I'll now make a lens, and do some magic." Then he went to the shore, picked up a small piece of brash ice, and started to fashion it with his knife into a lens about four inches across. It took him about thirty minutes, and he had to try it out several times before he was satisfied with the shape. Then with infinite patience he captured the sun, lit the tinder and transformed that into a blazing fire.

Over the next hour the four men enjoyed a small feast of grilled Arctic char followed by a few bilberries. That put a little colour back into their cheeks, although they looked haggard and unkempt. They had all lost weight. Since they thought that they were about to re-enter the civilized world, they cleaned their teeth with bits of dried grass.

Whiteside adjusted his silk cravat, which was now so greasy and filthy that one could no longer make out what colour it used to be. In any case, it was covered by his straggly beard. Then, with the sun at its zenith, they set out along the southern shore of the lake, heading for home.

The Frederiksdal party was now four days late, and there was a black mood at Base Camp. The three men in residence were convinced that something nasty had happened to their colleagues. They could not have been held up by difficult conditions on the fjord, for there had been four days of bright breezy weather with flat calms at night -- perfect for paddling canoes along the coast. Without any discussion, Joe Horton took command and decided that he would wait for one more day. If they did not turn up by tomorrow, another emergency rocket would have to go up and the whole expedition would have to be aborted.

In the meantime, they had needed to keep occupied. While Mortimer was still recuperating at Base Camp, Horton and Petherton had carried on with the business of moving food and other supplies northwards, on both sides of the Schuchert Valley, to the camp sites already planned for the final phases of the work programme. They had made several trips, heavily laden, but they were now so fit that they felt they could cope with almost anything.

For some days, Mortimer had been hobbling about, complaining that he felt useless and that he was a burden upon his colleagues. Horton had tried to keep up his spirits by pointing out that he was really no burden at all; his mobility was increasing by the day, and in any case somebody had to remain at camp, as agreed with Hanna before he and his canoe party had gone off up the fjord. He had given Mortimer the task of preparing all the meals while he and Petherton were out and about, but the poor fellow hated cooking, and hated it even more when they poked fun at his lumpy soups, burnt stews and Angel Delight with added moss and gravel. In fact all three of them moaned and groaned about each other's culinary disasters as a matter of course, but Mortimer seemed unaware of that. Horton was worried about him, for he had seen men with deep depression before, and he did not want to get into counselling sessions while there were other more urgent matters that needed attention. So he was delighted when, at breakfast time, Mortimer reminded him that tomorrow would probably be the day when the *Ymer* came up from Sandvig to Syd Kap, carrying the wives who wanted to visit the graves of the men from the *Mikkelsen*.

"I promised to help them," he said, "and I think I can do it, even though I'm still hobbling a bit. I won't have to walk there, since the inflatable is on the beach at Nordøstbugt, and I can take that round the coast to Syd Kap. Fuel isn't a problem. When we came back from Gurreholm the other day there were still three full jerrycans left."

"Very well, Griff," said Horton. "You can go. The Inuits may or may not come, but if there's no sign of them after three days we want you back here. Are you happy with that?" Mortimer nodded. "And another thing. You can't go alone. The inflatable is pretty safe, but you might have to cope with ice and big waves, and you must have somebody with you who's able-bodied. Andy, will you go with him? Once you are at Syd Kap, you can carry on with your work on the plateau while Griff stays at the Hotel Paradiso. Does that sound reasonable?"

Petherton protested at first, but then agreed to this plan. After breakfast the two of them took the supplies that they needed, and headed off, very slowly, for the depot on the shore of the bay.

Horton was now alone at Base Camp. He wanted to do some work on identifying plant samples -- a task that required peace and quiet, and considerable concentration. But first he wanted to collect some specimens from an unusual plant community on the edge of the Schuchert river plain, about ten miles inland from the coast.

As he walked along, late on a bright, calm afternoon with excellent visibility, he was just a mile or so from his destination. He heard a muffled explosion a long way off, maybe a little louder than the other explosions, cracks and thumps that came from the icebergs in Hall Bredning, especially when there was a stiff breeze and a falling tide. All of those sounds were insignificant in the context of the thundering roar that continued, day and night, all the way along the fifty miles or so of the Schuchert River. He stopped and listened intently, and decided there was no cause for alarm. He carried on along the grassy bank that marked the edge of the river gravels. But then, after a few minutes, he noticed that there was a change in the pitch of the sound from the river, and before he could react to the sound he saw a wall of water approaching fast from the north. He could hardly believe it. But there was no time for pondering on rhymes and reasons. He dropped his rucksack and ran for his life, first somewhat aimlessly and then towards a gigantic limestone erratic boulder the size of a house, about twenty feet above the flood plain. He flung himself to the ground in the lee of the boulder, and prayed that the force of the torrent was not sufficient to move it. If it had rolled over, he would have been crushed by it and never seen again. As the water overwhelmed him, he managed to get close to the ground and brace himself against the side of the boulder. The torrent poured over it and around it, and a huge eddy on the lee side almost sucked him away, but then the crisis was over, as suddenly as it had started. The water quickly subsided, and the flood continued downstream towards the sea, spreading sideways across the tundra and dissipating its strength. His rucksacks was gone, and so was the depot which he and Petherton had established a mile further up the valley.

Horton was badly shaken and soaked to the skin, but otherwise uninjured. He thanked his lucky stars that he had been close to that gigantic boulder, dumped millennia ago by a glacier streaming out of the mountains. he was appalled by the thought that if he had been anywhere else, across maybe 20 square miles of country, that would have been the end of him.

He turned and trudged back down the valley towards Base Camp, chastened by the conviction that the gods were clearly not on the side of the virtuous. Where on earth had that wall of water come from? There could only have been one source. One of the glacier lakes in front of Roslin Gletscher, which they had seen from a distance when they walked down the valley an age ago, must have burst its banks and emptied catastrophically. He knew that this sort of thing happened occasionally in

Iceland, but normally in connection with volcanic eruptions or earthquakes. He had never heard of such a dramatic lake drainage episode in East Greenland.

As he staggered southwards, shivering uncontrollably, Horton knew that he would not reach the camp site until the early hours of the morning. But he had to keep walking, and as he did so he saw with ever greater clarity that the strange happenings of the past few weeks had more than a little to do with Himmelbjerg and that strange fellow called Jim Wagner...........

CHAPTER 10
August 1962

Andy Petherton was out of breath, in spite of being fitter than he had ever been in his life. He had climbed up onto the Plateau from Syd Kap and had rushed to reach the radio shack on Pythagoras Bjerg. He looked around to make sure that the coast was clear, and then laughed at his own stupidity. Who was left to see him anyway? Nobody.

He went into the little hut which was carefully hidden among the boulders on a slope of rough scree, some way beneath the summit. It was dark inside, since there was no window, and he lit a small paraffin lantern which stood on a shelf. He settled onto a stool, which was the only piece of furniture in the hut apart from a packing case on its side, which contained several batteries and had a modified military radio set perched on top. He switched on the transmitter / receiver unit, and because it was set to a single frequency he established contact with Himmelbjerg almost immediately. The signal was excellent, and the batteries were well charged, so he put aside the morse code key and the headphones and switched to loudspeaker mode.

He asked to talk to Jim, and after a couple of minutes a familiar voice boomed out. "Hi Andy. Jim here."

"Jim! Good to talk to you. Did the flood happen last evening?"

"Yes, on schedule. Bloody good it was too. I got a grandstand view of what happened when the side of the lake gave way. Better than a disaster movie!"

"Excellent -- that should account for Horton."

"OK -- report back to me on that when you have confirmation from down at your end. Rucksack, boots, body, anything."

"If he did survive, he'll be walking back to Base, maybe badly injured. I'll go up the valley today and check for any signs of life."

"Best assume he is still around, for planning purposes. No trace of Hanna and the others from Frederiksdal?"

"None at all -- I think we can assume they can be crossed off the list."

"Any indications that they had rumbled what's been going on before they went up the fjord?"

"None at all. As I told you before, they've had their suspicions about Himmelbjerg, but in spite of all their training they seem to have accepted that all of the disasters have been Acts of God."

"Top brass will be delighted. Anything else to report?"

"Yes," said Petherton. "Horton and Mortimer discovered that Dr Jensen is dead."

There came the sound of a desk being slammed with a fist. "Bloody hell! How did they find that out?"

"Some Inuits turned up at Gurreholm in the small boat called *Ymer*. Looking for their lost colleagues..........."

"You mean that the bloody Danish Administrator allowed them to leave and travel to Hall Bredning?"

"Well, they might have left without permission......"

"Damn it all, man! That bugger Keppel is supposed to keep Sandvig watertight! By now it will be all around the village that something's going on up here -- the Inuits have nothing better to do than gossip and get pissed."

"Don't blame me, Jim. I've kept things really tight at this end. ...."

There was a long silence as Wagner calmed down. "OK -- what else does Horton know?"

"That the *Pole Star* and *Ellsworth* are in the area."

"What?! But they couldn't possibly have been seen from Sandvig when they came in past Cap Tobin. They were more than 30 miles from the village, and anyway, the nuke was submerged as it came in. Some bastard must have been talking.........."

"Not at this end, I can assure you, Jim. By the way, what news of Rowland Linney?"

"Oh, he died in the hospital in Reykjavik. He recovered consciousness, but our lords and masters decided that wasn't very convenient. So he had a visit from one of the top specialists from the

Keflavik medical unit, and died shortly afterwards. Very sad business.....
but one unnecessary problem out of the way."

"I get your drift, Jim. Handy people, these specialists. But I quite
liked Rowland -- a bumbling idiot, with not a bad bone in his body........."

"Not getting soft, are you?"

"No -- but I blame myself for that particular Act of God. I should
have triggered the landslide an hour earlier, when they would have seen
it without getting caught up in it."

"OK -- you probably will get to like some of these guys, even if
they're all as mad as hell. But we have to see this through now. Too much
collateral damage already to turn back. I hadn't planned it this way, but
Pentagon and Downing Street agree that we must press ahead regardless.
Get that?"

"Yep. I do what I'm told."

"Great. So if the guys who went to Frederiksdal have gone, and
Linney, that leaves just three -- you and Mortimer and maybe Horton......"

"Make that two."

"You mean Horton is disposed of? I though we agreed he might
still be alive?"

"No -- I'm talking about Mortimer. I took him to Syd Kap first
thing yesterday morning, and that confirmed my suspicions that he'd
gone native. Rambled on about the kindness of Joe Horton and the
tragedy that happened to the *Mikkelsen* -- and said he owed it to the Inuits
to show them the graves of their lost friends. He had to go......."

"Spare me the details. No traces left?"

"He's on the bottom of Syd Kap Bay, weighted down with stones."
Petherton spoke without a trace of emotion.

"And how will you deal with Horton? If he survived the flood, and
is badly injured, he's not gonna roll over and die quite as easily as the
others. Tough bastard. You knew he was a commando once?"

"Of course. It was all there, in our briefing. But don't you worry. I
might even take the gun from here. Clean and simple -- no point in
subtlety and subterfuge from now on. I'll do it this evening, at Base
Camp, if he 's there. Then I'll put up a rocket and you can send the
chopper down. We can use it to carry the body and dump it in the eastern

185

lake, with some stones as ballast. Then that'll be me finished. I'll write my report up at Himmelbjerg. I'll be glad to get out of this bloody place -- time to get back to Oz and start using my new name."

Suddenly the door burst open and Joe Horton rushed inside, carrying a large stone. Before Petherton could react he smashed it down onto the radio set over and again, putting it permanently out of action. "You bastard! You fucking bastard!" he shouted. "I heard all of that! I knew there was something going on -- and to think we actually trusted you..........."

A furious struggle ensued, mostly on the floor, with the two men locked in a desperate embrace in a very enclosed space as they each strove for some advantage, or for some lethal weapon made of metal or stone. The stool was smashed to pieces, and Petherton grabbed one of the splintered legs which he tried to use as a weapon, but Horton managed to seize his opponent's wrist and to smash it onto the stony floor of the hut several times until he was forced to drop it. The two men were evenly matched, and when they were both bruised and bleeding from kicks, strangleholds and blows from fists and head butts, they both began to tire. At last Petherton managed to kick Horton away. He was utterly exhausted, but his brain was still functioning. He reached into a corner and pulled out a gun that had been hidden behind a box. "Back off Joe, or I'll blow your brains out sooner rather than later!" he shouted. Horton retreated to the door, gasping for breath, and held up his hands. He stood there, framed against the light. "That's better." Petherton took a minute to catch his breath, and with his free hand he wiped blood from his mouth and from a gash on his scalp. Then he said: "So you heard all of that? Very inconvenient. But what the hell -- you're not going anywhere......"

"Don't be too sure of that, friend."

"I'm very sure of it. How did you find this place?"

"Just looked for it. I knew it had to be hidden -- so a big bank of scree was ideal. I also assumed there'd need to be a pretty clear line of sight to Himmelbjerg. So it had to be more or less here. And I knew there had to be some sort of aerial. Very discreet it is, but I found it in the end. And here we are, as cosy as can be."

"Smart arse. You always were a bit too inquisitive, Joe."

"Sherlock, they called me in the Marines. By the way, since this is my last chance to find out, you never were injured on that walk down the Sirius Glacier, were you?"

"Nah. I've always been a good actor, ever since my starring role as Aladdin's wicked uncle in a Sunday School panto when I was thirteen. I needed a few days with Jim at Himmelbjerg, so that I could get a proper briefing."

"Thought so. You were a bloody passenger on this trip, right from the beginning. Another crime to add to the list. But that was nothing, compared with your cold-blooded slaughter of your mate Griff Mortimer...."

"He wasn't my mate. Never liked the guy anyway. Too bloody soft for this line of work. He and I just happened to be on the same side."

"So you bumped him off because you didn't like him? Or because he had a streak of humanity in him? Charming."

"No! We had a disagreement. It was him or me."

"Him or you? The poor bugger was injured and defenceless anyway. Bloody miserable too."

"That's beside the point. We had a flaming row."

"Ah -- so that explains it. You bumped him off because you had a row. No wonder you have no friends left -- you're just a fucking psychopath. I hope your Sunday School teacher is proud of you."

"As it happens, she is............. "

"And then you tried to kill Rowland and me. Attempted murder, Alfred Jensen called it — and I couldn't work out what the hell he was talking about. Now the doctor's dead, and so is Rowland. So you triggered the landslide — God knows how, but I'm working on it. And you killed him, just as you might have killed him by plunging a knife into his back. Incidentally, I was rather fond of that peaceful and innocent young man. His death has to be avenged, and since nobody else will do it, I will have to kill you. I won't enjoy it, but duty comes before pleasure anyway."

Petherton spat blood onto the floor, and laughed. "You forget, Joe, that I'm in control here."

"I've heard enough. Careless people are never in control. Have you checked that that thing is loaded?"

"It's always loaded. I'm prepared for anything."

"Not, apparently, for an ex-Marine who arrives here half an hour before you do and knows how to disarm a good old-fashioned Walther PPK. Empty clip, old boy."

Petherton was furious with these taunts, and desperate at the same time. He pulled the trigger over and again. Nothing happened. "You bastard!" he shouted. "Nobody plays games with me!" He threw the gun at his adversary and then rushed at him, but quite calmly Horton grabbed a long-bladed knife which he had stuck into the outside of the door-post, prior to his assault with the radio-wrecking stone. He plunged the blade, without a moment's hesitation, into Petherton's stomach. With the same movement he ripped it upwards, as he had been trained to do. The result was appalling, and there was a deluge of blood and gore. Petherton gasped and staggered back into the hut, with terror in his eyes. He fell against the shelf supporting the paraffin lamp which had miraculously remained unscathed during the earlier desperate struggle. The shelf collapsed and the lamp crashed onto the floor. It was immediately smashed, and burst into a ball of flame. The conflagration spread with incredible speed, and since Petherton's clothes were now soaked in paraffin that is where the flames were concentrated.

For some minutes Horton stood back outside the hut and listened to Petherton's screams, which eventually ceased. Black smoke swirled in the breeze and climbed high into the evening sky above the funeral pyre. The smell of burning flesh almost turned his stomach. There was nothing more to be done, so he turned and walked away, saying to nobody in particular: "Justice done. Where I come from, the penalty for premeditated multiple murder is to be left dangling on the end of a rope. That would have been too kind............"

Professor Frazer Smith was in his room in New College when the phone rang. He was deeply engrossed in writing an article about the rights of citizens under authoritarian regimes, and the phone was buried beneath a pile of books and papers. He thought about not answering. But on the off chance that it might be something important, he dug out the handset and held it to his ear.

"Professor Frazer Smith?"

"Yes, that's me."

"Are you alone, sir?"

"Yes, I am. Term has ended quite some time ago, and it's holiday time, in case you hadn't noticed."

"Hold on please, Professor. I have a caller for you."

He waited for a while, and at last he heard a voice that he recognized. "Is that you, Frazer?"

"Yes, it's me, as already confirmed. Hello Giles. Keeping well?"

"Very well indeed. And you and Susanna?"

"Healthy enough, and making the best of things. I assume you haven't just rung to exchange pleasantries, my friend?"

"Not at all. Following your call, I've been making some enquiries."

"Ah, about those people who came knocking on our door the other day like a pair of doorstep evangelists?"

"Indeed. Well, I have inside channels to most places within the security services. Before I go any further, we may not be alone on this line. Your record of that conversation, when those people were interrogating Susanna — you wrote it all down, I take it?"

"Of course I did. I write everything down."

"Is the transcript somewhere safe?"

"Of course. I wasn't born yesterday."

"Good, good. Don't tell me where. I don't want to know. Next question. What were those badges like — you know, the ones they had in their lapels?"

"Rectangular, and about the size of business cards. The photos were good likenesses. The print was clear. The cards were mounted in little plastic folders and fixed with spring clips."

"Hmmm. That all sounds authentic enough. As I suspected………." Then there was a long silence.

"Are you still there, Giles?" asked the Professor after a while. "Stop suspecting things, and tell me the score."

"Very well, old chap. First things first. Our assessment is that neither you nor your daughter is in any danger whatsoever. Your visitors would not wish you any harm, and neither would their employers."

"Well, that's a relief — for Susanna more than for me. She's been very edgy since that visit out of the blue."

"Fully understood. Just in case there are other forces at work here, I'm putting your house under twenty-four hour surveillance, and both you and Susanna will be shadowed. Don't feel intimidated by that. Standard procedure when it comes to valuable people."

"Good God, Giles! This is all getting rather murky. Get to the point, man."

"The truth of the matter is this. Within the Home Office and the security services — all of them — there is no record of any agents or operatives with the numbers 24986 or 23724. And there are no records of any personnel with the names Mary Ellison and Jonathan Harries."

Just before six o'clock, the four members of the Frederiksdal party were trudging across the wide expanse of sediments between the two Holger Danskes Briller lakes. They were so tired that they did not notice much of what was around them, but they were shocked when they saw a gigantic landslide scar on the flank of the peak on the north side of the valley, and a spread of fresh rocky debris which almost reached the whole way across the valley. "God's teeth!" exclaimed Hanna. "That wasn't there when we left, that's for sure. I wonder when it happened? I hope nobody was in the way when it all came down............"

Three hours later, as they made their way cautiously through rough moraine and scrub on the shore of the eastern lake, they caught a glimpse of the plateau to the south. They saw a pall of dark smoke drifting down towards them from the flank of Pythagoras Bjerg as the evening air grew colder, and they wondered where on earth it might have come from.

At midnight, Hanna, Knudsen, Whiteside and Hughes limped and stumbled their way into Base Camp and promptly collapsed. For the last three hours they had been walking like zombies, hardly able to keep their eyes open, falling frequently, struggling upright again with the help of their comrades, only vaguely aware of where they were and how far it might be to their destination. They had hardly exchanged a word for two hours, and when they reached the shallow Parachute Ponds they had splashed through them like drunken idiots, cheering hoarsely and scooping up handfuls of water to quench their thirst. They had been using up their last reserves of adrenalin, and now it was all gone.

When Horton saw them, he could hardly believe his eyes. Each one looked as if he had lost half of his bodyweight, and sunken eyes and cheeks gave each one of them a skeletal appearance which convinced the single resident at Base Camp that they should really all have been dead, and that they had been kept alive by willpower or an insane determination not to let each other down. The ragged remnants of their clothes were doing nothing to keep them warm or dry, and if it had rained or snowed recently they would certainly have succumbed. But here they were, through another miracle, sprawled on the gravel in front of the tents, alive if not kicking.

Horton was exhausted himself, but somehow he dredged up some new reserves of energy. He dragged each one in turn into the mess tent, stripped off every piece of stained and filthy clothing and threw everything onto a pile on the gravel. To the accompaniment of mumbled protestations he gave each of them a wash with warm soapy water, got some fresh clothes onto them, and stuffed each one in turn into a sleeping bag. It was not particularly cold, but each of them shivered uncontrollably. Supper was long since over and done with, but Horton cooked up a pot of tomato soup and forced each of the new arrivals to drink a little of it. He knew that the four new arrivals would have to get back to full rations very gradually, and that all that mattered just now was warmth and sleep. There was important news to be exchanged, but that could wait until tomorrow.

Within an hour of their arrival, all four men were fast asleep, and they did not stir for sixteen hours. Later on, when Horton was in his own tent, trying to get to sleep, he heard the unmistakable call of the great northern diver, far away on one of the Holger Danskes Briller lakes. "Ah, the spirit of the wilderness," he thought. "On the edge of hearing, and on the edge of reason."

In the village of Sandvig it was four o'clock in the morning, and sunlight was already filtering through the cracks in the shutters which protected the privacy of the Danish Administrator's house. Harald Keppel lay on his back and gazed at the ceiling, pretending to be asleep. His wife Elise lay silently beside him, also pretending to be asleep. At last she cuddled up against him, kissed his forehead, and said: "Harald — awake again? You've slept hardly at all for the last three nights. And in the daytimes you've been more asleep than awake, and so lost in your thoughts that you haven't noticed the food on your plate and have participated hardly at all in our conversations as a family. This afternoon, Anyu asked me if you were ill, and I said I didn't think so.............."

"I'm sorry, my darling," mumbled Keppel. "I've got a lot on my mind just now. I fear that I'm a bad husband and a bad father."

"On the contrary, Harald. Too good, if anything. Do you want to share...........?"

"Deep matters of state, Elise. I'm sworn to secrecy, and I take my diplomatic oath very seriously."

"I know that. I would never ask you to betray your trust. But I'll not lie here and watch you passing through purgatory. So, as a good wife, I'll help you. First, I'll make you a cup of tea."

She slid out of the bed and walked through the open bedroom door and along the passage to the kitchen. Somehow, she managed to walk without making a sound as her feet touched the floor with every step, and she moved more like a phantom than a woman made of flesh and blood. She was quite naked and unselfconscious, and her body was the colour of ivory, glowing in the diffused light from a multitude of small cracks and gaps in the shutters which were closed across every window. She liked to be naked in the three months of summer within her own home, behind the shutters, when Anyu was fast asleep — maybe because the air was warm, and because for the rest of the year she had to wear layers of furs during the time of darkness, when temperatures plummeted down to minus thirty degrees centigrade. She had a Danish father and an Inuit mother, and she was taller than any of the other women in the settlement. Harald Keppel thought her twice as beautiful as any other woman he had ever seen — but then maybe he was prejudiced. He was aroused, as he always was when he saw her naked, for she had a perfect female form, with firm upturned breasts, not too large, and a slim waist, and broad hips. She had not an ounce of surplus flesh on her, because she was immensely careful with her diet and hated with a passion most of the staple foods that other Greenlanders adored. She had pitch black hair which was long enough to cover her breasts and which she let down at night, just for him. She was a conscientious and loving mother too. Harald Keppel was a very lucky man, and for a while he forgot about matters of state and watched her through two open doors as she boiled the kettle, poured water into the tea-pot and then carried it with two cups on a tray, back into the bedroom.

She sat on the side of the bed, handed her husband a cup of tea, and then said: "I'll ask you no questions, husband, since you won't be allowed to answer them. But it's not against the law for me to speculate, or for you to remain silent. Correct?"

"Correct," he smiled. "Elise, do you know that you are a very cunning woman? I appreciate your kindness in making me a cup of tea, of course, but you know full well, from our eight years together, that whenever you walk about naked in this house, I am reduced to a quivering wreck. Do what you will, now that I'm incapable of resistance..........."

"Don't be afraid, husband. I'll be very gentle with you. But first, there's serious business inside your head."

"And that business is.................?"

"The safety of the Oxford expedition."

"How d'you know that?"

"Harald, you must remain quiet, or you'll commit a crime. Do you promise?"

"I do, Elise."

"Good. Let me explain. I see things, Harald, and I listen, and I talk to the people in the village. I watch old Pana Naukun, and I listen to his songs. I know what they mean. When Pana comes to talk to you, and when you are dealing with messages from Copenhagen or from Himmelbjerg, something happens to you, and I don't like what I see. I know about NAPRE, for I heard you and Alfred Jensen talking about it, even before those young men from England arrived at Blyhavn. At that time, it seemed that the NAPRE experiments would be interesting and even exciting — and there was no thought in anybody's head that somebody might get hurt. NATO needed to keep one step ahead of the Soviets, and our Government agreed with the research programme. Maybe you agreed with it too, on the record. Then, if I read the signs correctly, the young men arrived and things immediately started to go wrong. That devil Wagner, whom I hope never to meet on Earth or in Hell, was careless, and he told lies. Pana told me that, in a song. And I guess that the expedition members were more intelligent and more inquisitive than he bargained for............"

She stopped and looked at her husband. He remained expressionless, apart from the slightest hint of a smile on his lips. He took a few sips from his cup of tea.

"Then bad things started to happen. I do not know what, but there were many messages between here, and Copenhagen, and Himmelbjerg, and London. A ship and a submarine came into the fjords. Three fighter jets flew north and then south again, and on the way back to Keflavik one of them was without its full complement of weapons. The radio shack picked up a message — by accident, when I happened to be there — sent by Wagner to NATO, saying that two Soviet spies had been eliminated. It was encrypted, of course, but encryption in such circumstances is worthless if the man in the radio shack puts humanity above power politics. Erland Pettersen is a very brave man........."

Elise looked at her husband again, and he nodded.

"Then that poor young man called Linney is almost killed, and dies in hospital. And Alfred Jensen has an accident that everybody knows is murder. And four of the best young men from Sandvig are killed, leaving wives and children and parents behind, mad with grief and despair. There is deep, deep anger in this village, Harald. You know it, even though the Greenland Office in Copenhagen appears not to have noticed. And d'you know why they are angry? Because at least eight people have been killed inside the last month. Because they see a war going on around them — a war against the fjords and the mountains, against the animals and the birds and the fish, and against Nanuk. We Greenlanders do not understand war. We can't understand violence, unless it's in the necessary and respectful pursuit of resources for food and clothing. Pana says that the land is screaming, and that the spirits of the ancestors are wailing, and that he hears all of this on the wind. He said it in a song yesterday, on his singing rock by the western bay, and only I was there to listen to him. So I know more than enough. I know too much."

She stopped. She just sat there, in the dim morning light, as naked as a newborn child, with tears in her eyes. She stretched her hand out, and her husband took it.

"Then you received a message three days ago, just after you had been talking to the old man. Immediately something happened to you, and you have been troubled ever since. I don't know what the message said, but I think I can guess, since Erland told me that you had sent a message to London two days before. Why would you send a message to London, and not to Copenhagen? I know you too well, Harald Keppel. It can only have been to express your concern about the safety of the expedition members, and to ask for the NAPRE programme to be abandoned, and to plead for safe passage home for the young men. Correct?"

Keppel closed his eyes, squeezed her hand, and nodded very slowly.

"And when the message came back, it was a refusal to accede to your request, and a confirmation that the research would proceed, even if it led to the deaths of some of those innocent scientists in what the Americans, in the manner of savages, call "collateral damage." Some of them? All of them, preferably — because I think I know enough about the workings of the world to know that if even one of them should survive, and get home safely, every single event from this hellish summer would be revealed to family, and friends, and the media, and the whole world." She paused for a long time, and sipped from her cup of tea.

Then she continued: "So now, darling, you must decide what you will do. Where does your greatest duty lie? To your country and your Government and this thing called NATO, or to humanity? You can't greatly influence the course of events, I suppose, because you're in Sandvig and they are a hundred miles away, but I think that perhaps you are destined to play some small part either in the elimination of these young men, or their survival. In making your decision, you need to know that every man, woman and child in this village hates the Americans. They hate the way in which they have presumed to take possession of this sacred landscape, to wipe Syd Kap off the map, and to force five families to move to Sandvig, where there are too many people and too few seals. And they hate the fact that they are banned from moving about in their traditional hunting and fishing grounds in Hall Bredning while American warships and fighter planes go where they will and do whatever they like. Maybe my people would hate the Soviets too, if they were to be brutalized by them in the same way, but they have never encountered any of them, and so they are mystified when they are invited to loathe them in this thing which is referred to, strangely, as the Cold War. Harald, you might not have noticed it, but I've thought very deeply about what the consequences for this beloved land would be if Jim Wagner and the Americans were to succeed with this monstrous thing that they call NAPRE. Speaking for myself, I think we would have a land that I would want nothing more to do with......... for it would have lost its soul."

"So, my dearest wife, do you presume to know what I will do?"

"Yes, Harald. You and I have never yet disagreed on anything in our married life, and I know you as a good and honourable man. That's why I love you more than anything else in the world. You want this place to remain a place of beauty and peace, and a place with a soul — for us, and for our daughter, and maybe for children yet to be born."

Harald Keppel smiled. "I've never heard you talk like this before, Elise. You should have been a diplomat yourself, or maybe a revolutionary leader! You might yet be the first woman President of an independent Greenland. But that's for the future. And you're right. I know what I will do."

"Even if you might place yourself at risk in the process?"

"If you are prepared to accept that risk, yes."

Without another word, Elise took the cups and the tray away from the bed and took them back to the kitchen. Then she returned to the bedroom, still moving like a phantom. She closed the door, and slipped into bed beside her husband. She made the first moves, because she knew her husband was exhausted. But as her hands explored his body she worked her magic. Sometimes she was a plaything or a temptress, or even a wild animal, always with his full acquiescence. Today she was a sorceress. They made love with a ferocity that surprised both of them. Eventually they lay back exhausted. Then their fingertips touched again, and then their hands, and then their bodies.......... The whole process started again, and with equal ferocity they gave themselves to one another, uninhibited, free, sighing and laughing and gasping with the ecstasy of the moment. When their passion was spent, they came down from the mountain, easily, gently. Elise rested her head on her husband's chest, sought for his hand, and held it with fingers entwined. Almost immediately he dropped into a deep sleep. Sleep well, beloved, she thought. Peace at last.

After a while Elise opened her eyes, and she realized that the bedroom door was open. At the bottom of the bed was a small girl in a white nightdress, holding a doll in one hand and rubbing her eyes with the other. "Mama," she said, "You and Papa woke me up. Please can I play too?"

While the Frederiksdal party was asleep, the weather broke. Heavy cloud started to drift in from the east, and as the wind picked up the only able-bodied inhabitant of Base Camp had to batten down the hatches. Soon he was having to cope with a full-blooded gale accompanied by driving rain. That was unusual weather for East Greenland, since most deluges occurred in calm conditions. After what Horton himself had been through he took it as an opportunity for dressing his own wounds acquired during the desperate struggle with Petherton, and for pondering on the events of the past two month. With the others still asleep, he ate a leisurely breakfast and an even more leisurely lunch. Then Whiteside woke up, followed shortly afterwards by his colleagues, and the process of recuperation began. They noticed immediately that three men — Linney, Mortimer and Petherton — were missing, but Horton said he would explain everything later in the day. Knudsen quickly recovered some of his strength and took over as expedition medic, proving himself to be both caring and competent. There had been many calls upon the medical kit, but there were still a few ointments, bandages and plasters left, and now Knudsen needed to use most of them in his afternoon surgery session. All four of the new arrivals had quite serious injuries including gashes and scratches several days old that had not been treated, and a multitude of bruises. It was a miracle that they had come through their ordeal without any broken limbs. Horton gave his colleagues vast quantities of hot liquids, then easy foods in the afternoon and a more normal meal in the evening -- and by 8 pm they were able, for the first time since their reunion, to sit down on boxes in the mess tent together and to discuss their situation. As the evening went on, the wind swung towards the north, and the rain turned to sleet.

The bad weather was now a blessing, and Horton knew that it would give them a respite from any further attacks that might come from Himmelbjerg. First things first. Belatedly, he had to tell the new arrivals that Linney, Petherton and Mortimer were all dead. This was difficult for them to cope with, but he relayed to his colleagues as much as he could remember of the overheard conversation between Petherton and Wagner. They could not fully comprehend what was going on, but when Horton had finished his narrative, Hanna said: "That bit about Rowland dying in the hospital in Reykjavik. Did I hear you right? Could you have been mistaken? Could he really have been visited by somebody purporting to be a doctor, in his room in the hospital, and been given some lethal injection or something? Because somebody wanted him out of the way? Things like that do not happen in a civilized society, Joe!"

"I'm afraid they do, Steffo. And this is not a civilized society. I discovered that a long time ago, when I was in the Marines. There are some very dark forces at work here. Rowland had seen too much and maybe understood too much, and a decision was made that he should never be given the opportunity to talk to the media."

"Oh my God, what's going on here?"

"I might have some answers for you, boys," said Horton. "But first, I want to know what happened to you and your canoes. Tell me everything."

Two hours later the story was told, in a somewhat chaotic manner, sometimes with all of them talking at once. At the end of the narrative, Horton was quiet for several minutes. Then he shook his head. "Oh my God," he murmured. "Yet another so-called accident. I still don't know what the hell is going on here, but whatever it is, it's clear that those bastards in Himmelbjerg will stop at nothing, and that this thing called NAPRE wants us all dead."

"And that Mortimer and Petherton were somehow got at by NAPRE and turned into spies and homicidal maniacs........."

"That description seems to fit Petherton pretty well," said Hanna. "But not Griff Mortimer. From what Joe has told us, I'm convinced he was blessed with a streak of humanity."

Hughes nodded. "I agree. I talked to him a lot. He was unhappy, and weak, and caught up in something he didn't fully understand. May he rest in peace."

Then Horton jumped to his feet. "That's enough bloody misery to be going on with," he said with a grin. "Now for a nice surprise. You have some letters from home which I promised to deliver at the earliest opportunity." He went to a food box designated for the last phase of fieldwork, and pulled out a small bundle of letters. "These have been waiting for you for some little time," he continued. "I thought I'd better put them somewhere safe. Before Petherton and Mortimer left for Syd Kap somebody searched for them in my rucksack. In retrospect, that would have been that evil bastard from Oz, desperate to find out if they contained anything important."

He handed the letters to Hanna, Knudsen, Whiteside and Hughes. "I had one myself," he continued quietly. "From my old mother. She told me to come back safe and sound, to let her know about anything exciting, and to bring back lots of pictures for her to see............" As he spoke, he was close to tears.

There was silence while the four men opened their letters. Knudsen had three letters, one from his fiancee Maria in Denmark, one with an Oxford postmark, and one with no stamp or external markings, apart from his name. When he opened the envelope from Oxford, he found that it contained another envelope with "Joe Horton" written on it. Knudsen expressed his surprise and handed it over. It turned out to be from Susanna Smith in Oxford. Joe Horton was also surprised. He read it quietly, swallowed hard, and said: "I think I had better read some of this out for you, chaps. It was written on 18th July. God, that's almost a month ago. Right. Let's start here -- *"Dearest Joe, I'm sending this to Lars, because I think it's less likely to be intercepted and read by somebody who might not have your best interests at heart. I took it upon myself to do some research on some of the things mentioned in your letter from Blyhavn........"*

"Bloody smart, that girl," said Whiteside.

"You mean you got a letter out to Susanna before we walked over the mountains?" asked Knudsen.

"I did — sorry I forgot to mention it before. I gave it to the Icelandair pilot and asked him to post it in Reykjavik. I don't really know why, but I had a suspicion that if I had posted it in the Blyhavn post office, it might not have reached her -- or might have been read by somebody else."

"You've got a nasty suspicious mind, Joe."

"So have several others, I suspect. I was intrigued by some of the things I saw at the airstrip. Two aircraft parked up with no markings on them, for example. More Americans than Danes. We've discussed all that before, haven't we?"

"Some of us have, for sure."

"Then there was the mine worker who saluted to one of his colleagues. Miners don't normally give salutes to their mates. Anyway, to continue: *The first thing I did was to contact the Danish Embassy. I spoke to Lena Larsson, who was so helpful in getting us all the necessary consents in Greenland. I asked her about American military activity at*

Blyhavn, and she went suddenly quiet before leaving me hanging on the line while she checked with a colleague. Then she came back and said she knew nothing of military activity, although it was possible that the airstrip was used occasionally for the support of scientific parties in the field, and for moving equipment through to Summit Camp and Camp Century up on the ice sheet. I got a distinct sense that she was on the defensive, and that she was choosing her words very carefully. Funny, don't you think? To continue -- I tried to find out about NAPRE and followed your suggestion that it might be a cargo handling or transport company. I tried the Department of Trade here and then the Danish export people -- and nobody had heard of it or anything similar. I went to the Bodleian Library and looked it up in trade directories, since they have a fantastic indexing system. Nothing. By this time I was more than a little interested, so I rang my cousin Ellie in Chicago and asked her to check it out. Things are much more open over there. She rang me back next day. NAPRE is the Natural Processes Research Establishment, set up about two years ago on the same lines as SIPRE -- the Snow and Ice Research Establishment. It has several hundred scientists working for it in various parts of the world. There's virtually nothing on the record about it, but there is some military involvement and somebody mentioned NATO. Is Denmark a member of NATO? I suppose it must be. Final thing. Jim Wagner. He's a colonel in the US Marines. Is or was -- can't be sure. Ellie found various mentions in the press of his exploits. In 1958 he was a military adviser in Vietnam -- they called him "Mad Jim" because he had little regard for his own safety. He was also a brilliant leader and got into and out of some pretty terrible incidents. He was pulled back to the USA after some scandal involving a massacre somewhere near the North Vietnamese border. He was decorated and promoted -- Ellie can probably find the citation if we ask her. Anything else you need? I'll send this to Lars c/o the Danish Administrator in Sandvig -- best not to get caught up in the Blyhavn post office, if the military are operating there. At the airstrip they'll probably open all mail and read it -- or am I just being paranoid? Don't want them to read THIS, that's for sure.........."

Horton blushed slightly, and then grinned. "I won't read more, if you don't mind, boys, since it gets a bit personal, not to say intimate, towards the end of the letter.."

"Hmmm," said Hanna. "You've got a bloody good woman there, Joe. Don't let her slip out of your grasp."

"I think she's slipped away already, boys. Or I have. She's in Oxford, and I'm here, with not much prospect of getting out alive."

"Something in my letter too," said Hughes. "From my old man. He likes to keep in touch -- I'm not sure why he sent this to Sandvig rather than Blyhavn. Probably because he knew we would be picking up the good ship *Kista Dan* there on its last visit of the season, early in September. It's mostly family stuff in the letter, but he's an inquisitive chap, my Dad, and did some checking up on mining matters. Arctic Mineral Resources, the old operators at Blyhavn and Himmelbjerg, went bankrupt a couple of years ago and were bought by this new outfit called Greenland Metals A/S. The thing that undid AMR was the relatively low quality of the ore at Himmelbjerg, and the incredible cost of getting it out, over the Mellem Pass or one of the others, and then out by sea through the pack ice belt. He also says that the price of molybdenum on the world market has dropped even lower. And finally, he checked out Greenland Metals. The company is registered in Denmark, with two directors whose names are unknown in the mining world. There seems to have been no trading activity, and the company has submitted no accounts."

"So the company is just a front?" asked Joe Horton.

"Seems like it," said Hanna. "There's something seriously dodgy going on at Blyhavn and Himmelbjerg, and it's our misfortune to be caught up in it..........."

Whiteside, who had been deep in thought, then chipped in to the conversation. "Gold? We discussed the possibility when we were burying those bits and pieces of bones and flesh in Frederiksdal. What if Himmelbjerg has the world's biggest deposit of gold deep inside the mountain?"

"That wouldn't explain half of what's been going on," replied Hughes. "So -- US naval vessels in Hall Bredning and US military aircraft in and out of Blyhavn. An exclusion zone in the inner fjords, with even the Inuits banned from their own hunting grounds. Some strange research organization called NAPRE operating in the area, under the pretence of conducting high-value mining operations. And a mad American colonel conniving with that bastard Petherton to try and kill all of us. But why? Why would these people want to kill off all of the members -- with the exception of Petherton and Mortimer -- of a perfectly innocuous Oxford University expedition doing some exploring and a modicum of scientific research? No threat to anybody.........."

"But we are all assumed to be intelligent men who know the natural world," said Horton. "I've been pondering for some time about these unfortunate accidents which have struck us down from time to time. Haven't we all? Acts of God, we might call them. How many have there been? Six? Seven? And the only ones not to be involved in any of the incidents were Petherton and Mortimer. Mortimer got trampled by the muskoxen, but that was his own stupid fault. Most of the other accidents happened in places where Wagner knew we would be working on a particular day and at a particular time -- we've known all along that Wagner at Himmelbjerg and Keppel in Sandvig had possession of our full expedition work schedule, as well as having all our personal details on file. And I'm pretty sure -- but can't prove it because I haven't been at Base all of the time -- that both Mortimer and Petherton visited that bloody radio hut on the plateau shortly before each incident..........."

"You're right, my friend," said Knudsen quietly. "As we've been talking, I've looked at my third letter delivered to Gurreholm. Another envelope inside an envelope. It's from Dr Jensen, intended for you, Steffo, as expedition leader., and somehow sent from Himmelbjerg to Sandvig. On the outside, written in Danish, are the words *To be personally handed to Mr Hanna when neither Mr Mortimer nor Mr Petherton are present*. So, Steffo, here is your letter." He handed it over.

Hanna opened it and saw that it was written in Danish, in terrible handwriting, probably designed to deter would-be translators. He handed it back to Knudsen, and said "You'd better translate it if you can, Lars."

Knudsen took the letter, looked at it, and frowned. Then after a few minutes of concentration, he read out the letter slowly, translating as best he could. It said approximately this:

"5th August, Blyhavn.

My dear Mr Hanna,

This is for you personally -- a sensible and intelligent young man whom I greatly respect. Time is short, and I must be quick if I am to get this to Sandvig with a government helicopter that is going that way, in the hope that you will receive it before too many days have passed.

I have tried to warn you on two occasions that something very unpleasant is going on, which I have -- to my eternal shame -- been a part of. I have a duty to my country and to the free world, but I also have a conscience, and I have been deeply troubled of late because of what is being done here in the name of freedom. When I was asked by Harald Keppel to represent my country and help Jim Wagner's project, I leaped at the chance, because I love East Greenland as much as I love my home region of Fyn in Denmark. The project called NAPRE sounded exciting, but I had no idea when the experiments were being planned that eight bright young men would be put in harm's way -- and that the mad plans of Jim Wagner had all been approved by NATO, and therefore, I suppose, by the British Government too. My warnings were made at considerable risk to myself, since the helicopter pilot, Art Ruckle, is Wagner's closest friend who watches every move I make.

By the way, I am not party to everything here -- far from it -- but I think all the key decisions are made by somebody called PG1. I think that's a code name for Wagner, but I am not sure of it.

Also, some days ago the helicopter was scrambled and went off over the Staunings. It is rumoured that there are two Russian spies in the region, posing as trappers. I don't know what happened, but apparently when the chopper came back, Wagner and Ruckle had quite a party.

The Americans do not, I think, trust the ten Danes who work at Himmelbjerg. (It was with great difficulty that I convinced Ruckle to take me on the trip to deliver your birthday cake -- but he agreed to do it when I said we needed to know if your Base Camp party had all arrived safely, and if your work programme was on schedule.) When Linney was injured in the landslide, and you put up the emergency rocket, Wagner and Ruckle wanted to ignore it, but I convinced them that they needed a report from me on the consequences of the landslide -- so that's why we came. I anticipated that medical help might be needed. By the way, Linney has been sent to Reykjavik on an Icelandair DC3 that came in earlier with some cargo -- he is stable, and I hope he might recover. But I still fear for his life.

I must rush -- my friend wants to take off for Sandvig. One last thing -- I have a colleague who does some spells of duty in the Himmelbjerg radio shack. He passed me the transcripts of three messages from Pythagoras. You will not know this -- but there is a camouflaged radio hut up there on the plateau. The messages are sent to PG1 and they are signed by AP and GM. You know who they are -- watch them carefully, for I fear that they are capable of anything -- including murder. I know for a fact that AP triggered the landslide that almost killed Linney and Horton, and that GM triggered the iceberg collapse and the long swells that almost overwhelmed you at the mouth of Konglomerat Elv.

I must go. God bless you all and keep you safe.
Your friend
Alfred Jensen."

For a minute or two, nobody spoke, but there was a lot of thinking going on. Then Whiteside said: "Poor old bugger. Now he's dead too, unless the Greenlanders are very much mistaken."

"Murdered, of course."

"But he fell into a crevasse..........."

"Nobody falls into crevasses on the lower parts of glaciers at this time of year," said Hughes. "Pushed, or thrown in -- but murdered, for sure."

"I agree," said Horton. "Mortimer knew about the warning scribbled onto the side of the package when they dropped the birthday cake. He must have reported that to Wagner. The doctor must have known that his days were numbered............"

There was another long silence as they all tried to digest the latest information. They were all having great difficulty in making connections and working out motives.

"So.........." said Hanna at last, with a frown. "One thing at a time here. Number one. We have two Russian spies in Frederiksdal -- murdered in cold blood and left for the hungry wolves. Not by Ruckle. He must have been piloting."

"Maybe by Wagner himself? He seems like the sort of fellow who would enjoy a jolly manhunt from the safety of a helicopter. Maybe he got lots of practice in while he was in Vietnam."

"Hang on for just a moment, boys," said Whiteside, groaning and dragging himself to his feet. "Time for exhibit number one. Joe, old fruit, where is my anorak?"

"In that pile of filthy rags that used to be clothes. Outside the door, to the left."

Whiteside went outside and returned a minute later with a metal cartridge case in his hand. "Picked up at the scene of the slaughter," he said. "I thought it might come in handy some day. It's been in my inside pocket all this time." He handed it to Horton, who examined it for some time.

"A standard brass M80 ball case," he said. "Can't be sure of it, but probably fired from an M60 machine gun. A few years back it became standard issue for the US Army and Marines. I used one myself in 1956. Perfectly easy to use from a small helicopter platform, and with 600 rounds a minute a man running away isn't going to survive for long.........."

"What were those Russians doing in Frederiksdal anyway?"

"A hell of a distance from Himmelbjerg. Maybe they were planning to reach it through the back door -- it would have been too obvious if they had approached from either Blyhavn over the mountains, or from Syd Kap and up the Schuchert Valley. Maybe they planned to walk through the Alps and then get to Himmelbjerg from the west, by walking down one of the glaciers?"

"That ties in with the ropes and the crampons in the hut close to where they were shot. So what were they planning to do when they got to Himmelbjerg? Just spy on it?"

"Maybe -- and then get out on a Russian nuclear sub, after a pick-up at Syd Kap?"

"God, this all gets a bit like a James Bond thriller -- too much, too much. We'll probably never know the full background. But it's the foreground that really worries me."

"So the nightmare unfolds," said Hanna. "Ten men dead already, by my reckoning -- four Inuits, two Russians disguised as Norwegians, Dr Jensen, those swines Petherton and Mortimer, and poor Rowland as well. And all because of some bizarre experiments involving simulated natural disasters or Acts of God, triggered off by one or other of those treacherous bastards who are no longer with us......."

"Or maybe by one or other of the warships?" speculated Horton. "If they really have been lurking about, out of sight, in Hall Bredning and in some hidden stretches of the fjords, they could have played an active role."

"You may be right!" exclaimed Whiteside. "Do you chaps remember that just before we were swamped by those waves in the fjord, we heard and felt a slight humming and vibration in the water. Could that massive tabular berg roll have been caused by a torpedo?"

"Distinctly possible," said Horton. "When I was in the Marines we did an exercise in Norway, and that involved subs and torpedoes. I was in the water wearing frogman kit, and heard every torpedo that was fired long before it hit the target..........."

"That must be it!" said Hanna. "And when the *Mikkelsen* was sunk we all noticed the strange smell in the air following the explosion. It was strange -- not quite the smell of diesel or paraffin fumes. Another torpedo strike on a big iceberg?"

"Those things I understand, friends," said Knudsen. "But what about the other explosions? Alfred Jensen said Petherton and Mortimer triggered off at least two of them, but how could that be? Were they prowling about in the mud, lighting fuses and then running like mad to get out of the way before getting blown up?"

"Not needed, Henrik -- in this day and age a radio signal is all that is needed. If Wagner has been a military adviser in Vietnam, he will know all about explosives, batteries and radio controlled trigger mechanisms. Remote control is the name of the game these days. Place the charges when it suits you, and set them off from the comfort of your own private radio hut."

"But we have seen no helicopters or other vehicles carrying and laying charges........... "

"There's been some helicopter traffic, but mostly a long way off. Remember that Wagner had our work schedule, and knew exactly where we were likely to be, and when. All of the charges could have been laid in the week or so before we arrived, or even earlier, if snow conditions allowed. People from Himmelbjerg might have set the charges in the north, and the crews of the *Ellsworth* or *Pole Star* could have done the work in the south. Now that I think about it, the vessels might even have specialist explosives teams on board. I wouldn't mind betting that there are still some other explosives out there, in places where they expected us to be working......"

"Let me help you with that, boys," said Horton, grinning through his bruises. "I have here a bit of paper....."

"Oh God, not another one?"

"It's my pleasure to collect them. I found this one in the radio shack, on a box next to the transmitter. It's a list of a dozen place names with codes next to them, which I don't understand. Some of the names are ticked, and some are crossed off. The ones crossed off are Nordøstbugt, Holger Danskes Briller, Roslin Glacier, Schuchert River, and Nordvest Fjord. All of those are places where we've had close encounters with the Grim Reaper. I assume that the other ones that are ticked are the places where charges have been set but not yet triggered."

"It all makes sense," murmured Knudsen. "Summer was early this year. When we arrived and walked over the mountains, most of the snow was gone, and the chaps at Himmelbjerg told us that they had had a long spell of warm dry weather in June. Setting the charges would have been very easy indeed."

"But why? Why? I just don't understand......"

"Excuse the pun, old man, but we're in the middle of the Arctic's own peculiar Cold War," said Whiteside, sounding like an old uncle explaining something complicated to a small child. "The Americans have hundreds of people working on future warfare planning -- futurologists, think tanks and scientists all beavering away, trying to work out what'll be going on in ten or twenty years' time. We probably have secret units in

Britain too, doing the same sorts of things. I've heard of SIPRE -- I was on a climbing expedition once with a fellow who worked on SIPRE projects. We were stuck in a bivouac for 2 days and passed the time by talking a lot. The real reason for SIPRE is to increase the capacity of the American military to operate in very hostile environments in the Arctic. That's why they have Camp Century and Summit Camp and also a presence at Station Nord — to the irritation of the Danes. Everything is tested to destruction at those places where temperatures go down to -50 degrees C -- aircraft landing gear, living quarters, tracked vehicles and sledges, cold weather fuel, rocket propulsion, radar installations and so forth. Camp Century even has a nuclear reactor. You aren't supposed to know that."

"But they could do all of that in Alaska if they wanted…….."

"Think strategy, old man. North Greenland is perfectly placed for long-range missiles, either coming from Russia or heading that way. Alaska's a long way from Moscow. Kennedy is just as paranoid as his predecessors, and I wouldn't mind betting that there are early warning installations up and running in North Greenland, and even long-range missile launch pads. There's something strange going on up at Station Nord, right on the northern tip of Greenland. That's only about 500 miles from the North Pole, and almost 800 miles away from the big American base at Thule. Keflavik in Iceland and Blyhavn in Greenland are key parts of the communications network if the weather shuts off the west side of the ice sheet."

"You are very well informed, Peregrin…….."

"My dear fellow, most of what I've studied on my PPE course has been way over my head, but the contemporary politics lectures are rather intriguing. My old man was a Foreign Office minister once, and although he was very discreet at home, I overheard a lot of dinner party conversations. Maybe I'll become a Prime Minister one day -- or maybe not, since I am probably not quite stupid enough…….."

That relieved the tension to some degree, and they were all able to laugh. But the fugitives from Frederiksdal were still very tired, and Hanna in particular could hardly keep his eyes open. So Horton said: "Boys, we need more sleep. As long as it's sleeting and raining, as it is now, we're safe, but if this weather clears we're in harm's way again.

Wagner will come looking for us, that's for sure........."

"Looking for me, more like," said Horton. "He'll assume, quite correctly, that I've killed Petherton and destroyed the radio hut on the plateau. He probably heard the commotion before the radio went dead. He seems to think the rest of you have already been safely disposed of."

"But he'll want to confirm that. Tomorrow we have some planning to do, if we're to get out of here alive..........."

CHAPTER 11
August 1962

On another day of low cloud and intermittent sleet and rain the seven survivors worked out how they might stay alive. It was taken for granted by all of them that the scientific work of the expedition was now at an end. Whiteside had even given up on his lettuce patch, since his seeds had failed to germinate. Not only would fresh work be impossible, but it was highly probable that the samples collected, maps made and surveys completed would all be lost to science. They regretted that, for some of them were young men set on finding jobs in science laboratories and in university teaching. They had been counting on publishing papers and reports which would, in normal times, have helped to further their reputations and their careers. All of their plans and aspirations had melted yesterday like snow in an oven, when the full horror and complexity of the situation had become apparent to them. Even if they managed -- by some miracle -- to get back to Britain, nothing would ever be the same again.

One advantage was that the bad weather gave the men from Frederiksdal one more day for recuperation, and another was that none of their injuries was bad enough to slow them down, should any forced marches prove necessary. They assessed their resources. There were just a few food boxes left at Base, but there were also half a dozen in scattered depots set up for future parts of the planned work programme, and some at Syd Kap and Gurreholm. Virtually all of their personal possessions including tooth-brushes and razors were gone. All of their cameras and the movie camera had been smashed or lost. There was still some fuel left at Base, and a full jerrycan down on the shore of Nordøstbugt. At Base they were left with just two two-man tents and the mess tent. The latter had to be used for accommodation as well as for eating and cooking. They assumed that the inflatable boat and motor would still be at Syd Kap, unless Petherton had destroyed them before climbing up onto the plateau for his last fateful radio schedule. Knudsen knew of five small depots in various places where food might be available -- these had all been left by geologist Lauge Koch and some of his field parties over the past decade. He also thought that there might be some tins of food in three trappers' huts which were within striking distance.

The nights were now starting to get gloomy, if not actually dark, and it looked as if the autumn storms were coming early this year. That was an advantage for them since Wagner and the forces of darkness would have to depend on helicopters and launches if it came down to a man-hunt. They had another advantage in that Wagner thought that only Horton was alive. But they were short of winter clothing, and although there were a few warm garments left behind at Base by the men who were now dead, they knew that they could not survive once the winter set in -- and they knew that they would be in serious trouble even if there should be a temporary snowy spell with sub-zero temperatures within the next few weeks.

"Now then, boys," said Hanna as they huddled into the mess tent at breakfast time, "we need to make some smart predictions. I reckon that as soon as the weather clears, Wagner will send a helicopter to that burnt-out radio hut on the plateau to check out the damage and to remove Petherton's body. He'll assume that the bastard is dead, because otherwise he would have put up a rocket. Agreed?"

"Perfectly logical, Steffo."

"And while they are on the way to Pythagoras Bjerg, it is not much of a detour for them to come here. They'll think that if Joe is alive, this is where he'll be. On the other hand, they might calculate that he'll go to Syd Kap in the hope of being picked up by the Inuits when they come to pay their respects at those graves."

Horton nodded. "Yes -- agree with all that. So we'd better get the hell out of here. Where to? Answers on a postcard, please......."

"Not Gurreholm or Syd Kap, that's for sure. Far too obvious. And not anywhere under canvas either. These bright orange tents are made to be seen from miles away, not to blend into the landscape. They'll be bloody obvious from the air anywhere within fifty miles of here, even with the flaming colours of autumn all around us."

Knudsen smiled and said: "So it has to be the cave on Karstryggen, gentlemen. It's quite big, and hard to find. D'you think that Wagner and the others at Himmelbjerg will know about it?"

"You're a genius, Lars!" said Hughes. "It's incredibly well hidden from the air, and even when you are right next to it you can't see the entrance........"

"Hang on a moment," said Horton. "Griff Mortimer was with us when we stopped at the cave on the walk down the valley. Andy Petherton wasn't -- he was in the sick bay at the time. Might Mortimer have told him about the cave? And if so, might Petherton have told Wagner about it?"

"Well, I've no recollection of us ever talking about the cave in Petherton's presence, when we were all at Base Camp."

Whiteside frowned and added: "Joe and I were at Desert Camp when Petherton arrived from Himmelbjerg with the helicopter. We were together for a few days, but I don't recollect that we ever went near that limestone plateau, or talked about the cave. Correct, Joe?"

"I agree. Maybe we'll just have to take a chance on it. There's another thing in our favour. Those guys at Himmelbjerg and Blyhavn don't go anywhere on foot -- so I'll bet my bottom dollar that none of them has ever walked across the Karstryggen or poked around among the boulders in that gorge. Any better ideas?"

Nobody could suggest anything smarter, and so it was decided. They would move to the cave, although it was almost twenty miles away and brought them closer to the enemy when all their instincts were to go in the opposite direction. Knudsen said that they had two or three days at the most, to make the move. "This bad weather will continue for several days," he said. "It always happens in late August when the summer comes to an end. Then at the beginning of September we will have cold nights and bright days. On some mornings there will be a film of ice on the water, if it's calm. Then it'll begin to snow. Then the lakes will freeze. And then the first new ice will appear in Hall Bredning, and it'll gradually thicken. By mid-September, nothing will be able to get in or out of Sandvig because the old sea ice and drifting bergs will be packed in between Cape Tobin and Cape Brewster. That's why the last boat always gets out by the tenth day of the month, to be on the safe side.............."

"The last boat out?" said Hanna. "Now there's a nice thought. Shall we aim to be on it, boys?"

There was no response to that, as the reality of their situation hit home with even greater force. They all knew that their chances of getting out of East Greenland via Sandvig on any boat at all were next to zero. But then Horton said: "We'll be on it, boys. I promise you..........."

"That's for the future," said Knudsen. "Thinking about today, what do we do about the people from Sandvig? They plan to come over today, if my calculations are correct, to pay their respects at the graves of their loved ones. They'll be very determined, and will come even if the weather is poor. Maybe they're at Syd Kap already. Griff Mortimer had promised to meet them and to show them the graves........"

"Only Steffo and I know where the graves are," said Hughes. "I can walk over to Syd Kap and help them, if they come."

Hanna frowned. "The Americans may stop them. After all, they've declared Hall Bredning to be a prohibited zone."

"I doubt the Greenlanders will be stopped," said Knudsen. "From what I know of them, they're pretty determined, and smart too. And the Americans will calculate that stopping them could cause an international spat with Denmark; these after all are devout Christians wanting to pay their last respects to loved ones who have died in tragic circumstances."

Whiteside said he agreed with that, and added: "The'll also calculate that nine out of the ten of us are probably dead. To cover all eventualities, I guess that they'll come with that American research ship in attendance, or even with a Yank on board, just in case Joe might be waiting for them at Syd Kap."

Outside, the sleet was still swirling around the camp site, and there was a bitter wind from the north. Some of the men were still very weak, but they knew that if they were to survive, they could not delay. It was decision time. On the assumption that the *Ymer* might come to Syd Kap at any moment, the decision was made that Horton and Knudsen should go to the old settlement to await its arrival, to check on the inflatable and the engine, and to work out how much food was available. If the Americans turned up, they would simply have to seek to avoid any

214

contact with them -- and maybe also avoid any contact with the Inuits. Hanna, Hughes and Whiteside would walk to the Karstryggen cave under cover of the bad weather and set up a base there. They would take as much food and vital gear as possible with them, including the two small tents. They would also pick up whatever food they could scavenge from the old Lauge Koch geology camps. The other two would join them in the cave as soon as possible. Then they would lie low -- maybe for a week or more -- while Wagner and the Americans from the naval ships searched the area and satisfied themselves that there were no survivors.

Three hours later, Horton and Knudsen were at Syd Kap, having walked over the plateau in appalling conditions, with wet sleet swirling around them on the lower slopes and driving snow on the plateau. As they dropped down the final slope towards the bay, the sleet turned to rain, and it looked as if the low cloud out in Hall Bredning was beginning to break up. They opened the door of Hotel Paradiso and peeped inside, satisfying themselves that nobody had been there within the last few days. They were cold and wet, but they dared not light a fire in the stove for fear that the smoke might be seen. More to the point, they could not even enter the building, out of concern that they would leave wet footprints and pools of water on the floor. They decided not to take off their wet things until they could settle into one of the semi-ruinous huts further along the shore, which was much less likely to be visited by those who would come in the boat from Sandvig. They found the inflatable boat and the motor, unharmed, on the beach where Petherton had left them, and hid them inside one of the ruined buildings. Then, with the weather clearing all the time, they waited near the "hotel."

Late in the afternoon they heard the sound of a boat engine in the distance, although visibility was too bad to see any vessel, big or small. Knudsen said that it sounded like the *Ymer*, with the "put-put-put" of an old-fashioned two-stroke engine. He was sure it could not be a modern launch that might have come from the USS *Ellsworth*. The men had worked out a strategy to cope with all eventualities. Horton went gingerly into the main room of the hut, trying desperately not to leave any footprints or water droplets behind him on the floor. He left on the table a battered copy of the map that Hanna and Hughes had made of the Bear Islands, showing the exact locations of the four Inuit graves. He placed next to it a note which Knudsen had written in Danish, saying *"If there are no foreigners with you, and if it is safe to do so, come and talk to me in the cellar of the warehouse next door."* Finally he took out of his inside anorak pocket four gold rings given to him by Hanna, and placed them on the map.

The pair of them then hid in the filth and debris beneath the semi-ruined warehouse, knowing that they were taking a calculated risk. There was a chance that an armed American might come and arrest them or even kill them -- but there was also a chance that a friend might come, and that the friend might speak Danish or English. At last they heard the *Ymer* running onto the gravel beach. They heard somebody jump down onto the beach and go into the house. They clearly heard heavy footsteps on the floor. One person, or more, pacing back and forth for several minutes? Whoever it was went outside again, and they heard the door slam. Then they heard footsteps crunching across the gravel to the warehouse. Somebody came round to the battered wooden door and opened it. From the darkness of the stinking cellar, they saw a figure silhouetted against the light.

"Lasse, are you there?" said a voice in Danish. They were amazed that the voice was that of Harald Keppel, the Danish Administrator.

"Good God! Harald, you are the last person I expected!" said Knudsen from the darkness. "Are you alone?"

"Yes. The Greenlanders have remained on the boat."

"No Americans on board?"

"No. But the *Ellsworth* is just off Syd Kap island. We're being watched, but with these flurries of rain and sleet, they won't see much. Best that we talk here in the cellar. But I must be quick."

The two men emerged and shook hands. But there was no time for formalities or niceties.

"How did you manage to get past the *Ellsworth* and into Syd Kap?" asked Horton.

"It wasn't easy. We were intercepted by the ship. I went on board and insisted to the captain (a tough fellow called O'Brien) that we were on a journey of great spiritual significance, and that as Danish Administrator I was accompanying ten Eskimos on a journey to find the graves of the four who were drowned when the *Mikkelsen* went down. He wanted to put an observer on board, but I refused point blank. I said this was Danish sovereign territory, and that I wouldn't allow any intrusion into the grief of my parishioners. In any case, I said, the boat was overloaded as it was, with eleven of us on board. He backed down, but I had to agree that he could keep us under observation here at Syd Kap, shadow us across to the Bear Islands, and finally search the *Ymer* before we make the return journey to Sandvig."

"Bloody paranoid, they are," said Horton, shaking his head. "So no free ride for any of us, back to the civilized world?"

"Afraid not, gentlemen."

"I assume that you know much of what has happened?" asked Knudsen.

"Only as much as Wagner has told me, none of which I believe, and what I have been able to piece together from Alfred Jensen's messages and from intercepted radio messages. We have a very good radio operator in Sandvig, and you would be surprised to know what eavesdropping he has been able to do. How many of you are alive?"

"Five of us. The others are Hanna, Hughes and Whiteside."

"And the two CIA men?"

"What? Were Petherton and Mortimer CIA agents?"

"Of course. Why else do you think you were "encouraged" by that Professor of yours to pull them onto your expedition in spite of them being unknown to any of the other members?"

"Are you suggesting that Davies was involved in this conspiracy?"

"I know it to be true. Another CIA man. Anyway -- those two colleagues of yours. Alive or dead?"

"Both dead."

"Hmm. That makes things even more complicated," murmured Keppel, with a frown on his brow. "The Americans get very upset when their agents get rumbled or bumped off. But thank God five of you are still alive. Now we have to make sure that we get you out of here and back to Britain. Forget about your plans for travelling home on the *Kista Dan*. She will be watched too closely. I've got other plans. Can you all get to Sandvig by 10th September?"

"We can try. That gives us just over three weeks to evade whatever search parties the Americans throw into the area. We can hole up in the cave, and maybe do a forced march to Sandvig at the last minute, hoping for bad weather and no aircraft overhead."

"I don't think they'll try very hard to find you. They think only Joe is still alive. If they can get him, they will call off the chase and concentrate on sweeping all the areas you have worked in, so as to remove all traces of your camps and your depots."

"I don't like the idea of being a sacrificial lamb," said Horton.

"Never fear, Joe," said Knudsen with a grin. "We love you too much to let you go to Heaven. Besides, we need you here on earth, since we have other things to do which might be just up your street."

"One last thing," said the Danish Administrator. "From now on, I have an intuition that timing will be critical. You know what date it is?"

"Yes — 18th August," nodded Knudsen. "I try to keep track, even if the others don't."

"And the time?"

"No idea. Maybe about seven in the evening?"

"Not a bad guess, Lasse. But don't you have any working watches between you?"

"All lost, Harald, in the assorted disasters that have overwhelmed us, except for the one picked up in Frederiksdal by Perry Whiteside. He's the only one who knows what time it is, and he's elsewhere."

"Very well," said Keppel, taking a Rolex watch off his wrist. "Lasse, this is rather precious — a gift from my father to commemorate my appointment as Administrator at Sandvig. Your need is greater than mine. You can borrow it for two or three weeks, as long as you promise to return it to me undamaged when you get to the village."

A seaman on the USS *Ellsworth* was carefully watching the shore through high-powered binoculars. Through a break in the flurries of sleet, he saw some activity at the top edge of the beach, behind the warehouse. "Captain!" he yelled. "There's something going on over there........."

The captain, and various others, watched intently as the Inuits jumped off the *Ymer* and milled about on the beach, finally getting some shovels from the big building and digging a deep hole in the gravel above high water mark. Then they went into the Administrator's House and carried out something heavy, wrapped up in tarpaulin. They placed it reverently into the hole, and then stood around it with heads bared and bowed while Harald Keppel conducted some sort of ceremony. To the watchers, it looked like a brief burial service. Then the participants filled in the hole and and stood together. They seemed to be singing a hymn, and this was confirmed when snatches of the plaintive sound reached the *Ellsworth*, drifting on the wind across the bay. Then the Inuits all filed back onto the boat and it was pushed off the beach before heading straight across to the Bear Islands, weaving in and out as it encountered the drifting icebergs coming out of Nordvest Fjord. O'Brien had a dilemma. Should he send some men ashore to check out what had been going on, or follow the *Ymer* across Hall Bredning in case Keppel and the Inuits try to pull some stunt or other? He chose the latter course, on the basis that he could always put a party of seamen ashore later, who could undertake a thorough search of the ruinous settlement.

The *Ymer* was heading south from the Bear Islands, en route for Sandvig. The weather was still calm and overcast. The sea was the colour of lead, with an oily sheen typical of the time when the freeze is starting. Ten miles offshore, the *Ellsworth* made the arranged rendezvous with the little green cutter, three hours later than planned. The Americans were not best pleased with that long delay, since they had other orders, and other things to do. Two seamen came aboard the *Ymer* and searched the cabin and the little hold meticulously, to make sure that there were no extra passengers who might have been smuggled on board in Syd Kap. Then Harald

Keppel went on board the *Ellsworth* and met the captain.

"Thank you, Captain, for your sensitivity," he said. "My parishioners appreciate the fact that you have not intruded into their grief."

"You found the graves OK?"

"Yes indeed. When I went into the Syd Kap house I found this on the table, with four gold rings resting on it." He showed O'Brien the scruffy map with the positions of the graves marked on it. O'Brien nodded.

"It must have been left there by one of the party which worked on the Bear Islands and witnessed the accident. The gold rings were from the fingers of the four dead men. Those Oxford fellows had been sensible enough to remove them from the bodies before they buried them, as a means of identification. I was able to return the rings to the four wives who are with us on the boat today -- they recognized them immediately as belonging to Christian, Joshua, Petter and Eskil. As you will understand, it was a very emotional moment for them. Many tears were shed.. ...."

O'Brian looked uncomfortable. "Quite so. I fully understand that..........."

"With the aid of the map we were able to find each of the graves. We covered them with the heaviest stones and with as much soil as we could find, and erected four wooden crosses brought with us on the boat. You'll understand, Captain, that these are not called the Bear Islands for nothing. There are possibly no polar bears here at this time of year, but in the winter this is a favourite haunt, and they can smell a frozen corpse even under five feet of snow. They may smell the bodies, but we hope that we've now taken sufficient measures to prevent them from getting at them and tearing them to bits. You understand the sensitivities of the wives in this matter?"

O'Brien looked even more uncomfortable. "Yes, yes indeed, sir."

"Anyway, we conducted a short ceremony at each grave, and then went on our way. The wives and families will now consider that there has been some sort of closure, and they can grieve properly at home, in their own community."

"What were you doing on the beach at Syd Kap? We could see that there was something going on."

"I was coming to that. We found a body in the house, on the floor just inside the door. We know his identity. I had met him once before, but that was before he grew a beard. This is what we found in the pocket of his anorak."

He handed O'Brien a weatherbeaten and stained polythene bag containing Horton's battered passport. It was wet and smudged, and was falling apart, but the photo was just about recognizable, and the name and number were legible.

"His clothes were covered with blood. When I examined him I found that there was a bullet embedded in his stomach. Poor fellow must have died in agony. He must have walked to the hut in Syd Kap from a long way off, in spite of his injury. He was thin and emaciated, and his clothes were soaking wet. His hands were lacerated and bleeding, and his trousers were worn through -- his knees were scratched and bleeding too. I think he must have staggered and even crawled across some very rough terrain. Not a pretty sight, captain..........."

"Bad business, Mr Keppel. May I keep this passport?"

"Indeed you may not! This is my jurisdiction, and I must report this death and give this passport to the Coroner. This has all the signs of a murder, as you'll appreciate. Murders hardly ever happen in Greenland, and the whole nation will be shocked when news of it gets out. There will have to be an inquest, as there'll have to be one for the deaths of the four Greenlanders. But feel free to copy down the details so that you can check its authenticity. The passport number is, I think, just about readable."

"Very well -- I accept that you must follow protocol. So you buried Horton on the beach?"

"What else could we have done? We couldn't have taken his rotting corpse on the *Ymer*, that's for sure. We did our best to give him a good Christian burial."

"That does you credit, Mr Keppel. I think we can now go our separate ways. I'll report the death of this guy Horton to Jim Wagner. I'm sure he'll be interested to know about it."

"Indeed he will. One last request, Captain. You are, I take it, a

Christian?"

"A good Methodist, and proud of it, sir."

"I might have guessed. Tell me, what's your procedure on board when you show your respects to someone who has just died?"

"Generally the crew lines the deck and salutes while we play the Last Post."

"I'd like to ask a favour, Captain. Would you do that as a mark of respect to those whose deaths have brought us here? And out of respect for Mr Horton, who has been most cruelly killed by some assassin or other -- presumably one of his own colleagues?"

Captain O'Brien spluttered but really had no option in the matter. So with as much good grace as he could muster, he called the crew to order. The wind had dropped away to the gentlest of breezes. The *Ellsworth* lay still in the ice-infested water, with the low hum of the engines hardly disturbing the silence. With the occupants of the *Ymer* standing on the deck of their little craft a hundred yards away, the Last Post was sounded. Keppel stood next to the saluting captain, and buried his face in his hands. It looked to the rows of naval personnel on the deck that he was overcome with emotion; but in spite of the solemnity of the occasion he was in fact trying to suppress a wicked grin.

The plaintive notes of the bugle echoed around Hall Bredning, and the sound reached the distant shore at Syd Kap. Horton and Knudsen, sitting at the table in the Hotel Paradiso, had been waiting for it, without believing that it would actually come. They burst into hysterical laughter, embraced one another, and congratulated themselves that another hurdle had been cleared. All being well, Wagner would now believe that all of them were dead. Then they became serious again, and talked for hours about dead friends and lost innocence, before settling down for the night.

CHAPTER 12
August 1962

The weather was clearing rapidly, and the sun was strong enough to wipe away all traces of the sleet and snow of the previous three days. Wisps of low cloud were swirling about in the Schuchert Valley as the ground warmed up, but the mountains were still hidden. A helicopter appeared from the north, flying very low and heading directly for Base Camp. All of those who heard it knew that it was the Bell 47 from Himmelbjerg, and assumed that it was piloted by Art Ruckle. It landed on a gravelly patch near the only tent still standing -- the mess tent -- and the engine was shut down. Three men climbed out. One of them carried an M60 machine gun and kept watch while the others examined the camp site minutely. There was one sleeping bag in the tent, left as it might be if somebody had climbed out of bed and left suddenly. They noticed that the sleeping bag had blood stains on it. There was not much else to be seen -- hardly any food, just half a jerrycan of paraffin, and assorted bits of scientific equipment. The pilot, who was indeed Art Ruckle, went back to the helicopter and talked to Jim Wagner on the radio. Then he returned to the camp site. The three men talked briefly, and then gathered up everything they could find, including scientific instruments and boxes of botanical and zoological samples. They piled everything inside and around the tent, splashed paraffin over the pyre, and set everything alight. While the fire raged they stood back and admired their handiwork, and then, when they were satisfied that there was not much left, they turned away from the smouldering pile of debris and climbed back into the helicopter. They were content that anybody who came here in the future would refer to the results of the conflagration simply as "a tragic mystery."

The Bell 47 then made the short trip across to the Gurreholm Hut, which was now bathed in beautiful autumnal sunshine. Ruckle and his companions satisfied themselves that there was nobody there and that there were no signs of recent occupation. Then they flew on to Syd Kap and landed on the beach not far from the big hut which others called Hotel Paradiso. They checked the elongated pile of stones and rubble just above high water mark and saw the name *Joseph Horton (1937 - 1962)* inscribed on a rough cross. They checked the house and the warehouse, and satisfied themselves that there was no sign of life anywhere. Ruckle called Wagner on the radio once again, and they had a brief conversation. Then they flew up onto the plateau, where there were several patches of thick cloud which forced them to proceed cautiously. But Ruckle had a good memory for landscape features, and he had been here many times before. At last they spotted the burnt-out remains of the radio hut on the side of Pythagoras Bjerg. They could not land next to it, because it was in an area of broken scree and large erratic boulders, so they had to land over a slight brow on a patch of flat gravelly tundra, about two hundred yards away. Ruckle remained in the helicopter while the other two went to the hut and confirmed that the radio was smashed to smithereens, and that the charred corpse of Petherton was still lying on the floor, three days after he died. It was not a pleasant sight, since it was starting to decompose and was buzzing with flies. The two men were under orders to remove all traces of the radio shack and its equipment, just in case anybody should pass this way in the future. They swore, and complained that they always got the filthiest jobs while all the others were swanning about at Himmelbjerg. They walked back to the helicopter and shouted to Art to come and help them to clear up the mess, to bury the corpse, and to dump all the charred cables, batteries and radio gear into holes among the rocks. He grumbled, but agreed, and the three of them returned to the site of the hut, carrying picks and shovels.

As soon as they were out of sight, Joe Horton jumped out from behind the huge boulder where he had hidden the toolkit from the hut and the clips of ammunition for the pistol. He raced to the helicopter, and worked quickly with a spanner and a pair of electrical pliers. He concentrated for a couple of minutes on the inside of the cabin, but he also had time to clamber up onto the roof. Then he sprinted back and hid beneath the rock again. He was well pleased. "Bloody good timing," he gasped. "Six minutes and twenty seconds." After about thirty minutes the three men returned to the helicopter, having completed their gruesome task. Ruckle started up the engine, switched on the radio and reported to Wagner: "All sorted, Jim. The body is buried and the radio and batteries are disposed of in a deep hole and covered with rocks. Now the site looks like a temporary camp of some sort, or maybe a bird watching hide, accidentally destroyed by fire."

"Any sign of how that miserable bastard Petherton died?"

"Couldn't tell. His body was in a hell of a mess. His guts were sliced open. But I reckon the flames actually killed him. The lamp was on the floor, and I suppose it must have got smashed in the fight with Horton............"

"OK -- he's now out of the way as well. You might as well come back to base."

"Will do. Over and out."

The helicopter took off and flew straight out over the steep edge of the plateau, setting a course directly back to Himmelbjerg across the eastern Holger Danskes Briller lake. A couple of minutes into the flight, when they were over the deepest part of the lake, the engine suddenly revved up and raced out of control, and a rotor blade flew off. The helicopter went into a vicious spin and then exploded into a ball of flame. From an altitude of about three thousand feet it spiralled downwards, spewing smoke and flames and bits of metal. It smashed into the milky glacial water and disappeared, leaving an oil slick on the surface.

Back at Pythagoras Bjerg, Horton and Knudsen heard, but could not see, the accident. Suddenly everything was quiet.

"Three less to deal with," said Horton. "How many more to come?"

"You are a ruthless bastard, that's for sure," said Knudsen.

"Survival of the fittest, old man. That's what I was taught in the Marines. Now then, shall we try to get some miles under our belts on the road to the cave, before they come looking for the chopper?"

All five of the fugitives were in their new home at last, and they had made themselves reasonably comfortable, given that the cave was dark, stony, dusty and smelly. It was a fine morning, and there was heavy helicopter and fixed-wing aircraft traffic up and down the valley. It had started at about 7 am, and as the hours passed the traffic built in intensity. The cave-dwellers peeped out every now and then, when they thought the coast was clear.

Just before noon, Hughes took a quick glance outside and immediately ducked back in again. "Bloody hell!" he exclaimed. "Don't like the look of this. Two heavy helicopters I haven't seen before — headed straight for us, flying maybe a couple of hundred yards apart and less than fifty feet up!" They were not really surprised, for they all knew now that this was a part of a systematic search across every square inch of the territory beneath the snowline. They were apprehensive to say the least, and their greatest fear was that military personnel knew exactly where the cave was, and were coming to check it out. Alternatively, troops might be landed in order to conduct a foot search across the bleak limestone plateau of Karstryggen. They took refuge in the back of the cave, not sure whether the extra boulders that they had placed across the entrance would render it completely invisible from above.

One of the fearsome monsters was now directly overhead, the downdraught from the heavy rotors drumming onto the ground and even causing hot fume-laden air to stream into the cave. The noise was so deafening that the inhabitants had to cover their ears. Horton whispered (unnecessarily in the circumstances) that he thought the helicopter was a Sikorsky Seahorse -- widely used by the military and capable of heavy lifting. It could not have been more than thirty feet above them, and they were convinced it was going to land. For an age it hovered overhead. Had the pilot spotted something from the air? They hardly dared to breathe, let alone speak --- but then the sounds of the beating blades and screaming engine changed pitch, and the helicopter moved off, and they breathed again. They thought that maybe the pilot had considered landing, but had been put off by the great boulders littered on the limestone surface.

After that, it was an afternoon of furtive glances up and down the valley and frantic retreats into the dark safety of the cave. The men saw that the light aircraft from Blyhavn had also been deployed, together with a Norseman float plane which they thought might have landed on Holger

Danskes Briller. They were not sure where that had come from, but knew that they must have been searching for the missing helicopter as well as for traces of the expedition members and their camp sites.

The activity continued for another full day, but nothing came as close as the Sikorsky. Then at about 8 pm the weather closed in again with grey cloud and drizzle, and the sound of aircraft and helicopters faded away. The men in the cave assumed that the search had been called off. They gained some reassurance from the fact that they had not seen any searchers moving about on foot, and this suggested to them that they had witnessed a futile airborne search for the wreckage of the helicopter which was now resting on the bed of the eastern Holger Danskes Briller lake.

Under the cover provided by the weather, the five comrades brought into the cave all the supplies they could find within striking distance, mostly from old research camp sites and trappers' huts. They ended up with a strange assortment of tinned and dried foods, some inedible and some so old that they were probably toxic by now; but they were in no position to pick and choose. They had more than forty tins without labels on them, and ran a sweepstake to guess what one of them contained. The bids on the table were carrots, potatoes, mackerel, peaches, sardines, pineapple slices and diced vegetable soup. Knudsen got it right, and so the others each owed him a pint of Heineken next time they came anywhere near a bar. They settled down to make the best of their voluntary imprisonment, with the Frederiksdal party getting stronger with every passing day as they worked their way through the bonus food supplies. They planned to start their walk to Sandvig between the first and fourth days of September.

Then Horton produced a bundle of documents which had been handed over by Harald Keppel when they met in the warehouse at Syd Kap. He had kept them in his rucksack for three days -- and having glanced at them in a rare moment of privacy, he had judged that they needed to be looked at when they were all in the right frame of mind.

"Now then, boys," he said. "Take a look at these. You'll not like what you read, but the words will help to stiffen your spines..........."

"Don't we know enough already to conclude that the whole bloody world has gone mad?" grinned Hanna. "Shock me if you can, Joe. Go on, read them out."

Horton shrugged, and explained that documents were all official messages which were supposed to have been encrypted before being sent from Blyhavn to NATO and the Danish and British Foreign Ministries. Probably they had gone to the Pentagon as well. He said that according to Keppel, these were the original drafts, kept by the radio operator when encrypted versions were transmitted, in contravention of the rules. Then he read out the first document, with the following text:

TOP SECRET. All versions encrypted

Stage 1 NAPRE Experiments East Greenland 1962:
1. Tsunami generated by iceberg rolling (various tests in Hall Bredning, where effects can be observed from Observation Post). Various sizes and types of icebergs, some stranded and others in deep water, various triggering experiments -- type 2 explosives, cold climate batteries, use of torpedoes if required for larger impacts.
2. Tsunami generated by cliff fall or landslide. Chosen locations: Hells Bells near Syd Kap and N wall of NV Fjord near Magetuen. Simultaneous explosions by 20 charges in a row along foot of cliffs.
3. Destructive flood associated with breach of ice dam at a glacier snout. Chosen location: The big lake in the area of ice-cored moraine around the snout of Roslin Glacier.
4. Landslides capable of taking out road or rail communications. Chosen locations: cliffs in valley near Syd Kap, and cliffs overlooking Holger Danskes Briller. (Note: There are bigger cliffs in some of the remote ice-free valleys, but these two are more accessible.) Late spring / early summer preferred.

Stage 2 NAPRE Experiments East Greenland 1963:
1. Tsunamis from ice front calving. Chosen site -- snout of Daugaard-

Jensens Glacier.
2. If these are successful, glacier surge triggered by melting of glacier base. Chosen locations: two glaciers known to have surged -- Oxford Glacier (very small) and Bjornbos Glacier (larger -- easily accessible from Himmelbjerg.)
3. Even more large-scale -- fracturing of winter sea ice to disrupt travel on "winter ice roads". Chosen research area -- coastal districts patrolled by the Sirius Sledge Patrol.

"So there we are then," said Hughes. "All neatly laid out. We thought we were coming to Greenland in order to undertake some research on rocks, plants, muskoxen and glaciers -- and all the time we were lined up to be the rats in a series of large-scale laboratory experiments."

"Bastards!" shouted Hanna. "This is more or less what we worked out for ourselves the other day. They probably expected at least some of us to die................"

"And remember, friends," said Knudsen quietly, "that this was not just the expectation of Wagner and the captains of the US vessels. The expectation must have been shared by NATO and the Danish and British governments."

"So much for our naive belief in the sanctity of human life," said Hughes. "I think I'm getting disillusioned and cynical in my old age."

"And this is just the start. Look at those Stage Two projects planned for next year -- the scale of those is phenomenal. Trying to break up huge areas of winter sea ice will involve explosives on a vast scale -- God only knows how they will keep the explosions quiet. Maybe they have a slow and quiet blasting technique? And triggering a glacier surge is something that will require heat above all else........enormous quantities of it."

"A nuclear reaction or nuclear waste? After all, they have nuclear submarines, and they have nuclear power at Camp Century. Not beyond the bounds of possibility..........."

"The rape of this beloved country," said Knudsen. "We are the only ones who can stop this happening. Are we agreed?"

"But how?" asked Whiteside. "We are effectively impotent, my dear fellows. We are woefully ill-equipped. We are low on food supplies, have no means of travelling about except on foot, and we've got no proper winter gear. Besides that, we're unarmed.............."

"Wrong, Perry," said Horton. "We've got one pistol and six rounds of ammunition from the radio shack up on Pythagoras Bjerg. It's a pity we lost those two Armalites that the Russians had in their possession. But on the positive side, we also have a few rocket distress flares and smoke canisters............"

"That doesn't exactly make us the best prepared guerrilla army in the world, does it?"

Nobody replied. No matter what their enthusiasm for a campaign of revenge attacks or sabotage might have been, the reality of their situation was beginning to hit home. Horton sensed that the atmosphere was becoming heavy with gloom. So he said: "There's more. Feel like another document, gentlemen, just to cheer you up? Here, Gwyn, you read this one."

This is what Hughes read out:

Press Notice 17 August 1962. Embargoed to 1 am on 18 August 1962
Danish Embassy, London
TRAGIC DEATH OF GREENLAND EXPLORER
The tragic death has occurred of Greenland explorer Rowland Linney (23), a member of the Oxford University Scoresby Sund Expedition which has been undertaking scientific work in the fjord country of East Greenland.

It is understood that Mr Linney and a colleague were caught up in a devastating rockslide that occurred not far from their Base Camp in Kjove Land. Fellow expedition members raised the alarm, and a helicopter from the Himmelbjerg Mine, about 50 miles away, was scrambled with a doctor on board. Mr Linney was unconscious at the time he was airlifted, and after further medical assessment at the Blyhavn airstrip, he was transferred to Reykjavik for expert medical treatment. Sadly, he died before it was possible to operate on his injuries.

Reacting to the tragedy, the manager of the Greenland Metals Himmelbjerg Mine, Mr Jim Wagner, said: "This is an appalling incident, and we send our deepest sympathy to Mr Linney's family. We did everything in our power to assist as soon as the expedition sent up a distress rocket, but there was nothing that our own medical staff could do for the young man. That having been said, we did warn the expedition members of the extreme dangers of working in this hostile Arctic environment, and we expressed our concerns about their lack of air support and their determination to manage without radio communications. Young men will always want to do adventurous things, but sometimes they take foolhardy risks, and place their own lives -- and the lives of others -- in jeopardy."

Commenting on the tragedy, Prof Adrian Davies, the expedition's home member in Oxford, disagreed that the expedition members were ill-prepared and inexperienced. He said that all ten members of the expedition had been hand-picked to give a balance of scientific expertise and Arctic field experience. But he did concede that the expedition would probably be the last of the old-style expeditions in which research scientists actually walked in and out of their field area and in which they had no radio or other communications with the outside world during the field season. "We were aware at the outset that such a degree of self-reliance and self-confidence would bring with it a high level of risk, given the likelihood of severe and dramatic natural events in a hostile field environment."

Mr Linney was a research student at Magdalen College Oxford, after obtaining a first-class degree in Zoology. He was working in Greenland towards his doctorate in marine biology, studying the feeding preferences of seals in the Greenland fjords. His parents and two sisters live near Edinburgh, and we send them our deepest condolences.

At the time of going to press, it has not been possible to contact the other members of the Oxford University expedition to inform them of the untimely death of their colleague. It is not known, therefore, whether the expedition will be continued or abandoned. The other members had planned to depart for home in early September on the ice-strengthened cargo vessel Kista Dan.

ENDS
Ref: PG1/01

"Oh my God. I wonder who wrote it?"

"It's in the reference number at the end. PG1 -- Jim Wagner. It's interesting that he had a quote from the Prof -- so there must have been radio messages flying back and forth between Himmelbjerg and England."

"He's another treacherous bastard -- and to think that we trusted him! Damning us with faint praise, and then putting the boot in by suggesting that we are — or were — a bunch of romantic and incompetent idiots."

"Look at the date -- 18th August. This will have been all over the media almost a week ago. I bet they had it written even before poor Rowland died. You can be sure that there will by now be widespread commentary in the papers about our supposed incompetence. Look at the way the whole thing is crafted -- the agenda is to refer over and again to the hostile Arctic environment in which almost anything can happen and in which lives can be lost in the blink of an eye. Wagner is pushing the NATO line just as he is paid to do."

"So what other delightful literature do you have for us, Joe?"

"Another press release, dated 20th August," replied Horton.

"So that, too, will now be in print all over the world?"

"Quite probably. This is what it says:

Press Notice 19 August 1962.   **Embargoed to 1 am on 20 August 1962**

Danish Embassy, London

MYSTERIOUS   DISAPPEARANCE   OF   GREENLAND EXPEDITION MEMBERS

A large-scale search has been under way in the fjord country of East Greenland for the seven members of an Oxford University expedition who have not been heard of since the beginning of the month.

Following the death some days ago of zoologist Rowland Linney in a Reykjavik hospital, attempts were immediately made to inform his colleagues, but it has proved impossible to trace any of them. The Danish authorities in Sandvig and Blyhavn have copies of the expedition's planned work programme, and searches have been made at all the locations in which the scientists might have been working. Helicopters and light aircraft from the Greenland Metals mine at Himmelbjerg have been deployed in scouring the fieldwork area, but no trace has been found of any of the missing men. Volunteers from the mine have also examined some of the key locations on foot, at considerable risk to themselves, and the US government has diverted two of its research vessels into Scoresby Sund to take part in the search by land, sea and air.

The only trace of the expedition is a burnt-out Base Camp not far from the old Eskimo settlement of Syd Kap. The mine personnel who found it said that there were no bodies there, but the conclusion is inescapable that some disaster -- or perhaps a series of disasters -- has befallen the expedition members.

Mr Jim Wagner, mine manager at Himmelbjerg, about 50 miles from the Base Camp site, said that he had used all the resources at his disposal in the search, but that he was now convinced that none of the missing explorers was still alive. "This is a very hostile environment," he said, "with rolling icebergs in the fjords, frequent snow avalanches, unstable rock faces and glaciers that behave unpredictably. The weather is now closing in, and when temperatures dip below zero the rivers and then the fjords will begin to freeze. Any men caught in the open without proper clothing will stand very little chance of survival. It's our belief that the expedition members were not equipped for survival in Arctic winter conditions."

The United States Embassy in London confirmed today that the two un-named American vessels have now been withdrawn from the search in view of the increasingly difficult ice conditions in Scoresby Sund. Also, with low cloud, sleet and snow now affecting the scientist's field area, searches from the air have also had to be called off.

Speaking from Oxford, a distraught Professor Adrian Davies, representing the expedition members, said he could hardly believe what had happened. "I have to accept now that the expedition members, whom I looked on as dear friends, have been lost without trace, and that they *may never be found. I now have the unenviable task of contacting all the the families of the missing men, to tell them that they must fear the worst."*

There have been occasional deaths on Arctic expeditions before, but the last time that a full expedition was lost without trace was in 1845, when a ship-borne expedition led by Sir John Franklin disappeared in Arctic Canada during the course of a search for the North-West Passage.

This is not a time for recriminations, but we understand from contacts within the community of Arctic scientists that the members of the OU Scoresby Sund Expedition were enthusiastic and skilled in their own fields, but were perhaps unprepared for the vagaries of the weather in the Greenland fjords and the dangers of travelling on foot in very hostile terrain. Questions will now be asked about whether any expeditions should be allowed in Greenland in the future without regular radio communications and planned helicopter backup.

The UK Foreign Office in London, which takes responsibility for foreign expeditions in the field, was not available for comment today, but a spokesman did confirm that the search for survivors has now been called off.

ENDS

Ref: PG/02

"So, gentlemen, we've been given up for dead," said Hughes. "Are we surprised?"

There was a long silence. At last Hanna shook his head and said: "I don't suppose we are. But what does surprise me is the extent of duplicity in all of this -- it looks as if the US government, and the governments of UK and Denmark, are all signed up to this version of events................"

"All members of NATO, dear friends," said Rasmussen quietly.

"Another press release written by Wagner. I can hardly believe the extent of his influence."

"True. But this goes far higher than Wagner. He's just the miner at the coal-face. We have to conclude that it's the policy of Her Majesty's Government that we should be dead, and that we should remain dead.

234

We're looking at highly sophisticated news management."

"They're lying, cynical bastards, the whole lot of them," said Horton in a voice surprisingly free of emotion. "I'm less surprised than the rest of you. Remember that I did a stint in the Royal Marines. Truth? Ethics? Loyalty? Don't make me laugh..........."

"But that press release is crap, Joe, from top to bottom. The whole story's fabricated. Surely any good investigative journalist will discover that most of the contents of the press release -- presumably now used worldwide -- are demonstrably false?"

"Demonstrably? And how the hell will they get out here to East Greenland to check the facts? Not the slightest possibility. Nobody can get in here this late in the season, and even if some journalists come rooting about here next season, what will they find? Nothing at all."

"But some people will talk, surely? Himmelbjerg staff? Harald Keppel and the Greenlanders from Sandvig?"

"The Inuits can probably be frightened into silence. They hate conflict. As for Harald Keppel, I think I might fear for his life. Look what happened to Alfred Jensen when he allowed humanity to trump his oath of secrecy."

"You mean that all these people swear oaths? I thought all that came to an end with the death of King Arthur?"

"Not so, my friend," chipped in Knudsen. "All of the Danes in East Greenland -- with the possible exception of some of the trappers -- are government employees, either inside or outside of the military. Even the Sledge Patrol members belong to the Army. Harald Keppel is a trained diplomat. If we don't survive, I suspect that the story he'll give to reporters will be exactly the same as that of Jim Wagner. He has a wife and family to look after, and he'll want to save his skin."

"And all of the Americans at Himmelbjerg and Blyhavn are probably military personnel anyway. It will be a clever reporter who gets a squeak out of any of them. Forget it.........."

"This has all been coordinated with military precision. At this end, Wagner gets rid of all of us, leaving no trace that we ever existed, apart from the burnt-out tent at Base -- and maybe, in months to come, some bits of flotsam and jetsam caught up in the sea ice or washed up on the shore. Out there, in the big wide world, they're selling two messages. One, that we are -- or were -- a bunch of irresponsible adventurers who disregarded the warnings of others and deserved whatever fate had in store for us. Two, that the Arctic is a place where Acts of God happen on a dramatic scale -- thus promoting the NAPRE mythology and military strategy at the same time. Bloody clever -- and the media know so little about this part of the world that they'll believe every word of what's in the press releases."

For a long time there was silence, as they all tried to work out the full implications of what they had just heard. There was fear in the air, thought Horton, but also a deep anger which had replaced the earlier pervasive gloom. "So, dear friends," he murmured at last, "we'd better survive. Agreed?"

"Agreed, Joe," smiled Hanna, getting up from the large limestone boulder on which he had been sitting. "And I think, all things considered, that I'm going to be very bored, festering in this miserable grotto for another eight or ten days. I feel a change of plans coming on."

"Quite understandable, my dear fellow," said Whiteside. "I really think that a trip up to the sunlit mountains and glaciers would lift the spirits enormously. I'm fed up with the morbid vapours of the Schuchert Valley."

"Ah! That reminds me," said Horton suddenly, digging into an obscure pocket in his anorak. "I knew there was something else! Another piece of paper........"

"Oh God! Another one?" groaned Hughes. "You're in the wrong profession, Joe. You should be a courier, or a postman. What have you got in your other pockets -- the Encyclopedia Britannica?"

"No, no," he laughed. "That great row of tomes is full of useless information. I know, because I ploughed through one volume after another when I was a kid. My speciality is useful intelligence. This is just another scrap of paper I found in that radio shack, in addition to the list of sites, when I had the unfortunate encounter with Andy Petherton. I didn't understand it before, but I've just had a flash of inspiration about its full significance."

CHAPTER 13
August 1962

On 23rd August the ragged and unkempt occupants of the cave heard aircraft engines a long way off to the north, but they saw no further planes. They assumed that Himmelbjerg was being evacuated or -- more probably -- made ready for winter. The weather was on the point of breaking, and soon it would be impossible to get anything in or out, either by air or through the use of the Caterpillar trains. They also accepted that USS *Pole Star* and USS *Ellsworth* would have left the fjords, heading for home, and would by now be out in the Atlantic, clear of the thickening pack ice belt.

Late in the afternoon Hanna and Hughes trudged across the Karstryggen limestone desert back to the cave entrance, carrying supplies which they had collected from locations within a ten-mile radius. Whiteside had arrived shortly before them, after visiting two sites where he had found explosives, just as predicted by Joe Horton. Horton himself, accompanied by Knudsen, was expected back at any moment from a long trek to depots in Kjove Land. It was Hanna's turn to make the supper, and so while he worked on his culinary delights inside the cave, the other two sat outside on the rocks, and relaxed. Whiteside immediately noticed that Hughes was tense and silent, and said: "What's the trouble, Gwyn? You look as if you have the weight of the world on your shoulders."

"Maybe I do, Perry," replied Hughes. "I'm probably six inches shorter than when we started, from being weighed down. I wonder how many tonnes of stuff we have lugged about since we arrived in this goddam country?"

"You're young and fit, old fruit," grinned Whiteside. "You can cope. And all this Sherpa portering stuff was not exactly our choice, was it? Force of circumstances. But we're after all still alive, and one has to plan to keep it that way. Think positive!"

"I try to, Perry, but we have one hell of a problem on our plates, and it's been bothering me today— going round and round inside my head while we were climbing up to rather precarious locations and picking up those explosives."

Whiteside slapped him on the back, and said: "I thought you were a bit off colour today, my dear fellow. Come on — spill the beans. Your secrets are safe with me."

"Very well. Yesterday we all decided, in a moment of euphoria, that we would attack Himmelbjerg, using all these explosives we've been gathering up. Do we actually know what we're doing, and why?"

"I think we know exactly what we're doing, Gwyn," said Whiteside, speaking slowly and deliberately. "And the decision wasn't made in a moment of euphoria. I think we all realized, simultaneously, that we have absolutely no alternative."

"Don't we? For a start, it's bloody suicidal, and I reckon our chances of getting away with it are a thousand to one, at best...........""

"And what other cunning plan might you have, my dear fellow, which might increase our chances of survival?"

"Well, we could march up to the mine, and offer a truce. Or maybe kidnap somebody, so as to improve our negotiating position?"

Whiteside smiled indulgently. "Gwyn, all of us will have thought of that scenario. But let's get real here. Wagner is a homicidal maniac. But he's just the chief executioner. The real decisions are made by the politicians. If Joe has reported correctly on what he heard in the radio shack on Pythagoras Bjerg — and we have no reason to disbelieve him — and if all those messages which we looked at yesterday are authentic, we have already been declared dead. All of us. That last press release that we looked at has already, no doubt, been given saturation coverage throughout the world's media. Radio, newspapers, television, you name it........ And government statements will have been made in the UK and Denmark. All of our nearest of kin will have been contacted by the Home Office or the Foreign Office, and our families, God bless them, will be grieving their losses. These people are all bastards, and if this hadn't happened to us, I would never have believed it as being possible in any civilized society. Don't you get that?"

"I do, Perry," said Hughes, with a flush on his cheeks. "But I still want to be sure we're exploring all possibilities here. Couldn't we miraculously appear, and be welcomed with open arms by Wagner and his staff, and by the governments of the UK and Denmark? There would be fantastic global publicity — "Explorers return from the dead" and so forth. One of the great survival stories of all time! Wouldn't that be good for everybody, including NATO, NAPRE and the politicians? A great feel-good story in the middle of the Cold War — just what the nation needs!"

"Gwyn, you are a bloody good member of this team, and I'm lost in admiration for the way in which you and and the others have coped with one disaster after another. But I'm afraid I can't sign up to your benevolent and optimistic view of the state of play. Let's look at the real world here, old fruit. OK — so we march up to Himmelbjerg, or even turn up at Sandvig after a long slog across Jameson Land. What then? D'you think they'll cheer and deliver us back to the UK and Denmark as heroes? There's zero chance of that happening. D'you know why? Let me tell you. Because whatever happens to us, there has been murder and manslaughter already, on a substantial scale. Four Greenlanders, Alfred Jensen, two Russians, and our poor friend Rowland. Add Griff Mortimer if you like. Nine men dead — and Petherton too, who got what was coming to him, thanks to Joe. So that's ten. God only knows — there may be more. We know all about those deaths, and they know that we know. We even have a bundle of incriminating evidence, including some rolls of exposed film and one box of exposed movie film that Lasse left at Base Camp before the movie camera was lost. If any one of us gets out of here alive, d'you know what'll happen? There'll be a media feeding frenzy, and whoever it may be will be cross-examined, and subjected to such intense pressure from all sides that the truth cannot and will not be suppressed. We know that, and so do they. And they know that we're bloody angry about what happened to poor Rowland. As for us, how many times have we all managed to escape from the Jaws of Death? More times than I care to count. Will we be able to go through the rest of our lives by maintaining a sort of diplomatic silence, or by telling an endless string of lies? Bloody impossible. Sorry, Gwyn. I have to say this, but you're being as naive and trusting as a newborn baby."

There was a long pause. Then Whiteside chuckled, got up and

slapped Hughes on the back. "Don't take that too hard, Gwyn. I mean no offence. But it's true. This Greek Tragedy's gone so far now that in the last act, it's us or them."

Unexpectedly, Hughes smiled. "Thank God for all of that. Those are exactly the sort of things that have been going round inside my head for hours — even for days. We Welshmen tend towards introspection. I hereby accept the decision of the Democratic Republic of Kjove Land, as the only means possible of defending our territorial rights in the face of unprovoked aggression."

"So do I!" shouted Hanna from inside the cave. "I heard all of that, while slaving over a hot stove in the interests of the starving masses. No sign of Joe and Lasse yet?"

"They're on the way, my dear chap," said Whiteside. "I saw them just now, maybe a couple of miles away, climbing up from the Gurreholm Gorge. Supper on the table please, in half an hour, with the best silver cutlery. If this is the Last Supper, we might as well enjoy it in style."

"One further moral dilemma, boys, if I may," said Hughes. "I haven't finished yet..........."

"Oh God, is there no end to this moral philosophy? And just before supper, too. Can't we leave it until later on, when we are sitting before the fire in our arm chairs, with port and cigars?"

"Sorry, but I need to clear my head on this one. And it's serious. I've never killed anybody before, and I don't want to start now. So we're resolved to attack Himmelbjerg with explosives. Regardless of what happens to us, what if those guys who work inside the mountain get injured or killed?"

"I'm afraid that casualties are inevitable, Ed. We've no option but to take them by surprise. Or d'you think we should politely ask them to get out of the mine and assemble on the glacier where it's safe, while we blow up everything inside the mountain? I'm sure they would be only too delighted to cooperate.........."

"And remember who these guys are," added Hanna, coming out of the cave and wiping his hands on his filthy trousers. "They're not mining engineers and geologists. They're probably all US Marines, seconded to NAPRE and fully signed up to what Wagner is doing as his contribution to the Cold War effort. Take it from me that they'll be heavily armed, and that they'll know all about hand-to-hand combat. If we get into any close quarters fighting with them, we all know who the winners will be. Joe might survive, because he's a tough bastard who knows what he's doing, but the rest of us will be dead meat."

"Very well — I think I can accept all of that. But what about the Cold War and the political decisions of the Government and NATO? The men in Himmelbjerg are not our enemies. They're our allies. Won't we be committing treason and assisting the Russians if we go through with this?"

"Thus spake Saint Edward of Cambridge," chortled Whiteside. "Again, commendable sentiments, my dear old thing. But once again, get real. I'm not sure I want to support the Americans in whatever Cold War stunt they are planning to pull — probably against the Soviets, and dragging along assorted reluctant NATO allies. Maybe they haven't learnt anything from the Bay of Pigs fiasco, or maybe they're intent on demonstrating that they're not always totally incompetent. I wouldn't mind betting that something big is planned, and it would give me some pleasure to stop the bastards."

"So, Lord Peregrin Whiteside, you're a man with politics in your blood. Is it possible to commit treason against your own country, when your own country is trying to kill you?"

Whiteside looked surprised, and then said: "Haven't got a clue, old fruit." He paused and struck a pose rather like that of The Thinker in the famous statue by Rodin.

After a while he continued -- and his face was serious. "My considered legal opinion. I should have thought that if a country abandons its moral code and does things that are inimical to the interests of its citizens, or becomes involved in brutal and oppressive behaviour, then those citizens could probably argue in the International Court of Human Rights that they have a duty to resist, and to seek to restore morality. In short, they would probably be justified in doing whatever it takes simply in order to protect their fundamental right to freedom of speech and freedom from fear and want — or just to try and stay alive. It may be that national laws, if they have been twisted or distorted against the interests of the populace, are then overridden by international law, or by some sort of common law or moral code applicable to the whole of humanity........"

"Good God, man!" said Hanna. "I didn't know you knew so many long words. That's all mightily impressive, I must say. Whatever you said, I'm sure you're right."

Hughes frowned. "But we might not even be killing our own countrymen here, if it comes to a matter of killing or being killed. We will be killing Americans. President Kennedy will not be best pleased. Mind you, those particular Americans have blood on their hands — lots of it."

"Retaliation is long overdue, old man," came the reply. "The only reason why we beat the Light Blues during the Varsity Match of 1961 was that we got our retaliation in first. We had five Welshmen in the team, and they argued the moral case very convincingly. Gwyn, I know you have an analytical mind and considerable moral scruples, but remember that we've no time here for contemplating our navels. Winter is coming, and we've neither the clothing nor the food supplies to survive, even if we retreat to somewhere like the Gurreholm Hut. Himmelbjerg will be evacuated within the next few days; if we don't deal with Wagner and the rest of those cowboys now, it'll be too late. They'll be off to Blyhavn and then away to Keflavik — and then they'll be back next year for the next phase of this insane project. And be sure of this — if we then return home from Greenland some time within the next few weeks, or reappear anywhere in the western world, we'll be quietly eliminated one by one, by whatever means may be appropriate. I foresee lots of unfortunate accidents — or at the very least we'll be arrested and shut away somewhere on some trumped-up charges of treason or whatever. The media will probably be prevented from reporting. We simply know too much to be allowed to live. I don't know about you, but I don't want to spend the rest of my life in hiding, and I don't feel inclined to die young either. Gwyn, you have a bloody good woman waiting for you, by the sound of what you have told us about her. And so do I. D'you want to see her again, or don't you?"

"Emotional blackmail will get you everywhere, Steffo," grinned Hughes. "I agree with everything you two have said, as it happens. So in this Strategy Committee we're agreed unanimously. I just wanted that established, beyond all doubt."

Just then there was a shout from a hundred yards away, and Horton and Knudsen were silhouetted against the reddening evening sky as they strode homewards, bearing bulky packs full of explosives. "Come on Steffo, you lazy bastard," shouted Horton. "We're starving. Isn't the tomato soup on the table yet?"

By the following day the temperature had plummeted, and the expedition survivors knew that from now on night-time temperatures would be well below zero. As if to emphasize the point, a skein of maybe sixty pinkfoot geese flew noisily overhead, in strict V-formation, heading south. There was snow in the air, and Knudsen thought that this might be the first significant snowfall of the winter. Maybe it would melt in September, and maybe not. It was time to go onto the offensive, and for the fugitives to become saboteurs. They already knew a great deal about what was going on, but there were other pressing questions to be answered, and the only person in Greenland who could answer them was at Himmelbjerg. Their assumption was that God would still be in his Heaven, believing that all was well with the world which he surveyed from his observation window.

They were 30 miles from the mine, but thought they could get there in two days if they travelled light. The twilight was becoming more pronounced each night, glacier melting was now much reduced, and they were sure they could cross the meltwater streams without ropes and maybe without even getting their feet wet. Plans were laid. They would take no tents or sleeping bags, no Primuses or fuel, and very little food. In other words, they would go for broke, as Shackleton and his colleagues had done when they crossed South Georgia at the end of the ill-fated *Endurance* expedition in 1916. Before they set out, they covered their already filthy red anoraks and orange over-trousers with mud and green slime from the cave. That made them look and smell disgusting, but Horton insisted on it, and said that the whole point of camouflage -- in

243

any environment -- was to be as socially unattractive as possible.

When they stepped outside the cave and headed north most of the weight in their rucksacks was made up of explosives. They had spent two days collecting them from the locations listed on the scrap of paper found by Horton in the radio shack. He had worked out that the code letters referred to the types of explosives set, together with the configurations designed by the Americans to achieve the greatest possible impacts. They were lucky that not all of the sites designated for Acts of God had been utilized and not all of the explosives planted had been detonated. They had investigated four sites, two of them very difficult to get at without helicopters, but Whiteside and Hughes had shown themselves to be first class climbers, and they had come down from their hazardous missions with enough explosives to have blown up the Pentagon.   They could have collected batteries and radio equipment too, but those items were too heavy and had less intrinsic value.

On the first first night out, the five comrades sheltered near the snout of the Roslin Glacier and saw the huge gap cut by the torrent which had almost cost Horton his life. In the distance, about fifteen miles away, they could see some lights flickering like stars at Himmelbjerg, so they knew that people were still in residence there.

"While we grovel about down here in the mud," grumbled Whiteside, "those fellows up there are probably in the canteen, enjoying their supper. Fish and chips, maybe? I'd die for fish and chips just now, with the Beethoven violin concerto in the background. Strange, what deprivation does to you……….."

"Don't be so bloody stupid," said Hughes. "Beethoven doesn't go with fish and chips. Anyway, it's scientifically proved that the Americans all live on hot dogs, popcorn and donuts -- and if they're listening to anything, it will be Elvis, at full blast. Seriously uncivilized they are, these ex-colonials."

They all slept fitfully under their bivouac sheets, and woke up to find that the cloud had come down again, and that there was incessant drizzle. Visibility was very low. The temperature was falling, and they knew from the rawness in the air that the drizzle would soon turn to snow, which would help to conceal them. They only had three pairs of gloves between them, and they took it in turns to use them in order to keep their hands from freezing. They ate a high-energy breakfast of chocolate bars and Kendal mint cake. Then they moved cautiously along the valley side until they came to the Schuchert Glacier moraine. By now it was snowing gently, but with enough breaks for them to make out the main features of the landscape. This was the point at which, as planned, they split into two parties. Knudsen, Horton and Whiteside were to continue on the west side of the valley, getting as close as possible to the mine before setting foot on the glacier surface. Hanna and Hughes would cross the valley and walk up the east side, climbing onto the chaotic piles of broken rock around the snout of the Sirius Glacier. Both groups had to gamble on there not being much of a lookout from the observation window high on the mountain, now that they were all assumed to be dead. They had only two watches — one on Whiteside's wrist and the other (belonging to Harald Keppel) in Knudsen's possession. On checking them, they found that they gave the same time, to within a few seconds. The Dane handed the borrowed Rolex to Hanna, urging him to look after it very carefully.

The parting was much more difficult than any of them had anticipated. They had been through more than a few life-threatening situations together, and there was now a tighter bond between them than any of them had ever experienced before. They knew that following this farewell within sight of Himmelbjerg they might never meet again. Every one of the five men knew that their chances of getting away from Himmelbjerg alive were very slim indeed, for they had no idea how well the mountain was defended. Embraces would not have been in order, but with lumps in their throats they all shook hands and exchanged muttered and very inadequate words of encouragement. Then they went their separate ways, without anything further being said.

After ten minutes of walking, Horton stopped and surprised his colleagues by saying, in a voice thick with emotion: "D'you know, boys, I really do love those bastards Steffo and Gwyn as if they were my brothers. Good men. Good men. And you too. I love you all. And I hope you'll all be OK, whatever happens to me........." His voice broke, and he had tears in his eyes.

The Schuchert Glacier trio had to cover the last four miles on the glacier surface without any cover at all. They knew that they were fully visible from the mine. There were fewer snow flurries than they would have liked, and they were initially worried that with an inch or two of fresh snow on the glacier ice their footprints could easily be seen from a distance. Then they stopped worrying and a kind of fatalism took hold. If they got away with this final stunt, all well and good, and if they didn't, at least they will have tried..................

They crept as close as they dared, following a dry stream gully on the glacier surface. Now they were within half a mile of the junction of the two glaciers. It was 7.25 pm. Occasionally, in the drifting cloud, they saw a bright light high on the front edge of the great triangular peak of Himmelbjerg. Through their binoculars they could see a long window curving round the mountain face. "Is God in his Heaven?" asked Knudsen.

"Yes, I think so," said Knudsen. "It's too far to see whether there's anybody in there, but as long as it's brightly lit on the inside, it'll be difficult for Wagner or anybody else to see whatever is going on out here, in the semi-darkness. I came here a few years ago. I'm sure that until recently there was just a ventilation tunnel coming out at this point. It's been considerably improved, for some purpose other than mining."

"Griff Mortimer told us it was a radio shack, built up there so as to reduce the magnetic interference of the ore body inside the mountain. That was just one of his little white lies. It has to be Wagner's control room and observation point. If he's still in residence, that's where he'll be. Can we get up there?"

"Yes, with a little luck. The sloping tunnel they call the Schuchert Adit enters the mountain about fifteen hundred feet up, on the west side. It used to be connected by steeply sloping tunnels to the other two adits, the Arcturus Adit and the South Adit, which are both lower down. The Schuchert Adit rises gently from the entrance, as I recall, running right into the heart of the mountain. They must've built a new tunnel up to that observation room, but to minimize effort and expenditure I'm sure they must have run it off the highest adit.

"So how do we get in?"

"There's no alternative, at least from this side. We have to go up that clean rock face and get in through the Schuchert Adit entrance. It'll be open and unguarded -- its main purpose is ventilation, and I bet that nobody has ever climbed that rock face before."

"Perry, can we do it, without ropes and decent equipment?"

Whiteside scanned the rock face with the binoculars. He frowned, and looked again, more intensely. Then he looked at his colleagues and grinned unexpectedly. "Well well. A jolly good challenge, I would say. There's a long diagonal fissure that runs up from the glacier. If we can get onto that fissure, I think we can traverse the rock face without too much difficulty. There's some fresh snow on it, and it will be bloody hard in places, but it's a piece of cake compared with climbing up the side of Nordvest Fjord. When's the diversion going to happen?"

"At 10.05 pm," said Horton. "What's the time now, Perry?"

"A minute after eight o'clock."

"Right. That gives us a bit over two hours."

"Can we reach the far end of the fissure in an hour, and get up to the adit entrance in another hour?"

"Yes, I think so. It's getting pretty gloomy now, and here come some more flurries of snow. Just the camouflage we need. Since the main mine entrance is on the other side of the mountain, nobody'll be looking this way. There's some heavy machinery moving about -- d'you hear it in the distance? That must be Caterpillars on the Arcturus Glacier. I guess that anyone still here will be busy with that. Let's go!"

The assault party had made good time, but the elements had been against them. They had reached the edge of the glacier, up against the flank of the mountain, in just over an hour, hidden from observation by drifting white cloud and flurries of snow. But the snow had been too wet for comfort, bringing with it memories of their trek across the mountains, a lifetime ago. It had soaked into their hair, saturated their gloves, and insinuated its way into their clothes, where it had melted and mingled with their sweat. Furthermore, it had stuck to their boots like heavy white tar, making progress difficult, given that they were each carrying around forty pounds of explosives.

Two minutes past nine. "Right, my dear fellows," said Whiteside. "The lower end of that fissure is just above us, but first we have to get up to the top of this bloody moraine, which has probably got an ice core. Agreed, Joe?"

"Don't ask me. I'm just an ignorant botanist."

"I'll be as unstable as hell, so be prepared to go one step up and two steps back, every now and then. Follow me — I'll try to find the most stable part of the slope........."

So Knudsen and Horton followed Whiteside as best they could, slipping and sliding and falling onto their hands and knees over and again, but managing somehow to keep moving upwards over a surface that was as smooth as glass, and even more slippery because it was lubricated with meltwater and falling snow. By the time they got to the crest of the moraine and set food on solid rock, they were covered with mud from head to toe, and they were hardly recognizable. They all collapsed, gasping for breath, temporarily incapable of standing up. They had to stop for five minutes while they regained their composure and gathered their strength. Horton looked at Whiteside and managed to laugh. "My God, Perry! You look a proper picture of masculine beauty!" he said. "If a Yeti saw you now, he would run a mile. And as for your cravat, it's a bloody disgrace. I'll buy you a new one for Christmas."

"You're too kind, my dear fellow. You don't look too smart yourself, if I may say so. Now then, onwards and upwards. Without ropes and ice axes, this is going to be tough. But needs must."

"Time, Perry?"

"Quarter past nine. We've got thirty minutes to get up to that adit entrance. If we are not inside by ten to ten, we have problems, since we have to get inside and find the way to that observation room before the decoy goes off. Let's go for it............"

Whiteside moved gingerly off along the narrow fissure. In places it was more like a ledge, and they were actually able to walk along it, but in other places it was such a tight crack they they had to inch along it, with their boot tips balanced on its lower edge and with their bodies spreadeagled against the rock face. That was hellishly difficult for them with heavy packs which seemed constantly to be dragging them away from the face and out into space. In some places fresh snow sticking to the rock face made it impossible to see where the crack was, and here and there they encountered effusions of old ice which they had to bypass by climbing either above or below the fissure. Luckily none of these effusions was too extensive to negotiate, and the four climbers thanked God in his Heaven that they were doing this mad thing in late summer rather than early in the season, when the whole face would probably have been blanketed in ice. In one place Whiteside encountered a boulder perched precariously on the ledge, and in trying to creep past it he inadvertently sent it crashing down. Horrified in case anybody inside the mountain had heard it, they stopped and froze against the rock face for a couple of minutes. But there was no reaction from anywhere, and they pressed on, with hearts beating wildly. Gradually they gained altitude.

They dared not look down, for although the rock face was not vertical it was clean, and if any one of them had lost his footing he would have been lost, ending up very dead on the moraine five or six hundred feet below. Several times they had to stop to catch their breath before inching onwards again.

Ahead of them, at last, Whiteside could see that the fissure levelled out and widened. And no more than fifty yards further on, he could see the disturbed rock that indicated the location of the Schuchert Adit. He breathed a sigh of relief, and panted: "Keep going, chaps. Almost there........" But he momentarily lost concentration, and suddenly he shouted: "Bugger! I'm going......" Horton, who was immediately behind him, saw that his hands were off the face and that had lost his balance. He reacted instinctively by jamming both feet into the crevice, throwing his full bodyweight onto the rock face and slamming one arm against his colleague's rucksack as he teetered in mid-air. Luckily Whiteside's feet had not lost contact with the rock. For an agonizing few seconds Horton's outstretched right arm took most of the big man's weight, but then, as if in slow motion, his centre of gravity was righted, and his chest thumped against the rock face again. Somehow he managed to find hand-holds, and then he stood there with his toes still in the crack, gasping with shock. Horton wanted to scream in agony and thought that he might have broken his arm because of the extreme lateral stress to which it had been subjected. For a moment he saw stars and thought that he might lose his balance as well. But he closed his eyes tightly and managed to keep quiet, and the stars drifted away. He knew, as did the others, that they were now so close to the adit entrance that any sound might have been amplified along the tunnel. For a minute or two nobody said anything. "Sorry about that, my dear fellows," whispered Whiteside at last. "Bloody careless. Not a good time to lose concentration. Thank you, Joe. I owe you a stiff drink........"

"Don't mention it, my dear fellow," whispered Horton as he tried to compose himself. "Make it an Ardbeg, if you will. No ice — just a dash of water. Not everybody likes it, but it suits my palate very well."

"Joe, is your arm all right?" whispered Knudsen. "I don't know what Ardbeg is, but can we talk about it later?"

Hanna reached the junction of the Arcturus and Sirius Glaciers, after leaving Hughes behind, just out of sight of the mountain, on the Sirius Glacier itself. He had been here before, following his encounter with the innards of a crevasse, right back in the early days of the expedition. He pressed on, encouraged by the fact that the ice was covered by a layer of broken rock debris and black windblown silt. Before long he got his first glimpse of the mine entrance and the collection of huts that made up the settlement. He could see through the snow flurries that men were loading up a train of very heavy sledges with boxes which had come out of the tunnel entrance on the small railway track. Through the binoculars he noticed that some of the boxes and crates had NAPRE stencilled on their sides. The last of the season's equipment moving out? Quite probably. There were six men working near the entrance. One of them was driving a small motorized vehicle which brought out the heaviest crates on railway bogies. Another man was working a fork-lift truck. A big Caterpillar tractor looked as if it was being made ready to drag the sledges over the mountains tomorrow, when full daylight brought improved visibility. He crept closer and closer, keeping on the blind side of a ridge of rocky debris which ran almost up to the mine entrance. Now he was within 200 yards of his objective, and it seemed impossible to get any closer without being seen. Suddenly he had a stroke of luck. A bell rang out, amplified by a loudspeaker. The Himmelbjerg workers looked at their watches, turned off the engines of all the vehicles, and sauntered into the tunnel. Hanna grinned to himself; ten o'clock was obviously the designated time for a late evening snack. The enemy would be back, but how many minutes did he now have to fulfill his objectives?

Hanna knew it was time to make his move — Hughes now had the watch, and it would be about four minutes to the diversion. He decided to take the Caterpillar tractor first and then the mine entrance. He sprinted across the ice, and fixed an explosive charge with a five-minute fuse under the ugly vehicle. He lit the fuse. Then he placed a much larger charge behind the massive metal door of the mine entrance and lit a four-minute fuse. Then he ran for it and took shelter beneath a spoil heap which projected out over the moraine. Precisely on time, Hughes played his part in the operation from lower down the valley. An emergency rocket went up as a decoy, lighting up the twilight sky with a red ball of fire beneath a drifting parachute. Somebody, presumably in the observation room high on the mountain, saw it, and within a few seconds a siren started wailing. There was an instant reaction from inside the mine. At least a dozen men came running out and stood near the mine entrance. Some of them were armed with rifles and what looked like Kalashnikovs. Somebody with an American accent shouted: "Where the hell did that rocket come from?" He never got a reply, for within the space of a few seconds two huge explosions sent rock debris, bodies and bits of metal high into the air, and deadly thunderclaps bounced off the steep valley sides. The saboteur saw at once that the metal door had been blasted clean away from the mine entrance and was now on the ground, twisted and shattered. The Caterpillar tractor was on its side, with the remains of one of the tracks draped across its contorted cab. Several of the huts and cabins on the moraine had been blasted over onto their sides, and one of them rolled in slow motion down the steep slope to the glacier below. There was smoke and fire everywhere, and inside the mine tunnel men were screaming. Outside, there was no movement whatsoever, since the men who had clustered around the tunnel entrance had not stood a chance, given the force of the two blasts.

His job done, and without waiting to see how many might be dead, Hanna ran back down the glacier, stooping low on the lee side of the lateral moraine ridge. He was afraid that a hail of bullets might follow him, but not a single shot was fired. At last he stopped, exhausted, and slumped onto the snow-covered ice. Then he ran on again, until he met up with his Welsh colleague.

"Dear God, I hope we haven't killed anybody," said Hughes.

"Don't say your prayers just now, Gwyn," gasped Hanna. "We came here to do a job, and NATO obviously expects that when a job is done properly, there'll be collateral damage. It's us or them, old man, as w've already established."

"I know, but.............."

"Phases one and two completed successfully," continued the saboteur, with evident satisfaction. "Now let's see if the invasion force is as competent as the diversionary unit."

Jim Wagner was in his control and observation room, shouting into an intercom microphone while an emergency siren blared somewhere in one of the tunnels. There were flashing lights on the control panel in front of the huge sweep of the panorama window which looked down the Schuchert Valley. "Bishop, what the hell is going on down there?" he yelled, but got no reply. He picked up a telephone handset and dialled a number. "Radio shack, are you there?" Again there was no reply. The siren continued. "Unbelievable!" he yelled, to nobody in particular. "An accident with fucking explosives at this stage of the game -- incompetent assholes!" He slammed his fist down onto the console, and turned to go and investigate. He came face to face with Joe Horton, who was leaning nonchalantly against the door-post. He was covered in mud from head to toe, and he was holding a long-bladed army knife.

"No accident, Jim," said Horton. "Just an Act of God."

Wagner staggered back into the room and tried to adjust to the situation. "Joe Horton?" he whispered. "I thought you were dead, and buried at Syd Kap..........."

"You must have been misinformed. So we meet again, here in your cosy apartment. Much more comfortable than the Nibelungen Arms."

"How the hell did you get in here? Nobody gets inside this place........."

"Wrong again, Jim. Now then, you and I are probably going to die together, because there are other explosive charges which will shortly be going off inside this mysterious mountain of yours..........."

"Where the hell did you get the charges?"

"Nothing but the best. Standard NAPRE issue, taken from the sites that you planned to detonate but never got round to."

"Fucking hell! How did you know where they were?"

"Oh, it was nicely written out on a piece of paper. I collect interesting bits of paper -- my friends say it's something of an obsession. And I've got another piece of paper telling me the quantities and types of explosives. Always good to know."

"And the fuses? You don't carry fuses around in your bloody expedition food boxes, do you?"

"Gurreholm Hut. The Lauge Koch geologists were doing seismic work there a few years ago, and the fuses were in a nice box in the corner, perfectly dry and usable. I picked them up when I was there a little while ago, thinking that they might come in handy."

"You bastard! You must have been very busy after climbing out of your grave. A pity we didn't have you on board, instead of those morons Petherton and Mortimer. You and I might have worked very well together."

"I don't think so, Colonel. Now, before I kill you, I want to ask you some questions. I know the answers to most things, but there are some little niggles that keep me awake at night...... and I could do with a good night's sleep after all this excitement."

He noticed that Wagner was sidling towards his desk, and said calmly: "Walk away from there, Colonel, and raise your arms. I dislike firearms intensely, but I'm very good with this trusty knife, as Petherton

253

might attest, if only we had the pleasure of his company." He walked up to Wagner until he was standing just a few feet in front of him. "If you move an inch closer to that desk, I'll slit your throat without the slightest compunction. And keep your hands in the air, palms towards me. Like you, I used to be a Marine."

Wagner held up his hands and smiled. He moved away from the desk. "OK -- I see that you mean what you say. Ask away."

The siren was still blaring. The phone started ringing on the console. Wagner moved as if to answer it, but Horton ordered: "Leave it! If it's your mother ringing from Austen in Texas, to check that you cleaned your teeth this morning or changed your underpants, she'll probably try again later."

"Well well! You're very well informed, Mr Horton, aren't you?"

"I have my sources. Now then, first question. What's all this nonsense about PG1?"

Wagner laughed. "Our little joke in NAPRE. That's me, as you have probably deduced. When we started with this project, somebody in the Pentagon got the bright idea of calling me Polar God One, since I was in the business of recreating Acts of God. The idea caught on — so we have TG1, DG1 and other deities as well -- Tropical God One, Desert God One, Ocean God One and so forth. We're the guys in charge of the research in all of the key global environments of interest to the military. A bit of humour to warm up the Cold War. Fun, don't you think?"

"No wonder you're a bloody megalomaniac as well as being a psychopath. Next question. Did you kill those two Russian spies? Apparently both of them had bullet holes in the back of the head. Standard issue cartridges, fired from an M60."

"How the hell did you know about them? Ah - I think I can guess. Probably from Alfred Jensen, who sadly fell down a crevasse. We knew they were prowling about, and then the U2 spotted them from the air. They were foolish enough to allow smoke to come out of the chimney of the Frederiksdal hut."

"So you gunned them down from your helicopter gunship, while they were running away? Charming. Good sport, was it?"

"Necessity, not sport, Mr Horton. It's my Christian duty to deal

254

with those who stand in the way of progress."

Now Horton laughed. "Your Christian duty, my arse! You call yourself a Christian, when you have the blood of God knows how many innocent men on your hands?"

"There's a higher purpose, sir, which I don't expect you to understand........."

"Enough crap from you. Let's get back to those poor buggers with holes in their heads."

"You found their skulls?"

"Not personally. My colleagues found them."

"Hmmm. Careless on our part -- we thought the wolves would leave nothing for anybody to examine.........."

"Dear Mr God, you appear to have been careless many times, ever since we arrived in East Greenland. Lastly, before I slit your throat, what's this NAPRE business all about? I've pieced together the nuts and bolts, and it's obviously of interest to the Russians -- but what's it REALLY about?"

"Loyalty to my country, sir. You might not believe that, but it's true. You may or may not understand Communism, but I've seen it at first hand in Vietnam and elsewhere during my career, and my stomach still turns at the memory of some of the things I've seen. Whatever I can do to defeat Communism, in the service of my President and my country, I'll do it."

"I'm not sure how the activities of NAPRE are going to deal with red insurgents in the steaming jungles of Vietnam....."

"Not this section, sir, but we've got four other sections working in different environments. As I've said, one of them is the Tropical Section, working in locations which I will not divulge. Like us, they try to trigger off natural catastrophes in a manner which allows them to be portrayed as Acts of God. Bloody successful they are too. Blowing things up is easy enough, but doing it in a way that attracts no attention and leaves no trace is much more difficult."

"And the value of working in an environment such as this?"

"Novaya Zemlya, sir. Nuclear testing facility, Arctic research station, nuclear submarine base, and advance warning radar installations, all stretched out along the coasts of two islands which are mostly covered with ice. Lessons learned here will be applied there, when we choose to cause a little inconvenience to the Russians."

"And the vessels in the fjords this summer -- **Ellsworth** and **Pole Star**. They are the ones designated for these covert activities?"

"Correct. They will be very high-risk operations -- and careful training is required by our top brass. They don't want us to turn the Cold War into a hot one."

"Colonel, I can understand your patriotism and your desire for complete secrecy in these insane operations, but I can't understand why you chose, before we even arrived in Greenland, to involve my colleagues and myself from the Oxford University Scoresby Sund Expedition........."

"Sometimes you're very bright, and sometimes very slow, Mr Horton. We chose you eight fellows because you were young and intelligent. All experts in the Arctic environment, and in the processes at work. We thought that if we could trigger off at least a dozen Acts of God in or near the places where you were working, and if we could convince you that all of the accidents were down to entirely natural causes, we would have a very powerful case to put to the Pentagon."

"So you placed all of us in harm's way as a part of some grotesque experiment?"

"Not grotesque, sir. I object to the use of that word. Highly sophisticated and scientific, more like........."

"And did you expect all of us to be killed?"

"No -- that wasn't in our plan when we first put it up to the top brass. We thought there might just be some collateral damage.........."

"Some collateral damage?" shouted Horton. "You bastard! Collateral damage? You mean deaths!"

"Well, yes, but all in a good cause. For the greater good. That's the way with war........" As he talked, Wagner noted with some satisfaction that Horton was getting angry and agitated, and that suited him perfectly.

"War? Which war?" raged Horton. "So you ramped up the explosions and then started using torpedoes. You must have known that deaths arising from the use of that sort of lethal force were inevitable. So eight innocent lives were to be sacrificed for the greater good........."

"Six. Petherton and Mortimer were supposed to survive……....."

"And then the Greenlanders found themselves in the wrong place at the wrong time."

"No, the **Pole Star** crew knew they were coming. Their instruments picked up every sound in Hall Bredning and Scoresby Sund, both natural and mechanical, while they were on station. They knew the signatures of all the boat engines based in Sandvig -- even the little 2 HP outboard motors like the one you were using. Oh yes -- they knew the **Mikkelsen** was coming, all right. Mind you, they expected it to ride out the swells. In the event, the torpedo they used had too much explosive force, and the reaction of the berg to the explosion was more violent than expected. But all things considered, they learned a great deal from that episode."

As he listened, Horton became more and more agitated. "You cold, callous bastard! You're completely insane. I've heard enough…………"

Wagner continued, unperturbed, as Horton stepped towards him: "The shock wave was very unusual -- unlike anything observed before. The captain's technical analysis of that event is there, on the notice board near the window. The graph, as you can see, shows two peaks……....." He pointed, and Horton was fool enough to allow his eyes to look in the direction indicated. For a fraction of a second he was off guard.

In a flash, Wagner pulled a pistol from his pocket and pointed it at Horton. "Pistol versus knife, Mr Horton? Knives are very good if you have a quiet death in mind, but pistols are better if noise doesn't matter, and you are in a hurry. Drop it and step back!"

Horton, cursing his own idiocy, had no option but to oblige. "You forgot lesson number one, sir," said Wagner, very calmly. "Don't get mad -- get even.   I'm fed up with this conversation, and I have work to do. Goodbye, Mr Horton."

A shot rang out. Lars Knudsen walked through the door, holding the Walther PPK which Horton had found in the radio shack on Pythagoras Bjerg. Almost simultaneously there was another shot from Wagner's pistol, but his bullet thudded into the floor. He fell very slowly as the pistol dropped from his hand. Horton calmly stepped across the floor and picked it up. Polar God One looked up towards Knudsen with pleading terror in his eyes. As blood trickled from his mouth, he managed to whisper: "More than one of you? I thought that bastard Horton was alone………."

Horton replied. "You've not been paying attention, Colonel. Or did I forget to tell you that I had my friends with me? Sad business -- it seems that you've been badly misinformed, on all sorts of things."

Knudsen walked up to him and said in a level voice: "Colonel Wagner, there are five of us, all committed to putting a stop to this madness. There'll be no experiments next year, and no future for NAPRE, if we have anything to do with it. It'll not be missed. Not even my colleagues know this, but while there was chaos in Europe, my father was the only Dane to be killed in Greenland during the last war. He died before I was born. Like you, I know what war does to people. Lieutenant Eli Knudsen died to preserve democracy and freedom, and to keep this place special. No man had ever been killed here before, at the hand of another man. But now you, with your hellish plans, have brought miserable death to how many? I have given up counting. So this is for the four Inuit hunters."

He pointed the Walther PPK at Wagner's body, and a second shot rang out. "And this is for my friend Rowland Linney and for poor Dr Jensen." Another shot. "And this is for Petherton and Mortimer, both led into a path of evil." Another shot. "And this is for your own men caught up in this carnage." A fifth shot. "And finally this is for the rape of Greenland, and for the sprinkling of innocent blood on the snow." A last shot rang out.

Knudsen was shaking uncontrollably, and there was blood everywhere, splattered onto the clothes of the two friends, onto the unmade bed near the window, and all over the floor. Horton put his arm around the young Dane's shoulders. "Thank you, Lars," he said. "Enough. Enough. He isn't going to be any more dead than he is already. Keep your last rounds. You may need them."

Whiteside came through the door and calmly placed a ten-minute explosive charge against the console, disregarding the bloodied body of

Wagner. Horton picked up the dead man's PPK and found another one in a drawer beneath the console. He checked that they both had fully loaded clips in them, and passed one to Whiteside. Then he turned to Knudsen. "Reload yours as well, Lars, if you will," he said, and Knudsen, still shaking and breathing heavily, took another clip from his rucksack and put it into his pistol.

"Are we ready for Phase Four, chaps?" asked Whiteside. His colleagues both nodded.

"Three Walthers," said Horton. "Not a lot of firepower, but better than nothing, and not bad in an enclosed space."

Whiteside was about to light the fuse on the charge he had just put into position when Knudsen noticed some small fragments on the floor. They were white, and covered in blood. He also noticed on Wagner's prostrate body that there was a leather thong around his neck, with another white fragment on it, also dripping with blood. It was very small, but the Dane could see that it was something made of tusk or bone. He looked more closely, and saw that it was a crude representation of a grotesque head with sharp teeth and protruding eyes. He stepped back, breathed deeply, and nodded slowly.

Pana Naukun woke with a start, and for a while lay perfectly still, aware that his heart was beating loudly and that his forehead was dripping with sweat. He gazed for a long time at the simple boarded ceiling of his hut, seeing nothing because the first glimmers of dawn had not yet started to lighten the sky out there, on the other side of the shutters. Everything in the village was quiet. He could not even hear the wavelets lapping on the shore, a few yards from his hut. Strangely quiet, he thought. Even his neighbour's huskies, who normally snarled and howled and whined and growled for twenty-four hours a day, were quiet.

So he listened. His hearing was not as good as it use to be, but at last he heard it -- so far away as to be right at the distant edge of his hearing. The sound of the great northern diver, which was never seen or heard around Sandvig or Hurry Inlet by anybody else, because the conditions were not to its liking. But Pana saw it and heard it now and then, when there was a message. It was done. It was done. He was not pleased, because these things were not pleasing to him. So he sighed, and closed his eyes again, and turned onto his side, and went back to sleep.

CHAPTER 14
August 1962

"Now we must get out of here," said Whiteside. "It's snowing heavily outside -- far too dangerous for us to go back down along the fissure. So it has to be Plan B, and the main gate, which we hope will still be open if the first blast has done its job. While Joe was having that pleasant chat with Mr Polar God, I set the other three charges in the most strategic places I could find. Follow me -- I think I know the way out now, and we'll light each fuse as we pass. Pistols at the ready, just in case. Let's go.........."

He lit a ten-minute fuse in the observation room, and then they ran off down a steeply sloping tunnel. All the lights were still on, and the siren was still wailing continuously, apparently without any response from anywhere. At the bottom of the incline there was a junction, where there was a signpost towards the exit. "Nine minutes left, at the most," said Knudsen. They lit the second fuse and ran on, clattering and almost tumbling down a steep metal staircase adjacent to the ore crushing plant. At the bottom there was another junction, with a tunnel containing a railway track. There was an unoccupied room with the words "Radio Shack" inscribed in English above the door. Inside, Whiteside had placed the explosives against a bank of radio and other communications equipment. He lit that fuse too, and Knudsen shouted: "Number three set to go! Six minutes, I reckon!"

They ran on, continuing downhill and following the railway track into a side tunnel that had a very large humming generator set inside. Here Whiteside had set the last charge and now he lit the fuse. "My dear chaps," he said calmly. "We have four minutes to get out, before the generator goes up and we are plunged into primeval darkness. Run! Run!" All three of them knew that if they were delayed from this point on, they would be blown to pieces and entombed within a mountain which would be as black as the deepest pit in Hell. They sprinted on, following the railway track downslope, and passed through a vast cavern from which thousands of tonnes of ore had been taken. There were six or seven tunnels to choose from. Which was the one which led to the open air? For a few seconds they were confused, and then Knudsen saw a sign above one of them that said "Strøget" and guessed that it must be the main exit tunnel, at least for foot traffic. They ran on, around a corner, and almost collided with three men who were running the other way. They were carrying Kalashnikovs, and one of them said: "What the hell......?" and tried to raise his weapon. But this was close range, and Joe Horton already had his Walther PPK in his hand. Three shots rang out, and all three Americans fell onto the railway track.

Now the saboteurs were all gasping for breath as the seconds ticked away. "Less than one minute!" said Whiteside as they passed a mess room containing a crowd of men. The door was wide open, and it looked as if some casualties were being treated inside. Knudsen shouted madly and instinctively in Danish: "Get out of here, for God's sake, before this whole place is blown to bits!" But the inhabitants seemed dazed and confused, and none of them seemed to react to the warning, since presumably none of them understood Danish.

At last the four men saw the light at the end of the tunnel, about a hundred yards ahead of them. They kept on running, and then they heard the first charge going off, probably in the observation room where Wagner's corpse lay. Then after another minute, the second explosion sent a shock wave reverberating through the tunnel network. Knudsen was by now completely exhausted, and he staggered and fell onto the railway track. In a panic, Horton grabbed him and pulled him desperately towards the light, with his feet dragging along the ground. Then Whiteside tripped over one of the railway sleepers and went sprawling. He smashed against the wall of the tunnel and fell to the ground. He gasped, and was temporarily winded, but he shook his head, and then stumbled and crawled onwards as Horton shouted "Keep going, Perry! Almost there!"

Ten seconds later came the third blast. The three men staggered into the fresh air outside and flung themselves away from the tunnel entrance just as the fourth and final charge went off, with a shock wave slamming out past the twisted metal door and causing further destruction outside.

For some minutes the friends gasped and coughed and tried to gulp fresh air into their tortured lungs as they lay on the ground. Then, as their breathing became more regular, there was an eerie silence. They picked themselves up, and realized that the men in the mess room -- and God only knows how many others -- had not managed to get out before being hit by shock waves, dust and burning fumes. "Bugger it," said Whiteside. "I know they were no great friends of ours, but I hoped those chaps would be OK -- jolly bad luck for them to be caught up in all of this bloody palaver."

"Idiots!" said Horton. "They must all have retreated into the mountain, thinking that was where they would be safe, assuming an attack from outside. And unforgivable from a military point of view. Never, never concentrate all your resources in one vulnerable place........"

"Not so simple, Joe," said Knudsen quietly. "I did military training too. They probably thought they were in the least vulnerable place possible -- after all, it's called Himmelbjerg, the heavenly mountain. Where the gods reside, there can be no harm."

They looked around. There were at least a dozen bodies lying in the snow close to the Caterpillar tractor, which had been keeled over onto its side, with one track ripped off, presumably by the explosions set off earlier by Steffo Hanna. Then they heard several fresh explosions in the heart of the mountain, maybe related to the ignition of diesel fuel supplies or mining explosives. Inside the mouth of the mine tunnel they could see flames, and heavy black smoke poured out to envelop everything within fifty yards of the entrance.

Out in the open, they were very exposed, and they still feared that there might be guards with automatic weapons in some of the mining settlement huts, or stationed in other strategic places. They decided to put as much distance as possible between themselves and Himmelbjerg..........

They sprinted down the gentle gradient along the moraine towards the confluence with the Arcturus Glacier. They stopped after a while to catch their breath again, and looked back. It was just starting to snow again, but through the swirling snowflakes they could see, high up on the mountain front, a raging inferno inside the observation room. The glass had been blown out, and flames were curling up into the twilight sky. Then, as they watched, something quite grotesque happened. The smoke that had been pouring out from the mine entrance was sucked back in again, to the accompaniment of a deep and terrifying roaring sound.

"Good God!" said Horton. "The mine is starting to act like a chimney. Air is being sucked in through the lowest opening in the mountain to feed the flames inside — God help anybody left alive in there. The temperatures will be phenomenal — it must be like a blast furnace. I suspect that even the machinery will all be melted......."

Five or six other massive explosions thundered inside the mountain, echoing round the valley, as they hurried southwards through the thickening snow. Knudsen looked back over his shoulder and caught a last glimpse of the red mountain, which now looked for all the world like an erupting volcano.

By the time the five saboteurs met up on the Sirius Glacier, as agreed, it was blowing a blizzard. There was no time for an emotional reunion, but Hanna asked: "Job done, boys? Sounds and looks like it............"

"All sorted," said Whiteside. "By all accounts Joe talked too much, as usual, and had to be rescued from that bloody maniac Wagner, but that's the end of nefarious activities inside the red mountain. Jolly good riddance, too."

"Were any shots fired?"

"Only by us -- at Wagner and three guys carrying Kalashnikovs. They were unprepared for an attack. They must have been completely convinced that we were all dead."

"Unforgivable complacency and negligence on the part of trained military men," said Horton. "I never thought for a moment that we would all get out of there alive........."

"And casualties on their side?" asked Hanna.

"God knows how many," sighed Knudsen. "Wagner is cremated

and is with his maker. Three others shot by Joe in the tunnel. Maybe a dozen inside that mess room, and another dozen or so bodies lying in the snow outside. Maybe thirty all told."

"Bloody hell," said Hanna. "That's a pretty big loss of life. How on earth will they cover that up?"

"Oh, they'll cover it up all right," said Hughes. "There's no way they can admit to it, when they get to discover what's happened here. But I agree with Perry — that has to be the end of NAPRE and Himmelbjerg."

"I only hope you're right, Gwyn. Will they ever be able to discover what really happened?"

"I doubt it," said Horton. "It'll look like an accident -- with one explosion triggering a fire and a series of other explosions, leading to a white-hot inferno fed by air sucked in through the mine entrance. Even if they manage to trace the explosive points, they'll simply find traces of standard issue US military explosives. I wouldn't mind betting that some of those which were used in the field, causing us such distress, came from storage depots inside the mountain. A most unfortunate Act of God."

They climbed off the glacier and found a hollow in an area of undulating morainic debris. They had to huddle together to keep warm, and they dragged their bivvy sheets over themselves, to keep off the snow. Then they ate their remaining chocolate and Kendal mint cake, and slept.

Twenty-four hours later they were back in the Karstryggen cave, where they dried out their sodden clothes, talked endlessly, ate too much, and rested their exhausted bodies. Through the snow flurries they caught just one glimpse of Himmelbjerg, and saw that there was still black smoke billowing through all of the upper adits and vents. Then they cleared everything out of the cave, strapped heavy packs onto their backs and started a fifty-mile trek to Gurreholm.

In spite of the fact that they travelled on the east side of the Schuchert Valley, where there were few major obstacles, the journey took them four days, in more or less continuous blizzard conditions. Most of what they were carrying was food, including the tinned items that they had scavenged from food dumps and depots left by earlier field parties which had enjoyed helicopter transport. Temperatures were now well below zero, day and night. They only had two two-man tents with them, so they had to take it in turns to sleep in the open, under a bivouac sheet. They thanked their lucky stars that the Schuchert River was now so low that there was hardly any water in it, allowing them to cross and recross it at will. And somehow, in spite of their inadequate clothing, they all reached Gurreholm without suffering from frostbite.

They stayed at Gurreholm for two days while they recuperated, dried out their clothes, and waited for a break in the weather. They allowed themselves the luxury of a fire in the stove as long as there was a heavy cloud blanket. Then there was a temporary thaw, on the last day of August.

On an overcast but calm day, with an easterly breeze, Hughes and Whiteside walked to Syd Kap to collect the inflatable, the engine and a jerry can of paraffin. They could have walked via Base Camp, but knew that there was nothing there any longer, and they had no wish to stir up unpleasant memories. They were more relaxed now, but they were still stranded in East Greenland, and their prospects of getting home to the UK unharmed were still very slim. They did their best to keep cheerful, and were able to marvel at the changes that had occurred in the landscape. With the approach of winter and the regular occurrence of frosty nights, the dusty greens of the tundra were now transformed into flaming reds and yellows and colours that reminded them of burnished copper, brass and bronze. The sunsets were wonderful too -- and they almost regretted that they were in no position to settle into Hotel Paradiso and enjoy them for an evening, or two, or three........

The two men brought the inflatable boat and a can of paraffin across Nordøstbugt and pulled it up onto the gravelly beach at Gurreholm. As they did so, they heard the unmistakable sound of migrating pinkfoot geese to the north. They watched, entranced, as one skein appeared high overhead, followed by another, and then another. Ten minutes later they were assailed by a chattering, gabbling cacophony of sound as thousands of the big birds swept overhead, clouding the sky from horizon to horizon, having no doubt flown over the Werner Mountains and Himmelbjerg and having used the Schuchert Valley as their route towards Scoresby Sund and the ice-choked waters of the

Denmark Strait. Some groups were in V-formation, and others simply flew in straggly lines. The two men watched them as they followed the coast of Jameson Land southwards. Then they were gone, and peace returned.

"I wonder how many times that spectacle has been repeated down through the millennia?" murmured Hughes.

"Who cares, old chap?" said Whiteside. "Mathematics is not my territory. Life goes on, in spite of the the species which stupidly calls itself Homo sapiens. Bloody arrogance, if you ask me. You don't have to be smart to understand what the pinkfoot geese are telling us. Time to go home."

CHAPTER 15
September 1962

Next day, on the first day of September, the expedition survivors started their long walk to Sandvig, choosing a route that bypassed the higher land of the interior of Jameson Land. They reckoned that they would need to cover well over a hundred miles in a week, allowing for four days of walking and three days for bad weather and recovery time. They were in good spirits, since they no longer had to behave like fugitives. They carried all their remaining food with them. Their packs were still heavy, but for the first part of the journey, along the gentle sandy coast of Hall Bredning, those who were walking on the beach had the luxury of watching the inflatable craft piled high with their rucksacks gliding along at the same pace, twenty yards offshore. So they walked unencumbered. They took it in turns to pilot the boat, and were amazed that they had clear water all the way to the point at which they planned to head inland. They could see thick pack ice a mile or so offshore, but there was no sign that it might move in towards the coast.

Far away to the north, they heard the distant sounds of aircraft traffic, and they assumed that the Americans and Danes based at Blyhavn were involved in frantic attempts to get to Himmelbjerg, given that there was by now thick snow on the glaciers and bad visibility throughout the Werner Mountains. They could only imagine what the reverberations might be within NATO when the first reports began to come through of the damage done by the explosions and the fire, and the appalling loss of life.

On the second night of the walk Knudsen, Hughes and Hanna were in one tent and Horton and Whiteside were in the other. It was Horton's turn to be in the bivvy bag, and he had found a comfortable spot about ten yards from the tents. They were camped on the soft grass just above the limit of storm waves, adjacent to a long sandy beach that ran for miles, backed by sand dunes. They could hardly believe that this benign

268

environment was just a few miles from the vertical black cliffs of Nordvest Fjord, which had terrified them on more than one occasion when they had been out on the water. They were tired, and they were complacent. In fact, they were all asleep. Knudsen was sleeping in the tent nearest to the sand dunes when something woke him up. He could not be sure what it was. There was a movement outside the tent, and at first he thought it might be Joe, stretching his legs or having a piss. But then he heard some low grunts and became alarmed. He sat up, and as he did so a giant paw smashed through the tent canvas and onto the folded sweater he had been using as a pillow. There was chaos. Knudsen screamed: "A bear!" and as his colleagues woke up the tent collapsed on top of them. The bear was tangled in the guys and as it struggled and lashed out with its claws the frail cotton fabric was shredded. The three men tried to roll away from the creature's slashing paws, and their thick padded sleeping bags probably saved them. There was goose down everywhere, swirling about like snowflakes in a blizzard. The bear tried to run away, but it was so tangled in the guy lines that it dragged the groundsheet and what was left of the cotton tent with it. Hanna and Knudsen managed to slip out of their torn sleeping bags and escape, but Hughes was so tangled in the lines that he was dragged along by the bear. After a few yards the bear realized what was happening, and turned on him. He covered his head and closed his eyes as the bear stood on its hind legs. Then three shots rang out, in rapid succession, and the bear crumpled, slamming down onto his legs. It struggled for a while, and then was still.

Hughes opened his eyes and saw Joe Horton standing a few yards away, with a Walther PKK in his hand. "Sorry, Gwyn," he said, his face red with anger and guilt. "Bloody negligent of me. I should've been awake, and keeping watch........."

Luckily, Hughes was not injured, for although the bear must have weighed the best part of a ton, its thick fur and the padding of the sleeping bag had cushioned its fall. They rolled it clear, and pulled the very frightened Welshman to his feet. "Bugger me," he gasped. "A bit too close for comfort, that was. We don't see a single bear for the whole of the expedition, and then, just as we're heading for the fleshpots of Sandvig, one pops out of the sand dunes and almost does what Jim

Wagner and the combined forces of NATO failed to do."

They were all shocked. There was no chance of any more sleep that night, no matter how tired they were, so they made some tea and lit a fire on the beach, using a few scraps of driftwood that had somehow found their way into Scoresby Sund from the outer coast. There was now quite a deep twilight, and for the first time it was dark enough for them to see the stars. The temperature was around ten degrees below zero, and when they looked to the north they could see a faint flickering green glow in the sky above the Stauning Alps. It was their first sight of the Northern Lights.

As they sat around the fire they held an inquest. Joe Horton was mortified, since what might have been a fatal accident had happened on his watch. He kept on apologizing, but Hanna put his hand on his shoulder. "Forget it, Joe," he said. "We've never kept a proper polar bear watch -- not on the Bear Islands, not at Base Camp, not in Frederiksdal, not anywhere. We've just assumed that we would not see a bear, and that a bear would not see us."

"Quite so, old chap," chipped in Whiteside. "Calculated risk. You tend to keep a bear watch in the winter, but not in the summer, since the bears are usually out on the sea ice. But some bears stick to the mainland, and some even go up onto the glaciers in order to keep cool. Some of the females keep close to their breeding areas, and the males wander far and wide. Good God, for most of the nights since we've been here we have all been utterly clapped out, and would've been easy meat for any passing polar bear that might have felt like a little snack."

"You're right," said Hughes, still with a quiver in his voice. "I've seen polar bears often before, but they generally keep well clear of camp sites with several people in them. I'd hazard a guess that this one was old and starving."

They examined the creature that lay covered in blood a few yards from where they were sitting, and found that it was indeed emaciated, with several teeth missing and with a bent leg that looked as if it had been broken at some stage in its life. "Poor old bugger," said Horton. "He was probably on his last legs anyway, and was just poking around in the hope of finding something edible now that all the eggs are hatched and the birds are gone."

The tent had to be dumped, but they managed to cut off the groundsheet in the expectation that it could be used by somebody sleeping in the open until they reached Sandvig. Two of the sleeping bags had to be dumped too. From now on they would have to use the remaining bags in rotation, with three sleeping and two staying awake and keeping watch. They dared to hope that there were no more polar bears wandering around in this barren wilderness of tundra, rocky hills and undulating gravelly lowlands.

As they talked and watched the sky lightening in the east, Whiteside suddenly said: "D'you realize, my dear fellows, that on this very day it is two months exactly since we set foot in Greenland, and..........."

"Bloody hell!" exclaimed Hughes. "Is that so? Feels more like two years, or two centuries."

"Kindly don't interrupt, old fruit. To continue. And in celebration of this fact I think we should enjoy a wee dram."

"Poor thing," sighed Hanna. "He's finally flipped. Used to be such a nice fellow, too. Never mind, Perry, we'll look after you in your old age."

Then they all noticed that their eccentric colleague was holding a small metal hip flask in his hand. There was a gleam in his eye.

"Hallucinations have set in," murmured Knudsen. "I think I see something with whisky inside it."

"It's for Joe," grinned Whiteside. "I owe him a stiff one, for services rendered. Isn't that right, Joe? I always pay my debts." He handed it over to Horton, who was lost for words.

Whiteside continued: "If you all promise to behave, he might even share it with you, together with a toast to our safe homecoming. Sadly, I don't think it's Ardbeg, but I did test it a little earlier, and it's quite a good one. Try it, my dear fellow, and if there's any left, we can maybe all have a sip."

Horton took the hip flask, pulled out the cork, and took a sip. "Good God," he said. "Single malt! It's a good one, too! Here, boys, there's probably enough for all of us."

Each man in turn took a sip, and said: "To our safe return." Then Hanna turned to his angelic colleague and said: "Come on, Perry. Spill the beans. Where the hell did it come from?"

"Manna or nectar from the heavenly mountain, dear boy. When I was setting the charges in the radio shack in Himmelbjerg, there it was, on the desk next to the radio console. It looked like a nice hip flask, and when I shook it I discovered it was half full, and decided it would be a pity for it to go to waste.."

When the colleagues moved on a couple of hours later, they had buried all their ruined camping gear beneath a pile of stones. They left no trace of their visit apart from the bloodied carcass of the polar bear, still on the beach where it had fallen. They were in no mood to try to take a polar bear skin home with them, whatever its value might have been....... and the foxes, skuas and owls would make short work of it.

The inflatable boat and its motor were abandoned thirty miles down the coast, and they too were buried beneath a stony cairn. Then the five friends walked due east on Days Four and Five across the semi-desert of Jameson Land until they reached the shore of Hurry Inlet. By this time they were very tired, and were effectively living in the open for twenty-four hours a day because they had only the one remaining tent. They were however now well attuned to the Arctic environment, and had no further serious problems. They saw a few muskoxen, and some Arctic foxes and hares, but no more polar bears. They had a brief break in the hut at Constable Pynt, and then had to slog all the way round the head of Hurry Inlet before following the eastern shore southwards on Day Seven.

By now the concept of exhaustion had no meaning for any of them. They had long since gone through the pain barrier, and several of them suffered from intermittent cramps. Although they were fit, their shoulders ached from the continuing pressure of heavy packs, and their limbs stiffened up if they stopped for just a minute or two. But they kept going by thinking simply of one step at a time. One step at a time......... over and again, onward, over and again. Towards the end, they walked for three hours with hardly a word passing between them.

From southern end of Hurry Inlet they headed cross-country again for the final few miles of their journey. They passed a number of small lakes, and as they were plodding along the shore of one of them, they heard the unmistakable sound of huskies howling in the distance. "Sandvig, boys," said Hanna. "Just over the skyline. I think we've made it. Time to get rid of the guns." They threw the three Walther PKK pistols and their remaining cartridge clips as far out into the water as they could manage, and watched them sink without trace.

They reached Sandvig in the middle of the night, and were alert enough to notice that there was no sign of the famous red-painted **Kista Dan** out in the bay. But there was another ice-strengthened vessel there, which none of them recognized. Knudsen led his colleagues past thirty or so small houses, and countless growling and howling huskies, to the residence of the Danish Administrator, and knocked on the door. Harald Keppel looked more asleep than awake when he opened it, probably in the expectation that he might have to sort out yet another domestic dispute between an inebriated local man and a long-suffering wife.

When he saw the weather-beaten and bearded explorer standing before him, he could hardly believe his eyes. "Lasse?" he murmured in Danish. "Is it really you? I can hardly believe it...... and your friends?"

"Five of us, Harald," said Knudsen quietly. "We've come to give your watch back." Then he stood aside so that Keppel could see the other four clustered in a little group at the bottom of the steps. They must have looked grotesque, if not comical, to a gentleman in carpet slippers and a dressing-gown who was framed in the warm glow of his own front doorway. They all had wild eyes, unkempt beards and long matted hair, and in truth their ragged anoraks and trousers appeared to be held together by nothing more than accumulated filth and grease. Keppel looked at their feet, and was amazed to see that they were all still wearing serviceable boots. That appeared, to him, to be another small miracle. But they were clearly on their last legs.

"Thank God, thank God," said the blonde Dane, switching to English, and then he said it again, with his voice breaking, as tears began to roll down his cheeks. "I was absolutely convinced that they would get you, and that I'd never see any of you again. But don't just stand there. Come in! Come inside, all of you!"

They only just found the energy to climb up the steps. As they stumbled into the warm comfort of the Keppel household, the Dane closed the door behind them and ushered them into the living room. Then he insisted on embracing each one of them in turn, giving the lie to the idea that the Danes were incapable of displays of emotion either in public or private. Suddenly waves of euphoria overwhelmed all of them, and the exhausted comrades laughed, and cried, and embraced one another. Keppel had to ask them to make less noise, for fear that his small daughter might be woken up. Each one of the explorers realized that they had been living on adrenalin for days, or for weeks, or for what seemed like a lifetime.........and that they had forgotten what it was like to sleep easy, or to relax. Now the bow-string was released, and after a few minutes of euphoria all they wanted to do was sleep. They slumped onto the floor, mindful enough of their social responsibilities to know that they would have ruined their host's armchairs and sofas if they had sat upon them.

"Five of you still?" Keppel asked quietly, just to make sure.

"All present and correct, Harald," replied Hanna, with a weary grin on his face.

"And here's your watch, as promised," grinned Hughes, handing over the Rolex borrowed at Syd Kap. "It came in very handy."

Just then Keppel's wife Elise came into the room, no doubt disturbed by all the commotion. She was wrapped in a colourful dressing gown lined with white fox fur. She was tall and very beautiful, with fine Inuit features, bright eyes and long black hair which cascaded over her shoulders. She smiled, and the five explorers all instantly fell in love with her, for they had not seen a woman since the day that they had left Reykjavik a lifetime ago.

"A very warm welcome to you, gentlemen," she said in impeccable English. "We've been hoping and praying for your arrival, but hardly daring to expect you. I can't tell you how relieved I am to see you. You've done much for our people since the terrible episode on the Bear Islands, and as you have kept faith with us, we will keep faith with you."

The weary explorers looked mystified. Keppel laughed. "What Elise means is this," he said. "Everybody in the village knows that you are here. They were woken by the dogs, of course, when you walked through between the houses, for their sleep is much shallower than that of a European like me. But you may take it from us, on a solemn oath, that not a word of your arrival will be uttered by anybody in this community, by radio or by written message; and if there should be interrogations, many lies will be told............."

"Thank you both for that assurance," nodded Hanna. "In the circumstances, the fewer people who know that we are alive, the better."

Keppel nodded. "My inclination is to give you breakfast and to ask you about everything that has happened. But that will have to wait. One day we will get together somewhere, and talk about old times. You need to know that *Kista Dan* has come and gone, having been searched by the Americans prior to departure. The captain was furious, but the Yanks are very afraid. They flew in from Blyhavn to check, just in case any of you had managed to survive and get on board. The *Ella Brae* has just come in, on an unscheduled visit, and is ready to go. You heard about the disaster at Himmelbjerg?"

"Yes, we heard about it," said Knudsen. "A terrible thing. An Act of God, I suppose."

"Thirty-six people dead, including Jim Wagner, and the whole place destroyed in an inferno. Not a single survivor. That's off the record. The press releases are already out, saying that there was a small explosion in a mine in East Greenland, with three men injured and nobody killed."

"Oh God," moaned Hanna. "And the world will probably believe what it is told..........."

"Leave God out of this, Steffo," said Hughes. "Not appropriate, in the circumstances."

Keppel continued. "You'll now go on board the *Ella Brae*, and captain Peter Eliason will take you home. He's an old school friend of mine, and he's supposed to know nothing, but knows everything. Nobody tells him what to do -- not the Americans, not the Danish Government -- nobody. He owns the ship and takes it where he will, and when it suits him. He knows the ice in these parts better than any other man alive, and the ice strengthened hull on this ship is as good as any other in the world. There's a lot of ice out there now, and it may take weeks, but he will get you out. You can trust him with your lives. During the voyage, he will maintain complete radio silence. I know that'll be frustrating to you, since your loved ones will be grieving, and you will be desperate to contact them. But in the circumstances, there is no option in the matter."

Then the Dane went into his bedroom and came out again with a folded piece of paper in his hand. He gave it to Hanna and said: "Take this with you and look after it very carefully. It should have been destroyed, but shall we say that there has been an unfortunate oversight? I've been keeping it for some time in the hope that I would one day get the opportunity to hand it over to you. If you had not turned up, it would have gone into the fire……….."

Hanna glanced at it. "A typed-out radio or cable message?" he asked.

"Don't read it now. Read it when you're on the *Ella Brae*. You'll find it entertaining in a gruesome sort of way — it's just a death warrant for all of you, signed by your Prime Minister in London, probably with the backing of my Prime Minister in Copenhagen. Thankfully, it's of historical interest only, since the appointed executioners themselves have, according to reports, been caught up in several unfortunate Acts of God."

"Götterdämmerung," said Knudsen.

"Pardon?"

"Oh, it's just something that struck me. There's this opera about the twilight of the Gods and the end of the world, by a chap called Wagner…….."

Without further ado, Keppel got dressed, and led the five men down the steps and onto the filthy trackway that led to the shore. They turned to look back, and exchanged waves with Elise, who was still standing in the illuminated doorway of the house. Somebody on the *Ella Brae* had been keeping watch, and as soon as they reached the shore they saw figures moving on the bridge. Within a couple of minutes a small boat was let down onto the placid water surface and started to glide towards the beach. The sound of its engine echoed around the bay, amplified and distorted as it bounced off half a dozen vast grounded icebergs. After a few minutes the boat's bow bumped onto the gravel, and five filthy rucksacks were thrown on board. There was not much in them, but they were the only possessions the men had. Before climbing on board themselves, each of the surviving members of the expedition once again embraced the young Dane who had effectively been their salvation. He was again moved to tears, and as the boat reversed off the beach, he waved and said simply: "Bon voyage, gentlemen. Tell the world."

It was about three o'clock in the morning. As the small boat made its way out to the waiting ship, half a mile offshore, the men noticed a very old man sitting on a smooth rock on a little peninsula, just a few feet from the water's edge. He watched them for a while, and then smiled and waved. They waved back.

Ten days later, on the 20th of September, after escaping from unusually heavy pack ice outside the mouth of Scoresby Sund, and having battled its way through a storm in the Denmark Strait, the *Ella Brae* was off the east coast if Iceland, close inshore. It had been an exceptionally rough voyage thus far, and several of the ship's passengers had been violently sick; Hanna and Hughes had hardly been out of their bunks for four days. Captain Peter Eliason had slipped into the fishing port of Seydisfjordur during the night for refuelling, since he had used much more fuel than anticipated while the ship had been in the grip of the ice. Now they were on their way out again, heading down the fjord towards the open sea.

For a change, all the men were in the mess room, tucking into a substantial breakfast. Eliason came in and threw his captain's cap onto the breakfast table. "Good morning, boys," he said with a grin. "You've slept well, I hope, for the first time since we got out of the ice? Anyway, enjoy your breakfast. There's rough weather again later today, when we are clear of land. But that suits us fine. By the way, this might be of interest………….."

He threw down onto the table a battered newspaper and helped himself to a substantial fried breakfast. Horton picked it up and saw that it was the *News Chronicle*, dated 13th September.

"Left behind by the captain of an English trawler that came in for fuel yesterday," the captain said. "Mostly dull English politics and tittle-tattle, but there's something intriguing on page five."

Horton opened it up, and was amazed to see a prominent photograph of Himmelbjerg and the mining settlement as it must have appeared a year or two earlier. It was obviously a photo obtained from some previous visitor -- maybe a member of some geological field party or even somebody who had worked at the site. Beneath the photo was a prominent headline which read:

SOVIET - AMERICAN SPAT OVER GREENLAND MINING ACCIDENT.

Then came a long article. He read out its contents so that everybody could hear.

"A remote mining settlement in East Greenland has become a focal point in a new dispute between the Soviet Union and the American government, lowering the temperature of the Cold War by a degree or two.

News of the accident at the Himmelbjerg molybdenum mine was first released at the beginning of this month, in a statement from Greenland Metals A/S which said that there had been a small explosion at the mine in which three miners had been slightly injured. It was assumed that there had been no deaths. The story received little attention from the media, except in Denmark. Now it appears that there was more to the accident than meets the eye. In a statement to the press, US Secretary of State Dean Rusk confirmed that the mine was run by an American company, and that some American nationals worked there alongside Danish colleagues. He said that accident investigators had encountered great difficulties in reaching the remote mine because of the onset of winter weather, but that they had confirmed beyond all doubt that there were several explosions, triggered as an act of sabotage by Soviet agents operating in East Greenland. It is very rare for material evidence to be placed in the public domain in cases like this, but Mr Rusk reported that investigators had found a sophisticated Russian wrist-

watch -- manufactured in the Russian Sturmanskie factory -- in the mouth of the mine tunnel. He said that the watch was badly damaged, and that it had stopped at 22.37 on 25th August -- at precisely the time of the explosions. "We know that such time-pieces are routinely used by Soviet special forces," he said. "We have other evidence, which we cannot disclose, that points to covert Soviet operations in Greenland designed to disrupt the export of certain valuable minerals used in the manufacture of specialist steels." Mr Rusk confirmed that a stiff protest had been delivered to the Kremlin by the US Ambassador in Moscow.

In a furious response, the Soviet Foreign Minister Andrei Gromyko issued a statement to the press in which he claimed that the Americans had fabricated evidence in an attempt to worsen relations between the two countries. "We categorically deny that we had any agents in the area at the time of these explosions," he said. "Furthermore, we have issued a formal protest to the White House relating to another recent incident which we had -- in the interests of good relations -- previously left unreported. This involves the sinking of a Russian fishing vessel which was working in international waters off the Greenland coast on 8th July. As a result of a completely unprovoked attack by US Phantom jets from Keflavik, four innocent crew members were lost. We have identified the precise location of that attack, from other fishermen operating in the area who found an extensive oil slick. The attack cannot possibly have been down to a mistake, and we have demanded an apology and restitution for the families of the lost men and their vessel."

According to defence expert George Jenkins, these incidents fit into an ongoing sequence of claims and counter-claims involving the two global super-powers. "It's difficult to know what to believe and what to be sceptical about in these statements," he said. "As far as the mine incident is concerned, we should note that the Americans now refer to "explosions" rather than "an explosion" -- so the damage to the mine must have been much more severe than previously admitted. And could there have been a covert Soviet operation in the area involving personnel from crack "Spetsnaz" or special forces units? Yes -- it's quite possible. They have used disguised fishing vessels and sealers in the past, to get into and out of target areas. Reading between the lines, it's a distinct *possibility that the so-called fishing vessel sunk by the Americans was strengthened for ice work and used by the men who went ashore on the Greenland coast. The saboteurs would have had to walk to Himmelbjerg from the coast, but that should have presented no problem to highly trained men. And finally, the watch. Its provenance can easily be verified. The Americans have released a photo of it, and it looks identical to the Sturmanskie chronometer -- giving very accurate time and the date as well -- used by Yuri Gagarin on the Vostok orbital flight last year." Asked how he would assess the overall impact of these incidents on international relations, Jenkins added: "Probably not that great. Certainly less significant than the Bay of Pigs fiasco and the shooting down of that American spy plane a couple of years ago. Tit for tat, I suggest, and honours even."*

Notwithstanding this Jenkins assessment, it must not be forgotten that Greenland is an autonomous province of Denmark, and that Cold War power politics do not play out well in the local community. In a statement just issued by the Danish Greenland Department, the Greenland Minister Borup Jespersen said: "We are shocked and saddened by the revelations of these events on our sovereign territory. We will now assess very carefully our relations with NATO and with the governments of the United States and the Soviet Union. We will also be conducting our own enquiry into what happened at Himmelbjerg. Until that is complete, we are placing a moratorium on all further research and commercial activities in Greenland, and will cancel certain agreements already in place." Our Diplomatic Editor, who has read the full Danish press release, says that this is one of the strongest statements he has ever seen from a small country, given that it constitutes a direct rebuke to the two super-powers. He says that it stops short of a withdrawal from NATO, but he suggests that behind the scenes there has been a very forthright exchange of views.

In a grotesque coincidence, this is the same area which featured in the headlines of the world's press less than a month ago, during the desperate hunt for eight members of an Oxford University expedition who had disappeared without trace. Sadly, with the onset of winter, the hunt for survivors had to be called off, and it is now accepted that the young explorers are all dead. **When questioned by this newspaper about possible links between the mining accident and the disappearance of the explorers, a Foreign Office spokesman was quick to damp down speculation. "These very sad incidents are quite unrelated," he said. "The mine is a hundred miles or more from the area in which the expedition members disappeared, and all of the evidence in our possession suggests that they died in a number of accidents in the Scoresby Sund fjord system. We accept the evidence of our American allies that the Himmelbjerg incident, far to the north, was related to covert Soviet operations in the area, carried out for reasons that are currently unclear."**

By the time Horton had finished reading the press report, Peter Eliason had finished his sausages and eggs. He downed what was left in his coffee cup, grabbed his cap, and got up from the table. "Well, that was interesting, boys, wasn't it?" he said with a grin. "Life's full of surprises." Then he went off to resume his station on the bridge, as the ship slid out from the fjord and into the open sea.

The expedition members were left alone in the mess room, and there was a very long silence while they all tried to digest what they had heard. At last Hanna said: "Good God! I really don't know what to say......."

"Me neither," said Horton. "It's not often that I'm lost for words, but I'm rendered speechless."

There was another long silence, broken only by the sound of Whiteside crunching his teeth on a crisp slice of toast at the far end of the mess room table. One after another, his colleagues looked at him, and he said: "Can't a fellow eat his toast in peace without being stared at? It's jolly good toast, and I'm enjoying it very much indeed."

Then Hanna said: "Perry, you are a crafty bastard, and I smell a rat. Whatever happened to that nice watch of yours?"

Looking as innocent as a six-month-old baby just out of a bubble bath, Whiteside said: "D'you mean that one I found lying on the ground in Frederiksdal?"

"Yes -- the one that presumably belonged to one of those Russian trappers, or whatever they were."

"Oh, that one!"

"Yes, that one. You and the watch have been inseparable ever since you took possession of it. It doesn't appear to be on your wrist any longer. I've only just noticed."

"Oh, bugger! I thought there was something missing from my life. I must have lost it."

At this, Knudsen and Hughes, who were sitting closest to him, leapt upon him, knocked him off his chair and pinned him to the ground. Amid gales of laugher, Whiteside struggled and protested that he was being murdered, and it was lucky that no great damage was done either to the furniture or to the crockery. At last order was restored, and Horton said: "I still don't know what to say. Bloody miraculous. I thought I knew a thing or two, but this takes the biscuit....."

"Come on then, Perry," added Hanna. "How did the watch get to the entrance of the Himmelbjerg mine tunnel?"

Then Horton recovered the power of speech and said: "Now I remember! Just as we reached the mine entrance, with those explosives due to go off any second and blow us to kingdom come, Perry stumbled and fell against the wall and ended up on the ground. For a moment he looked winded, and I thought the poor bugger might not get out in time -- but then he got back onto his feet and flung himself out after the rest of us, just as the explosions blew the place to bits............"

Whiteside resumed his chair, and took another slice of toast, grinning ear to ear. "This toast is quite perfect, my dear fellows, with this particular marmalade on it," he said. "Even better than Cooper's Oxford thick cut. Must ask the chef where he got it."

"That dive was either the stupidest or the cleverest thing I ever saw," said Knudsen. "I was pretty well done in, and only got away thanks to Joe. But I caught a glimpse of Perry falling down............" He looked at Whiteside, who was spreading butter onto his toast. He jabbed his finger towards him. "What this fellow really did, if I am correct, was maybe not carefully planned and executed quite as he had hoped -- but he must have had the watch in his hand. He smashed it against the wall of the tunnel, with enough force to ensure that it stopped working, then threw it onto the ground and got out of there like a cat with its tail on fire.

He knew that whatever happened from that point on, some accident investigation or forensic science people would turn up, find the watch, and put two and two together in order to make twenty-two. Correct, Perry?"

"Oh, bugger again!" said Whiteside, with his mouth full of toast. "Rumbled yet again…………"

"So when did you realize that the watch was a Russian one?" asked Horton.

"Can't exactly remember when. The face of the watch looks just like any other high-class instrument, with Roman numerals. But when we got back to Base camp after that hellish walk from Frederiksdal I examined the back of it one day I saw the brand name Sturmanskie. You might agree that that doesn't sound very American."

"But what about finger-prints, Perry? Won't the Americans find yours on the watch?"

"No chance, old fruit. They haven't got mine anyway, so they have nothing to compare. But I like to be careful, and before we went into the tunnel I wiped the watch very carefully with my handkerchief. I carried it in my pocket, still wrapped up, until we were making our escape. My fingers didn't come into contact with it at all before I chucked it onto the ground at the side of that little railway track."

"Bloody hell!" said Horton. "We have an evil genius in our midst. That sort of cool thinking under extreme pressure -- I'm lost for words again. Don't have ambitions to take over the world, do you, Perry?"

"Afraid not, old fruit. If I ever get a degree, which I doubt, I have every intention of retiring to the country where I can spend the rest of my days tending the dahlias and collecting rents."

"One last thing, Perry, if I may," said Knudsen. "When did you hatch this cunning plan of yours? You must have given it a good deal of thought."

"It just sort of materialized. And after those endless discussions we had in the cave before we attacked Himmelbjerg it became even more obvious to me that we could achieve a great many things by diverting the responsibility for the attack onto those poor fellows whose remains we found in Frederiksdal. So that was that. The Americans and the Soviets both mystified, and blaming each other for things only partly understood. The Danes furious with everybody else. The Greenlanders angry with the government in Copenhagen. And the end of NAPRE."

"And why did you go it alone?"

"Because, my dear old thing, life was complicated enough for everybody else, as it was. In all seriousness, I didn't think I'd see it through, because I didn't really expect to survive, but I thought it was worth a punt."

After that, euphoria returned, and in a very noisy mess room the five blood brothers cleared away the breakfast things and did the washing up. Then they spent several hours in deep discussion, both before and after lunch. At the end of it, Hanna said: "Right, boys. We're agreed. Our own governments, British and Danish, have connived to get us killed, and they have to face up to the consequences of that. From this point on, truth in all things. We have done nothing — NOTHING -- to be ashamed of. But there are two things that are wiped entirely from our memories. Number one, the discovery of those human remains in Frederiksdal. Number two, the assault on Himmelbjerg. Never to be mentioned again, even to those who are nearest and dearest. Not even in pillow talk. Before we walked across Jameson Land, we simply laid low at Gurreholmsdal and rested. Agreed on oath, between brothers?

"Agreed, on oath, between brothers," they said, in unison, with five hands clasped in the centre of the table.

The *Ella Brae* slipped through the Minch and into the inlet at Leverburgh, close to Hanna's home on the island of South Harris. There was just a glimmer of light in the pre-dawn sky, and Hanna had to guide the ship in, very slowly, to the jetty. If anybody had been watching, they would have seen five men jumping ashore. Nobody spoke. Then the ship backed away from the jetty and turned its bows back towards the island's southernmost point, where it would swing north. Within twenty minutes it was out of sight.

The shadowy figures, carrying just a few possessions, passed through the village as silently as ghosts and climbed up the track to the converted croft which was home to Stephen Hanna, his parents and his sister. He knocked on the door, several times, until it was obvious that the house was deserted. He was not surprised by that, for they had been listening to the BBC World Service while they had been aboard the *Ella Brae*, and they were fully aware of the great news stories of the day. Hanna went round to the back of the house, where he looked for the spare front door key inside the peat shed. It was hanging there, as it had done whenever the house was empty, since he had been a very small child. Then the five men let themselves in, dumped superfluous belongings, and freshened themselves up. They were clearly in a hurry.

Half an hour later Hanna went into the kitchen and picked up the key for the long-wheelbase Land Rover that was parked in the yard behind the cottage. He locked up the house again. Then the five friends piled into the vehicle, and set off for the ferry quay at Tarbert.

CHAPTER 16
September 1962

Great Tom, the famous bell in the tower of Christchurch Cathedral in Oxford was tolling slowly. It was fifteen minutes before two o'clock on 26th September. Countless people streamed into the church, from all walks of life -- for a memorial service to the eight members of the OU Scoresby Sund Expedition who had been so tragically lost in Greenland in mid-August. The tragedy had stirred the nation, for although there had been occasional losses among expedition members in various parts of the world in the past, this was the first time in the history of British exploration that ALL of the members of a single party had been lost without trace. The Bishop of Oxford was officiating, and there were many members of the university hierarchy in the congregation. The Duke of Edinburgh was there, in his capacity as patron of the Royal Geographical Society. Even the Prime Minister was present -- and indeed he had asked if he could give a short eulogy. Senior officers from all of the funding bodies were present, along with representatives of the Danish and Greenland governments, NATO and the armed forces. The families of the lost men were there too, facing up to the ordeal of receiving multiple condolences, just as they had faced up to the gross intrusions of the press over the past six weeks. Those intrusions had not been unkind, but they had been insensitive, and some of the families had found it almost impossible to cope. They had done their grieving, with the love and support of friends and family members, but now they had another ordeal to face..........

Hundreds of students and members of the public were already installed in the pews filling the nave, all wishing to pay their respects. The other parts of the little cathedral, including the north transept, had also been pressed into service, although from some parts of the complicated and beautiful building there was no direct view of the pulpit or the altar. Before long there was standing room only. There was also a considerable media presence, and the TV cameras had been allowed inside the cathedral as a special concession for a live transmission, in view of the overwhelming public interest.

Great Tom stopped tolling and the service commenced, with the TV pictures beamed round the world. The Bishop of Oxford said this: "Your Royal Highness, my lords, ladies and gentlemen, we are gathered here today in this ancient place to commemorate -- and celebrate -- the lives of eight brave young men, tragically cut short in the beautiful yet unforgiving environment of the High Arctic. We remember Stephen Hanna, Gwyn Hughes, Rowland Linney, Griffith Mortimer, Andrew Petherton, Joseph Horton, Lars Knudsen and Peregrin Whiteside. Let us remember them for a moment in our private prayers....."

There was a deep silence in the cathedral, broken only by a few sobs from the pews occupied by the families of the lost men.

Next came a hymn, chosen by the families because it was a favourite of the leader, Stephen Hanna. The stirring words and music of "Guide me, oh thou Great Jehovah" resonated through the magnificent building and at last faded away. There was a long prayer, followed by a short eulogy by Professor Adrian Davies, the expedition's home member, who was so deeply affected by the occasion that his voice could hardly be heard, even though he used the microphone. An anthem from the choir, with an ethereal climax from the boy choristers, moved many to tears.

Then the Prime Minister stepped into the pulpit, and spoke to the world.

"Your Royal Highness, my Lord Bishop, my lords, ladies and gentlemen -- this is one of those moments when a nation stands united. United in grief for the loss of eight young lives, tragically cut short among the magnificent fjords of East Greenland, whence they had travelled for what was expected to be the adventure of their lives. They were not ordinary young men, and indeed their exceptional qualities as individuals have become more apparent over past weeks as news of their disappearance has been reported and has gripped the attention of the world. As a nation, we have felt their loss as keenly as we might have felt the loss of eight of our own sons -- and indeed our hearts go out to the families whose grief we can never fully understand............"

At this point the intermittent sobs coming from the pews occupied by the grieving families intensified, and the mother of Lars Knudsen started weeping uncontrollably. Only a few knew that she had lost a husband in Greenland, and now a son as well. She was quite inconsolable, and at last some of the other members of his family helped her to her feet and guided her towards the vestry with the assistance of two concerned and compassionate cathedral officials. At last calm was restored, and the Prime Minister, with his composure considerably disturbed, coughed and continued.

"............For these were young men from all corners of the country -- and, let us not forget, from Denmark and Australia as well -- who were driven by the spirit of adventure and by the desire to contribute to the sum total of our knowledge of the natural processes that operate within the High Arctic. They were not in Greenland to climb new peaks or to follow frivolous pursuits as "Arctic tourists." Let us be in no doubt about this -- they were all skilled scientists, working in their chosen laboratory beneath a wide sky. They had a range of approved scientific projects in place, a detailed plan of action, and an aspiration to publish at lest ten scientific publications on their return. They were fit and well prepared, and had the best equipment and the best possible backup. They had the full support of the Royal Geographical Society and the Mount Everest Foundation, and of other august funding bodies as well -- and they had taken advantage of the accumulated wisdom of many previous polar scientists and travellers. They would all have been future leaders in their chosen fields -- of this I have no doubt at all.

"So what happened to them all? There have been losses on Arctic expeditions before. Gino Watkins is but one of many who have died through accidents or because of the unforgiving nature of the Arctic environment in which the cold -- even at the height of summer -- is the implacable enemy. Young men have gone into this environment for many, many years, driven by the urge to test themselves and to move forward the frontiers of science. Some of them -- like the unfortunate Rowland Linney -- have been brought home. Others have sadly been lost without trace. But never, since the loss of the Franklin expedition in Arctic Canada in 1845, have all of the members of a single party been lost.

"So I ask again -- what happened to them all? We will probably never know. We know that Mr Linney was caught in a landslide or rockfall, but were the others lost in a sequence of unfortunate accidents, or in some all-encompassing tragedy? Since news emerged that contact had been lost with the expedition, and speculation increased that something terrible might have happened, my Government has been in the forefront of attempts to find these young men. With the unstinting support of the authorities in Greenland and Denmark, we have followed up all possible leads and have deployed all available resources in order to find them. The Americans diverted two naval vessels into the East Greenland fjords to look for them; the manager and staff of the metal mine at Himmelbjerg, almost a hundred miles from where the men went missing, searched systematically for them, on foot and with the use of their helicopters and sea planes. No clues have been found, apart from a burnt-out base camp, a few food boxes, and some items of equipment scattered about in different locations. Was fire, the other great enemy in the Arctic, responsible in some part for this tragedy? No bodies have been found in spite of a meticulous search of hundreds of miles of coastline and thousands of square miles of mountains and tundra -- with search parties placing themselves in considerable danger as they battled against the elements. At last it was the approach of winter and plummeting temperatures that forced us to abandon the search, with snow falling and the fjords caught in the inexorable and unforgiving grip of the ice.

"It is no part of my brief to apportion blame or to criticize in any way the young men who have died in these most mysterious circumstances. There will of course be a full inquiry and an inquest into the death of Mr Linney. There will be further inquests conducted by the Greenland authorities relating to the deaths of his seven colleagues. No doubt certain matters will emerge during the deliberations of our experts. But my main message is one of consolation for those who have lost loved ones in this appalling tragedy. I say this: the Arctic world is a place of cold and terrible beauty, where avalanches, landslides, floods and mighty waves generated by rolling icebergs can transform landscapes in an instant. In the face of such powerful forces the works of man may be destroyed and even obliterated, and those who have the misfortune to be in the wrong place at the wrong time have little chance of survival. Perhaps it was the misfortune of these brave young men to have encountered not just one Act of God, but several. We will never know. May they rest in peace."

Then, as he started to descend from the pulpit, there was a slight movement from a dark corner of the north transept. The sounds of chair legs scraping on ancient stone echoed around the cathedral. Heads were turned. A young man with a heavy beard stood up and walked quietly to the front of the church. Then another. Then another -- until five men were standing silently in front of the congregation. They were all heavily bearded, and they looked exhausted. They wore an ill-fitting assortment of clothes, most of which had been given to them by the officers and crew of the *Ella Brae*. Some of them were recognized by friends and families, and gasps and sobs echoed around the lofty pillars of the nave. An elderly lady shouted: "Joe! Joe! Is that really you?" and tried to get out of her cramped pew until she was gently discouraged by those sitting alongside her.

Then everything became quiet, as a packed cathedral and millions of television viewers tried to adjust to the reality of what was happening in front of them. As the world watched, the television cameras homed in on the ashen face of the Prime Minister as he started to shiver uncontrollably. At last the silence was broken.

"My name is Stephen Hanna, age 23, of Jesus College."

"My name is Gwyn Hughes, age 27, from Emmanuel College and the Scott Polar Research Institute in Cambridge."

"My name is Joseph Horton, age 28, of Merton College."

"My name is Lars Knudsen, age 23, from Copenhagen in Denmark."

"My name is Peregrin Whiteside, age 24, of St John's College."

Joe Horton had been chosen as their spokesman. He stepped forward. He was clearly so nervous that he could hardly speak, but then Stephen Hanna moved up and stood beside him, and put an arm around his shoulder. Spontaneously, the others followed, so that they stood in a row, linked together as if to tell the world that the words to be uttered by Horton were their words too. They looked at their families and friends, who were sitting just a few feet in front of them, and gave them brief smiles. The smiles were returned, and any doubts the men might have had about actually uttering their carefully rehearsed words disappeared like fresh snowflakes under a midsummer sun. So Horton swallowed hard and said in a halting voice, heavy with emotion: "Ladies and gentlemen, you are, we hope, pleased to see us here today. Five of us, as you may observe, are not dead, but in good health. We grieve the loss of our dear friend Raymond Linney, not in an accident but in a cold act of murder. You have just heard the Prime Minister speak most eloquently about our expedition, our adventurous spirits, and the events surrounding our apparent demise. What he has said is embroidered upon a fabric of lies. The Prime Minister knows it, for he helped to make that fabric. He is personally complicit in the murder of one innocent British citizen and in the attempted murder of four others from Britain and one from Denmark. Five minutes ago copies of his personal authorization for us to be killed were handed to the world's media. We make no apology either for our accusation or for our release of sensitive classified information, even though some may accuse us of treachery or treason; for if truth ceases to have any meaning in this country, and if the sanctity of life is no longer respected, democracy is dead and our nation loses its soul."

He paused and glanced at the Prime Minister, who was slumped forward, holding his head in his hands. Then he looked resolutely at the sea of faces in front of him, every one registering shock and disbelief. He continued. "Now, if you'll bear with us for a little while, we'll give you an abbreviated account, leaving out the most distressing details, of what happened in Greenland."

END

ACKNOWLEDGEMENTS

As usual, I have received great help from many quarters during the journey towards publication. Early drafts of the text were kindly read by Robert Anthony, Ian Richardson, Keith Mann, David Sugden, Ken Brown and David Llewellyn. My wife Inger has read the manuscript several times, and as ever her editorial input has been invaluable. I have also appreciated the advice of my sons Stephen and Martin -- and Martin has created another wonderful book cover designed to sell the book to the world! I hope that the final product will be something that they are happy to have been associated with. And — after an interval of 52 years — my grateful thanks to my seven colleagues on the 1962 Oxford University Expedition to East Greenland. That was one of the most wonderful experiences of my life, and I cherish many memories of our camaraderie and our adventures. That expedition, enjoyed when I was young and very foolish, planted the seeds of the story which I have now put together. Thank you all!

FURTHER INFORMATION

If you would like to know more about this novel, its background, and how it came to be written, check out the following web sites:

http://actsofgod.weebly.com/

The author's home page, with details about his other books, is here:

http://www.brianjohn.co.uk/index.html

The Amazon author's page is here, with details of all the titles available in Kindle and paperback editions:

http://www.amazon.co.uk/Brian-John/e/B005SAZ200

Signed copies of all Brian's books (fiction and non-fiction) can be obtained here, with a Paypal payment facility:

http://www.angel-mountain.info/

And here is a photo album with images from the spectacular landscape within which the story is set:

http://uk.pinterest.com/brianjohn526/acts-of-god/

OTHER FICTION BY BRIAN JOHN

On Angel Mountain (Part One), Greencroft Books 2001.
ISBN 9780905559803. A5 paperback, 328 pp, £6.99.

House of Angels (Part Two), Greencroft Books 2002.
ISBN 9780905559810. A5 paperback, 432 pp, £7.99.

Dark Angel (Part Three), Greencroft Books 2003.
ISBN 9780905559827. A5 paperback, 432 pp, £8.50.

Rebecca and the Angels (Part Four), Greencroft Books 2004.
ISBN 9780905559834. A5 paperback, 432 pp, £8.50.

Flying with Angels (Part Five), Greencroft Books, 2005.
ISBN 9780905559841. A5 paperback, 400 pp, £7.99.

Guardian Angel (Part Six), Greencroft Books, 2008.
ISBN 9780905559865. A5 paperback, 256 pp, £6.99.

Sacrifice (Part Seven), Greencroft Books, 2009.
ISBN 9780905559902. A5 paperback, 352 pp, £7.99.

Conspiracy of Angels (Part Eight), Greencroft Books, 2012.
ISBN 9780905559933. A5 paperback, 352 pp, £7.99.

These books make up the Angel Mountain Saga, and together have now sold about 75,000 copies in paperback alone.

ABOUT THE AUTHOR

Brian John was born in Carmarthen in 1940 and brought up in Pembrokeshire. He is married and has two grown up sons and two grandsons. He studied at Haverfordwest Grammar School and at Jesus College Oxford, where he read Geography and obtained his D Phil degree for a pioneering study of the Ice Age.

When he was a student he led two University expeditions, to Iceland and Greenland, and thinks it is a minor miracle that he survived. He then worked as a field scientist in Antarctica and spent eleven years as a Geography Lecturer in Durham University. He has travelled widely, mostly in cold places.

In 1977 he and his family moved to a smallholding near Newport in Pembrokeshire, and since then he has made his living as a writer and publisher. He is also actively involved in environmental and community organizations.

He has published hundreds of articles andmore than 80 books, and among his publishers are Collins, Pan, Orbis, Aurum Press/HMSO, Longman, David and Charles, Wiley and Edward Arnold. His published output includes university texts, walking guides, coffee table glossies, and books of popular science. Many of his titles have been published by Greencroft Books, and have been of particular interest to readers in Wales -- for example tourist guides, books of local jokes, walkers' handbooks, and titles on local folklore and traditions.

Then came the Angel Mountain Saga. The novels have received wide acclaim for their narrative skill, their strong sense of place, and their historical authenticity. Much to Brian's surprise, the Saga has been a runaway success, and the heroine, Mistress Martha Morgan, now has a cult following of readers from all over the world.

Sales of the paperback editions of the novels are holding up well, and "On Angel Mountain" has now sold about 33,000 copies, excluding Ebook (Kindle) sales. The accumulated paperback sales figure for all the titles in the saga currently stands at about 75,000.

Another recent book (reprinted several times) is *The Bluestone Enigma*, which takes a controversial look at the various theories used to explain the transport of certain bluestones from West Wales to Stonehenge.

Brian's recent children's story called *The Strange Affair of the Ethiopian Treasure Chest* has been well received, and won the 2011 Wishing Shelf Gold Award for books aimed at the 6-8 year-old age group. That's a great accolade, since the judges were all primary school children from the appropriate age group.

And since 2012 he has been hard at work on "Acts of God"............